FOSSIL COVE PRESS

NEW WORLD WAR

Part Two

Of

AXIS OF ANDES

By

D. G. Valdron

NEW WORLD WAR,

Part Two of AXIS OF ANDES
FOSSIL COVE PRESS, Winnipeg, Manitoba
Copyright © 2019 by Denis George Arthur Valdron.
The right of Denis George Arthur Valdron (D.G. Valdron) to be identified as the author of this work is asserted. All rights reserved.

Fossil Cove Publishing
1301 - 90 Garry Street
Wpg, Man, Canada, R3C 4J4

Cover: Ewen Campion-Clarke, artist & designer. All images public domain.

Issued in electronic and print formats
ISBN: (ebook) 978-1-7778108-0-1
ISBN: (IngramSpark paperback) 978-1-990860-90-4

Text set in Garamond
Printed and bound Canada

NEW WORLD WAR

Part Two of

AXIS OF ANDES

Table of Contents

NEW WORLD WAR INTRODUCTION

This is a work of historical fiction. But it isn't the history that you know. In our world, as Germany and Japan overran Europe and Asia, two South American nations had a brief conflict. Peru made war on a poorly prepared Ecuador; the conflict lasted less than a month, killed fewer than a thousand people and saw the loss of 40 percent of Ecuador's empty interior. Today, it is all but forgotten.

But it didn't have to be like that. The Peru-Ecuador War of 1941 lasted only a month, but its origins stretched back a century. If things had turned out a little differently, everything could have gone very wrong.

In this alternate history, beginning in **Axis of Andes**, a fascist government comes to power in Ecuador, a government prepared to fight. This sets in motion a chain of events, not just of a more ferocious local war, but one which, step by step embroils neighboring and rival nations. Peru attacks Ecuador, Chile attacks Peru, and the dominos start to fall.

The story you are about to read, New World's War, flows from the events of **Axis of Andes**. The Andean War spreads to Bolivia, to the highlands of the Andes, to the rain forests of the interior, and draws in country after country. This conflict turns out very differently. This is the history where things went very wrong, and a continent was bathed in flame.

The history of the nations of South America is well worth studying. It's a history of idealism and cynicism, greed and generosity, comedy and tragedy. I commend the reader it. You will be well served.

This is a work of fiction, we make no apologies. Much has been taken from real history as we know it, of economics and geography, of various historical persons. But I warn you, liberties have been taken with characters and personalities, they may be different in greater or lesser degree than the men who actually lived and died. No disrespect is intended. In a few cases, they have been made up altogether, but represent the sorts of personality that turn up frequently and so people very much like them have lived.

Although this is fiction, there may be errors of various sorts in the portions that purport to draw from actual history. These errors are mine and no one else, and I certainly acknowledge them.

In the Previous Volume
AXIS OF ANDES

Book of Ecuador

Book of Peru

Book of Chile

Book of Alba

Book of War

Aftermath

Chronology

***

New World War – Page 4

BOOK OF BOLIVIA

July 1, 1941, Bolivia

If the average Bolivian citizen knows anything on July 1, 1941, it is this: They don't want to get involved.

Bolivia has lost every war it has ever been involved with; has been defeated by every country it has ever crossed swords with; has lost territory to Peru, Brazil, Chile and now to Paraguay.

Bolivia finally, in 1938, signs off a peace treaty formally ending the Chaco war. But it is still licking its wounds. The economy is in ruins, unemployment is high, there are vast numbers of former soldiers, the politics are fractured, the spectre of famine lurks around the corner. The country is held together by threads.

So, the average Bolivian knows one thing: They don't want to be involved in the bloodbath taking place on their borders. It is the one thing that every Bolivian, Indigenous, mestizo or Criollo, rich or poor, fascist, communist, conservative, whatever; all agree on.

They are going to sit this one out for a change. They know that.

No good can possibly come out of it. They know that too.

One out of two isn't bad.

Bolivia in the Great Game, 1936 to 1941

Bolivia has been wooed nonstop since 1933. Initially, this was primarily Ecuador's doing. In their quest to deter a Peruvian invasion, they came to La Paz seeking an ally. That is the whole point of the Sorzano-Ibarra Treaty.

After that, from a diplomatic point of view, things got complicated. Under pressure from both Peru and Chile, Sorzano-Ibarra is repudiated, and Bolivian neutrality is agreed upon.

And, as irony would have it, in 1940 the treaty ends up being cause of the war that Velasco Ibarra worked so hard to avoid.

Respect for Bolivian neutrality lasts until the Peru-Chile side of the war actually heats up in July and August, 1940, when Peru enters increasingly intense secret negotiations with Bolivia for their intervention on the side of Peru.

Peru at this time is fighting a two front war, Alba's begun his march. Things are looking bad. The focus of negotiations is the former Bolivian (now Chilean province of Antofagasta), whose recovery Peru guarantees if only Bolivia will enter the war.

At the same time, Chile wages an equally intense diplomatic war to keep Bolivia out of it, with a combination of threats of military reprisal and promises of commercial benefits and preferential access to seaports on better terms.

At this point though - June through November, 1940, the Penaranda regime has no intention whatsoever of getting involved in the conflict. Penaranda has only recently taken power, his government is dominated by the traditional right wing elites which desperately seek stability above all else, and the country is basically broke and broken. Remember that Penaranda's predecessor was desperately looking for foreign loans to avoid starvation in the cities.

Bolivia's a mess. They're heavily in debt; socially they are politically fractured all the way from extreme nationalists, extreme socialists and extreme oligarchs. The Indigenous don't like the Hispanics, the Mestizo don't like anyone. Veterans remain a huge constituency just waiting to be animated. The backbone of the remaining economy is the tin and silver mining industries, but those are having problems, and their response to a softer market was to screw the workers. In addition, the geography of the country makes communication and transportation between different regions a costly undertaking.

The Peace treaty with Paraguay provided for mutual disarmament, and Bolivia's forces are restricted to about 15,000 troops. But even that is almost impossible to maintain. During 1940, Bolivia's actual military strength is probably around 12,000 to 14,000.

So despite increasingly generous Peruvian enticements right up until August 24, 1940, the Penaranda government has no intention of committing. And truthfully, it's pretty much a pipe dream. Even if they do commit, Bolivia might be no more than a minor distraction to Chile and they would require substantial aid to function.

This frenzy of diplomatic promises and threats lasts until August 24, when Peruvian forces push through Tarapaca and actually attack Antofagasta. At that point the Peruvians decide that they don't need Bolivian help, and that Bolivian intervention might actually undermine their claim to a province they now believe that they can make their own. The Peruvian mission in La Paz abruptly packs up and goes home with barely a word.

When the Peruvians lose interest, so do the Chileans, and promises of preferential trade and access privileges vanish. The threats remain though. The Chileans don't want the Bolivians supporting Peru in any way whatsoever. From the Peruvian point of view, even negotiations are beneficial, however, since it raises the possibility of a Bolivian intervention and forces Chile to keep a reserve against a possible attack. That actually works for a while.

But it's the 'Boy who Cried Wolf' syndrome. Eventually, the Chileans lose their fear of a Bolivian assault and their situation grows desperate enough that they commit all their reserves anyway. This is part of the reason why the war see-saws back in their favour in September.

Why do the negotiations even occur? Although Penaranda has no intention of being dragged into this war, there are good reasons to entertain both sets of warring diplomats. The Chileans are pretty threatening, so it's important to make nice to the Peruvians just in case. And to a lesser extent, vice versa.

The promises are enticing. Regaining Antofagasta and access to the Pacific coast was and is a central feature of Bolivian politics for half a century. Even if it is out of the question in practical terms, it's just not culturally possible in Bolivia to simply shut the door on that kind of discussion. The Chilean promises - privileges and access, are much more modest, but far more realistic and achievable.

But of course, as of September, 1940 on, the 'Battle of Temptations,' as it's called in La Paz, abruptly comes to an end, the respective combatants thoroughly engaged with each other, and their respective mobilizations reaching the point where the comparatively small force Bolivia can project will cease to be able to make an impact.

From October, 1940, onwards, Bolivia drifts towards the Chilean diplomatic and economic orbit. As noted, it desperately needs sea and trading access, and must curry favour to maintain it.

History can be a harsh teacher. Bolivia's always getting dragged into these regional wars. Back in 1828, the Peruvians frustrated Simon Bolivar's dream of a great Latin American state by splitting Bolivia from Gran Colombia, leading directly to the War between Peru and Gran Colombia. A few years later, Bolivia's relationship to Peru developed into the Peru-Bolivia Confederation, which in 1839 resulted in war with Argentina and Chile and the collapse of the Confederation. A few decades later, the War of the Pacific comes along, with Peru and Bolivia once again battling Chile in 1883 and losing badly.

Geography and politics conspire to drag Bolivia into every major war in the region. In the long run, their chances of staying out of

New World War – Page 8

this one are nil. The only questions are who, what, when, where and how? But luckily, those are the good questions. Bolivia's not interested in getting involved. It's learned its lessons.

As for Paraguay, forget them. They want in on a war even less than Bolivia. Their military is restricted by treaty to about 8,000. And while it might be tempting to bite off more of the Chaco, particularly those oil producing areas they just handed over, which are the only valuable part, there's no popular support for it, there's no money for it, and they're now at the wrong end of logistics. Their best strategy is to hold what they got and hope no one notices them.

* * *

Bolivia, 1941 - The Penaranda Regime

The Enrique Penaranda government takes power after the death of German Busch, and the overthrow of Quintanilla, and represents the re-establishment of control by the right wing traditional elites. Like all reactionary governments it rules by excluding various interests, the working classes of the mines and urban centres, the nationalists, the leftists, the middle class, the indigenous peoples.

In such a situation, the crown sits uneasily upon the head. Penaranda's government lacks a clear congressional majority and acceptance of its authority is far from complete. The response, of course, is increasing repression. Lacking a genuine consensus, the next best thing is to imprison, beat or shoot the opposition.

But the Penaranda government has another deeper problem. Fundamentally a reactionary regime, it really doesn't have the intellectual tools to deal with Bolivia's ongoing economic crisis. Government for and by conservative elites always harkens back to some idyllic past and is never well equipped to deal the problems of the present. And in this instance, Bolivia is faced with very unconventional problems posed by the war and the Great Depression.

The usual solution for such regimes is to tighten their belts, let the poor suffer, keep the elite in power and ride it out. Such a solution works best when those below are quiescent and submissive, not engaged and increasingly angry.

You have to keep in mind that Bolivia is a fairly stratified society, particularly prior to the Chaco War. Its motto is a place for everyone and everyone better be goddam well in their place. Miners mined, the elite ruled, the Indigenous stayed in their villages, etc. Bolivia's geographic and regional divisions, and a modicum of force, ensured this unhappy order.

The Chaco war is transformative. The rapid expansion and mobilization of the Army suddenly provided an avenue for social mobility that never existed before. Within limits of course, social mobility doesn't exist all that much for the Indigenous conscripts who formed up to 85 percent of the Army. They just get siphoned up, moved around, and used as cannon fodder.

But an army needs NCO's, it needs field officers, it needs an officer class and staff. A rapidly expanding army needs a lot of new leadership. And an army suffering heavy ongoing casualties needs even more leadership, or needs to replace that leadership fast. These are drawn mostly from middle classes, the intelligentsia, the smarter or more organized portions of the working classes, from entrepreneurs, from the ambitious. Essentially, from people who, left alone, might have gone on to be mildly successful leaders of their village or relatively competent shop stewards or foremen in their mines.

Now, of course, they are catapulted into a wider social forum, one where they might arise far faster and much further than previous Bolivian opportunities could provide. In a society which has previously enforced a lot of stability, suddenly a lot of smart people were being brought into an organization which offers the potential of both rapid advancement and exposure to cutting edge technology and social and administrative organization.

And of course because the expansion of the Bolivian military made it desperate to hoover up literate, relatively educated persons for an officer class, they ended up siphoning a lot of Marxist and socialist theory and analysis, and a much broader range of social perspectives beyond simple elitist stability. Inevitably, all of these new young officers are talking to each other, exchanging ideas and notions, trading books, arguing about the world's problems. So idealism and ideologies migrate rapidly. Radical notions migrated especially quickly as the old elitist ideals and methods were proving themselves bankrupt by losing their war.

There is a further component, and that is the structure of the military itself. The new officers, ideology aside, are being trained up in a military way of getting things done. It is a hierarchical social structure of orders and obedience, goal oriented, intended to be flexible in organization and deployment, emphasizing lines of communication, open to technology, and with a window onto the outside world. So at the same time as many in the military are radicalizing, they are also training up to see military command structures and military methods of organization as a way to implement their radicalism.

All of this goes to show that the Military Socialism of a David Toro is not some freaky notion of a singular man, but rather a kind of inevitable social trend that persists through Busch, Quintanilla and eventually Villarroel. The Army isn't completely a radical organization, of course. There are a lot of reactionaries ready to turn machine guns on striking miners or to support a right wing coup. Still, radicalism and progressivism remain firmly ingrained in elements of the military, despite the best efforts of the elite to purge it. Over time, such efforts will inevitably succeed, but for the present, it remains a force. A leaderless disorganized force pushed from power, but still a force.

In slightly more modern times, we saw an analogue to this development in the Middle East, as reformist left wing or socialist movements in the military pushed aside traditional oligarchies in Egypt, Libya, Iraq, Syria and Algeria.

Major Villarroel is the last gasp of Military Socialism. The elite continually attempts to purge radicalism from the military. This arguably begins as early as 1939, with continuing demobilization after the formal peace treaty, reducing the size of the army and releasing many officers into civilian life.

By 1940, leftists Siles and Estenssoro formed the Revolutionary Nationalist Movement (MNR), a civilian radical political party, which seems to have took up the mantle of social transformation

***

July 20, I would sooner lie in a bed with pigs....

"So much for Europe," Paz Estenssoro says, "but I still fail to see why Franco does not join in."

"He can't," General Villarroel responds. "Three years of civil war? I'd wager that Spain is worse off than we are."

War, whether in South America or in Europe, General Villarroel reflects, sipping his port, is a popular topic.

There is another round of bitter strikes in the mine, and rail workers have walked off the job. In the central square at La Paz, troops have fired on demonstrators, killing over a dozen. Rumours of starvation are going around. The unemployed flock to the cities like La Paz and Sucre, milling aimlessly, as opportunity fails to materialize. Things are going to hell in Bolivia.

But then again, when hadn't things been going to hell in Bolivia?

He can't actually imagine Spain being worse off. He can't imagine any place being worse off.

In any event, it isn't his problem. Villarroel is only technically a general now. He retains his staff title and a stipend, but that ass Penaranda made sure he isn't in command of any troops.

Careful, he tells himself. These days, you can lose more than a commission. Bodies keep appearing at the bottom of the Old Man Cliffs, with no one quite knowing how they'd gotten there. Gravity is now a mysterious subject. I'm drunk, he tells himself, but not sloppy.

He looks around at the men who occupy the salon at Madame Rosa's brothel, a mixture of civilians and military officers. Detached military officers mostly.

A few years ago, the Bolivian Army stood 250,000 strong, the largest army in all South America. Now it is 13,000, and struggling at that.

New World War – Page 13

Most of the Army are Indigenous conscripts of course. They'd gone back to their villages, the haciendas and farms, taking their wounded and injured and a disturbing number of weapons with them. There, they minded their own business, and once again slipped out of the mainstream of Bolivian life.

Presumably, Villarroel reflected, they are not starving, or at least not much. He imagines he would have heard something if strife or suffering had broken out among the Indigenous. They'd be flocking into the cities with their hand out like everyone else then, and there's been no sign of that.

At least, Villarroel thinks, Penaranda is wise enough to leave the Indios well enough alone. Bolivia has enough problems without stirring up that hornet's nest.

Still, you never know. Some of the greedy Latifundista bastards who form Penaranda's base would happily squeeze a mouse until it shit itself.

But an army of 250,000, even subtracting all the Indo conscripts, that was still immense. Even after the reductions, Bolivia is oversupplied with corporals and sergeants, Lieutenants, Captains, Majors and Generals. Particularly Generals. Things being what they are, it is hard to show a General the door.

But Penaranda, whatever else Villarroel thinks of him, is no fool, and he's relatively astute in his management of commissions, carefully trying to purge the officer corps of all the Military Socialists. No easy thing, since any officer who's been through the hell of the Chaco war was likely to be socialist.

Instead, with the meticulousness of a chess player, Penaranda is slowly moving people around, neutralizing popular officers, retiring some, discharging others for trivial offenses, making sure that his own loyalists, his own, more ideologically compatible officers, are placed in key commands.

Which is why Villarroel has no troops to command. He is safe enough, he thinks, you can't arrest a General after all. Not even Penaranda is that much of a fool.

But he has, ever so carefully, been neutralized. All he wants is to help his nation, but Penaranda, the bastard, has him sitting on a doorstep.

What would German Busch have done with a humiliation like that? Revolted, almost certainly! Stormed into the Presidential Palace, swearing a string of curses, and then punch El Presidente in the nose.

Villarroel smiles at the thought. There was a real man for you.

Poor German, he reflects, things ended so badly for him. He'd deserved better.

"The war," Estenssoro prompts.

Paz Estenssoro is one of the leading civilian socialists, a noise maker of such stature that Penaranda cannot yet have him thrown off the Old Man Cliffs. Aside from Villarroel himself, he has the most stature of anyone in the room.

He needs to be cultivated.

Or perhaps Paz needs to cultivate. People keep disappearing these days, after all.

It was a sign of the times now that a brothel has become one of the only safe places for men in certain circumstances to meet.

"The advantage now," one of the other officers, a Colonel Gutierrez, says, "lies with Chile. Ibanez offensive succeeds in the south, where Peru's offensive failed in the north."

The conversation moves from Europe to the Andes? Villarroel has allows himself to be distracted.

"Ibanez made some good progress," Villarroel replies. "But I am not so confident. All he's done is extended his lines. Can he hold them? Can he break through? The Chileans are good troops, but the Peruvians have numbers."

A lawyer, Chavez, offers, "True enough, the Peruvians have the numbers, but all the quality is on the other side. Lima has nothing of the quality of an Alba or an Ibanez."

New World War – Page 15

The discussion shifts to an involved examination the details of the campaign. Everyone has an opinion. The wars have replaced sports and weather as a top of conversation. Certainly the newspapers find it safer to report the details and claims of a war going on in neighbouring countries than questionable the activities of its own government, or the strikes and conflicts which seem unending. You have to read the socialist newspapers to even know that there are strikes and demonstration, though you can see the evidence everywhere in real life.

"I think," says Villarroel finally, "that we can all agree on this, it will be good for all of us when their war is over."

"I will toast to that," replies Estenssoro.

Even without participation, the war is an ongoing nightmare for Bolivia. Deserters from both sides flock across the borders, many of them settling into banditry, taking up begging or otherwise making a nuisance of themselves.

Then there are the swarms of spies and diplomats. Spies from everywhere it seemed. Chilean spies, Argentinian spies, Peruvian spies, American spies, British, even German and Italian, all of them flashing around money and promises, scheming endlessly. There are times when Villarroel isn't able to throw a rock without striking some obnoxious diplomat or spy. In a nation wracked with poverty and despair, they wear their wealth and scheming like badges. You can always pick a spy out of the crowd.

Villarroel has come to despise the breed. The Peruvians make promises, treating Bolivia like a whore to be seduced. The Chileans offer threats, like his country is a dog to be whipped. As the fortunes of war shift, their interest waxes and wanes. It is a particularly obnoxious humiliation to have the coast provinces offered on a platter one day, and the next to find that your letters are returned unread. And more humiliation to realize that the American spies care more about the Germans, and the German spies care more about Argentina. Too much exposure and you want to build a fence around the whole country and shoot foreigners on sight.

But of course, that isn't possible.

"I would sooner lie in a bed with pigs," he says when the discussion turns that way, "than side with Chileans."

"And Peruvians?" Chavez asks.

"I'd sooner lie in a bed with dogs!"

That earns a laugh, a palpable relaxing that warms Villarroel's heart. He needs friends.

Bolivia's lifeline is its exports, and those exports depend on passage through its former provinces, now held by Chile. But the war has destabilizes the passage.

Exports go through; the Chileans have no desire to antagonize the Americans who are rediscovering a hunger for Bolivian tin. But prices and demand vary wildly, and all too often, bewildered mining companies discover that shipments which promised wild profits would arrive at port forced to deep discounts or with the contracts abandoned. At that point, all you can do is sell for a pittance to whatever Chilean warehouse merchant is willing to make an offer and hold it until the prices jumped. There are killings to be made, but somehow, it seems that these are made by Chileans, and the Bolivians always get the short end.

Hard pressed mining companies have no options left but to squeeze their workers, and the workers, so long squeeze, have less shit in them than a mouse. Which explains the constant cycle of escalating strikes. The saying going around is that it was better to be a slave these days than a miner.

Then there is the matter of imports. When there are any. Chile, on a war footing, has made a habit of seizing imports and simply offering credits to La Paz. It isn't quite robbery, technically, Chile has paid for it, though you have to go to Santiago to spend the money.

But it hurts. Mining equipment and railway locomotives are going unrepaired. The stressed Bolivian economy creaks louder than ever, with shortages appearing everywhere. Luxury items often make it through for the rich, but that only adds to tensions, that awkward gap between the oblivious rich and the increasingly desperate everyone else.

New World War – Page 17

Bolivia has not lost a single man, Villarroel thinks, but despite that, it suffers more than the actual combatants.

The conversation reflects his thoughts. As the night wears on, and wine is drunk and cigars smoked, the conversation turns more and more to Bolivia's seemingly insurmountable problems.

"I'll say this," Villarroel says at the end of the night, "Penaranda and I have our differences, but in his life, his only good idea was getting rid of Salamanca."

He pauses and licked his lips. Did he mean it to come out sounding like that, so close to sedition? But his companions applaud and toast him, and so he smiles and raises his glass.

****

The Embassy Letter, July 18, 1941

Douglas Jenkins, US Ambassador to Bolivia, watches the little comic opera General read the letter. The man reminds him of Peter Lore. He seems diminutive, shallow, his eyes too large, his chin too weak. The man is covered in gold brocade and medals, a cavalry sabre hangs from his belt. He seems more a figure from a Marx Brothers movie than any kind of leader.

Does he go to work in that outfit?

Or has he just gotten dressed up for the occasion?

He looks up.

"Is this true?" he asks. "Is this letter true?"

Ostria Gutierrez, the Bolivian Foreign Minister, nods soberly.

"So far as I know," he says, "it was delivered to us by the Ambassador. If we cannot trust in the Americans…"

Worm, thinks Jenkins. You can't trust these Latins as far as you can throw them. Not one has a spine.

General Enrique Penaranda, President of Bolivia, turns to face the Ambassador. Jenkins puts on his most honest look.

"Your Excellency," he lies, "I can't verify it one hundred per cent, but it was intercepted, and I can't see any other honest way, than to share it with you. The Nazis are plotting to overthrow you."

The chubby general's face is red. With fear or fury? Jenkins can't say.

"I think," he says, squeezing the letter in his fist, "it is time to… as the Americans say… clean house."

"Who?" Gutierrez asks.

Penaranda's face is like stone. "All of them."

✷✷✷

New World War – Page 19

July 21, 1941, Outside Madame Rosa's, La Paz, Bolivia

It is early in the morning, the first light of dawn visible on the horizon as a half drunk Villarroel and his bodyguards staggered out of Madame Rosa's brothel.

Men are waiting for them. Villarroel's face freezes, and he finds himself sobering up fast. As casually as he can, he puts his hands in his pockets, fingers tightening around the pistol he carries in one of them.

The men, black clad in expensive coats walk toward him. With a small gesture, Villarroel halts his bodyguard.

As they approach, he can see by their faces that they were not Bolivians. They have that pinched pasty look he associates with Germans, as if the entire nation has grown up sucking on sour fruit.

Canaris' men. What do those fuckers want? He toys with shooting them on general principles.

"Herr Villarroel," one of them says, in that queerly accented mix of Spanish and German that Canaris' spies are so well known for.

"General Villarroel," he corrects.

The spy blinks.

"General Villarroel," the man says, "come with us if you want to live."

***

Tin Smiths of Bolivia

At the centre of Bolivia's economic malady is its main export, tin. This is the major source of Bolivian foreign revenue, and with the Great Depression it takes a huge hit. One would think that WWII would result in a boom, and it indeed results in a sudden sharp increase in tin prices, but that is followed as quickly by an equivalent collapse.

The trouble is that fairly early into WWII, one of the biggest markets for tin, Continental Europe, goes offline, blockaded by Britain. The British market alone cannot make up for the loss of the European tin market. Japan for a time remains a steady and expanding market, but eventually British and American hostility bring an end to that, reducing the market even more.

During this time, the first few years of World War Two, America was neutral and its demand for tin is pretty small. The American market for tin doesn't really ramp up until around 1942 or 1943.

The result is that during the critical period of 1939 to 1942, tin prices experience a few sudden sharp peaks, more dramatic collapses, and tend to dwell in the basement. Without foreign exchange from the tin exports, the Government is crippled, the economy is crippled, and there isn't anything anyone can do about that. It is only after 1942 and a steady huge American demand that the economy recovers somewhat, but by then it is too late. Even then, the wartime price that the US strong arms is not terrific.

The stresses of the war on its borders, particularly the need to maintain a significantly larger army, the added uncertainties to the export market, the difficulties with imports, the larger number of foreign agitators and the money and influence they bring with them, and a host of factors are adding stress to the equation.

Not a huge amount of additional stress, but still stress which tended to exacerbate or accelerate the problems. So there are more strikes, they happen earlier, they're a little bit bitterer earlier. Penaranda is a bit more repressive and more willing to eliminate his enemies earlier. Resistance to him is accumulating more quickly. Bolivian society is more fractured and volatile.

The History We Know

Even without a war on its doorstep, the Penaranda government was deeply reactionary and repressive.

It was also a focus of deep interest to foreign powers, primarily the United States, which, as WWII grew closer, was interested in securing sources of oil in the western hemisphere. Chaco oil, even if it was remote, expensive and difficult to procure, made Bolivia a priority. At the same time Nazi Germany's agents were active in the country, perhaps more so than any other Latin state except Chile and Argentina.

In July 18, 1941, the American Ambassador, provided to Penaranda a forged letter, allegedly from Berlin, to one of Penaranda's ministers in La Paz, plotting a coup. This letter triggered a wave of political repression at home, and catapulted Bolivia strongly into America's orbit. But in the absence of a regional war, the purges of the political class were not as intense.

Despite repression, Penaranda continued to mismanage Bolivian economy and society. Through 1941 and 1942, Bolivia experienced a number of crippling strikes, as miners protested their worsening conditions. Having no actual skills and no ideas, the odious Penaranda frequently resorted to repression and murder, eliminating some, torturing others, opening fire on demonstrators, and perpetuating atrocities and massacres.

This culminated in a major army massacre of miners and their families in Catavi, on December 21, 1942. In this case, the army fired on a group of 8,000 striking workers and their families, including women and children. As many as 700 were killed and 400 wounded. The Catavi massacre did much to discredit the Penaranda government and galvanize opposition.

The Penaranda government continued to flounder for another year, struggling with increasingly bitter strikes and undertaking vicious repression. Things boiled over with a massacre of striking miners and Penaranda was overthrown in December 1943 by General Villarroel, the last of the military socialists.

Villarroel's regime was quite a mixed bag. On the one hand, like so many of these guys, he comes into power with high hopes and an effort at real social reform. He enacted a number of labour protection measures, including pensions and official recognition of unions.

On the other hand, he was seen by the United States as having significant Nazi sympathies. In this respect, he was like Penaranda's predecessor, Quintanilla. What he really was, was an extreme nationalist, and his ideals and ideology were a mixture of right and left. He believed strongly that Bolivia needed structural reform. But like his predecessors, Toro, Bush and Quintanilla, his background and outlook was that of military autocracy.

Nationalist military autocrats with radical and socialist tendencies? It made it easy for the traditional conservatives to paint this new wave as essentially Nazis or Fascists. And there was an element of truth to this. In the late 30s after the Chaco war, German capital and German influence flowed into Bolivia. And there was substantial contact and borrowing of Nazi and Fascist thought.

In the late 30s, the United States would look at these developments with a certain amount of concern and paranoia, but perhaps retained some nuance. By 1943, and the War in Europe, America was no longer concerned with nuance and tolerance was zero.

To obtain American support, Villarroel actually had to dismiss several cabinet Ministers and to break relations with the remnants of Toro and Bush's military socialist party.

The situation in Bolivia remained dire. Even though the Great Depression had ended and the war was lifting economies, Bolivia's problems remained huge and intractable. In a sense, Villarroel made things worse for himself by raising expectations rather more than he was able to raise conditions. As the gap between expectations and demands rose beyond Bolivia's actual performance, Villarroel faces increasing opposition, not just from the elite, but from many constituencies that had supported him.

The answer that Villarroel turned to, as people in this situation always seemed to do, was repression. Like Penaranda before him, Villarroel was losing his grip, and like Penaranda before him, his response was to cling to power with increasing brutality. There were massacres. We saw the beginning of the Latin American military fixation with exotic brutality, as enemies of the state were thrown from a 3,000 foot cliff.

And in the end, it didn't work out any better. Nationwide strikes and demonstrations escalated into open rebellion. The Presidential palace was besieged by angry crowds. Villarroel resigned, but it was far too late.

Ultimately, a mob of civilians, whipped up by his enemies and driven by conservative elite interests rose up against him, stormed the Presidential Palace and literally tore him limb from limb. It was not a good death. In many ways, it was reminiscent of Mussolini's degraded demise.

His body was tossed from a balcony onto the street below, where it was mutilated by the crowd and eventually hung from a lamppost.

After him, Bolivia pretty much fell to the rule of conservative elites which kept the army just strong enough to slaughter the population when required, maintained repression, and spent the next several decades mismanaging Bolivia in service to their own interests.

Bolivia became a by-word for backwards and repressive Latin autocracies. It was no wonder that so many ex-Nazis wound up there. And it was no wonder that Cuban revolutionary Che Guevara would decide that the place was ripe for an uprising.

****

The Nazi Intervention, History of the Andean Wars, Prentice Publishing, 1972

One of the minor historical mysteries is the extent and role of Nazi Germany at this crucial point in the histories of Bolivia and the Andean Wars. Specifically, a single young Nazi spy of Chilean-German origins intervened to save the life of General Villarroel, setting off a chain of events which would shake the continent.

To begin with, despite the later conclusions of the United States, Villarroel was never a Nazi asset. Villarroel can look at a map as easily as we can, and he's well aware of how useless Germany and Italy are too him. Although Military Socialism has some correspondence with National Socialism, it really was an indigenous movement. And although German ideas and German advisors were big in Bolivia, and particularly during the war German spies were all over, Germany doesn't really have even the sorts of ties that were present in Ecuador and Chile.

There's no one in Bolivia who is saluting portraits of Hitler. The personality cult, such as there is, is about venerating the nationalist hero German Busch. And there's no one in Bolivia, certainly not Villarroel, who went cap in hand to Berlin as the Ecuadorans did. So as far as Villarroel is concerned, German interests and concerns are only slightly more important than the desires of Penaranda's pet goat. Villarroel was prepared to accept German help, if it was useful. But he was well aware of the importance of the United States, and prepared to throw any Nazi influence overboard in a heartbeat if that's what it took. For Villarroel, it was simple pragmatism.

But it is also well established that the German and Italian regimes, had extensive espionage networks in Bolivia at the time. German espionage was regional, not country by country, so the operatives in Chile and in Bolivia worked under a single command. The German network also had clear linkages to the Chilean Nazi movement for obvious reasons.

In the simplest terms, it is clear that the local Nazi intelligence operatives got wind of the purges, realized that a lot of people who they were on speaking terms with were going to disappear and their position would worsen. This was apparently a snap decision in the field to intervene to try and keep Villarroel alive. The decision certainly hadn't come from Berlin, there's no record of notification of Admiral Canaris, or any other senior German within the region. Nor does there seem to be any coherent thinking behind it. It was just a reflexive reaction to preserve a possible ally.

Had the Nazi agents stopped to work things out, they'd have minded their own business. It might hurt to lose Villarroel, but they could still try and build relationships with whoever is running things - they do have money and connections. By intervening, however, they had taken a big risk, an unacceptable one, because now, when Villarroel goes down, they're going down with him.

And there's also the act that the German intelligence network in Bolivia is compromised by and somewhat influenced by the Chileans. Most of Canaris' agents in Bolivia are not from Berlin directly, but recruited from the Chilean German and Nazi communities. This isn't an issue because the perception is that these two nations' interests are in no way contrary.

But this does suggest more complex motivations. Was that critical young spy simply acting recklessly in a manner his handlers would not have approved? Or was his spontaneous and sentimental gesture an act of Chilean patriotism, the decision that Villarroel's survival against Penaranda was in the best interests of Chile?

****

July 21, 1941, La Paz, Bolivia, the street outside of Madame Rosa's Brothel

Major Villarroel sits in the passenger seat of the German spy's automobile, his bodyguard in the back seat. The young spy sitting behind the wheel is sweating.

Dawn is beginning to break, the streets are lightening. It is fifteen minutes now.

"What was your name again?" Villarroel asks.

"I should not say," the spy replies.

"You speak Spanish well," Villarroel says.

The spy nods. Villarroel heard the lilt of a foreign accent, a bit of Chilean lingo, perhaps? Canaris' bunch are very strong in Chile. He's heard that there are those in Santiago and Valparaiso who salute portraits of the German Fuhrer. Madness.

It is a delicate thing. Canaris has money to spread around, and promises of more. Villarroel and most others take little stock of the promises. True, Germany and Italy do great things in turning their country around and there is hope that similar tactics might save Bolivia. But beyond an example, there is little tangible that they can offer.

Except money. Not even a lot of money, but in a place as poor as Bolivia, even a few Sucres goes a long way.

"Tell me your story again."

The young spy looks awkward, as if rethinking the wisdom of his actions.

"My superiors received information that President Penaranda was about to launch a purge of political malcontents."

"That included me?"

"Your name was on the list."

There is a list? That is new information. Villarroel feels a chill down his spine. There's been that massacre of the miners. Villarroel like other officers had signed his name to a petition denouncing the action. His sympathies for Bush and Toro were well known. He's spoken frequently with both socialists and fascists.

Villarroel supposes that if there is a list, he's probably on it. He sighs.

More interesting is that this young man's superiors had access to the list. Canaris money greased high ranking palms. Or perhaps not everyone in Penaranda's secret police is as loyal as they thought.

It wouldn't surprise him. No man could go through the Chaco war unchanged. Bolivia is a stinking mess, and it needs deep reform. The old ways had led to one disaster after another.

Military Socialism, Villarroel reflects, is still the best chance Bolivia has. He wonders if his association with Fatherland's Cause has been found out. There are grounds for arrest right there.

"Something's happening," the bodyguard says suddenly.

A military truck is pulling up in front of Madame Rosa's. Soldiers come boiling out. Villarroel squints, but does not recognize the officers. They are too far away.

Villarroel's guts churn. The pup is right after all. They had been coming.

They watch as soldiers race in. Squawking prostitutes, half-dressed customers are pushed out onto the street.

"That's Paz," Villarroel says suddenly, recognizing the distinctive build of the tiny, wiry socialist. "Paz Estenssoro."

As Villarroel watches, the small man is jostled back and forth roughly. He protests loudly, Villarroel can make out his voice but not the words. The soldiers shove him. Then on the apparent command of an officer, a soldier strikes him in the face with the butt of his rifle. Paz struggles, reached out, grabbing at the officer. Suddenly, they are all on him, soldiers kicking and striking the little man. A shot rings out.

New World War – Page 29

"Jesus Christ," Villarroel says, "they killed Paz!"

He wants to vomit. His blood runs cold, his mouth is dry, his heart pounds against his ribs. He wants to run, wants to gear the car and drive off. It's true. That bastard Penaranda was clearing the deck.

"We've got to get out of here," he says.

"We need to wait," the bodyguard says.

"To hell with that," Villarroel replies, "start the automobile."

The Nazi turns pale. The boy seems paralyzed, sickened. Villarroel glances at him.

Spy? No, some youth playing at being a spy. A lark. He's probably recruited from Chile by Canaris' men, probably thought that La Paz is a safer docket than the Chilean front. And now he's just witnessed a murder.

The boy is no help. Villarroel tries to master his surging fear.

"Andre," he says to his bodyguard, "get your pistol ready."

Hesitantly, the bodyguard draws it but keeps it covered. Villarroel reaches into his pocket feeling his own. With the cold steel in his hand, Villarroel feels a little better.

"Boy," calling him that seems to startle the Nazi, "do you have a gun?"

The youth shakes his head.

A Nazi without a gun, thinks Villarroel. Ridiculous. What are spies coming to? He begins to suspect that his rescue owes more to a foolish youthful gallantry than any of Canaris planning.

"Andre is right," he thinks aloud. "We can't move now. We'll have to wait for them to leave, and we've got to pray that they don't pass this way, or if they do, that they don't look our way."

The raid, however, turns out to be brief. Within half an hour, everyone who seems important is being hustled onto the military truck. The prostitutes repair back to the brothel. The handful of regular clients are sent packing.

The truck starts up, makes a u-turn in the street and drives off without coming near them.

"Notice that?" asks Villarroel.

"What?" asks the young Nazi.

"More came than are going. Some of the soldiers were left in the Brothel."

"Penaranda wants to make sure that the word doesn't get out," Villarroel says, "the sweeps are still going on. He doesn't want any birds to fly."

Villarroel has a sinking feeling in his gut. This isn't what it was like in the Chaco. For all of its barbarity, the Chaco was a war, you'd known whose side you were on, you could trust the men who fought with you... well, trust was too strong a word, but despite incompetence and recklessness, you could at least feel that they were on your side.

This is being hunted. This is the awful feeling of a knock on the door at night, of not knowing who to trust, or where to turn.

"I can't go home," Villarroel says suddenly. "They may be waiting there for me. Or they will be."

His wife, he thinks suddenly. Do they already have her? What of his children? Were they there yet? Can he get a message to them to flee? Go to their mother's house, they'll be safe there for a spell.

In the blink of an eye, his life turns inside out. Paz Estenssoro was just murdered in cold blood, and he, and how many others, are now hunted men. He shivers.

Can he flee? He needs to get out of the country. Take the car and drive for the border.

He looks at his hands. They are shaking.

Calculates his chances.

They'll never make it.

And even if he does escape, what about Paz? The bastards murdered him. What about justice? What about everyone else? The

Radelpa group in the army, or 'Fatherland's Cause' as they called themselves, what happens to them if he runs?

Damn Penaranda.

Fine, Villarroel thinks, no choice but to strike back. The bastard's administration is rotten to the core. Bolivia, poor bleeding Bolivia, is rotten to the core. But there are still good men.

"Do you have a phone," Villarroel asks the young Nazi. The boy nods.

Of course. Canaris' boys will have phones, and radios, and messengers, and they will have contacts in the newspapers and radio stations, and who knows what else. He can use that.

"Get me there," he says. "I want a phone, and paper, a lot of paper."

Already, he is composing new lists in his head. Lists of names, reporters, supporters, sympathetic officers, reservists. And letters, he is already composing letters.

That bastard, Penaranda isn't going to get away with it.

****

Headlines, Bolivia

Newspaper Headlines from July 2, 1941 to July 26, 2011. Bolivian Civil War

Infamous Murder! Paz Estenssoro, founder of MNP Murdered by Soldiers on orders of President Penaranda!

Penaranda Denies Charges. Blames Communists. Denounces Conspiracy.

Major Gualberto Villarroel Demands Resignation of Penaranda, Formation of Unity Government

General Strike in La Paz!

Massacre at the Plaza! Soldiers Open Fire on Demonstrators!

Penaranda Declares Martial Law!

Fighting At the Armory!

General Strike Spreads Across the Country

Major Gualberto Villarroel Announces Formation of National Unity Government, Calls for Army to Lay Down Weapons

PRESIDENT PENARANDA DENOUNCES VILLARROEL AS FOREIGN TRAITOR, CALLS FOR ARREST

Fighting in La Paz! Civil War!

Major Villarroel Accuses President Penaranda of Foreign Conspiracy

National Unity Government Overrun! Villarroel Escapes!

Villarroel Government

Established in Sucre, La Paz Under Siege

Excerpts from: The Centre Could Not Hold, A Chronicle of the Andean Wars. Pennyworth Press, London, Hugh Fitz-Castro, 1991

***

The Bolivian Theatre In Review, Journal of Latin American Studies, 4th Ed.

In assessing the outbreak of the Bolivian Civil War, the central controversy is whether it is a genuinely indigenous conflict or a proxy driven by the conflicts going on outside its borders.

During and in the immediate aftermath of World War II, it is impossible to see the conflict as yet another conflict in the three cornered struggle between Liberal Democracy, Fascism and Communism.

But this narrative does not hold up particularly well. Among other things, it overlooks the reality that the so called 'Liberal Democrats' are nothing of the sort, but rather, under General Penaranda represent some of the most repressive and elitist elements of the reactionary Bolivian oligarchy. Far from Democratic, Penaranda's group are committed to Bolivian society as they had known it, a society of landowners, mine owners, and a tiny oligarchic property class, which is prepared to go to any length to maintain and enforce its privilege.

Oddly, Penaranda himself is not a member of the class he fought for, a man of mixed Indigenous and Mestizo parentage; he is put forward by the elites as a figure of national compromise and unity, and wins election handily. But the Bolivian economy, shattered by the Chaco War, the toll of the Great Depression and the wars on its border is unable to sustain any kind of growth. This leaves the property owning oligarchy with only repression to maintain their position. Their appeal to the Allies is never one of ideology, but merely of tradition and entrenched interests.

Much has been written of Major Villarroel and his Nazi movement, with some justification. But this is inaccurate. Villarroel is an ardent follower and disciple of German Bush and David Toro, the founders of Military Socialism. Military Socialism is often confused or considered to be interchangeable with National Socialism.

The Bolivian Army, since the turn of the century, had retained literally hundreds of German advisors. This is natural, since Germany has established pride of place as the dominant land power, with the most advanced weaponry and tactics. Germany replaces France and Britain in Latin America as the most prestigious source of advisors and armaments. Latin American military officers often travel to or study in Germany, even before the rise of the Nazi party. Bolivia is no exception. Indeed, Prussians rose high in the Bolivian military, culminating in General Kundt during the Chaco War. Busch himself is part German, and it is no surprise that his administration and military contain a number of German advisors.

The United States, of course, rising to dominance in Latin America, in the twenties and thirties, particularly in the rising international tensions, views any German presence with extreme suspicion and hostility. Busch's alleged pro-German views cause him quite a bit of trouble in Washington, despite his own insistence that his movement is 'made in Bolivia.'

For the most part, Military Socialism really is a made-in-Bolivia phenomenon. It emerges out of the disaster of the Chaco War and the profound challenges that war posed to Bolivian society. The dramatic expansion of the Bolivian military results in wide range of individuals, including educated individuals, entering service, and a proliferation of ideas. Socialism and Socialist ideas were incorporated and wedded to concepts of social management by military institutions. Unlike National Socialism, Military Socialism really does embrace socialist views.

This is seen in Bolivian politics with the willingness of civilian socialists to embrace, at least temporarily, military socialists like Toro, Bush and Villarroel. Indeed, Villarroel's Civil War government includes a number of personalities that the United States object to as being too close to outright communists.

The reality was that Bolivia in the early 1940s is a desperately poor country out of options. Avenues of compromise have vanished. It was a nation heading relentlessly towards a class war between the oligarchs and the dispossessed. It is Penaranda himself that provokes the civil war with new rounds of repressive measures.

Eventually, opposition to Penaranda has no choice but to coalesce into an organized resistance, or end up dead in ditches. If it wasn't Villarroel, it would have been someone else. Had it not been 1941, it would have been 1942.

Indeed, the nature of the civil war shows that it is essentially reactive. Neither Villarroel nor Siles nor any other leading member of the Military Socialist government is properly prepared; otherwise they would have engineered a coup. The entire progress of the Bolivian civil war is a series of incremental steps, with the revolutionaries literally making things up as they go along in an ad hoc way.

How else to explain that Villarroel in La Paz sets up his headquarters at a radio station? How else to explain the failure to coordinate different factions of the general strike? Or to coordinate the general strike with military action? Both the Penaranda and Villarroel regimes vie for the loyalty of troops and officers and put out calls for general mobilization, but Villarroel is critically late in his attack on the armory, which leaves his troops critically under supplied and his position in La Paz untenable.

In contrast, Penaranda consistently retains the initiative, breaking the General Strike, re-taking the essential tin mines which are critical to American support, and re-establishing control over the city of La Paz. But beyond that, Penaranda hits his limits.

The cult of German Busch, is strong among many military officers, who establish a secret network called Radelpa ('Razon de Patria', translated loosely as 'Fatherland's Cause') prior to the civil war.

Penaranda works assiduously to purge the military ranks of 'socialist' elements, but a clear balance of forces outside La Paz are resentful and came down in support of Villarroel. The unwieldy ad hoc coalition against Penaranda includes just about everyone, including miners, unions, socialist intellectuals and members of the middle class. Indeed, the size of the coalition makes governance difficult, and consensus slow to achieve.

Although Penaranda is able to establish order over La Paz and critical economic interests, he is unable to control the countryside. Villarroel's opposition government re-established itself in the city of Sucre, and his call for a national army results in a huge mass militia emerging, poorly armed, poorly supplied, but easily two to three times the size of Penaranda's loyalists.

For a month the civil war seesaws crazily, with La Paz itself under siege on occasion, and as much as 3/4 of the country in Villarroel's hands. But neither side can successfully evict the other from its beachheads. Villarroel can't defeat Penaranda's professional army; Penaranda can't overcome the Villarroel's numbers. Matters are well on the way towards a stalemate and a slow grinding campaign, similar to the Spanish civil war, and most outside observers see it ending similarly, with Penaranda in the role of Franco.

However, at the centre of South America, intervention in the Bolivian situation is inevitable. Even before the Chaco War, foreign interests are actively engaged in Bolivian politics. British interests in the tin industry in the 1920s are supplanted by American interests lead by Standard Oil in the Chaco region. Then comes Ecuador, looking for an ally against Peru. As the thirties draw to a close, American presence increases, looking upon German immigrants and German advisors with suspicion and hostility. Left to itself, it is likely that there would be a gradual but steady transfer of authority and loyalty from England and Germany to the United States.

But in the context of war breaking out between Peru and Chile, suddenly, everything changes. Bolivia becomes potentially vital, not just to the United States, but to Peru and Chile, who assiduously work to get Bolivia into or keep it out of the war. Driven in part by Chilean interests, the German Intelligence service invests heavily in Bolivia, followed by both Italian and Japanese interests. By 1941 the joke is that a typical Bolivian family consisted of a man, a woman, a child and two spies. There is an endless series of spies, conspiracies, covert actions, plots, counterplots, all of which attempt to read and manipulate the subtle pathways of Bolivian society, all of which struggle for the ear of Penaranda.

This almost certainly has an effect, although that effect can be hard to trace. Do American backers and their strong ideological hostility to apparent fascist and communist influences embolden Penaranda to step up his repression disastrously? Who can say? Do conflicts between German and American agents help to polarize Bolivian politics? Arguably.

Once the civil war begins, it is clear that neutrality is not an option anyone favours. The United States clearly approves the Penaranda government. Ideologically, Penaranda's ruling oligarchy finds its closest kinship with the Peruvian Criollo, and looked to them for aid, support and advice.

Peru initially sought to involve Bolivia in the war. This initiative vanishes during the period of Peru's success, when it seems that they will not need Bolivian help and thus have no reason to share the spoils. When Peru bogs down in trench warfare they once again seek Bolivia on side, but their argument at that point is basically hopeless.

When the civil war breaks out, Peru, already stretched, has little interest in getting directly involved. Nevertheless, it sees a compelling need to have a sympathetic government on its border. Peru makes no secret of its diplomatic support of Penaranda, and follows this up with a steady stream of money and munitions, and voluntarily acts as a conduit for American support.

Much is made of alleged Peruvian involvement. During the civil war, there are accusations that Peru invested troops in Bolivia first. This does not appear to be the case for the most part. Peru does send a number of military advisors and technicians, it does enter into arrangements to 'clear the border' allowing Penaranda to move troops from border duties, and there are documented reports of relatively small numbers of Peruvian troops inside Bolivia, mostly in a logistics capacity. But the Peruvian armies alleged by Villarroel are simply not there.

Whether Villarroel's charges are mistaken, or knowingly false, is a question for the historians. But certainly, in Villarroel's government there is a growing and widespread sentiment that they are fighting not just Penaranda but the Peruvians as well. Faced with this, an increasingly desperate Villarroel has only one option left...

****

Chile - July/August, 1941

As July turns into August, it is becoming clear that the bold gamble that is the Landing has not paid off. Despite the expenditure of vast amounts of blood and treasure, despite the deployment of the navy, air forces and army, despite a hideous cost in casualties, there was no break out.

Peru was not knocked out of the war.

Ecuador's Alba, with far less, has done far more.

Day by day, the hard won mobility decreases, as bloody skirmishes moved the front back in one place, forward in another, shortening lines and shifting towards a resumption of static trench warfare.

Chile's meaningful gains, if any, amount to an advance of less than a couple of dozen miles.

It is in this context that Ibanez and his high command are looking desperately for a new way to break the stalemate....

****

August 13, 1941, Sucre, Bolivia - National Unity Government

Villarroel sits with his cabinet. It is raining outside the Palace of Government. The day is cool and overcast. President Villarroel, he still can't quite get used to the title, sits pensively. Once again, he wishes for German Busch. Busch had presence and charisma, could dominate the room with the sheer force of personality, could get people moving in one direction. In contrast, people don't seem to listen to him, he speaks and they keep on talking.

"I have come to a decision," he says. He repeats it, more loudly. "I have come to a decision."

The cabinet quiets, looking at him.

"I'm going to ask Ibanez for five thousand troops."

Silence.

Villarroel feels sweat pooling down his back.

"Discussion?" he asks.

"This is outrageous," Emil Lozada spits. "To invite the goddamned Chileans in, after they raped our country?"

"That was a long time ago," says another cabinet minister.

"They're still sitting on our coastal provinces. Now you want to get in bed with them?"

"The Americans are against us already. They think we're in Hitler's pocket. This will decide them, surely."

"As you said," Villarroel says, "they're already against us, so what does it matter?"

"Why do we need them?" asks Siles Zuazo, the leader of the socialists in cabinet. "We have three times the men that Penaranda does."

"And Penaranda has three times the guns that we do," Villarroel replies. "You see my problem."

"But still, to invite the Chileans.... this will embroil us in their war."

"We're already in it. Right now, we're fighting Peruvian armies in Bolivia. Penaranda and his gang are tight with them. Peruvian armies and American money," Villarroel snaps.

"But this..." says Lozada, "this is insupportable. I call for a vote."

"Military matters are my exclusive province," snarls Villarroel. "I'm entitled to make my decision."

"Yes, of course," Siles replies, "but still, you should consider the wisdom of the cabinet."

"The vote!" says Lozado.

Every hand is raised against it.

"Will you reconsider, Mister President?" Siles asks.

"I will not," Villarroel replies stiffly.

He watches as several cabinet members stand up and walk out of the room. He prays that they will return after they come to their senses. One of the socialists has not left. It is the Union Man, the Trotskyite, Juan Lechin. He leans back, making notes.

"I'm not a military man, and I won't pretend to know soldiering. But I know this, Penaranda controls the tin mines," he says finally.

"As long as he controls that, the Americans will back him. If he controls the capital of the country, he will win."

Villarroel watches him.

"So I ask you, Mister President, with these foreigners... these mercenaries from Ibanez... these brigands... can you take the mines away from Penaranda?"

Villarroel nods slowly. "I think so."

"Then do what you must."

***

Bolivian Civil War, July 31, 1941

Actually, the traditional export route for Bolivian Tin is west, through Chilean territory and Bolivia's former provinces. One of the few concessions they received from the War of the Pacific was free trade and customs exemptions through those ports.

But that's solid Villarroel territory, and Penaranda's forces makes no headway there. Which means that Penaranda sits on the mines, and Villarroel sits on the export route. If Penaranda could take that, he would, but so far, he hasn't and he has no real prospect of doing so.

Penaranda is trying to remedy that by switching to overland export through Peru (which is more time consuming and expensive), and by maintaining production through any means necessary, which at times verges on slave labour. He's also selling tin, and even worse, tin futures, at deep discounts to the Peruvians, who then resell - he's being screwed on the deal, but he's desperate for foreign exchange and Peruvian support.

Villarroel has no interest in shutting down the mines. He's got control of the more efficient trade route, and mining country is labour country, and labour is very strong in his coalition. Organized Labour is pushing for him to take the mines, nationalize them, and subsidize the workers. Policies that he's not adverse to. Penaranda may control the mines, but the miner's hearts are with Villarroel. All he needs now are their bodies.

In Penaranda's hands, the mines are all still privately owned; the conditions that the miners work in are deplorable. It's the usual story of company towns and company stores, no shopping anywhere else, paid in company scrip which isn't redeemable for money, poor and dangerous working conditions, being paid by lot or production rather than a flat rate, being cheated at that and prices dropping.

Prior to the civil war, things got so bad in the mines that there was a lot of labour unrest, sit downs, wildcats, riots, and even full-fledged strikes. A precipitating incident was Penaranda using soldiers to break miner's strikes and committing full-fledged massacres. Now, in many ways, it's steadily moving towards slave labour, the scale of repression is upped considerably. Penaranda would like to enlist the mining communities by offering a better deal, but his hands are pretty much tied and his options are limited both politically and economically. So it's basically all repression all the time.

The miners definitely resent their situation under Penaranda and feel that they're under occupation. On the other hand, Penaranda has a great many soldiers in these communities, it's the sort of hill and mountain country that is very easy to defend, and the soldiers aren't fooling around.

Villarroel's position is better, but it's not enough. He needs Chile's support. For many nationalist Bolivians, Chile is the devil incarnate, the country that raped away Bolivia's access to the sea.

To be fair though, pretty much every country in the region, Peru, Chile, Argentina, Chile again, Brazil and Paraguay, have carted off bits of Bolivia in one war or another, so it isn't like the Chileans really stand out. Still, Chile is a nationalist bete noir, and Chilean assistance hurts Villarroel more than Peruvian assistance hurts Penaranda.

As we see, his entire Cabinet votes against it, and half his cabinet walks out on him. Villarroel comes to it only reluctantly. Recall that when we first see him, he is comparing an alliance with Chileans to sex with dogs or pigs. Now he's forced to put lipstick on, he doesn't like it, no one else does. But he doesn't see a choice.

However, we will put a caveat on this. Bolivian nationalism is still a relatively recent development. Bolivia as a national identity doesn't really start to gel until or shortly after the Chaco War. It's true that the war of the Pacific and the loss of the coast provinces is a big national trauma, and there's a serious grudge against Chile. But in the particular time frame we're talking about, a country in the aftermath of the Chaco War, struggling with the Depression, the succession of radically different governments represented by Sorzano, Toro and Bush, and Penaranda, the escalating class conflict and now the civil war, Bolivians are pretty much shell shocked. Rabid Anti-Chileanism takes a little more psychic coherence than many have left.

In addition, many of Villarroel's followers believe that the Peruvians actually have armies in Bolivia. Whether they do or not, it's propaganda that Villarroel is desperate to spread around. And it's not entirely false. Whether they have actual troops in Bolivia, the Peruvians are certainly in it up to their elbows.

The question that you have to ask however, is whether Peru is prepared to see Ibanez intervene decisively to put an end to the Bolivian civil war, and risk a Chilean ally on a large stretch of their southern border?

Order of Battle: Bolivia

In June of 1941, Bolivia has 12,500 troops under arms. The army consisted of six infantry regiments, each of three battalions, two light and one heavy; three cavalry regiments, each of four squadrons; two artillery regiments, each with four batteries, each battery equipped with four guns, field, mountain or howitzer; and two engineer battalions.

There were also small cadre infantry units known as the columnas stationed at the chief towns, usually of 100 to 200 soldiers. Somewhat bigger detachments of frontier guards of 300 men each perform security and border guard functions in the country's peripheral regions.

The air force has just been designated a separate branch of the armed forces (Fuerza Aerea-Air Force); the air force is composed of two flights by 1941. These flights contain fighter, army co-operation, and light bomber escuadrillas-squadrons, there were nine to 12 planes in each squadron. Most planes are of U.S. origin, and most are effectively obsolete, the last major purchases being 1937. The main air fields are located at La Paz, Oruro, Cochabamba, Santa Cruz de la Sierra, and Puerto Suarez.

Military service is compulsory for all males capable of bearing arms and in the 19 to 50 years old age group, but in practice this is restricted to the Criollo and Mestizo, the Indigenous who formed the bulk of the population are historically excluded. Exclusions are also made for mine workers and agricultural workers. Active service lasts for a period of two years.

The country is divided into eight military districts, every single of these military districts is supposed to raise a single division in case of war. The divisional district headquarters were located in the following cities and towns: La Paz, Oruro, Sucre, Camiri, Puerto Suarez, Riberalta, Cochabamba, and Santa Cruz de la Sierra.

The Bolivian military was undergoing active attrition since the Chaco War. During the Chaco War, the Bolivian army at its height reaches approximately 60,000 men. No more than two thirds of the Bolivian army was ever in the Chaco at any one time.

Through casualties, attrition and rotation, the total numbers that pass through the army reached 250,000. 90 percent of these are Quechua and Aymara Indigenous conscripts, led by cadres of mestizo and white officers and non-coms. Collectively, there were 57,000 casualties, weighted heavily towards the Indigenous, and 17,000 deserters, most of which end up back in Bolivia. Another 20,000 were captured.

Following the Chaco war in 1935, the Bolivian army rapidly demobilized, most Quechua and Aymara conscripts were released or discharged, and the army became heavily Mestizo. As peace negotiations dragged on, Bolivia re-armed for a possible resumption of the war, the re-armament reaching 25,000 in 1937. The peace treaty or truce was finalized only by 1938.

Due to its rapid expansion during the Chaco war, and the huge enlistment or conscription of educated whites and mestizo as officers, the army became a place of intellectual ferment and social critique. This lead to the Military Socialism movement of Toro and Busch.

Under the Penaranda regime, which was a major conservative push back, there was a consistent campaign to attempt to depoliticize the army and root out military socialism in favour of conservative views. This was to be achieved through the continuing overall reduction in the size of the army as a whole, something also driven by economic factors. It was also pursued through policies of dismissing officers, removing officers from command of troops, or reassignment of suspect officers to remote towns or outposts, retarding promotions, early retirements, and rapid recruitment and promotion of the 'right sort' of officer with the proper political views and social connections, but often unqualified.

The outbreak of war between Chile and Bolivia slows down the attrition of the army considerably. It is estimated that without it, the Army would decline to a low of approximately 9,000 in 1942 or 1943. Despite the war on the borders, however, there is no real thought given to mobilization, and Bolivia is utterly unprepared to confront either country, or any significant fraction of either country's military might.

Nevertheless by the eve of Civil War, the Bolivian armed forces are in sad shape. Morale is poor, paranoia and attrition are widespread and politics of the worst sort infects the body. For the most part, the army is under equipped and much of the equipment is obsolete, although selected divisions and battalions will be much better armed than the average. Soldiers and officers are, on the whole, well trained, with notable exceptions, but the organizational structure is poor.

The hidden strength of the Bolivian military, however, is in its veterans. Numbering roughly 200,000, Bolivia has an immense cadre of combat aged males who have received intensive military training and even combat experience - by which I mean they know how to march, they knew to look attentive when an officer is around, to do what they are told with speed when a non-com yells, and obey without thinking too much, they know to dig holes fast, eat as they move, sleep where they can, stick close to their peers, rely on their unit, and crouch rather than run when someone is shooting at them.

The veterans include a large cadre of displaced or dispossessed Mestizo officers and non-coms, many of whom are politically and socially incompatible with the Penaranda regime.

It also includes a vast number of Quechua and Aymara, mostly infantry but including some non-coms and some trained personnel, who have made friends and contacts and connections with each other while in the army, but who surrendered their weapons and returned to their villages, their experiences in the army little more than a bad memory, but retaining and even passing on their training and experience to their peers.

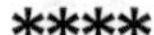

Bolivia - Order of Battle - the Civil War, Early State

The first month of the civil war sees the partition of the Army between the warring camps of Villarroel and Penaranda, but the partition is neither easy nor stable.

Essentially, Penaranda retains control of roughly two thirds of the active army, including all of the cavalry and artillery battalions, roughly 7,000 to 8,000 troops.

Villarroel's supporter ranged between 4,000 and 5,500 troops, mostly infantry, but with one engineers battalion and a surprising amount of loyalty from air force wings. One flight goes over to Villarroel; another is severely sabotaged by ground crews

Many of those who declare for Villarroel are stationed in towns and outlying communities, while Penaranda almost immediately concentrates his strength in La Paz and the mining district.

In the opening phases of the civil war, both sides put out immediate calls to reserves, and numbers escalate rapidly. During the first month, enlistment under the Penaranda banner climbs to slightly over 10,000. For the most part, Penaranda's forces are well armed and well supplied. But inexperienced and often inept leadership at the officer level often hampers operations. Despite overall greater quality, Penaranda's army finds it difficult to mount aggressive operations, logistics being a short suit. These drawbacks are being addressed.

In contrast, Villarroel's call ups exceed 15,000, with numbers continually climbing. However, Villarroel's forces are chronically short of weapons, ammunition, and even shoes and uniforms. Villarroel's communications, however, are excellent, and his logistics and mobility surprisingly good. Villarroel is able to establish loyalty and control over much of the countryside, and even in outlying areas nominally under the control of Penaranda, he often has a hidden presence.

For the most part, the Quechua and Aymara Indigenous avoid voluntary call up, and are at best passive in the face of conscription moves. The civil war armies that face each other are initially almost wholly white and mestizo. Nevertheless, as rival armies reach saturation, conscription begins to be implemented by both factions, and there is a battle of the white men for the hearts and minds of the Indigenous they want to die on their behalf.

Neither of the combatants at the early phase of the civil war - July/August, even at their strongest, is sufficient in numbers or equipment to confront even a fraction of the military strength of the belligerents on their borders. Whether that will remain the case, has yet to be seen.

****

Battle for the Top of the World

On the west side of Bolivia is a young steep mountain range called the Corderilla Occidental. Volcanic, jagged, fierce, the Corderilla Occidental forms part of the border with Chile and extends both south into Argentina and north into Peru.

Travel due east, and you come to another mountain range, older, granitic, a product of continental flex, the Corderilla Oriental. Keep travelling east, and you get to the Bolivian lowlands, and eventually to rain forest jungle barely above sea level, and even the remnants of the Bolivian Chaco, which a humorous god deigned to place the Chaco's oil fields, the only valued raw materials to be found in the Chaco.

But we've gone too far. Step back. Between the two mighty ranges, the Corderilla Occidental and the Corderilla Oriental is a broad plain running north and south called the Altiplano. Homelands to both Quechua and Aymara, the site of Lake Titicaca and Lake Poopol, the highest lakes in the world.

The Altiplano averages 12,300 feet (3,750 meters) in elevation, just short of the Himalayas themselves, and is the largest high plateau outside of the Himalayas.

In particular, the Altiplano and its monstrous companion ranges, and the networks of hills, valleys and mountains that represent the Andean highlands runs beyond Bolivia, south into Argentina, and perhaps more critically, north into southern Peru, all the way to the Peruvian city of Cuzco....

For Peru the Altiplano is of little strategic significance. It offers little in the way of opportunities, since the Corderilla Occidental forms a mountain barrier making an Altiplano route invasion of Chile impractical. Equally, the Altiplano blocks any possible Chilean attack.

Chile, on the other hand, should it gain access to the Altiplano...

***

New World War – Page 54

Santa Cruz de la Sierra - August 30, 1941.

Colonel Ramon Valpes is having a bad day. It doesn't help that the little shit, Major Gustavo was underfoot.

Valpes signed. Gustavo isn't so bad. It's just that they have so little in common. Ramon Valpes is a historian by trade, drafted into the Chaco war; his education made him automatic officer material. He's risen quickly, and somehow lingers on, out here in the lowland town.

At times, he almost misses the Chaco war. Not the Chaco, of course. By his mother's name, God himself would not miss the Chaco, the heat, the drought, the flies, the endless mud and marching. At times he thought that they should fight to make the Paraguayans take it.

Rather, he misses the camaraderie of the officers, the free ranging debates and discussions that were almost collegial in their breadth. He misses the sense of purpose.

After the war, he finds that there are no opportunities for historians in any of the cities. Reluctantly, the army becomes his home.

Slowly with Penaranda, the chill sets in. Gradually, you start watching what you said; then you start watching your back.. And even that isn't good enough for those high nosed bastards.

Still, he keeps his nose clean. Not that it matters. In the end, he's assigned to the lowlands, commanding a stick of a town called Montero. It is hot, it is humid and unbearable. The place is full of Guarani Indigenous, who are too much of a reminder of the Chaco. There are even Jews here. Jews? Who would have thought?

He corresponds with his peers, hears reports and rumours of disappearances. After a while, Montero isn't so bad. He keeps his head down and hopes that Penaranda's inquisition might pass him by in this remote backwater.

An undercurrent of fear worms its way into his life.

Then comes the National Unity Government, like a breath of fresh air. Finally, we'll all be rid of that butcher, Penaranda!

The news comes rapidly, the headlines contradictory, a breathtaking succession of claims, counter claims, and occasional struggle. Santa Cruz quickly declares for Villarroel. For the first time in weeks, Valpes thinks he can breathe freely.

Then within a week, the Garrison at Santa Cruz, led by that arrogant bastard, Aguilada, rises up, putting the city under martial law, and declaring for Penaranda.

Within days, riots begin. The troops themselves split.

Valpes finds himself thrust forward. At the head of several local garrisons, he marches into Santa Cruz. The Penaranda loyalists flee without a shot being fired, Valpes find himself the hero of the day and commander of the city, and by extension, of a fifth of Bolivia.

But now?

He wads up the letter and throws it across the room.

Gustavo starts. The bookkeeper disguised as a major looks up, puzzled.

"Merde," Valpes swears. He studied in Paris, and he likes to throw in a foreign curse or two. It made him exotic to the whores down in the brothels.

"What is it?"

"President.... 'President' Villarroel made us all the whores of Chile. He's invited Chilean armies in."

"That cannot be good."

"It is an outrage, after the War of the Pacific, after the rape of our cherished country. He does this?"

Valpes stands up and strides around the room, burning off nervous tension.

"Bah... hopeless. I'd go over to Penaranda this minute, if I didn't know he'd shoot me the moment he has a free bullet. It is insupportable! What are we to do? Our choices are a butcher on one hand, a traitor on the other?"

"Well," says Gustavo, "they're both far away, and more concerned with beating each other, so that's not so bad. It's too bad there's not a third choice."

Valpes stops, letting the words sink in. He stares out the window.

"President Valpes?" he whispers to himself. He sort of likes the sound of it.

Santa Cruz Rebellion - September, 1941

As Penaranda jockeys for position, and Villarroel struggles to hold his disintegrating coalition together, the logical, inevitable point for the next fracture is Santa Cruz. This is only large city outside the range of the Altiplano, and therefore beyond the easy reach of either faction.

Santa Cruz also guarantees effective control of the lowland hinterlands. In the struggle between the two factions in the main population centers, the lowlands are ignored, their interests are divergent enough that they want a seat at the table, or perhaps, their own table.

Initially, Valpes is claiming, somewhat dubiously, Presidency of all of Bolivia. To be blunt, he's got no legal case at all. His claim amounts to 'those other two guys are assholes, so why not me?'

Actually, it's a little better than that. Pretty much no one but Penaranda's own backers like Penaranda, and that's a narrow class warfare group of elites.

Villarroel risks his constituency, his national unity government, with the Chilean invitation. Villarroel is taking a calculated risk that he can use the Chileans to win control of the mining district, overrun La Paz and take out Penaranda. And once he does that, he needs to make sure the Chileans go away.

It's a gamble, but if it works and he wins big time, he figures everyone will fall in behind him. If it doesn't work... well, odds are the Penaranda will grind him down like pepper in a protracted war. So this is his best bet.

But Villarroel's coalition fractures over dealing with the Chileans, so Valpes is hoping to pick up support and supplant Villarroel in a new National Unity Coalition, while at the same time establishing a distinctive power base in the lowlands to draw people and factions to him.

He's also making a calculated gamble, that Villarroel's followers will eventually fall his way. If it works, he gets the whole country. Or at least he gets Villarroel's mess. If it doesn't.... well, either Villarroel or Penaranda is going to swat him real hard.

He's commanding a fairly large city, which dominates the lowland, so he's controlling a fairly large territory, although with very low population density. His real advantage is that he's out of the way of the two big dogs.

The military forces at his command are almost trivial. Roughly 3,000 to 3,500 troops, no artillery, some ad hoc cavalry, poorly armed and equipped. Villarroel's sucked up the best of the countryside's men and equipment to face off against Penaranda. Even with his best efforts, Valpe's own resources aren't enough to make him a real contender. Fight either one, his loss is ordained.

Nor is the hinterland economy of Santa Cruz really up to sustaining a fight. It's basically an agricultural hinterland, some mining, a bit of oil production in a remote province. But most of the export trade goes through the centre, held by the warring rivals. Most of the imports come from there, and they're heavily dependent on imports.

So basically, Valpes bites off way more than he can chew. And unless Villarroel's coalition falls apart decisively, opening the way for him to step into the vacuum, he's going to be in trouble.

Unless he can think of something....

✳✳✳

Paraguay and Argentina

Paraguay isn't nearly as bad off as Bolivia. But it sustained a ruinous war, colossal casualties, and massive expenses. So it's not a happy place. It goes through many of the same sorts of social disruptions and instability as Bolivia.

Arising from the Chaco treaty, Paraguay's military is only 8,000 men, and while they're lean, mean, fighting machines and pretty well equipped, there's just not that many of them, and the Bolivian frontier is a long way away, through some really hard slogging.

During the Chaco war, Argentina supported Paraguay behind the neutrality facade. Paraguay received military supplies and daily intelligence from Argentina. Argentina provided Paraguay with critical economic and military backing throughout the war. And what did they get for that? Nothing. The oil turned out to be in Bolivian territory. The Argentines won no real advantage for their efforts, no reward for their investment.

The thing is, no one really wants to get involved in a war. Certainly not the Ecuadorians under Bonifaz, Ibarra and Alba. Certainly not the Peruvians under Benavides or Prado. And certainly not the Chileans under Ross or Ibanez. The Bolivians under any regime, Penaranda or Villarroel, going all the way back to Bush, Toro and Sorzano were all uniformly appalled at the thought of getting dragged into a foreign war.

Really, the only one who actually wanted a war is probably General Ureta, and he certainly didn't want the war he got.

So the Argentines don't want to be involved. They're not champing at the bit. The Depression has been bad for them, and in particular, they're discovering the downside of not actually being a British colony. They have huge economic problems. They can't afford and don't want a war.

On the other hand, they don't actually want to see a Bolivia dominated by Chile. A Bolivia dominated by Peru is almost as bad.

They don't like to see the current balance of power being altered in Latin America; they don't want any of their neighbours getting too strong. So there's going to be a temptation to meddle in Bolivian politics, to get a client, to back a favourite, to send, as Warren Zevon said, lawyers guns and money.

A Bolivia that ends up as an Argentine satellite... that doesn't sound bad at all. Not when considering the resources that Argentina could access from Bolivia.

But it's not worth sending an army in for. Just worth meddling, stirring the pot, sending arms and money, making life interesting, maybe diplomatically finessing their favourite into a leadership position.

What happens is that President Ramon Valpes, contender for rule of Bolivia, current le Jefe of the lowlands, finds he desperately needs a patron with an open checkbook. One without the baggage of a Chile or Peru. One with the resources to support his efforts. And where it goes from there....

But remember, nobody actually wanted to be in this war, they've all more or less been dragged in unwillingly by circumstance. That's something that the Argentines might ponder.

****

Calama Base, the Bolivian Altiplano, September 2, 1941

Colonel Sebastian Milero sits down on and tries to catch his breath. For some reason, even the least exertion leaves him gasping, heart pounding. He is cold, shivering cold, and yet he is sweating. It feels like he is coming down with something.

"It's just the altitude," his friend, Colonel Penzance says, handing him a canteen.

Milero nods and takes the canteen, drinking hungrily. It is so dry up here a man can feel all the liquid boiling away out of him.

Calama base is nowhere near the Chilean towns of Calama or Chuqicamata which supplies them, but farther inland inside Bolivia, high up on the Altiplano, south of an immense salt flat, and near a lazy brackish river.

What is it called? The Lipez? More than it was worth to drink from that he thinks. Better to drink his mother's toilet water.

By Christ, but this is a horrid inhospitable land.

"So, how's it going?" Penzance asks, sitting down beside him.

"Still having trouble with the trucks, they overheat, they sputter and stall," he replies, he is finally catching his breath, "I've never seen anything like it."

"Altitude," Penzance says. That was is answer to everything. "It makes a difference; we're up, what ten thousand feet? That's half way up Mount Everest. We could look down on half the mountains in the world. The thin air, it makes water evaporate away, it probably does something to the gasoline."

That makes sense, Milero thinks. But then Penzance has to ruin his point.

"Add oil," he says, "that should thicken things up."

Milero shudders.

He hands the canteen back.

"How does it go on your side?" he asks, "With the Boliviano recruits?"

"Well…" says Penzance reflectively, "very well indeed. Frighteningly so. These Indios, Quechua they call themselves, it is like they are made of stone. The altitude does nothing to them. All us Chileans, we fall over at the least little thing, but these damned Indios, you can't see it in their expression, but they must be laughing as they trot around like spring deer carrying packs that would cripple a mule."

"They're used to it," says Milero, "this height. They grew up with it."

"True enough," Penzance replies, "they're farmers too. Lots of manual labour, it makes them strong, especially up here. And they make good soldiers. A lot of them, I think, are veterans of the Chaco, so they know a bit of soldiering. Some bad habits they pick up, but many good ones. But even the conscripts who weren't in the army before, they're good. They know to march and salute, they pick it up fast. All they need are decent boots and rifles, and they are the match of any soldiers we've seen."

Milero grunts. As the war goes on, he's lost a certain respect for Chilean soldiers. In his experience, their patriotism is thin, and they complain almost constantly. Where is the love for the fatherland? Look at an average infantryman, he's just as happy to leave the war and go home.

"If they're such good soldiers," Milero asks, "how was it that they lost the Chaco war?"

Penzance shakes his head.

"Maybe they didn't have decent boots and rifles, or enough of them. Maybe leadership…"

"Careful."

It won't do to insult the leadership. The officers who lost the Chaco war are the same ones inviting them into this desolate country, and the ones they'll have to fight beside. The Indios are one thing, they don't seem to care one way or the other, white men are all of the same to them. But the Boliviano officers and NCO's are all over the place; and they are a prickly bunch.

Desperate, yes. Impoverished, yes. Needing the Chileans, of course. But still bitter over the war in the Pacific, despite that it was half a century ago, and resentful of the men they have just invited into their country. And by god, they were prickly over the Chaco.

The two men glance around, to make sure that there are no Boliviano in earshot. As far as Moreno is concerned, maybe if the bastards grow up and stop being such whiny bitches they might someday win a war with someone. But that was an opinion he keeps to himself.

"So," Moreno says, to change the subject, "what do you think we're up to?"

Penzance spreads his hands. "Not sure, counting the Indio, we're past ten thousand though, and more coming in every day... from the Indios at least."

Not so many Chilean soldiers though. Oh there are a few thousand of them, but more supplies. Even now, the trucks come mostly loaded with supplies. Blankets and uniforms, rifles and ammunition, water, lots of water, and rations. Calama base is a small town all by itself, nestling in the Altiplano desert. It is an expensive base, to be sure. It is not cheap to truck thousands of tons of supplies out to the middle of nowhere.

On the other hand, the Peruvian front isn't cheap either. Ibanez has to supply his men at the outer limits of Chilean territory, through the inhospitable Atacama Desert and the barren regions of Tarapaca and Antofagasta. The Peruvians defend on their doorstep, the bastards could go home to eat their lunch. But the Chilean forces are maintained only through elaborate supply networks and large bases.

Against such, Calama base is merely a drop in the bucket.

"Big meeting tonight?"

Moreno nods.

"I hear President Ibanez is flying in personally."

Added to that hideous expense is Ibanez 'brilliant' but ruinous strategy of the 'Landing', which turns the compact stable line into horribly overextended frontiers that are causing the Chilean budget to haemorrhage in arterial spurts of red ink. Only Ibanez pride keeps it going.

Back in Santiago and Valparaiso, Ibanez enemies like to say that one more victory like that, and the country will be forced to surrender.

But they don't say it loudly, not yet.

"And the Boliviano, Major Villarroel."

"It's President Villarroel!"

They glance around, wary of some prickly Boliviano walking by.

Moreno wipes the sweat from his brow. Even sitting he pants slightly. Damn this place. Who could possibly want it? When the is was over, he'll gladly leave it to the Indio.

Still, it is better than being on the Peruvian front.

****

September 2, 1941, The 'Calamity Summit', Calama Base, Altiplano, Bolivia

Colonels Morena and Penzance stand with the Chilean delegation, off to the side of the big tent. In front of them are the aides and higher officers, the various specialty officers. President Ibanez and his generals, the high command, sat on one side of the makeshift table. They flew in direct from Santiago, and will fly out again, once the summit was over.

The Bolivians, led by President Villarroel, sit on the other side. No Indios, Morena noted, all white men or Mestizo. Villarroel's team are a rather motley assortment of civilians and military men. Villarroel wears a general's uniform and medals, but it was common knowledge that he'd risen no higher than Major. There isn't a man on the Chilean side, Morena reflected, that does not outrank Villarroel, and that tells you something.

Morena has no idea who the Boliviano are, apart from Villarroel. The corpulent, thick faced President has a kind of stolid dignity to him. The civilians are a mixed lot, thick working men and bespectacled academics. If Morena knows anything, he knows a communist when he sees one. The military men are similarly unimpressive, hardly a professional in the bunch, their uniforms sloppy, buttons missing, threads loose.

Some of them are doubtless genuine fighting men; a country can't go through the Chaco war and not produce some real ass-kickers. Here and there in the group, there are some hard stares. They all look tired though. Moreno knew that they came by truck, navigating the dirt roads from Sucre and Potosi. Again, Morena sees this as a marker of the differing quality of Boliviano and Chileans. The Chileans fly, the Boliviano ride.

"What about this Colonel Valpes?" Ibanez is asking.

"He is of no consequence," Villarroel responds. "He has nothing; he'll be swept away like that." Villarroel snaps his fingers.

"He broke away from your command," Ibanez prods, "I hear that many of your officers have some sympathy for him. He controls a good chunk of territory."

"Allying with your country is controversial," Villarroel replies. "But the ones who would rebel over it, have rebelled. I remain in control. The country he rules is worthless."

Except, of course, for the Chaco oil, Morena thinks, which is how the argument started. Morena prays that they won't get back into it again. He couldn't stand yet another half hour of it. Ibanez clearly thinks of pursuing it, but decides not to.

"Valpes is a problem for another day," Villarroel repeats. "When we defeat Penaranda, he'll fold like a house of cards, if he even bothers to fight."

"Well enough," says "Ibanez, let us return to the main strategy."

Morena struggles not to roll his eyes. Here we go again.

"We have no quarrel with Peru," Villarroel says, "we will permit your forces to cross our territory, on our conditions, but we will not supply troops."

As if we need that collection of inbred mestizo and Indio peasants, Morena thinks, allowing himself the slightest smirk. But at least the discussion is moving forward. Initially, Villarroel is adamant that no attacks on Peru be made from Bolivian soil. That is a condition that would make the whole venture pointless. They might as well pack up Calama Base and go home. But both sides know it is just a negotiating stance. The Bolivian puta pretends to be a virgin, so that she can negotiate a higher price.

"You think Lima will appreciate that distinction?" Ibanez replies sarcastically, "We will attack through Bolivia, but Peru will hold no hard feelings because you did not send a brigade along. Hell, Ramirez already has his hand up Penaranda's rear. Mark my words, either we are partners in this, or your country will be Peru's puppet."

Ibanez pauses, looking at the faces of the Bolivian delegation. They've all turned to stone. Time to walk back, Morena thinks.

"But as partners, we respect your wishes. The struggle against Peru is ours; we will not compel you to more than you wish. We appreciate your support, and of course we pledge our support against La Paz."

"La Paz is but a rest stop on our road," Villarroel replies. "We need to take the mining districts."

"Go ahead," Ibanez snaps. "Take it."

"I need artillery, and air support. I need engineers," Villarroel replies. "We must cooperate on this."

"Giving you this support will undermine our offensive," Ibanez says.

Ah, thinks Morena, now it comes out, after an hour of dancing around.

"Why should we do this?" Ibanez demands. "What you ask may mean the difference between victory and defeat."

"We need the mines," Villarroel replies. "We need the capital they produce."

"You need it," Ibanez says almost silkily. "We don't."

The Bolivians don't have a pot to piss in, they are desperate for cash. Morena hears that in Sucre, government officials are paid in vegetables. Well, now that they are admitting they are broke, the real concessions will come.

"You need it too," Villarroel replies. "You forget the Americanos."

"What about them?"

"They're up there, watching this war. Sooner or later, they're going to pick a side," Villarroel tells him. "And when they do, this war is over. Now, it would be good to finish things up so that they don't have to make a decision. But if we cannot do that, well then, they will pick the side that benefits them most."

"And so...." Villarroel pauses dramatically, about to play his Trump card. Moreno almost admires his theatricality.

"Bolivia has tin and other metals. The Americanos are hungry for both of these, they need them. If we control them, then they will support us, and we'll give them a good price. If we cannot control it, they'll throw their weight behind anyone they think can give it to them, and at best, we're in a bidding war."

"Tin is not so much," Ibanez says, he pauses. "We have copper, they need that more."

Villarroel does not reply immediately. Ibanez looks thoughtful.

"You were telling us all how important Chaco oil is," Villarroel says quietly.

Finally, Ibanez nods.

"I see your point. You'll have your artillery and engineers."

"And air support?"

"Yes, that too." Ibanez snaps. "But we don't undermine the offensive; I'll find new resources for you. And in return, I want Bolivian infantry support when we go into Peru."

"Done."

Finally, Morena thinks, it's all over. Four hours of arguing, over what should be sorted out in fifteen minutes. I could learn to despise politics, Morena decides.

"Now," Ibanez says, "turning to the next matter..."

****

Battle of Lake Titicaca, Peru

September 27, 1941, the Battle of Titicaca officially commences, ending with the decisive defeat of Peruvian and North Bolivian armies and opening the Peruvian Altiplano to Chilean forces.

Named after the Altiplano lake, a combined force of 15,000 Chileans and Bolivians move up the Altiplano, sweeping away the forces of the Penaranda government (approximately 7,000 men, plus 25,000 unarmed conscripts, and a Peruvian expeditionary force of 5,000), reaching the shores of Lake Titicaca and entering Peruvian territory in numbers along the west coast of the lake.

By October 10, 1941, Chilean forces penetrate as much as one hundred miles into Peruvian territory on a broad front. Large populations of Quechua refugees are pushed before them, or withdraw further into the hills. Peruvian army units are caught mostly unprepared and retreat into foothills, where they struggle to reconnect and reorganize.

Despite these successes, the Chilean/South Bolivians are unable to fully capitalize on their advances. Pockets of resistance remain throughout the areas overrun, and the geographical barriers of the mountain and hill ranges slow mobility.

Eventually by late November, the Chileans drive into Peru is contained, and while there are sorties into the Peruvian Altiplano, most of the combat operations are taking place in the Bolivian north and centre.

Initially overwhelmed by the combined advance of Chile and South Bolivia, Penaranda's army withdraws to La Paz, where Villarroel lays siege. La Paz holds out until surrendering on October 29, 1941. By this time, the Penaranda government has already moved its seat officially to Cobija in the north. But for all practical purposes, the Penaranda administration is running its affairs from Puerta Maldonado just over the border in Peru.

The Chilean intervention does not go unopposed. As early as August 15, Peru formally protests alleged Chilean intervention in the Bolivian civil war. September 8, in response to news of the build-up of forces at Base Calama, Penaranda's government signs a mutual defence pact with Lima.

By September 22, Peruvian military forces are in northern Bolivia conducting joint defence operations. Penaranda, supplied with Peruvian weapons and equipment, begins a massive conscription program among the Quechua and Aymara. The magnitude of the conscription is such that entire villages and districts are emptied of combat age males. This causes a further erosion of Penaranda's support, never high, particularly in Quechua areas.

Unfortunately, these moves come too late, and the Chileans and Southern Bolivians attack with superior organization and effective numbers. Despite commitment to joint efforts, the Peruvian and Bolivian militaries fail completely to coordinate, making them easy prey for the more organized attacking forces. The disintegrating Penaranda military establishment is eventually subsumed in late October by Peru, and while his government retains nominal independence, most of the Quechua conscripts end up under Peruvian command.

During September, Villarroel begin a second thrust of 7,000, mostly Bolivians with a smattering of Chilean specialists, attacks the mining district. The fighting is heavy, going from town to town, village to village, but by November 10, 1941, the entire area is under the control of the Villarroel administration, which pronounces the nationalization of mining assets, and resumption of operations under workers collectives. By December, 1941, Bolivian mines, shipping through Chilean ports return to almost full productivity. Dissidents return to Villarroel's coalition.

On November 15, a sortie by Villarroel's forces on the city of Santa Cruz is decisively defeated. Villarroel's staff begin to plan a campaign against the rival Valpes government. By November 24, Villarroel formally asks for Chilean assistance, including contributions of trucks, artillery and air support. The Chileans, at this time entirely overstretched, can contribute little.

Montevideo Peace Conference, Encyclopaedia Britannica, 1973 Edition.

The Montevideo Peace Conference, September 23 to 25, held in Uruguay is an unsuccessful diplomatic attempt to resolve or at least bring a cease-fire to the Bolivian Civil War. The conference is undone by its refusal to accept the participation of either Chile or the Villarroel government.

Parties to the Peace Conference include the interested and neighbouring governments of the region - Brazil, Argentina, Peru, Paraguay, Uruguay, the Valpes and Penaranda factions of the Bolivian civil war, plus the United States and United Kingdom.

The Conference agrees on basic principles. i.e. - To whit (1) the immediate withdrawal of all foreign troops from Bolivia, except for an independent Brazilian peace-keeping force to be authorized by the Conference; (2) the elimination of 'foreign influences', generally understood to be Nazi/Fascist and Communists; (3) immediate cease-fire by all combatants; (4) free trade and respect of foreign investment; (5) the recognition or establishment of an interim national government; (6) Free and fair elections to follow.

The Conference explicitly excludes the Villarroel faction of the Bolivian government, together with its Chilean backers, which creates major obstacles to implementation of the agreed positions.

Initially the Penaranda government is supported by the United States, the United Kingdom, Brazil, Peru and Uruguay. Dissension breaks out when first Argentina and then Paraguay back the Valpes faction. An attempt by the United States to arrange a Penaranda/Valpes coalition falls apart when a meeting between the two factions degenerates into a brawl. Uruguay moves to a position of neutrality.

Thereafter, the two factions, backed by Argentina and Paraguay and then Peru and Brazil respectively, struggle to persuade the United States and the United Kingdom to extend their support. But both major powers are reluctant to commit either way. In the end, the conference ends without resolution.

The failure of the Conference means that the Bolivian situation continued to disintegrate and the lack of a clearly dominant player means that neighbouring countries intervene in a variety of ways. The Bolivian civil becomes a central theatre of the Andean wars.

Initially at least, the Peace Conference is seen by several parties as an attempt to end the civil war by consolidating effective support, and garnering support for an intervention on Penaranda's side. There is a reason that Villarroel's faction isn't invited.

Sadly for Realpolitik, Valpes also gets an invite through his Argentinian backers. The thinking of the other parties is that folding Valpes into a 'coalition government' will give Penaranda some further legitimacy. But when Argentina insists on backing him as a real player, things go down the toilet.

But the Conference is probably doomed anyway. In the end, only Peru is really committed to intervening on Penaranda's side. Without a joint coalition, the Brazil, the United States and United Kingdom are not sufficiently invested.

As far as an arms embargo goes though, that horse has long left the barn.

****

Ecuador - The Third Northern Offensive, Prelude

The failure of the 2nd Great Northern offensive leaves the Commander of the Northern Army Group, General Markholtz, facing disgrace. By the end of April, the head of the Peruvian Junta, General Rodriguez issues letters on April 20 and April 26, relieving him of his command and ordering his return to Lima. The Junta has utterly lost faith in him.

Markholtz chooses to ignore both orders, refuses to relinquish command and refuses to leave the north. These acts of insubordination would normally provoke a crisis in the Junta. By mid-May it becomes clear that Markholtz is effectively in rebellion.

However, events are moving quickly. On May 26, 1941, the Chileans launch the 'Landing' a land and sea offensive that almost overwhelms the Peruvian front and pushes the line up along the coast in a new jagged perimeter. Suddenly, the Junta is fighting for its life, and the problem of a recalcitrant general far away in the north seems unimportant. The confrontation with Markholtz is forgotten for the time being, and although the letters are never recalled, there is no further action.

Instead, during the crisis, Markholtz is allowed to pledge fealty once again to the Junta, and signify his good faith by contributing levies from the Northern Command to the Southern Defence. Mostly, however, these are not seasoned troops, but relatively raw and under equipped Quechua and Mestizo. Unwilling to part with his already attenuated Criollo Officer and NCO corps, Markholtz compromises by promoting able veterans of his Mestizo and Quechua infantry to lower ranking officer and NCO positions. This is not particularly well thought of in Lima, but it is accepted.

The 'Landing' is a blessing for Markholtz, providing him with a vital reprieve. During this period, spies and intelligence reports from Ecuador provide him with a steady stream of information, and it begins to dawn on Markholtz just how close he came to overrunning Alba. Each succeeding report confirms that the Ecuadorians are broke, that they are stretched to the limits, that Alba was literally running out of ammunition as they'd fought.

Markholtz decides that a third northern offensive cannot fail. Even more critically, his survival and reputation depends on a clear victory. Crushing Alba is not simply a national priority; it is a vital personal necessity.

Unfortunately, through the months of May and June, the 'Landing' is ongoing, and the High Command in Lima absolutely refuses to countenance or supply a further northern invasion. Instead, they demand that Markholtz send troops south. In a letter received from Rodriguez, the prospect of a Northern Invasion during the Landing is described flatly as 'treason,' notwithstanding Markholtz assurances that this time, Ecuador will be crushed.

By July, the situation in the south stabilizes, at least as far as the front goes. The Bolivian Civil war is rapidly escalating, and this preoccupies the Junta, leaving Markholtz with a relatively free hand in the north. Unfortunately, even if Alba is down to his last few rounds of ammunition, Markholtz forces are only a little better off. His secondments to the southern front are gradually returning back to him, better armed and better equipped, but for the most part his demands for more equipment, more weapons and ammunition are ignored. He receives but a trickle of what he asks for.

But it is a steady trickle. With only moderate support from Central Command, Markholtz works relentlessly to build his army back up. He undertakes massive conscription from the Quechua interior, at times triggering conscription riots. He also requisitions every firearm he can lay his hands on, in some cases literal museum pieces, hunting rifles and bandit weapons. He offers a cash bounty for weapons. Regular forces are bolstered with secondments from central command as he cashes in favors. Policio are requisitioned as officers. In all this, he acts with almost complete independence, a nearly autonomous Prince bound only lightly to the commands of Lima.

The promotion of Quechua and Mestizo to positions above their 'proper' station, originally implemented as a means to preserve his own officer corps becomes a fact of life as conscripts swell the ranks with non-Spanish speakers, and numbers grow beyond the ability of his existing officers to manage.

Throughout, it becomes an article of faith that the Ecuadorans are near collapse. The realization of how close he's come to achieving victory rankles him deeply. Markholtz becomes obsessed, ignoring any argument or evidence that threatens his coming vindication. As August comes to a close, he is almost ready.

It is in late August that an American peace initiative is advanced, essentially calling for a cease-fire between Ecuador and Peru and a return to established borders. Not directly involved in the talks, Markholtz contacts in Lima keep him apprised.

By early September it appears that the Junta is preparing to enter a formal cease-fire and truce with Ecuador, in order to free itself to deal with the enemy to the South. The Bolivian situation has the Junta spooked by both reports of an alliance between Villarroel and the Chileans, and the emergence of a third faction. The Junta comes to believe that Chilean forces are massing in Bolivia, although they've taken no action to date. For its part, the Junta is drawing close to the Penaranda government, and struggling to bring Brazil and Argentina on board as guarantors of Bolivian neutrality and the primacy of the Penaranda government.

Hostilities with Ecuador are a very unwelcome distraction. Peace with Bonifaz is about to break out any minute now.

Markholtz cannot abide that. On September 6, 1941, he launches the Third Northern Offensive.

***

Demographic Shifts

During the Chaco War in Bolivia, as much as 90 percentof the Bolivian soldiers are conscripted Mestizo and Indigenous, principally Quechua and Aymara.

The proportion isn't quite so high for Peru, but traditionally, the Peruvian army has always conscripted Indigenous and Mestizo for the lower ranks.

Historically, the Indigenous have passively avoided conscription by making themselves scarce when the press gang comes along, or even by local riots or aggressive resistance. But enough still got conscripted to fill out the ranks, and local resistance was tolerated. They didn't need that many Indigenous.

Both the Bolivian and Peruvian ruling class seem to have regarded the Quechua and Aymara as convenient and useful, but low quality, cannon fodder. Because the Indigenous are out of the cultural and economic mainstream, you can harvest as many of them into the army as you want. Theoretically you can conscript without putting any real stress on or removing manpower from your 'real economy.'

Of course, during the Depression, there is a lot of surplus population in the 'real economy' but the war is soaking that up really fast.

While the Indigenous aren't participants in the real economy, they're important to their local economy, so communities are not thrilled with conscription. Historically, the Indigenous and Mestizo who get conscripted or drafted into the army are people that were, for one reason or another, surplus to the community. Sometimes they're actively unwanted in the community. But as the war goes on though, and conscription in these communities gets heavier and heavier, it begins to produce real tension.

Another interesting thing that's starting to happen by this phase, is that due to the dramatic expansion of the military, and severe

attrition in the officer and non-commission corps (this is
particularly bad with the Ecuadorian campaigns - Alba & Co are
hell on officers and sergeants. The Chilean front on the other hand,
tends to keep officers safe and secure as infantry rushes the
machine guns), we're starting to see increasingly Mestizo and even
some Quechua moving into the positions of lower ranking officers
and non-commissioned officers.

From the Chaco War to the Civil War

Bolivia fared extremely poorly in the Chaco war for a number of reasons. We've discussed the ingrained social problems, the conservatism and relative ineffectiveness of the elite etc.

But there are reasons to believe that Bolivia could be a much more effective combatant in this new war.

In the Chaco war, Bolivia was hampered by extremely long supply lines. It took Bolivia an average of three weeks to get its troops to the front, as opposed to one week for Paraguay. This meant that Bolivia's movements were comparatively slower and less flexible, and it was far more expensive to supply and maintain its troops at the front. In this war, it's right on Bolivia's doorstep. The issues of logistics are much more favourable. And in fact, Bolivia's infrastructure and roads orient in this direction, running directly into Peru and Chile.

Another factor was that many of Bolivia's troops in the Chaco were Altiplano Indigenous, who found the low elevations of the Chaco to be severely debilitating. Here, they're fighting close to home territory, and there isn't the same degree of climactic and environmental disruption.

Because many of Bolivia's troops are and will be drawn from the indigenous population, it's worth noting again that much of this population is essentially outside the mainstream economy, engaged in traditional subsistence activity. So Bolivia can draw fairly large armies up without actually disrupting its economy. High unemployment in the mainstream economy also helps.

And, given the large number of veterans, Bolivian forces will have some prospect of an edge over green troops.

<u>Return to Table of Contents</u>

***

BOOK OF ARGENTINA

The Rain Forest War - January to June, 1941

As the rainy season wears on the campaign in the Oriente/Selva/Amazonas swings slowly back towards General Blandon and his Ecuadoran Expedition.

The Peruvian offensive gradually stalls out due to unceasing rains. The makeshift road to Pucallpa floods out again, ending the stream of manpower and supplies from that region. In the north, currents and flooding shut down operations out of Tarapota.

With the Peruvians cut off from supplies, their units spread wide and overextended all the way out to Brazil, it's now Blandon's turn. He pushes back from bases in Brazil and using his carefully hoarded weapons and ammunition, begins systematically eliminating Peruvian units and looting the corpses.

But as much damage as Blandon does, the real enemy is malaria and other tropical diseases.

A significant portion of Blandon's original complement of soldiers hail from the Ecuadoran Oriente and have some inbuilt tolerance to tropical diseases. This is a deliberate recruiting strategy by Alba who studied jungle warfare, and has at least a notion of the issues.

The local Ecuador recruits were not particularly good soldiers, not in conventional terms. But they survive and adapt to the campaign. Balanced against these were soldiers and officers from outside the Oriente, but most of these are already several months in field. Those who are unlucky have already died; those who fall sick mostly recover.

To make up for losses through tropical disease, Blandon recruits native auxiliaries, at first on an occasional basis, and then later in a systematic fashion. While not immune, the natives are more resistant, and in most cases, are not prone to becoming sick during the campaigns.

The Peruvian expeditions are not so favored. These largely consisted of conscripts, mostly Indigenous and Mestizo, pulled from the coast or the highlands. Almost none of them have any experience with the tropical diseases of the rain forest and casualties are high. Overall, the troops are poor quality; the younger, fitter, more robust soldiers divert into the northern or southern theater. Instead, what is sent into the jungle are the marginal soldiers, the short, the fat, the lame, the lazy, the discipline issues, and the inept.

By sheer numbers, they might still crush Blandon's forces. But sheer numbers in the rain forest simply means a larger pool to be infected. Malaria and other tropical diseases ravage the Peruvians, medical care is haphazard. As much as 85 percent of the Peruvian expeditions are infected during this period, and as many as 50 percent of them die.

There was one Peruvian General with direct experience of Jungle warfare, who could have explained the risks and hazards, and perhaps organized an effective systematic campaign under these difficult circumstances. General Oscar Benevides. But he was executed in the Coup of September, 1940.

As the rainy season goes on, they Peruvians become less and less effective, and Blandon counterattacks more and more aggressively, always careful to seize boats, weapons, ammunition and supplies, in campaigns that resembled piracy as much as warfare.

By May and June, the Peruvian expeditions are a few sick remnants huddling around fortified positions, unwilling to go out and challenge, committed to waiting out the season.

Nevertheless, the Peruvians can at least claim a form of victory in having pushed out or blocked Blandon from large parts of the Selva, and pushed some of his operations into Brazil.

****

August 22, 1941 – Guayaquil

Bonifaz, Velasco and Alba sit at a table with the Japanese representatives. The Japanese ambassador is there, of course, together with his aides and translators. A second Japanese Ambassador, this one visiting from Chile, clearly outranks the local ambassador. And then there are the dignitaries from Tokyo, two men in tailored black suits, and a third in what is recognized as a naval officer's uniform that the others defer to.

The conversation is achingly slow. The two sets of interpreters are careful in relaying the Japanese speech first to English, and then from English to Spanish.

"So," says Bonifaz, "we have an agreement?"

He waits for the phrase to be translated, and then translated again. The Japanese seem to nod. They speak a rush of unintelligible gabble to the Ecuadorians.

"Yes," comes the answer back. "The funds will be routed through Bogota, Colombia. We trust that they will be adequate to your purposes."

Ibarra winces. The Colombians will take their cut, of course. The Bogota Donkey gorges at the grain trough, but hopefully a few grains will make it through for the sparrows in Quito.

Alba nods. He'd have rather have weapons, but the Japanese aren't willing to part with more than a handful of near obsolete field artillery pieces. Even now, they are offloading at Guayaquil harbor.

He supposes it doesn't really matter; Alba is dubious about the quality of Japanese arms and munitions. In the long run, whatever capital the Japanese put their way is the better choice. But it takes time to convert money to munitions. He isn't sure how much time is left.

"And the Islands?" comes from the Japanese through their translators.

"A ninety nine year lease upon the Galapagos Island of Baltra. Yes," Ibarra says.

"Among other things."

"Fishing stations, airstrips, weather and electrical research stations," Ibarra confirms.

The Japanese, hearing these things through the translator, nod.

"No military usage," Alba insists. "We have no intention of provoking the Americanos."

"Of course not," comes the reply. "But you must appreciate that we will require absolute jurisdiction over our leased territories. And in any event, some of our fishing vessels are quite large, and require elaborate harbor facilities."

Ibarra finds himself blushing at Alba's gauche remark.

"Of course, of course," he says. "No one expects otherwise."

Things proceed to the technical details, and the meeting drags on for another hour. At the end of it, the Japanese delegation bow and depart.

Alba looks at Ibarra. Ibarra shrugs eloquently.

"I hope that we do not come to regret this," Ibarra says.

"It is not," says Bonifaz, "as if there are a lot of other choices available to us. The war is ruining us, and we need cash. We will deal with the Americans when we must."

***

The Town of Milagro, October 4, 1941

"What do we have left for rounds," Pepe asks.

Omar is already rooting around in the stores at the back of the makeshift trench.

"One box."

Pepe nods.

"After that, we just spit at them. I hope the truck gets here soon."

Omar nods. "This is what? The fifth retreat? The sixth?"

"We'll have our backs to Quito soon enough," Carlos says sourly. "And then what?"

Carlos is the third in their little group, a replacement for Hugo who was unfortunate enough to catch a bullet during the last retreat

"Well, if you'd like to have a glorious last stand, you can always stick around," Pepe says. "But Omar and I? We'll be getting out of here."

****

Peruvian Northern Command, October 4, 1941,

General Markholtz surveys the field of battle, and finds it to his liking. He puts down the spyglass.

"The legend of Alba is over," he tells his aide, Captain Aguire. He basks in the exquisite satisfaction. "As with all too many legends, it was mostly luck and a few tricks. Like a child's balloon, tap it with a needle, and it is gone."

"Yes, General," Aguire replies, "Tomorrow, you will have the field. It will be your sixth victory?"

"Seventh," Markholtz corrects him. "The seventh. And in a few more days, an eighth. In a week, the ninth and tenth. We are on the verge now of cutting Quito from Guayaquil. By next month, we'll have the coast and split the whole country in two, and then we'll have the leisure of deciding which fragment to devour first."

"Remarkable!"

"Bah," Markholtz says. "This would not be necessary at all, if Ureta hadn't been such an incompetent fool. I'm sorry to say, Aguirre, Alba could only succeed because we allowed ourselves to grow weak. The rot set in with Benavides. He was a soldier once, you know. But he lost his taste for it. Sanchez, that was a fighting man, but Benavides? He had no stomach for it."

"Yes, Sir."

"Weak men rose up under Benavides, Aguirre. That was our problem. Fine men, certainly. The best of the Criollo, assuredly. But not soldiers. Not truly like us. It's still there, I think, the weakness is not yet purged in the south."

Aguirre begins to sweat. Sometimes, when Markholtz talks like this, he drifts dangerously close to sedition.

"You're certainly beating Alba," Aguirre says cautiously. "He's met his match. He's retreated every time he's met you. It should be apparent to everyone that you rolled up his March on Lima."

New World War – Page 85

Markholtz nods. In his mind, the past is subtly reconstructed. Alba and his Ecuadorans were already returning home when Markholtz took command against him.

But to Markholtz, this is alchemically transformed to Alba's cowardly flight from his pursuit.

"Alba's a shopkeeper," he says. "He's better suited selling shoes to women in Guayaquil. They call him the Accountant, did you know that? His own officers! I'd have them flogged for such disrespect, but there you go. Still, it turns out, we need accountants in war, he had a few tricks."

"Indeed, Sir." By this time, Aguirre has heard it all many times.

"Well, I've mastered those tricks. Soon enough, Aguirre, soon enough, I'll be bringing the bastard back in chains to Lima, and then he can stand trial for his crimes."

***

The Third Northern Campaign, September 1941

The Peruvians come in force in September. Overwhelming force. General Markholtz, astonishingly, pulls together close to a hundred thousand men, though a good portion of those were shoeless Quechua. Even more remarkably, he's armed many of them.

Not all, not even close to all. But that is fine with Markholtz, since an army requires many supporting roles to maintain the man shooting the rifle. An old Criollo, he has no particular love for putting weapons in the hands of Indigenous. Many of the Quechua are relegated to organization and support, transportation, cooking, digging latrines. Since so many of them are ignorant of even basic Spanish, Markholtz designates some Quechua as de facto corporals and sergeants, even a couple of lieutenants. Outrageous, of course, and it will only last till the untutored brutes could learn enough Spanish to do what they are told by proper officers and sargents.

The practical result of deploying so many to support duties, however, is that it gives Markholtz forces logistical depth. He doesn't appreciate the significance of this, but he takes advantage of it. Markholtz is able to maintain full supply lines as he pushes into Ecuador, overwhelming local defenses with a continuous stream of firepower and manpower.

The apparent weakness of the large Quechua portions of his army is more than offset by regiments of crack troops. These are trained soldiers that Markholtz is holding back from the southern front, sending raw Indigenous conscripts in their place. These are bolstered by more regiments of trained soldiers and their officers who, for one reason or another, have enough luck or wits or enough political pull to avoid the meat grinder that is the southern front. There is friction with Lima, and particularly with the southern front Generals. But in the end, it doesn't matter. Success is all that matters, and Markholtz can smell victory.

Peruvian forces overwhelm the coastal provinces of Ecuador and then push inland. Facing the onslaught, the Ecuadorian forces retreat towards the hills and mountains, where Markholtz ignored them, or back towards a series of defensive lines, which Markholtz relentlessly picks apart. By early October, Markholtz overruns as much as 15 percent of Ecuador's territory.

Markholtz will crush Ecuador, and then he will return in triumph to Lima, with a victorious army at his back, ready to turn now on the perfidious war weary Chileans who can no longer count on a two front war to distract Peru. He will be the hero who wins both wars.

It will all be over by the New Year.

****

Town of Milagro, October 8, 1941

Gomez pulls up in the truck; he squints as a gust of wind blows smoke from the bonfire. Bits and pieces of wood and furniture, he makes out the outlines of a chair, supporting timbers. The sandbags are gutted and their sacks thrown on the blaze. The fortified position is mostly ruined.

"You men ready?"

Pepe laughs with relief. "By Jesus, yes! For half the day, we've had nothing to throw at them but harsh words. I'll be glad to get out of this shithole."

Through the haze of smoke, Gomez can see the steady flash of Peruvian firearms in the distance. The invaders are advancing cautiously; so far as he can tell. They've learned bloody lessons about coming on too fast. But they come on, nevertheless. Another fifteen minutes, half an hour, they will overrun this position. The truck is late, and Pepe and his boys were far closer to being dead men than they want to think about.

"That's your trouble Pepe, everyone tells you. Dig the latrine, don't live in it."

Omar and Carlos have no time to talk. They are busy tossing bundles to the waiting arms in the back of the truck. It is already packed to the top. Omar wastes no time, climbing aboard, trying to find a place to hang on.

"Funny, so funny. You're late, did you get distracted feeling up little boys."

"A truck broke down," Gomez replies, "we had to redistribute the jobs. And we lost time stripping it down."

Everything is stripped down. As the Peruvians advance, the defenders pour fire on them, selling every foot of ground dearly, and then they pull up, withdraw, and entrench further up. There was always a desperate but organized flurry of activity, crops harvested early, or abandoned or burned, houses stripped, valuables buried or hidden. The campaign is nothing more than a series of well-mannered retreats that allows Markholtz to march half way to Quito.

Gomez glances over at the heaped trench.

"That machine gun any good?"

Pepe shakes his head.

"Kept overheating faster and faster. It was close to junk toward the end. When we ran out of ammunition, I poured water on the barrel to cool it."

"Still looks okay?"

Pepe shakes his head. "But woe to the man who tries to use it next."

"Good enough," Gomez says, "climb aboard."

"If I can find a place."

"Not to worry, I can strap you to the fender if we need to. Compared to some of the trucks, you'd still be riding in comfort. They're packed."

"Funny man, when the war is over, you should look up Bob Hope."

"Hang on to the running board, and hang on well. We're taking the old carriage road."

"The carriage road? I thought we were going along to Vasquez."

"Change of plans, your friends down there, they got ahead of themselves, they overran parts of the Vasquez road."

"Where at?"

"Old farm."

"We didn't have anyone there?"

"No, it was undefended. They moved faster there than we thought, some Lieutenant out to make his name or something."

The old farm part of the road is considerably inward from the lines, and very exposed. Hard to defend.

"They seem insistent on holding it, makes not much sense to me, since they take fire from both up and down the road and no cover at all. Peruvians, what can you say. But if they want to put their men in a shooting gallery, why should we say no?"

"Anyway," Gomez says, "it's too hot to go there."

"Alright, alright," Pepe snaps, "you going to start this thing? There's still Vielle to pick up."

Gomez shakes his head.

"Vielle is gone, and Morena too. You're the last."

He throws the machine into gear, and it rolls away down the road. Behind them, the Peruvian attackers crawl forward, pouring firepower at the empty outpost.

****

Behind the Lines, Ecuadorian Army

"Shut your mouth," a soldier snaps, a heavy lipped thug with a scar along one side of his face that pulls his eye down. The old injury makes his voice slur.

But his fist is hard enough, and Carlos would have fallen, but for the press of soldiers. Carlos has gotten used to griping; the sudden violence it earns startles and frightens him. He looks around for Omar, but the man, crowded over to the side, might as well be on the other side of the town.

"I'm just saying we need to stand and fight," Carlos says. "We keep running away, soon enough we'll be backed up to Quito, or fighting from the border at Colombia."

"Yes," the soldier says, "oh so brave, so wise. Yes, let's fight like they do in the south. Nose to nose, and the grass choking on soldier's blood. The Colonel is smarter than that. He knows not to throw away soldiers' lives."

"But we keep retreating," Carlos spits. "How do you win that way?"

Some rational part of himself says that he should just shut up while he still has teeth left. But he can't help it. It's all so unfair. He is the only one who wants to fight, and they all treat him like a coward and a fool.

"Trust the Colonel," the soldier says. "I was with the Colonel, right through Peru we walked. Right up to the gates of Lima. They just about surrendered. Everywhere we went, the Peruvians they ran away, or we cut them to pieces. The Colonel knows what he's doing."

"But now we're running."

"Leave the kid alone, Miguel," an old soldier says.

"He's just a punk," Miguel snaps.

"We were all punks once. If he stays stupid, he'll get himself killed, and that's worse than anything you can do. And if he wises up, well then, he won't need you rattling his brains."

Miguel snarls and turns to the side, in the crowded truck, that is all the movement he can make

"Kid," the older soldier says, "you got a cigarette?"

Carlos shakes his head.

"Too bad. You weren't in the March on Lima were you?"

Carlos shakes his head again. "I volunteered though."

"More the fool you. Never volunteer. These officers will get us killed fast enough, they don't need our encouragement. Ever been on a retreat?"

"Too many lately."

The soldier laughs.

"These? No, these aren't retreats. Not like we saw of the Peruvians. Just running and trying to get something together, scrounging whatever you can of whatever anyone thought to take with them. No, this isn't a retreat at all. More like a relocation. We stand and we kill Peruvians, then when it gets to be the time when we should do some dying, we pack up all nice and neat, and move ourselves up the road. Every step that bastard Markholtz takes is paid for with Peruvian blood.... Not Ecuadorian mind you, Peruvian blood."

"It's no way to win," Carlos says obstinately.

"You'd be surprised. Trust the Colonel. His family came from Alba, you know that place?"

"No."

"It's in Italy; it's an island I hear. When they finally packed away Napoleon the Frenchman, it was to Alba that they put him. Well, I've heard it said that the Frenchman, he had trouble keeping his pants, if you know what I mean."

Some of the soldiers laugh.

"Now, the Colonel's family, they come from there, if you see where I'm going. Now, I'm not saying anything, because that would be disrespectful.... But...."

"I heard that too," another soldier in the packed truck says.

"You see where I'm going then."

"So you just trust the Colonel."

****

The Japanese Perspective

The Japanese aren't nearly as heavily involved in the Andes as the Germans are. This is fairly obvious, less money to throw around, less capital investment in the region, fewer nationals.

However, the Japanese are rather more involved than one might initially expect. The Japanese embassy in Chile in particular is a hotbed of spies and spying. Chile is the best place to assess southern hemisphere shipping - particularly British and American naval movements coming up from the South Atlantic, and the movement of freight shipping.

The Japanese espionage and political networks tend to cooperate with and overlap with the Germans. In the Chilean election of 1938, the Japanese actually invest heavily in trying to sway the Presidency to Ibanez. He receives support and money under the table to finance his bid.

With Ecuador and Chile forming the Andean Axis and Ecuador brutally cash starved, there are potential opportunities for the Japanese to exploit. The Japanese focus on use of the Galapagos for shipping, radar and radio surveillance and as a submarine operations base. Extensive plans are drawn up for a ship re-fitting and resupply complex, although there is an element of unreality to it. The designers, for instance don't reckon with the very limited availability of potable water, and consider the landscape more arable than it actually is. Ironically, there are actually plans for a commercial fishery based out of the Galapagos.

Ultimately though, it is one of those situations of 'eyes bigger than stomach' which the Japanese Empire is so prone too. The Galapagos planning group is largely unaware of other plans or high ranking strategies. By the time Pearl Harbor comes along, work has barely begun.

****

New World War – Page 95

The War No One Wanted, Quixote Press, 1984, Mark Weinbaum (excerpts)

General Markholtz unilateral invasions of Ecuador are in many ways repeats of General Ureta's own actions at the beginning of the Andean War. Like Ureta, Markholtz is acting with almost complete autonomy, making his choices and presenting them to a frustrated Lima as a fait accompli.

But Markholtz position is far more tenuous than Ureta's ever was. General Ureta had, for all intents and purposes, been a prince, a feudal lord, master of all he surveyed.

Peru is a large country, and in dividing the nation into military districts, President Benavides tried to reduce the risk of coup and insurrection which had arisen from a centralized military command. Autonomous regional generals are less able to conspire successfully against the central government. Unfortunately, the corollary is that autonomous regional generals were more likely to simply do what they wanted in their own territory, and tell Lima to live with it.

Thus, when Ureta made the decision to invade, there was little that Lima could do but follow after the fact.

Markholtz situation was similar but different. Colonel Alba's spirited defense and his subsequent March on Lima devastated the military command structure in the north. And it provoked the overthrow of the Prado government; and its replacement with a military Junta, whose focus almost immediately is forced to shift to the Chilean war.

The result is an effective political and military vacuum in the north, into which General Markholtz steps. No one, not the Prado government, nor the Ramirez Junta, ever designated him as Commander of the North. There is not a single document in the military archives in Lima which appoints him to any field command. He simply assumed authority, and the Junta went along with him.

Markholtz first comes to prominence in the wake of Alba's 'March on Lima.' Originally commander of the Huanaco army group, Markholtz stands by while Alba destroyed one army after another on the way to and from the capital.

Markholtz first sortie against Alba is disastrous. The 1st Battle of Cajamarca, on October 20, 1940, saw the obliteration of half of Markholtz army group through casualties and desertions, the destruction of almost the entirety of the staff, and the full-fledged rout of Peruvian forces. It is barely short of a miracle that Markholtz himself survives.

Only the arrival of General Boaz's force from Lima allows the fleeing Huanaco group to reform in any semblance of order. Markholtz career seems at an end. Then, during the 2nd Battle of Cajamarca on October 24, 1940, a miracle takes place: The cautious General Boaz is killed by a sniper's bullet, and Markholtz, as the senior ranking officer assumes command.

He never relinquishes it. Following the inconclusive battle, Markholtz holds back his forces, following in Alba's wake and declaring victory, but refusing to actually engage.

Legend has it that Markholtz is enraged by a contemptuous note he received from Alba on November 3, resulting in the burning of the town of Chiclayo, but this may well be apocryphal. Certainly there is never any love lost between the two men.

Alba's departure from the field, however, leaves Markholtz as the undisputed commander in Peruvian territories, there are literally no rivals left, every other general in the north is dead or in disgrace, or has returned to Lima to be part of the Junta. And the Junta itself, though smarting from the humiliations Alba inflicted, finds itself overwhelmed dealing with the war with Chile. The sentiment is simply to leave Markholtz where he was. There are simply too many real problems to deal with than the question of a single commander of dubious authority.

Between November 1940 and March of 1941, Markholtz proves to be an able politician. He successfully defends the bulk of his forces from demands by the Junta for redeployments to the south.

This results in lifelong enmity from many of the southern generals. General Corona, for instance, writes bitterly of Markholtz as one of the inadvertent architects of disaster, and makes the case that Markholtz refusal to part with men and munitions cheated Peru of an early victory against Chile. Markholtz himself argues strenuously that his forces are needed to prevent a second March on Lima. Certainly there is a hugely exaggerated reckoning of Alba's capabilities, the Junta genuinely fears a second March.

Markholtz advances the thesis that Peru cannot turn its full strength on Chile until Ecuador, the lesser threat, is decisively defeated. On this basis, he is able to compete successfully for scarce war materials against desperate southern commanders. Despite his success, his tactics leave the Junta deeply divided about him.

It is his weakness, however, not his strength, which drives his actions. Markholtz position, in regard to his fellow generals, is always precarious. His command was assumed on the battlefield, not conferred through normal channels, and even if he presents himself as the hero of Alba's retreat, there are those who point out his failure to engage Alba initially, his disasters on the two occasions he actually crossed swords, and his reluctance (cowardice) to pursue him closely.

As early as November and December, 1940, the Junta is actively looking at replacing him, or reorganizing the northern command. Markholtz is slated to return to Huanaco, as a commander of training garrisons. This is going to be a big step down for a man who is effective sovereign of almost half the country. Markholtz is certainly aware of these discussions, and aggressively opposes them. Even international peace negotiation efforts are seen by Markholtz as a serious threat to his position. He enlists his own supporters, and successfully maintains his position.

But he cannot stand still, that option was simply not available. His only choice is to go forward to victory. Every other path leads to personal ruin.

The culmination of his efforts is the disastrous Second Northern Campaign in March and April, 1941. After initial successes, the campaign falls apart rapidly. Markholtz promises of victory blow up in his face, and despite his reconquest of some (but not all) Peruvian territories, his detractors are ascendant.

Orders are issued relieving Markholtz of his position, and relieving him of command. He ignores both of these.

Luckily, the Junta is distracted by new Chilean offensives and has neither the ability nor the inclination to discipline the wayward General. Markholtz is able to curry some favor with supporters by conscripting and supplying northern troops to the southern war machine. But this earns him no points with his enemies. It is generally accepted that Markholtz is due for a reckoning when time permits.

Once again, there are peace negotiations and an imminent ceasefire. If these succeed, it would be his ruin. The Junta will be in a position to recall him to Lima, or to crush him if he rebels. Once again, the Junta is distracted by the south. Once again, opportunity is before him.

The Third Northern Campaign, of September/October, 1941, began on Markholtz decision. Lima, once again, is notified after the fact.

The Ramirez Junta, Lima, Peru, September, 1941

News of the Third Northern Campaign causes a furor in the Junta. The high command divides almost equally for and against Markholtz. In the end, however, there is little that they can do.

A public motion of support is issued. But privately, the Junta settles on Markholtz court martial in absentia, as of September 7. Daily, the Junta debates what support to provide Markholtz, and what needs to be held in reserve for the southern front.

During the initial phases of the campaign, Markholtz star rises as he racks up an impressive string of victories, overrunning occupied Peruvian provinces and pushing deeply into Ecuador's territory.

The United States on the Sidelines

The American position at that point is definitely not sympathetic to Ecuador. But at that point, as at others, American policy is hung up at cross purposes.

The Peruvian government is nominally America's favorite child. But the trappings of democracy and the pretense of civilian government have been tossed away, there is a military junta in place and frankly, they act badly. The Peruvians started the war, and they keep launching awkwardly timed offensives in the middle of American sponsored peace negotiations. It makes for a frustrating client.

But still, if the conflict is simply Ecuador vs Peru, American dithering would not have lasted and the U.S. would have decisively weighed in. The trouble is that Chile is more important economically to the United States than Peru. So some in Washington argue in support of the southern state.

But then again, Chile is chock full of Nazis. But then again, Ibanez isn't actually a Nazi. Etc. The debate in Washington see-saws back and forth and no coherent policy emerges.

The preferred US outcome is for everyone to just sit down and shut up, for the war to go away while the US concentrates on real conflicts, but a ceasefire seems elusive as locals kept launching offensives. The second best outcome would be for Peru to wrap things up, but that is not happening. The third best outcome is for someone to win decisively, make nice with America, and guarantee an uninterrupted supply of critical resources.

America is prepared to tolerate Franco's Spain's closeness with Nazi Germany, and to tolerate the Thai regime which quietly supported Japan, so long as they shut up and play nice at the proper times.

***

New World War – Page 101

The 3rd Northern Campaign Re-Evaluated, Journal of Military Studies, Cambridge, 1956. Ed. R. Peabody, Wr. B. Windsor-Montgomery (Excerpt)

.... the conventional narrative is that by November, Alba and the Ecuadoran forces are bolstered by dramatic infusions of money and armaments from Colombia, and were able to sustain a dramatic counterattack that brings about the collapse of Markholtz offensive.

Like so many conventional narratives, this does not hold up in the face of examination. The records clearly indicate that Ecuadorian forces begin to rearm almost immediately after the depletion of the 2nd Offensive in April. By June, levels of equipment and ammunition stores are largely been replaced. By late August inventories averages 50 percent larger than at the start of the first offensive.

Financially, Ecuador's position, at least temporarily, improves during the hiatus. Large tracts of the disputed Oriente are licensed to Colombian interests, and extensive futures in Cacao are pledged. With Colombia as an intermediary, Ecuador assembles a short term financial package that sees it flush with cash from sources as disparate as Japan and Brazil.

That cash does not immediately amount to munitions. It takes time to order or to build, time to replenish and rearm. There is often a significant lag time in mounting Japanese artillery, or in constructing the Ecuadorian 'half side' tanks or partly armoured trucks.

The perception of the Ecuadorans as under-equipped to deal with the offensive comes primarily from the extreme rate of munitions exchanged. Markholtz approach is not particularly subtle; it amounts to a doctrine of overwhelming force and firepower deployed rapidly. The rate of fire is dramatic, as much as a week's worth of Peruvian ammunition would be expended in a day. Even modest rates of return fire find the Ecuadoran defenders rapidly running out of ammunition, and as supplies are depleted, it is easier to simply relocate to supply depots.

Through much of the campaign Markholtz has the advantage of extremely effective logistics trains, and is able to maintain high rates of fire. This continues into October, despite the outbreak of fighting in Bolivia.

The real story, however, lies not in the rates of ammunition expenditure, but the rates of attrition suffered by each side. The Ecuadorians hold fortified positions which they defend up to a point, before retreating backwards to yet another fortified position, all the while continually pouring firepower into the enemy. Casualty rates are lopsided, often three to one or four to one, in some cases, reaching ten to one. Markholtz is literally buying land with blood, while Alba continually retreats and redeploys, maintaining his forces intact.

By the time Markholtz marches to disaster at Portoviejo on October 20, 1941, he has sacrificed most of his combat effectives, his supply lines are badly overextended, and in fact, he is on the verge of collapse. Even his elaborate supply lines are not sufficient to continue to supply ammunition and equipment at his prodigious rate of usage. The extension of his force over two hundred miles only increases the demand for ammunition and gasoline.

Markholtz gambles that he could bypass major population centers and achieve victory by seizing and holding key strategic points. This is not fundamentally an unsound plan. But it depends on Markholtz maintaining sufficient integrity to his forces to hold the strategic points.

Markholtz in his own self-serving memoirs blames Lima for a lack of support, but there's very little evidence of this. The later phases of the campaign feature an increasingly desperate series of demands for more men and munitions, but the inability or unwillingness to meet these escalating demands is a far cry from lack of support. There is an element of unreality to some of Markholtz' demands in terms of numbers and timing which suggest that they were written for posterity, not practicality.

Faced with organized counter-offensives from the North, from the Mountain regions and from Guayaquil, Markholtz found his supply lines cut in several places. Without logistics supply, his offensive degenerated into a series of independent units which were, one after the other, overcome.

Peru lost two thirds of its northern army including almost all of its officers. Markholtz himself was forced to surrender. The reformed northern army that was allowed to retreat was almost entirely Quechua, with de facto field promotions of illiterate Indigenous as high as Captains and Majors.

Ultimately, Markholtz defeated himself, the strategy of overwhelming force and firepower was only effective as long as it could be sustained. On the other side, Colonel Alba's forces retained their cohesion and effectiveness throughout the campaign. Markholtz was never able to degrade the effectiveness of the Ecuadorians, and when he ran out of steam, it was the end.

Alba took advantage of the disarray in Peruvian forces to re-occupy Peruvian territory, including once again taking control of the Peruvian oil districts, by December 1, 1941. There was simply no effective Peruvian government left in the north.

The Rain Forest War- June to December, 1941

The coming dry season finds Peru desperate and aggressive on all fronts. In the north, Markholtz launches his third and final northern offensive. In the south, Ibanez desperate gamble is barely foiled. Southeast, the Peruvian Junta goes all in on Bolivia's Penaranda government.

In this sense, it is inevitable that there will be a renewed effort by Peru to rid itself of the irritant that was Enrique Blandon and his cursed Matilde.

By July, the road to Pucallpa is once again open, and the town is rapidly built up. One of the new facilities is a hospital. There is also a lagoon for float planes, a series of new docks for river boats, munitions dumps, barracks, all guarded by low earthworks. Pucallpa is to be a fortress and launching point. The northern military bases at Lamas and Tarapota also expand.

The new strategy is a repeat, simply overwhelm Blandon and force him into a war of attrition until he has nothing left. The Peru correctly assesses that his stockpiles are limited, no matter how much he hoards, and the supply chain from Ecuador is thin to nonexistent. The Ecuadorans are nearly bankrupt, and can spare little for Blandon. The use of aircraft will neutralize Blandon's few planes, most of which are now grounded for lack of fuel and parts, and allow pinpointing of his forces.

Most critically, with the dry season, water levels are down, minor tributaries disappear or are no longer navigable; Blandon's freedom of movement is confined to a series of principal waterways, all of which are or are being mapped.

Unfortunately, Blandon anticipates all of this, and shifts his tactics accordingly. Somehow, he manages to acquire and mount a small anti-aircraft gun for the Matilde. During the rainy season, many of his supply depots and stations relocate inland to secured locations, largely undetectable and inaccessible to the Peruvians, and he establishes overland routes and portages through several areas for ambush and kill zones.

Even worse, Blandon continues to arm and train the natives, having spent the year carefully recruiting and building alliances. During this time, he takes his first and second native wives, and adopts a youth as a native son. Several of his surviving officers also take native wives.

What the Peruvians stumble into is not a mad river pirate with a sloppy retinue of followers and a dwindling cache of supplies, but rather an evolving native insurgency. In particular, it is a native insurgency with comparable weapons and training and tactical and strategic leadership. Every colonialist's worst nightmare.

Blandon's alliances are not continuous; many tribes are neutral or even hostile, innately suspicious, or more concerned with local rivalries. His patchwork insurgency extends across the northern Selva into Brazil. Nor are his native supporters as disciplined or reliable as he hopes. They are as likely to turn their new weapons and training upon each other or their rivals, and inclined to conquer new territories while abandoning old ones. Entire noncombatant or neutral tribes are wiped out, some neutral tribes sent fleeing, and populations shift, unpredictably. The Peruvian Selva is a much more dangerous place for everyone.

Peruvian casualties are high, far higher than anticipated. But as the months wear on, the Peruvian missions adapt. As they come to understand the nature of the native insurgency, tactics shift to scorched earth, purging all natives they encounter. This is successful. The worst victims are the relatively innocent neutral or refugee tribes. This drives population and refugee movements throughout the region, with many tribes making their way into Brazil or the Ecuadoran Oriente.

Eventually, the Peruvians attempt to form their own native auxiliaries, but this effort comes late in November and is not particularly successful. By that time, the Peruvians established that they are no friends to the natives. Recruitment attempts founder.

It is not all one sided. Despite best efforts and continual raiding for supplies, Blandon's stockpiles dwindle rapidly. His Ecuadoran manpower also diminishes, with perhaps a third of his original force remaining; his lost numbers are replaced by natives. The Matilde and his river fleet is regularly hunted and spotted by river planes. Despite his anti-aircraft gun, he must take evasive measures, scattering his fleet, making use of camouflage and cover.

The most important development, however, is that in late September, the Brazilian government begins to receive reports that Ecuadoran and Peruvian forces are crossing into Brazilian territory. The Vargas government sends an expeditionary force down the Amazonian River from the town of Manaus, to secure Brazilian borders and evict trespassers.

In November, that expedition disappears without a trace.

December 7, 1941

Pearl Harbor!!!

***

December 8, 1941, Quito, Ecuador

Velasco Ibarra marches stiffly past President Bonifaz's secretary into his office. The white haired old man looks up from his desk. Any recrimination dies on his lips as he stared at the frightened appearance.

"What is it?" Bonifaz asks.

"Pearl Harbor," Ibarra replies.

"What?"

"Can we call Alba back?"

"What are you talking about?"

"Doom."

"Pull yourself together man, what's this about?"

"You haven't heard?"

"Obviously not."

"The Japanese launched a surprise attack on the American naval base at Pearl Harbor. Japan and America are at war."

For a few minutes, there is silence, as the older man considers this news.

"The same Japanese that we just leased islands in the Galapagos to?"

"Yes. Them."

Bonifaz nods.

The moments grows long.

"Two things," he says finally.

Ibarra looks expectant.

"First, burn all records of our dealings with the Japanese."

"They'll have their own copies."

"Good, if they win the war, they can use them. But I doubt they'll be sharing them with the Americans."

"Very well, the second?"

"Declare war on Japan...." Bonifaz says. "But do it courteously, let's not upset them more than we need to."

∗∗∗

December 8, 1941. A Prison Cell in Ecuador

General Montaigne Markholtz receives the news of Pearl Harbor.
He spends the day alternately laughing, weeping, cursing god and
calling doom down on Alba.

***

America Goes to War!

In the months immediately following Pearl Harbor, it becomes clear that the focus of American attention is on Europe and Asia, where clear antagonists and protagonists simplified the social narrative.

In Europe, Hitler is clearly a bad guy, Churchill clearly a good guy. The British are an English speaking democracy under threat from an inhuman war machine. This simple black and white dichotomy provides a strong enough moral freight to allow the communist menace of the USSR to slip into the 'good guys' camp.

In Asia, there was a lack of a clear 'good guy' apart from the Chinese government, battling both Japan and its own insurgencies. But Japan is clearly a menace, and now openly attacks America. In the next few weeks, Japan will attack and overrun American and British possessions in the region, including the Philippines, Hong Kong, Malaysia and Burma. For the American people and the American government, this crystallizes the Asian front into black and white.

In Latin America, however, the situation remains clouded. The metrics of aggression bring mixed results, American financial and commercial interests come down on both sides, particularly with respect to Chile and Peru. South America is, to American planners, militarily far less significant than either the European or Asian theaters. But it is also a critical producer of resources needed to fight wars in those theaters. The United States priority is to end the Andean wars once and for all, so that America can set itself to the real tasks at hand.

Within days of Pearl Harbor, the Roosevelt Peace Plan is announced. As an initial step, all Latin American nations, including the combatants, are asked to break all ties with the Axis nations. All do so, with the notable exception of Argentina.

Chile breaks ties, but its considerable German/Nazi constituency leaves American intelligence services with severe doubts as to its bona fides. On the other hand, the other Latin Axis member, Ecuador, muddies the waters with its fervent though ineffectual declaration of war upon Germany and Japan, and an offer of basing rights to the Galapagos.

In the ensuing weeks, the elements of the Roosevelt Peace Plan will emerge. The key principles were: 1) Immediate ceasefires throughout all Latin theaters of war; 2) Removal of foreign troops from all territories and a return to pre-conflict borders; 3) Eventual Independent adjudication of border disputes in a binding fashion by a neutral party, the United States, or alternatively a triumvirate panel of the United States, Britain and Brazil. 4) Free and unrestricted trade, without interdiction by national disputes.

This plan is not presented as a package, but articulated through a series of embassies and diplomatic missions to the various capitals. Bilateral meetings take place in Mexico City and Rio de Janeiro. All of the parties agree in principle.

And then, of course, the bickering starts.

Ecuador promises that it would immediately withdraw from captured Peruvian territory in return for the United States guarantee of its security from renewed Peruvian attack. More critically, it requires the interim recognition of its territorial claims to the Oriente. To say that these demands are not well received by the United States is to put it mildly.

The Americans take the view that they are being maneuvered into potentially defending or even waging war on behalf of an Axis power, and giving credence to a border claim that it has no sympathy for. Still, there are ongoing negotiations for basing rights to the Galapagos which might be useful to the United States. So the Americans, while refusing to say outright yes, keep avoiding a flat 'no', and continued to press for both basing rights and Ecuador's withdrawal from Peruvian coastal territory.

Peru protested vociferously against what it perceives as favorable treatment of Ecuador, but supports the principle of withdrawal from its territory, and recognition of its claims to the interior. Following private talks with American officials, Peru finally agrees to an interim arrangement wherein the disputed Oriente will remain in Ecuadoran hands, and Ecuadoran jungle forces will withdraw from Peru's rain forest regions.

The result is at least a nominal ceasefire and withdrawal, and by June of 1942, the northern border along the coastal and highland regions of Peru and Ecuador returns to their pre-war state, albeit the disputed Oriente remains in Ecuadoran possession.

A major challenge is Ecuador's failure to cease hostilities in the Peruvian Selva, due to Quito's increasing inability to control Blandon.

South is an entirely different matter. Much of Peru's war in the south is fought on Chilean soil, and in provinces formerly belonging to Peru and Bolivia.

Ibanez in Chile wholeheartedly accepts American terms. Ramirez in Peru wholeheartedly rejects them. The best American diplomats can arrange is a ceasefire along the front.

It is in Bolivia that the war continues to rage unchecked. Despite American demands for a ceasefire, none is forthcoming. The United States recognizes the Peruvian-backed Penaranda government, and this recognition, together with fresh infusions of Peruvian troops, mostly Indigenous conscript infantry freed from the Northern and Chilean front, give it a new lease on life.

By this time, the Chilean-backed Villarroel faction is now firmly in control of the mining districts and the export channels through Chilean territory. With this advantage, the Chileans are unwilling to abandon their claims, and they too pour more and more troops in.

The third Bolivian faction, led by Valpes, funds itself outmanned and outmatched, but finds a powerful backer in Argentina. Relatively secure in the interior, Valpes is sustained by an increasingly ambitious and overt Argentine commitment. Valpes policies change from day to day, ranging from claims to all of Bolivia, to a separatist movement, the 'Republic of Los Chaco', to a repudiation and renegotiation of the outcome of the Chaco war in favor of Bolivia. Valpes and Argentina win some degree of favor from the Americans with proposals for a coalition government with Penaranda.

The complete failure of American diplomacy to resolve or even bring a temporary halt to the Bolivian civil war underscores the ultimate contradictions in American foreign policy.

The reality is that the United States pursues two contradictory agendas. On the one hand, it presents as a neutral independent party, guaranteeing the rights of all parties. On the other hand, American policy makers are inevitably biased in favor of Peru which has the most significant American commercial investments, and against Ecuador and Chile, which are, in the words of one diplomat 'lousy with Nazis.' The problem is that Peru's ambitions and positions, in the north, the south and Bolivia, were simply contrary to stability.

Ultimately, the best efforts of American diplomacy simply put a lid on the pot. But beneath, things continue to boil, and in Bolivia, it boils over.

The Combatants at the Breaking Point

America's demands for a ceasefire come at an opportune time. By the beginning of 1942, all of the combatants are nearing breaking points.

Peru found itself fighting major wars on three fronts: the north, south and Bolivia, while simultaneously engaging in lesser, but still expensive, conflicts in the jungle and at sea. It has suffered at least 130,000 military casualties, killed or wounded, plus another ten thousand in civilian casualties. This is half again larger than its entire military force at the beginning of the war. These ruinous casualties have all but destroyed the army. The cream of professional soldiery, non-commissioned officers and field officers is gutted.

Numbers were made up from the civilian Criollo and Mestizo classes, who are at least literate and Spanish speaking. But the bulk of replacement infantry is Quechua. The Peruvian army is larger, and more combat experienced, but far less professional. The military represents over 20 percent of the combat age male population, which is only bearable because of the large number of Quechua conscripts who were never part of the commercial economy. Conscription efforts are massive, as are efforts to avoid conscription. In the mountains, entire villages are conscripted, or flee.

The Peruvian economy continues to function after a fashion. Trade and exports to the United States are uninterrupted, and this is a major part of government revenues and lowland economies. Still, war is ruinously expensive and the Peru regime struggles to cope. One approach is increasing government control over the economy, with wage and price controls, and the state actively dictating business decisions. Peru comes close to a full command economy.

The only limits are the competence of the Peruvian government officials, and the need to avoid stepping on American toes. Apart from that, the major asset the Peruvians command is a steady flow of financing, along with overt civilian and covert military aid from the United States.

Peruvian society, however, is up against the wall. The wars are not popular, conscription is incredibly unpopular, and the government's attempts impose wage and price controls, and to direct businesses and workers is hated. Despite martial law and curfews in almost every community, there are recurring riots, strikes and uprising. The government's response to resistance is an extreme degree of repression.

On the other side of the battle lines, Chile has experienced at almost 90,000 military casualties, as well as thousands of civilian, either through enemy action or repression. This represents 1.5 percent of the population. The military now constitutes over two hundred thousand, at least 10 percent of the combat age male population.

The richest and most advanced of the South American regimes, Chile is nowhere near the levels of command economy control or of repression seen in Peru. Nevertheless, tension is everywhere. First the Communists, then the Socialists, abandon Ibanez coalition. As his political base narrows, Ibanez relies increasingly on the Nazis and the Army. Each military success brings a degree of social order and stability, each defeat brings waves of strikes and riots.

The Ibanez regime attempts to control information, suppress resistance and maintain order, but it is like trying to plug a dyke suffering a thousand small holes. By 1940, underground newspaper circulation is exploding.

In the north, Ecuador has gotten off lightly with less than forty thousand casualties, and their military record is enviable, having repelled three invasions, and launched two substantial invasions of their own. Almost 25 percent of the combat age males are involved in some way in the military, a ridiculous and unsustainable number, that is less an indication of military strength, than an indication of the collapse of the civilian economy.

Ecuador's triumvirate rapidly blew through resources carefully hoarded over a decade. They have moved rapidly to wage and price controls, and a command economy focused principally on holding the country together. The struggle to avoid collapse lead to bouts of hyperinflation followed by mass devaluations. The country is sustained by massive borrowing from literally any party - Particularly Colombia, but also Mexico, Japan, Italy, Venezuela, Brazil, all of which is funneled through Colombia.

While each of these countries is approaching collapse, by far the worst off was Bolivia, now a battleground between three competing governments, each of which was backed by external military supporters. It is a war with no end in sight, the local factions blow through their resources, but the foreign interests refuse to let the fighting end. For Chile and Peru, victory in Bolivia promises to win the entire regional war. Argentina wishes to frustrate both and see its own opportunities for expansion.

Casualties in Bolivia are impossible to calculate, perhaps thirty-thousand. The numbers of active military, both native and foreign are a substantial part of the population. There are massive movements of internal refugees, comparable to Peru. The economy is literally fragmented, with only the mining district functioning with anything resembling normal operation, and that only because of foreign demand.

In barely a couple of years, the scale of carnage and loss is proportional to that experienced in World War One. Each of the parties faces disaster, and it is entirely possible that the war will be decided not on victory, but on which of the parties collapses first.

Inadvertently, the American attempts to impose a ceasefire and resolve the conflicts create the breathing room that each combatant needs to eventually continue the war.

****

Stumbling Into History, Argentina and the Andean War

H.M.S. Peabody, ed., Naval Press, Dublin, Ireland, 1979

The original Spanish settlers of Argentina were second generation, farmers coming down the river Plate from Peru, Chile and Paraguay.

During the sixteenth and seventeenth centuries, piracy was a problem for Spain. In dealing with its colonies, exports were off loaded in Central America and then traveled overland through Peru and Chile before being delivered. Pacific trade went to Lima, and then traveled north to Central America. This was time consuming and costly.

As a result the port of Buenos Aires on the Atlantic coast became a haven for smugglers and smuggling. It was immensely cheaper for smugglers to simply sail down the Atlantic to Buenos Aires and pick up or offload goods. This threatened the revenues and power of the Spanish establishment in Peru. But economics is its own force, and this contributed to the culture of Buenos Aires as a kind of rogue city, an accidental metropolis slowly dominating the cities and towns of the La Plata region, and undermining authority from Peru. Elsewhere in the river basins, Asunción and Montevideo also emerged as smugglers ports.

In 1776, the Spanish establish the Viceroyalty of La Plata, which included the territories of northern Argentina, Paraguay, Bolivia and Uruguay with its capital at Buenos Aires. This marks a decline in the authority of the Viceroyalty of Peru, which previously ruled these territories as dependencies. Buenos Aires is the new capital and emerges as a city on both sides of Spanish law.

From there on, the history of Argentina is checkered. The Viceroyalty of La Plata is hardly a unified territory, but amounts to the most remote and inaccessible parts of the Spanish Empire sandwiched together into an unwieldy adminitrative district.

Spanish authority, even the authority of the Viceroyalty is thin on the ground, local rivalries are strong, the La Plata provinces are successful, but often frustrated by Spanish rule.

In 1780, the revolt of Tupac Amaru II in Peru incites the Aymara of Bolivia to their own bloody revolt by Tupac Katari. In 1806 and 1807, British invasions of Montevideo and Buenos Aires are thrown back by local militias.

The Napoleonic wars, as elsewhere, are the gateway to the Argentine war of independence. The La Plata region has always been ambitious and independent, and steeped on the circulating ideas and ideals of the French revolution. They produce 600,000 head of cattle a year, of which a quarter are consumed locally. But their economies are strangled by Spanish policy.

During the Napoleonic wars, they had been left to themselves and successfully fought off the British. The topsy turvy events of the Napoleonic Wars left the La Plata reeling. Portugal was an enemy? Or was it now a friend? The British were opponents? Or allies? Were we with the French? Perhaps not, since the French had overrun Spain. Who were we loyal to? The Bonaparte pretender? Or the opposing Regency Junta? And when the Junta fell apart... Then who?

'Then who?' was the question asked by Buenos Aires in the May, 1810, uprising. Their answer then was 'ourselves.' Maybe? Or maybe Spain? Or some faction of Spain? Or something? They were very earnest, but not all that clear. They issued the call for revolution....

And just about every other major center in the La Plata answered with a resounding and occasionally violent "NO WAY!"

Buenos Aires was declared a rogue city. Montevideo in what is now Uruguay became the new capital of the Viceroyalty of La Plata. The Viceroyalty of Peru took back Bolivia. It all turned into something of a mess. Spanish loyalists organized a counter revolution, but their army deserted before it could go to battle.

Invasions of Bolivia failed. An invasion of Paraguay meets with some success, before the Paraguayans throw it out, and then a year later quixotically stage their own revolution and declare independence. In 1817 the Buenos Airians, decide that the way to attack Spain is to hit Peru.... through Chile.

It is all like that. Armies without leaders; freebooters and adventurers; generals waging campaigns in defiance of orders; generals without authority; goofy flounderings. Were it not so tragic, it could have been comic. But people die. On the long run, it works out; by 1818 Spanish power is broken.

By 1822, San Martin, the hero of Argentina, would momentously meet with Simon Bolivar to plan the future of Latin America, to absolutely no effect.

What the revolution produced was a Bolivia or Bolivia/Peru in the north, an independent Paraguay, a Uruguay, and finally a Buenos Aires which forms the center of gravity around which the remaining provinces and communities of La Plata involuntarily arranged themselves, like iron fillings around a magnet.

But that isn't the end of the story. The history of Argentina in the 19th century is a history of uprisings, civil wars, insurrections, secessions, invasions, rebellions and coups almost all of which involved Argentines doing dirt to each other.

Most of these struggles come down to the simple reality that Argentina was actually two nations, two classes, two groups irresolvably in conflict with each other: Buenos Aires... and everyone else.

Buenos Aires and the rest of La Plata had completely different origins and evolution. Most of the La Plata communities seem to be second generation immigrants from the Pacific coast. These were Criollo or Mestizo from Peru and Bolivia who headed inland for one reason or another, forming small self-sustaining agricultural communities, largely independent of the rest of the world.

Buenos Aires and the other 'smuggler' ports served these populations, but they were not especially derived from these populations, but from sailors, factors, merchants and others from outside. The La Plata knew each other, Buenos Aires knew the outer world, but fundamentally, they were evolving as two independent but interdependent nationalities.

Montevideo the ruling city of Uruguay had a similar history, but was able to impose its identity on its hinterland.

But with Buenos Aires the La Plata hinterland was simply too vast and robust for Buenos Aires to impose its identity upon; but not strong enough to avoid being ruled by the metropolis.

The overall impression of Argentine history and politics through the 19th century is that there's a huge lack of overall consensus among elites and proletariats, no class identity or interests seemed to form as they did in other Latin nations. In any issue that comes up, there almost seems to be a range of positions taken, and a fluidity in approaching same.

In a sense, Argentina avoided a lot of the sharp edged distinctions that plagued other Latin American societies. This was not a land divided between Indigenous and Spanish, as in Bolivia and Peru, or between landowners and traders. It wasn't so much economic or social classes. No, it was just Buenos Aires.... versus everyone else.

Was Argentina to be a unitary state? Or a federation? If a unitary state, then who was in charge? Buenos Aires tried to rule. A couple of times it attempted to secede. Like an unhappy marriage, the Argentines couldn't seem to stay together, but couldn't seem to leave.

What resolved the Argentine quandary was not ideology or compromise or good wishes, but a very simple notion: A rising tide lifts all boat. Argentina in the 19th century, particularly in the late 19th century was very well situated. A lot of land and European climate which supported a fertile agricultural and ranching base, a world class harbor located smack dab on the route to Asia. The Argentine economy could not help but thrive, Argentina's landowners, ranchers and entrepreneurs could not help but feed a thriving export market, and those exports didn't have anywhere to go but through Buenos Aires.

Argentina experienced prosperity, and more importantly, it was a broad based prosperity not dependent on a key resource, like

Bolivian Tin or Chilean Nitrates, or on a key crop like Ecuadorian Cacao. Not dependent on a key resource or crop, it was difficult for an elite or government to monopolize resources. Broad based prosperity was a magnet for trade and immigration and investment. Buenos Aires became a world class city. The country saw railroads and factories opening up.

Much of this trade was with and through England. England, or more accurately, the British Empire, was an insatiable market for Argentine beef and wheat and other production. British business invested in Argentine infrastructure to support and sustain that pipeline. By the late 19th century, the Argentine economy was so heavily intertwined with British interests, investment and trade that it was sometimes considered a British colony in all but name.

From this, we may gather that Argentina, for most of its 19th century and early 20th century history probably didn't pay a lot of attention to the rest of South America. When the Argentines looked upon the world, they saw England, they saw Europe, they saw America, they saw India and China.

Their actual neighbors? They could give a rat's ass maybe. Possibly two or three. That was it though. There were practically no economic ties to other South American nations. Argentine trade was exclusively focused on the British Empire, Europe and perhaps the United States. Geography made Paraguay and Bolivia inaccessible, Chile remote, and Uruguay untouchable. As far as Argentina is concerned, Peru might as well be on Mars, and Ecuador on the Moon.

Despite this, Argentina did occasionally get involved in local conflicts.

There was the war of the Confederation in 1840. This featured both Chile and Argentina separately going to war against a Confederation composed of Peru and Bolivia. Bolivia became an independent state, and that resolved that.

There was the famous War of the Triple Alliance, where Argentina, Brazil and Uruguay teamed up against Paraguay.

A potential conflict with Chile over Patagonian claims was averted when Chile, busy beating Bolivia and Peru in the War of the Pacific abandoned claims to the Patagonian desert in favor of wresting more valuable provinces from its neighbors.

Argentine foreign policy, when it came to Latin America was largely twofold. The first and foremost was to preserve and maintain a perceived and entirely hypothetical Argentine economic and political primacy in Latin America. This was to be achieved by maintaining a vague concept of 'balance.'

Balance essentially meant maintaining a vague status quo. Nobody else could get too big. That was the whole point of the War of the Confederation. The old Peru-Bolivia Confederation, that was too big, it disturbed the balance. Rather Paraguay balanced Bolivia, Bolivia balanced Chile, Chile balanced Peru, Peru balanced Colombia, everyone held Brazil in check, South America was a set of dominos propping each other, no one too powerful or upsetting a balance that left Argentina sitting pretty. That was the point of the War of the Triple Alliance: Paraguay was disturbing that delicate balance. The War of the Pacific? That was a concern, but really, it only amounts to small territorial adjustments between Peru, Bolivia and Chile, and more importantly, it allows Argentina free rights to Patagonia.

Coming into the 20th century, Argentina is sitting pretty. It is one of the ten richest countries in the world. The future is looking bright. Funny how things can just go to hell.

The promises and hopes of the 20th century prove to be short lived.

The big disaster for Argentina, as it is for all Latin American countries, was World War One. None of them are directly involved. But all their economies, to a greater or lesser extent, are tied to Europe and Britain by strings of exports, imports and investments. With the war, these dry up. European partners like Germany and Austria are taken out of the equation. Britain and France, even Italy, are still in the picture but all their resources are devoted to the war. It makes for lean times.

After the war, it gets worse. The Argentine economy, tied to exports, is not quite large enough to generate an internal economic or consumer base and is literally set adrift. Europe is in ruins and destitute. Demobilization and reparations leads to an economic depression. The Argentines are in trouble

A brief recovery as the twenties wore on bottoms out completely as the Great Depression rolls around, as it does for all the Latin American nations. If Argentina is different, then it is because Argentina has further to fall being European or almost European in its outlook and economy.

Nor is the option of falling into the American orbit all that available. Ecuador might sell its cacao to the US. Peru an assortment of minerals and crops. Chile its copper. Bolivia its tin. But what are Argentina's big exports? Cattle and wheat. What does America produce? Cattle and wheat. The US isn't a market, it's the competitor.

The last thing that the American's own shaky economy want to import is its direct competitor's products. Tin, Chocolate, Sugar, Copper? It wants all that. More wheat and cattle... Nope.

The Great Depression devastates the rural landowners. There is a surge of population into cities, creating large impoverished urban proletariats. Argentina does its best to diversify its trading networks.

The British, at the Ottawa Conference in 1932, humiliate the Argentines, effectively shutting them out of the commonwealth system. The result is a wave of nationalism and Anglophobia.

The German economy in the thirties is revving up. Germany and Italy seems to offer a new solution, a new working ideology, an answer to the economic morass that is dragging down the world. American foreign investment os also sought.

In this sense, perhaps Argentine involvement in the Chaco War is a sign of renewed local interests. Argentina heavily supports Paraguay in the war. Nominally neutral, Argentina provides daily intelligence in Bolivian movements and supply lines running along the border. Argentine officers provide advice and support to the

Paraguayan command. An Argentine pilot becomes the Paraguayan director of Military Aviation. A number of Argentine citizens, largely from Corrientes and Entre Rios volunteer for Paraguayan service, mostly in the 7th cavalry. Argentina provides crucial military supplies, including arms and munitions, and military and economic support.

Argentina's bountiful natural resources do not include oil. So it's hard not to see Argentina's ultimate objective being to ensure significant oil supplies in the hands of a friendly or subordinate state in debt to Argentina and whose trade routes and access led through Argentina.

If that was the case, it doesn't turn out well. Argentina's great resource gamble and experiment in regional power politics largely flops. Paraguay wins most of the Chaco, but the oil fields end up in Bolivia anyway. The Bolivian and Paraguayan armies are by treaty reduced to skeleton forces, their economies and populations are devastated. If Argentina hoped to make Paraguay a client state, the outcome is a client too destitute to be of any worth. That's the Chaco war for you, everyone comes out a loser.

The Argentines adapt as best they can, with the usual political and economic shake ups. The immediate response to the Great Depression, as in so many places, is a coup attempt, in which Augustin Justo is a participant. Justo later becomes President in 1932 through a fraudulent election, and holds the position until 1938. As with many other leaders of the period, his approach to the Depression is austerity, in the later period shifting towards more active measures.

Justo received the Ecuadoran entreaties during the 1930s with cold indifference. Ecuador and Peru were far away, and a minor border dispute there is of no relevance to Buenos Aires. Besides which, Argentina lacks the money or the ability to intervene significantly. Nor does he give much regard to other Ecuadoran efforts, treating its 'volunteer' mission in the Chaco as an affront, and passing word to the Chileans that an Ecuadoran alliance will damage relations with Argentina.

Despite this, there are significant pro-German and even pro-Nazi constituencies in the Argentine army and society, and notable German immigration. The Germans are not as significant a constituency as in Chile. But Argentina is a minor hotbed of Nazi spying and sympathy. There are some channels from Argentina to fascist allies in Chile and Ecuador.

In 1938, Justo is replaced by Roberto Ortiz, who pursues a more interventionist approach in the economy. Protectionist measures are undertaken, efforts are made to develop an internal manufacturing base, protectionist measures and import substitution was the rule of the day, practical substitutions are made for shortages of raw materials - coal fired steam trains switched to wood.

But by and large, Argentina sits out the prelude to war, focusing instead on domestic matters. Unlike the Andean countries, Argentina makes no effort to militarize. Its navy was already superior to Chile's and on a par with Brazil. There are no security issues on land: Uruguay is a non-threat. Paraguay is emasculated. Bolivia a basket case. Brazil looks after itself. And Chile lies on the other side of the Mountains.

War between Ecuador and Peru is greeted with indifference. Ecuador's string of victories produced a wave of popular sympathy and a burst of enthusiasm for fascist causes. Chile's entry into the war is received with considerable surprise, but even Justo's mild condemnation is lacking, it is no business of Argentina's who Chile got in bed with. Bad judgment by Chile is not Argentina's concern.

None of this is cause for anything more than polite salon conversation in government circles. None of it affects Argentine interests or provided opportunities in any material way.

For the first two years of the war, Argentina undertakes no military preparations or build ups. Its principal role is attempting to secure a role for itself as a diplomatic broker.

The Bolivian civil war breaking out in July, 1941, and the near concurrent entry of both Peruvian and Chilean armies in August and September, on the other hand, is not taken lightly. Suddenly the equation changes. The policy of balance is at risk. Two rival

New World War – Page 127

powers are fighting it out over Bolivia, and presumably, the winner will inherit Bolivia as an effective chattel.

In the 19th century, Argentina fought a war to break a Bolivian/Peruvian axis. It has no desire to see a new Peru-Bolivia, and even less desire to see a Chile-Bolivia. Argentina doesn't want either a dominant Peru or a dominant Chile. It prefers things to go back to everyone balancing everyone, with Argentina on top of the heap. In a sense, Argentina is nobody's friend. It is definitely opposed to Chile's ambitions in Bolivia and bent on frustrating them. But then again, it won't be thrilled to see Peru taking over.

Either outcome threatens the balance which is the cornerstone of its foreign policy. But still, Argentina make no real efforts to militarize, although it views these developments with increasing trepidation.

The rebellion of Colonel Ramon Valpes in the southern Bolivian city of Santa Cruz is a godsend. Valpes subsequent appeals to Villarroel's alienated supporters and his establishment of a splinter regime in southern Bolivia, a regime which includes the Chaco oil fields offers new diplomatic and political opportunities.

As the Ortiz government sees it, Penaranda is clearly the legitimate claimant, but fritters away his legitimacy and finally abandons it by becoming a Peruvian catamite. Villarroel has a claim to legitimacy through his National Unity coalition, but that coalition fractures and his credibility vanishes with the invitation of the Chileans.

Ramon Valpes in this light, is as legitimate as anyone else, and has the advantage of being nobody's tool, despite the comparative weakness of his faction. He has the further advantage that his lowland regions are relatively accessible to Argentina. And most significantly, it is Valpes, who shortly after establishing his rebellion, reaches out to the Ortiz government, which immediately begins to provide a trickle of military and economic aid to prop him up.

And still, the Argentine government does not prepare for war.Rather, the first major offensives are diplomatic. Their first effort is to organize a Neutral Powers diplomatic alliance, including Brazil, Uruguay and Paraguay, to throw its support behind Valpes.

Efforts are largely unsuccessful. Brazil maintains neutrality. The eventual alliance includes only Uruguay and Paraguay.

Seeking great power support from the United States and Britain, Argentina enters the Montevideo Peace Conference on September 24, and again Argentina throws its support heavily behind Valpes with Paraguay at its side. Brazil maintains neutrality but weighs in on behalf of Penaranda. The United States and Britain, after attempting to broker a coalition government fail to commit to anyone. The lone Argentine success is in excluding Villarroel and his Chilean backers from the talks.

It is in October, following Montevideo, that the Argentine government finally begins to commit to a campaign of quiet mobilization and armament. Conscripts are called up, forces redeployed to the Paraguayan and Bolivian borders. Munitions orders are placed. The buildup is gradual and covert and takes place with the concurrence of the Paraguayan government.

The Argentine government at this time does not contemplate war, and certainly goes out of its way to avoid war. The Andean wars are an obvious disaster for all concerned, and no one in the Argentine regime wants into that meat grinder. On the other hand, a limited expedition to support the Valpes government might pay dividends; the lowlands seem accessible, defensible and contain Chaco's oil deposits. Argentina has no oil deposits of its own, and acquiring direct or indirect control of Chaco oil might be vital to national interests.

Argentinian diplomatic efforts intensify through the months of October and November, with little result beyond the consolidation of a Paraguayan diplomatic alliance. The Paraguayans hope to renegotiate the results of the Chaco War and secure some form of border adjustment or access to Bolivian oil reserves. This is a wish that the Ortiz regime coyly cultivates, being careful not to let it come too prominently to the attention of the Valpes regime. For obvious reasons, all three parties prefer Argentina to take the lead.

Also through this period, there are streams of reports from Argentinian military attaches giving increasingly critical opinions on Valpes military organization. Despite substantial amounts of

Argentinian aid and military supplies, his forces are still dramatically understrength in comparison to his rivals, deployments are poorly organized, discipline and effectiveness was judged to be low. Valpes proves to be a far better politician than a general.

For its part, Argentine ambitions grow exponentially between September and November, quixotically fed by the weakness of the Valpes faction.

At first the Ortiz government merely sought to prevent either Chilean or Peruvian domination of Bolivia. As time goes on, and as Valpes becomes more dependent, this outlook changes, and the Argentines begin to contemplate Bolivia, under Valpes, as an Argentine satellite. Indeed, the Argentines begin to envision a renewed Viceroyalty of La Plata, a federation encompassing almost all the Spanish southern cone nations, with Argentina as head. Even the worst possible case contemplates a splintered Bolivia, divided like Poland, with the oil-rich southern territories being either an Argentine client or outright Argentine territory.

The Depression remained an intractable problem. But suddenly, the situation allowes the Argentines to dream, and dream big. If the economy cannot be fixed, then political and military victories, a greater Argentina, can secure Ortiz legacy.

Then the dream comes crashing down. On November 24, 1941, with the Penaranda and Villarroel factions stalemated in the north, Villarroel suddenly turns a portion of his forces around and attacks the Valpes regime.

Outnumbered, outgunned and caught by surprise, the Valpes faction begins to collapse like a house of cards. The situation is beginning to look like the Chaco War all over again, a heavy commitment reduced to futility.

President Ortiz faces a profound choice. Argentina can cut its losses, abandon Valpes, abandon all its recent hopes and dreams, and resign itself to Bolivia as a pawn of a rival state in a redrawn map of South America....

Or it can dramatically escalate its commitment....

****

New World War – Page 130

Order of Battle - Argentina

Population: Thirteen million

Area: 2,778,400 square kilometers / 1,200,000 square miles

Army: In 1938 the army numberd 47,467 personnel, organized into five infantry divisions of the military districts, spread across the country. Aside from these five divisions, there were also two cadre regiments of mountain infantry, three cavalry brigades, and several independent and service detachments. Training was generally modeled on that of the German army, pre-World War I, with an emphasis on discipline, organization and lines of authority.

The primary military challenges, as perceived by the Argentine command were in order (1) the maintenance of domestic tranquility; (2) Brazil; (3) the suppression of the Indigenous population of Patagonia; (4) Chile. Deployments were made accordingly, with the majority of army forces distributed along populated areas in the north or the border regions with Brazil.

The primary weakness of the Argentine Army is mobility. Even into the late 30s and early 40s, the Argentine Army has shortages of trucks, armor or mobile artillery. Efforts to address these were hampered by fuel shortages and poor roads in outlying areas. Most infantry transport was by rail.

Military service was compulsory for all males capable of bearing arms and between the ages from 20 to 45 years old (one year of which was in the active service and 24 years in the reserve), following European models of universal conscription, but in practical terms, this was largely overlooked.

Navy: Argentinian navy (8th largest in the world during this period) stands at 12,000 men.

Ships included four line vessels (two of them old), two coastal defense armored ships, three light cruisers, 16 destroyers, and three submarines. The main naval bases are at Puerto Belgrano and La Plata, in the north of the country.

The Argentine navy is comparable to the Chilean one at the outset of the war. Chile has suffered losses, only partially balanced when the former Graf Spee, the Toro, returns to service. But in practical terms, the two navies sit on different oceans, and chance of conflict was remote.

The Navy is an entirely separate command from the Army, to the point that it has its own cabinet level Minister. Inter-service rivalry was high, the two military cultures are alien to each other, and cooperation was low.

Prior to the start of war, there is no Argentine Air Force. Rather, the Army and Navy each maintain separate air fleets. In 1937 the army has 106 airplanes while the navy has 46. The Aircraft were a grab bag of craft, but most were relatively modern 1930s standard. The primary weakness of the Argentine air forces are limited ranges and basing/airstrip issues.

Overall, Argentina is potentially one of the most powerful states in Latin America, and on paper its military is formidable. But in many respects it is a paper tiger, unprepared for war with significant handicaps in logistics and transport.

***

Order of Battle - Paraguay:

Population: 1,000,000 (in 1938)

Area: 406,752 square kilometers.

Army: The peace treaty stipulated that the country's peace-time armed forces could not exceed 8,000 personnel. The standing army of Paraguay consisted of four infantry regiments, one cavalry regiment, and two artillery batteries. It's a telling sign of how utterly destitute the country was that this relatively tiny armed force consumed 45 percent of the government's budget.

All the units and regiments were typical cadre formations; capable of increasing in size several- fold at a moment's notice. Paraguay was notable in having large numbers of fresh, combat blooded veterans, and was generally conceived to punch far above its weight class.

Although victorious, the Chaco war devastated the country. War losses touched every family. The country was largely bankrupt and anti-war sentiment was profound. Bolivia's attempts at re-armament did not provoke a similar response in Paraguay; and neither the Andean War nor the Bolivian Civil War provoked any nationalist sentiment. War was a touchy subject, and the Paraguayans had no stomach for it.

Despite this, there was resentment over the Chaco War outcome, and in some circles, particularly political; there was some sentiment to revisit the results in some way.

Other relevant factors were economic devastation from the War and Depression, a high degree of Argentine influence in some circles due in part to economic dependency on Argentina and some dependency on Argentina for rail access to the coast and international shipping. Both Italian and German agents and sympathizers were far more active in Paraguay in this time period, part of an overall more robust Axis network.

***

Meanwhile in Paraguay

For Paraguay, the scars of the Chaco War are very fresh. Felix Paiva, who took office as President on October 10, 1937, is the bridge between the old war and the new war, and wants little enough to do with either. It is in the first year of his rule, in 1938, that he signs the final peace treaty in Buenos Aires which settles the Chaco War. The war effectively ended in 1935, but the peace took another three years. Paiva's Presidency sees the beginnings of the Andean wars, but considers them irrelevant to Paraguay.

The next President was Jose Estigarribia, sworn in on August 15, 1939. An agronomist by training, Estigarribia is the war hero and brilliant general who won the Chaco war for Paraguay, consistently outwitting and outmaneuvering Bolivian forces. He casts a long shadow. But it is harder to be a President than a General. He assumes dictatorial powers by February of 1940, as a response to the intractability of Paraguay's economic and social problems. Foreign wars matter little to him, and he has less than no interest in the Andean conflicts which break out in June through August, 1940, between Ecuador, Chile and Peru.

On September 7, 1940, President Estigarribia is killed in a plane crash. His Minister of War, Higinio Morinigo is sworn in as interim President, and with the support of the army rapidly assumes dictatorial powers, postponing Presidential elections for two years, dissolving all political parties, instituting a secret police, exiling rivals and critics and implementing a campaign of totalitarian rule.

Resistance to the Morinigo regime is constant and varied, up to and including general strikes. To maintain control Morinigo relies heavily on the loyalty of the army and imposes extreme repression.

In a country battered by a ruinous war, the Great Depression and now a new set of economic dislocations flowing from both the Andean/Bolivian War and the outbreak of WWII, there is little Morinigo can do at home to stimulate the economy. Paraguay is utterly destitute. Its tiny army of 8,000 consumes almost half of government revenues, leaving almost no room for social or economic initiatives. A population of one million is far too small for any substantive domestic economic reform or initiatives. Most Paraguayans live at subsistence levels in rural areas and are able to survive the Depression, but the urban centers are devastated.

Morinigo is a soldier, not an agronomist, economist or businessman, and poorly equipped to deal with these issues. His best idea is to seek international assistance and investment. He flirts with both the British and the Nazis, but correctly assesses there will be no help there. Brazil shows no real interest. Argentina is by far the best option, but has very little motive to help out Paraguay when it us struggling itself. A proposal for Argentine assistance to build a railroad through the Chaco is met with polite bemusement.

In an attempt to distract from domestic problems, he focuses on international relations, building diplomatic bridges to both Brazil and Argentina and making various public pronouncements and offers to mediate about the Andean war and Bolivian Civil War.

This is a risky policy, since the prospect of re-involvement with war actually increases resistance in the population and erodes some Army support. Morinigo turns increasingly to Argentina as an ally, potential economic partner, and diplomatic conspirator. Unwilling to actually commit troops, Morinigo nevertheless sees tangible advantages in Argentina's increasing involvement in the Bolivian conflict.

As Argentina begins to back Valpes, Morinigo throws his support behind both. Suddenly, Bolivia's Chaco oil deposits are back on the table, and the prospect of a railway through the Paraguayan Chaco becomes a serious matter. His efforts to get Argentina to help rescue Paraguay's economy, or to fund railways or infrastructure for the region that will benefit Paraguay are suddenly well received.

A rail line through the Chaco will not only unify Paraguay and create a vital economic boost, but it will link the Bolivian Chaco oil fields to industries and markets in Buenos Aires. Paraguay will at the very least, benefit as a trans-shipment point. It will also be invaluable to Argentina in supporting its ally Valpes, and helping get troops and supplies to him.

New World War – Page 135

During the Chaco war, Bolivia actually developed war industries. Paraguayan factories developed a form of hand grenade the carumbei (Guaraní for "little turtle") and produced trailers, artillery grenades and aerial bombs. With the end of the war, the war industries become moribund. But Argentina's military adventure and a Bolivian civil war ally can provide a market to revitalize these industries.

And more! Examinations of Morinigo's private papers show a variety of scenarios. On one extreme, a gloriously short sharp war, assisted by Argentina, against an immeasurably weaker Bolivia, which will resolve all territorial issues completely in favor of Paraguay. More realistically, a renegotiation of the Chaco peace treaty, conferring more territory and oil territories to Paraguay. Or at the very least, intervention offering the prospect of key commercial concessions which will give Paraguay a stake in Bolivian oil.

Any of these will immensely benefit Paraguay, revive the economy, open the door to prosperity and most importantly consolidate his own position beyond challenge.

Morinigo too is beginning to dream big. Indeed, there is a personal stake in it. Morinigo is a man in a shadow, a shadow cast by his predecessor President Estigarribia. A man who has won the Chaco War, a man who had actually been elected President, and who had enjoyed overwhelming support in both the army and with the public. Morinigo sees involvement as a chance to step out of Estegarribia's long shadow, to be his own man.

Ironically, Morinigo's quest to prove himself, would become the greatest threat Paraguay faced. But not even Morinigo would understand this, until it was too late.

***

Argentina Struggles

Argentina has little interest in direct conflict with Chile. There are a number of obstacles. While Chile is embroiled in two wars and being bled white, its active military buildup is still substantially larger than Argentina.

Argentina, of course could initiate conscription, and spend a lot of time and money building up. But that will require a massive investment, and money is tight. And it will take time, and there doesn't seem to be an urgent need. There are other barriers The Andes themselves are a major one, a mountain barrier the length of the country, with a limited number of viable passes. The Andes Mountains are tough country to fight a war in.

Another issue was that while Argentina is a big country, most of its population centers are far away from the border. It will have to move and supply its armies through a lot of empty territory of its own to even get to the border and the Andes. There is a rail line from Argentina to Chile through Valparaiso and Santiago, but that is at best a partial solution. Logistics are not the Argentines strong suit.

Instead, of a direct confrontation with Chile, the Argentine theater will be the Bolivian civil war. Everyone is at least nominally promoting the legitimacy of their ally/pawn as the true ruler of Bolivia. Armies are in or going into Bolivia as unofficial guests at the invitation of and under the theoretical command of their Bolivian counterparts to 'help out.' That provides a reasonable fig leaf for Argentine involvement.

Officially, Argentina remains neutral and at peace with all parties. What is going on in Bolivia is legally a struggle between Penaranda, Villarroel and Valpes. In early phases, this was even mostly true. But that fig leaf of non-involvement becomes less and less true as time goes on.

***

Villarroel's Southern Bolivia Campaign, the Four Day Siege, the Argentine Intervention

Starting from his declaration of independence in October, 1941, President Ramon Valpes manages to sit out the larger part of the Bolivian Civil war. He establishes control of almost a third of Bolivia with little resistance.

For the next few months, Valpes actions largely consists of dealing with bandits and deserters, and repelling occasional sorties from Villarroel or Penaranda. Both are focusing on each other, and see Valpes as either a potential ally or a minor nuisance. If one can decisively beat the other, Valpes third movement is finished. For his part, Valpes correctly assesses that the battleground will be the mining districts and that his own forces are too insignificant to play a part.

But the writing is on the wall. Valpes military forces are weak, but his intelligence and contacts prove to be excellent. He is well aware of the increasing build ups and involvement of both Chilean and Peruvian forces. Survival is going to require a patron.

Valpes first choice is Brazil, but the Brazilian regime maintains neutrality and nominally favored Penaranda as the legitimate government. This leaves only Argentina. A surprisingly skillful diplomat, Valpes is able to enlist Argentinian support by appealing to Argentinian foreign policy priorities of 'balance' and waving the prospect of access to Bolivian Chaco oil fields. It works, and from September onwards a stream of Argentinian money, supplies and armaments flows north.

Through October and November, Villarroel and the Chileans score a series of decisive victories against Penaranda and the Peruvians. La Paz is taken by October 29. The mining districts are overrun by November 10. Penaranda's seat of government withdraws to Peruvian territory but still holds the northern reaches of Bolivia. Villarroel is reaching the limits that he can effectively push north with his forces, Penaranda's remnants are too entrenched. Then again, with the mining districts and key cities in his hands, all he needs to do is hang onto them, and ultimately, the war will be his.

Penaranda is down. He's essentially lost control of his government and army to the Peruvians from this point on. But the Peruvians themselves are still in the game in Bolivia, although it will take time for them to organize a counter offensive against Villarroel's nationals.

Villarroel, a competent military man, sees the opportunity to win total victory. He decides to use that time to consolidate his position; politically within his faction, diplomatically with the Chileans and militarily against Valpes. Starting in November, he begins planning a campaign against the Valpes faction.

Throughout the month of November, Valpes forces in the south encounter a series of sorties and feints by units of Villarroel's campaign. To the delight of Villarroel, and the growing dismay of the Argentines, Valpes soldiers uniformly perform poorly, at times throwing down their weapons and fleeing. Only against Santa Cruz itself are Villarroel's men decisively thrown back by Valpes forces.

Villarroel demands Chilean assistance, particularly trucks, artillery and air support, in a campaign to crush Valpes and establish his rule. The Chileans, focused elsewhere, provide little.

Instead, Villarroel gathers a force of primarily infantry, ten thousand strong and begins to march south, overwhelming and rolling up Valpes' forces wherever he finds them, until by November 24, 2012, he reaches the gates of Santa Cruz, Valpes' capital, once again encountering stiff resistance. Unable to breach the city, he begins the 'Four Day Siege.'

Throughout November, the Argentinians are viewing the situation with increasing dismay. From September onwards, Valpes hosts a series of Argentinian military advisors and attaches, who send a distressing stream of reports back to Buenos Aires expressing skepticism about the viability of their ally.

The Argentine government dithers, continuing to supply weapons and aid, seeking to advance the matter diplomatically. Troops are called up and remobilized to the Paraguayan and Bolivian borders, but they are reluctant to commit.

The March on Santa Cruz forces the Argentines to finally take a stand. On November 23, with Villarroel almost on top of Santa Cruz, an expeditionary force almost ten thousand strong crosses the Bolivian border. The force is well equipped with trucks and fuel but proceeds cautiously. A second force of five thousand enters through Paraguay, crossing the Chaco into the Bolivian foothills. The intent is for both forces to link up at Santa Cruz, but the Chaco expedition has a secondary purpose of securing the Bolivian oil fields.

The Argentine expedition moves cautiously, during which time, Valpes in Santa Cruz endures a four day siege. On the evening of November 28, shots exchange between Villarroel's forces and the Argentines. On November 29, the battle begins in earnest.

Villarroel's force is primarily an infantry force, moving on foot, with a limited baggage train of supplies and ammunition. The Argentine force, less the divisions securing the oil fields, number almost thirteen thousand, substantially outnumbering Villarroel, and with the further advantages of artillery and supplies.

Despite this, Villarroel refuses to retreat, committing his forces to close heavy fighting and riding a white charger among his men to urge them on. To retreat would be a political and military disaster undermining Villarroel. In turn breaking the siege would confer upon Valpes a credibility as a candidate for national leader he never before possessed. The battle is on.

Fighting is savage; casualties reached 3,000 on both sides, before Villarroel's forces begin a retreat on November 30. Among the casualties was Villarroel himself. His horse stumbles in a gopher hole, throwing him and resulting in a broken leg. Using rum as a painkiller, Villarroel continues to direct his forces until passing out through intoxication.

The Argentines initially show no desire to pursue, and Villarroel's forces, although badly mauled are allowed to retreat in good order, giving the day to Valpes faction. During the retreat, Villarroel's broken leg becomes badly infected and he passes in and out of delirium. This is the Argentines best chance to sweep the table and win Bolivia, but they hesitate, waiting for orders from Buenos Aires.

With Villarroel out of commission, his faction is paralyzed. Villarroel's ruling coalition falls into disarray, unable to forge a consensus without him, they flounder. A number of Villarroel's coalition members defects to the Valpes camp. The political balance shifts towards Valpes, now for the first time a serious contender.

Finally, the Argentine expeditionary force, after consulting with Valpes and eventually receiving further orders from Buenos Aires, embarks on a campaign to recover territories lost to Villarroel, and to add to those territories. They avoided the heavily defended mining district and the cities of La Paz and Sucre, but push up along through the east, reaching as far as Penaranda's rump forces by December 7, 1941.

By the time of the Japanese attack on Pearl Harbor, the Valpes/Argentine faction could claim control over almost two thirds of the country.

✳✳✳

American Policy in Bolivia, Three Dogs Fighting

It is in Bolivia that American policy is simultaneously most cynical and most unsuccessful.

Anti-fascist sentiment wars directly with realpolitik. The reality that neighboring countries are supporting or even animating factions in the civil war clashes with the reality that the civil war is a fundamentally indigenous conflict between increasingly irreconcilable factions of Bolivian society represented by Penaranda, Villarroel and Valpes.

American demands for a ceasefire are honored on paper and nowhere else. Attempts to arrange a reconciliation and coalition government do not outlast the meetings held to broker them. An American demand that foreign troops withdraw receives immediate consent, and is immediately ignored... even by the Americans. Recognition or support of Penaranda or Villarroel shifts from day to day and from policy maker to policy maker.

Ultimately, the United States finds itself unable to affect the Bolivian situation, and settles on a priority: There should be no significant interruptions of Bolivian mining production or exports. The bottom line is that whoever controls the mining districts is eventually going to be recognized as the de facto Bolivian government. The result is a continuing escalation of the Bolivian civil war.

Chile's ally, the Bolivian Villarroel government holds the mining district, and in Santiago, Ibanez concludes that continuing to hold them is vital to Chilean interests. It is by far the most significant piece of leverage he can exert on the Americans, and key to regional hegemony. If Chile loses control of the Bolivian mining district, then he foresees America falling heavily into the Peruvian camp. If Chile can keep it, then victory is assured on all fronts and regional dominance inevitable. Bolivia becomes the fulcrum for the contending parties; everything comes down to the Altiplano nation.

The ceasefires on the northern and southern fronts, free up both Chile and Peru to flood Bolivia with ever more troops, coming in under the flags of the Villarroel and Penaranda regimes. The Bolivian leaders are steadily losing control of their own civil war.

Despite American hostility, Argentina, for its part, is dragged further and further into support of Valpes. Despite misgivings, the Argentine regime lacks clear focus or goals. It does not see victory as a key to solving all issues and achieving regional hegemony, and on that basis argues with the United States that it is the only true neutral, and Valpes is the only credible representative of an independent Bolivia.

What drags Argentina deeper is the sunken cost fallacy. The choice Argentina continually faces in the Bolivian conflict, is to withdraw and essentially lose its entire investment to date and all further hope of advantage, or to increase its commitment incrementally, to stay in the game, committing more and more and hopefully recoup.

The wiser decision might be to withdraw, but no one in the Argentine junta is prepared to accept responsibility for failure. The choice is to pass that decision down for another day. For gamblers, the phenomenon is known as doubling down, and it seldom pays off.

December, 1941 - August, 1942 - The "Tranquility" of Peru

The period between December 21, 1941, and August, 1942, is known in Peru as the 'Tranquility.' The ceasefire imposed by the American entry into the World War, endures through most of the southern hemisphere fall and winter.

Far and away, Lima is the greatest beneficiary of American involvement. Even before Pearl Harbor, the frameworks of a lend lease and aid program are being put into place for Peru. Following Pearl Harbor the taps open wide, and money and material flows into Peru, rejuvenating the economy.

With this flood comes a host of American advisors, both military and civilian, and a host of informal consultants and business interests purchasing Peruvian assets, resources and production licenses, entering business partnerships. By March and April, 1942, Peru's economy and resources are being integrated into the emerging American war machine.

This clear favoritism contradicts Roosevelt's official 'even handed' policy. Protests from Chile and Ecuador, and Chilean supporters in the American government, result in some lend lease aid going to Chile and Ecuador, and some even earmarked for Bolivia. It also explicitly excludes military supplies being provided to any party. But Peru continues to receive the lion's share of aid, and, despite official policy, a quiet trickle of munitions and weapons.

Despite the immense advantages which come from allying with Brazil and the United States, there are downsides.

The Peruvian economy and social infrastructure is poorly equipped to handle the sudden influx of money and materials from the United States. Distribution is highly uneven. The new wealth is almost uniformly captured by the upper classes and educated classes, who use it to fuel acquisitions and luxuries.

Private land holdings and small businesses are eaten up or wiped out by new 'combines', enterprises of Peruvian wealthy, who seek land and resources for everything from airstrips, to roads, to factories in anticipation of an American driven boom. Ironically, although the Peruvian economy is flush with cash, the positions of workers, small businessmen, small farmers and landholders, actually declines. The Peruvian middle class grows even more attenuated, surviving as an appendage to a resurgent elite.

Corruption and graft is endemic, and many American advisors write extensively about the greed and dishonesty of Peruvian government officials, traits that reach all the way up to the Ramirez Junta. Ramirez himself is recurrently singled out for criticism, both by the Americans and by members of his own Junta, for his conspicuous luxuries and the increasing acquisitiveness of himself and his cronies.

The Mestizo and Indigenous of the highlands see no benefit at all, in fact their conditions worsen as inflationary spirals make their way into the interior, and the central government increasingly shifted to demanding cash from previously traditional economies. In the interior, the twin influxes of American cash and demand are expressed in the dramatic growth of haciendas and plantations and the rapid taking up of Indigenous land interests. Indigenous communities, many of which have seen their male populations reduced by conscription drives are often poorly positioned to resist encroachments of landowners.

With American assistance, Peru finds itself in possession of large quantities of trucks, gasoline, all the necessaries to move and transport armies, the tools and components to build weapons and ammunition. It even receives road construction equipment, and an ambitious highway was commenced to link Bolivia, and particularly its mining district, to the Peruvian coast, a plan with obvious military applications.

On May 23, 1942, a Brazil-United States political/military agreement 'The Washington Accords' sets the stage for a tacit arrangement which among other things, provides for direct American military aid to Brazil. This is followed a week later, on May 30, 1942, with the 'Lima Accord' in which Peru and Brazil formalize a trade and political alliance. Falling short of committing Brazil to military action on Peru's behalf, it nevertheless allows Brazil to provide military supplies received from the United States to the Lima government. With this legal fig leaf in place, the United States begins arming Peru.

Most of the new military procurement is directed south, to the Chilean and Bolivian fronts. Comparatively little is assigned to the northern command, largely because of growing antipathy of most of the junta to General Markholtz, increasingly seen as incompetent and unreliable. Despite Markholtz demands, he is actively denied reinforcement and rearmament, a clear revenge for his earlier conduct. This is cold comfort to Ecuador, which still fears a new offensive and is poorly equipped to fight one off. Ironically, during this period, Ecuador's best protection is dissension between Peru's generals.

In the south, Chile's Ibanez doubles down, fortifying a defensive position along the Chilean frontier and struggling to hold key districts of Bolivia against the looming threat of attack from a temporary alliance of Argentina and Peru.

Increasingly, the sentiment in Lima is that the ceasefire was temporary, and that a new offensive in August or September will end the war decisively. For the Peruvian Junta, victory is no longer a matter of 'if', but 'when', the only real question being the magnitude of the victory, and the shape of things to come.

Emboldened by alliances, a revived economy, massive infusions of cash and war material, the Ramirez Junta dares to dream of reversing the results of the War of the Confederation and War of the Pacific, regaining lost provinces, claiming new territories, rewriting maps wholesale.

***

The "Desperation" of Ecuador

Peace proves a greater threat to Ecuador than war. The ceasefire and subsequent declaration of war on Germany and Japan produces a short lived wave of optimism. It seems to Ecuadorans that the war is over, that the United States has weighed in on their side. A return to normal life is just around the corner. Instead, things seem to get steadily worse.

As matters develop, the average Ecuadoran finds themselves disenchanted by a continuing American policy of neutrality. The United States, by decree, brings an apparent end to the war and promises grants and loans, non-military supplies and materials to all parties. In a sense buying peace.

But the economic benefits from American aid are lopsided. Between December 7, 1941, and October 31, 1942, Ecuador receives roughly six million dollars in American non-military goods and non-repayable loans.

As significant as these sums are, it is paltry compared to the fifty-eight million provided to the Peruvian government, the twenty-four million provided to Chile, or even the twelve million set aside for Bolivia but never provided.

Ecuador fails to see even this minimal benefit. As much as eighty-five per cent of American funding directed to Ecuador is re-directed to or secured by Colombian interests, to which the Ecuadoran government is by this time deeply indebted.

As a result, Ecuador sees almost no advantage from American capital at all. The Ecuadoran government remains seriously cash strapped; the civilian economy finds itself with almost no investment capital. Infrastructure and machinery degrade steadily from shortages of cash and spare parts. Businesses fail, unemployment climbs, the economy is in desperate straits, and the little commercial activity taking place is increasingly captured by Colombians.

As an example, consider shoes: At the start of the war, 90 percent of Ecuador's shoes are produced locally. Guayaquil alone listed eight shoe manufacturers. Initially the war proves a boon for shoe manufactures and production rose 150 percent. Expansion leads to consolidation and the reduction to five Guayaquil shoe manufacturers, although production continues to rise, driven by military procurement.

However, with the ceasefire following Pearl Harbor, and the subsequent freeze on military purchases, compounded by the ripple effects through the civilian economy, the bottom drops out of the marketplace, with production declining a precipitous 70 percent, by April, 1942. Several manufacturers go out of business. Surviving manufacturers encounter difficulties procuring raw materials, difficulties keeping their equipment running.

The Ecuadoran economy, with its weak, piecemeal industrial and manufacturing sector, finds itself shuddering on the verge of collapse. Flood of imported cheap American or Colombian goods feed a thriving black market. Ecuadoran businesses regulated by increasingly draconian wage and price controls cannot compete and either fold their operations, or sell out to foreign interests, mostly Colombian

By July, 1942, there were only two domestic shoe manufactures left in Guayaquil, and domestic owned production accounted for less than twenty per cent of shoes produced or sold in Ecuador. And even those sales are lower than in the teeth of the Great Depression. No one has money.

These grim statistics repeat everywhere throughout the nascent urban economies. Domestic production is in steep decline on almost every level. Manufacturing and production sectors, never very strong, are eroding rapidly, and the Ecuadoran economy is being rapidly colonized by Colombian interests.

Compounding the freeze on military and government expenditures, the ripple effect through the civilian economy produces a rapid economic downturn. Suddenly, hundreds, even thousands are out of work. These, together with waves of bankruptcies and business failures, produce runs on banks.

Through the Depression, and through the war, of course, Ecuador's triumvirate encountered recurrent crises again and again of similar nature. But through them all, Bonifaz and Velasco successfully employed a series of tactics to regain control of the situation. In some cases, they practiced or indulged forms of Keynesian economics; at times they founded and funded credit unions to dispense capital, at times they bullied banks or businesses and elites into social generosity, or begged or borrowed money from abroad. There were mild experiments with wage and price controls. The war was used for a patriotic rallying point to suspend economic realities.

But now, in the post-Pearl Harbor world, they are out of tricks, they've used up all their cards, and the Ecuadoran economy is entering a state of free fall.

Less than two months after the ceasefire, February 11 through 14, 1942, Ecuador experiences its first great currency collapse of the Bonifaz era. The crisis begins with a financial panic, and a run on banks. In desperation, Bonifaz issues a decree freezing all bank transactions, a measure which only fuels panic, and leaves many citizens and businesses scrambling for funds.

As the crisis mounts Prime Minister Ibarra, issues a 'Peace Dividend', essentially printing money. This begins a hyper-inflationary spiral through March, which the regime attempts to halt with the imposition of wage and price controls on April 22, 1942.

This produces a quixotic situation where Ecuadoran cash is both worthless and impossible to obtain. Wage and price controls become even more punitive when Bonifaz decrees that businesses will be forced to sell products at the government rates. The result is a wave of de-facto business shutdowns, and a runaway black market. There is no way that Ecuadoran society can cope with these dislocations, and several days of fierce rioting break out in Guayaquil and Lima, quelled only with the use of troops through the end of March, 1942.

The crisis ends when Bonifaz and Ibarra declare martial law on May 2, 1942, and re-launch a new Ecuadoran currency. Behind the scenes, banks and commercial houses are strong armed, sometimes violently, and a measure of stability is arranged through a new round of loans from Colombia, and through the promise of American money and goods. Ibarra's promises of American money are made liberally to all parties, far eclipsing the amounts the Americans are prepared to contribute - Ibarra essentially promises the same money again and again to different parties.

Ultimately, Bonifaz and Ibarra are unable to resolve the crisis, merely defuse it somewhat, and push it further down the road. Lesser financial crises erupt again on June 9, and on July 27 and again on the week of September 11, 1942.

In the countryside, things are no better. Many Haciendas find themselves capital starved, unable to afford or obtain the necessary credit to maintain operations to bring in the cash crops. Many go bankrupt or simply abandon operations. Others survive by withdrawing from the commercial economy and embracing a form of local barter and feudalism. Agricultural production and exports decline.

Bonifaz, a major landowner himself, attempts to deal with the rural crisis by engineering a system of labor conscription - temporary forced labor granted to the haciendas or landowners, mostly drawn from the Indigenous population. But this in turn produces its own crises - the rural interior is peppered with violent uprisings and demonstrations, both by the Indigenous who are resisting conscription, and by the Mestizo class who traditionally labor on the haciendas and find their wages and entitlements as workers are being usurped by unpaid Indigenous labor. Nevertheless, despite the social conflicts which emerge, the forced labor system works for a time, and some commercial agricultural productivity is regained.

As economically damaging as the crises were, the political effects are far reaching. Ibarra and Bonifaz are often at loggerheads over how to respond, with each, at times, issuing contradictory directives. Political dissension at the highest level often produces inaction or worsened conditions. Alba, appalled by the use of troops against civilians, threatens to resign his commission.

Dissent gathers. Several newspapers are openly critical of the Bonifaz regime, and are subsequently shut down. Meanwhile,

Velasco loses complete control of the Ecuadoran Congress. On July 28, 1942 a vote of non-confidence in Velasco Ibarra's cabinet is narrowly avoided. Then on September 13, 1942, the 'revolt of congress' occurs with a bare majority calling for the resignation of President Bonifaz. Arising out of this, a group called the Congressional Governing Council is formed and promptly arrested.

Bonifaz, over the objections of Alba and Ibarra shuts down Congress. Within a month, Congress is reconvened, but it is notable that over a third of the sitting Congressmen are removed from their seats, banned for 'treasonous sympathies.' The reconstituted Congress is further tamed by a series of de-facto procedural rulings which make it the puppet of the Ibarra cabinet.

On the military front matters are equally dire. Ecuador's military is already stretched to the limit; almost every form of military material was in short supply. At interior military bases, troops train and march with wooden sticks because rifles and ammunition are reserved for the front. Protests and minor mutinies break out over shortages, including shoes, ammunition, and in some districts food and water. Despite Alba's fixation on logistics, there is only so much that can be done.

Although a ceasefire is in place, Ecuador's Blandon continues internecine warfare through the Amazonas / Oriente / Selva region beyond the reach of the central commands. Closer to the coast, both sides maintain high levels of troop numbers, and there is a constant series of border incidents.

Nevertheless, the ceasefire produces widespread expectations of demobilization. When this does not occur, desertions become an endemic problem. Originally, desertion is treated harshly, but on several occasions, troops balk at inflicting punishments. A steady low level of attrition takes place. By August, 1942, different sources place anywhere from five to fifteen per cent of Ecuadoran troops are classified as deserters or irregularly reporting, and the 'refusados' become a political issue.

Rather than confronting this directly the Ecuadorans choose to make up this continuing attrition through redistributions and redeployments of military assets, and through a campaign of conscriptions among the Quechua Indigenous of the highlands, both of which meet with considerable resistance and pose their own problems. In particular, the Quechua engage in anti-conscription riots which are brutally put down.

Struggling with military manpower issues Ecuador seeks, or Colombia offers, 'volunteer brigades' - Colombian companies staffed by Colombian officers, supplied through Colombian resources, nominally under the direction of Ecuadoran leadership.

Wary of the Americans objections, and concerned for their own soldiers, the Colombian troops are subject to a number of status of forces restrictions limiting their use. Despite this, they become a common sight throughout many northern and coastal towns and cities, excepting only Guayaquil and Quito.

During this time, Ecuador withdraws slowly from occupied Peruvian territories. Slow because these occupied territories are among the very few bargaining chips left to the Bonifaz regime. But American and Peruvian pressure is continuous. The public neither understands nor approves the drawn out process, which play as a series of continuing concessions and defeat.

For the Ecuadoran population, a sense of dismay and disappointment take hold. Having courageously won their war, they can see no benefit. Banks are failing, businesses are closing, haciendas can no longer pay their workers, the Indigenous were caught between the lashes of conscription and forced labor, the poor drift in from a countryside that can no longer sustain them, to put increasing pressure on cities already at their limits.

For the Ecuadoran government, the problems are intractable. Policy deteriorates to a combination of repression, showmanship, and desperate ad hoc measures intended to stave off crises rather than resolve them. In the speeches of leaders, and the writings of newspaper editorials, a sort of magical thinking emerges during this period, an exhortation to hold on and hold out for some miraculous intervention which will rescue them.

✳✳✳

New World War – Page 152

The 'Deception' of Chile

Following Pearl Harbor, Ibanez of Chile is the first nation to accept the American offer, or demand, for a ceasefire, beating out Ecuador by a full eleven hours, and Peru by thirty-two hours.

In particular, he enthusiastically accepts the demand to return to original borders. Not surprising given that the trench war is mainly fought on Chilean territory in the provinces of Tarapaca and Antofagosta. By this time, Ibanez is more than willing to settle for an end of war that restores the status quo and all Chilean lands.

Ibanez also supports the ceasefire in Bolivia, and presses for recognition of the Villarroel regime as the legitimate government of Bolivia.

In hopes of currying favour, Chile breaks relations off with Germany, Italy and Japan. Ibanez formally outlaws the Chilean Nazi party, giving while giving former Nazis an amnesty. Nazi representatives are removed from Cabinet.

In Santiago, and up and down the length of Chile, the ceasefire is treated as a victory. The Americans have come to the rescue; they have weighed in on the side of righteousness. After all, wasn't this war about curbing Peruvian expansion? Fighting Peruvian designs on Ecuador, Bolivia and even Chile's sacred soil. Spontaneous celebrations break out everywhere. People dance in the streets. There is a sense of relief, even joy.

Ibanez himself is tired of war. He finds that despite his military background, he's more a leader than a general. He's a businessman, a politician, a skilled negotiator. A man who understands give and take, hard bargaining and how to get a deal.

Like a poker player or a chess master, he considers his hand. The Americans are going to war with Germany and Japan, they'll need war materials. In particular, they'll need metal, particularly and vitally, copper. Which Chile happens to produce.

They'll need Tin, and right now, the world's greatest source of Tin is in Bolivia, particularly, in the Bolivian mining districts which his ally, General Villarroel controls with his assistance. And the only way to procure that tin is to ship it through Chile.

Their warships will pass through the Panama Canal, of course, but some of them, both British and American will pass through Cape Horn. They'll need friendly harbours.

That's a good hand. And what does he want in return? Nothing really. Chile wasn't the aggressor, it was responding to aggression. Everyone goes back to their respective borders. Ecuador will probably put up statues to their rescuer. As for Bolivia, there's really no other choice than Villarroel. Valpes is a clown, and Penaranda, before he became a finger puppet, was simply a butcher. Butcher or puppet, he's disqualified either way. So it's not unreasonable at all – particularly since Villaroel and Ibanez sit on the only real estate in Bolivia that the Americans care about.

When you look at it like that, everyone in Chile's expectations are going to be sky high.

At first, it seems to be working. There's a hiccup, the Americans change their position, abandoning the demand to return to original borders. Recognising troops on foreign soil. That's frustrating for Ibanez, with Peruvian troops entrenched in his provinces. But then again, it's plainly good for Ecuador, which Ibanez doesn't truly care about… except that it discomfits the Peruvians. And it's very good for Ibanez, in that it entrenches his position in Bolivia and the key mining districts. All in all, he can live with it.

Negotiations commence and are initially positive. The Americans appreciate his shedding of the Nazis, they're more than willing to bargain for copper and tin. There's a flush of American cash, the ports are busy, the minerals are moving, the mines are active, the economy, previously on the verge of collapse, is rescued. Ibanez star rises high in Chile.

And then? Nothing exactly happens. Perhaps that's the problem. Nothing happens.

The Americans are willing to deal, but they're somehow not quite willing to make a deal. As much as Ibanez strives for a commitment, a grand bargain, a contract, a treaty, it's never quite there. The Americans don't reject it out of hand. They don't say no. They're willing to sit at the table. They have requests and suggestions and demands, which are met. But at the end of the day, there's nothing signed on the dotted line.

Starting in March, the trench war slowly resumes. No big operations, but artillery fires back and forth, snipers target the unwary. The lines are tested. There's a trickle of casualties. Ibanez has been contemplating demobilization, but it's clear that won't be happening. Bolivia also remains volatile, the Peruvians slowly testing and testing. The violence escalates in both theatres.

Ibanez complains; the Americans listen and are very concerned. But that doesn't resolve things.

Still, Ibanez has other cards to play, other players to talk to. The Peruvians are the enemy. The Argentines? Possible allies. There are secret negotiations between the two countries which result in an accord on March 30, 1941. The remainder of the Chaco will be ceded to Paraguay, including the oil producing regions, in return for the division of Chaco oil production between Argentina and Chile. Neither Villarroel or Valpes are part of these discussions of course, and are kept in ignorance. Why does Valpes need to know that his usefulness to the Argentines is at an end? It should come as a surprise. And as for Villarroel, well, with two great countries backing him, he'll soon be the ruler of Bolivia. But his nationalism makes him tricky to deal with.

With the two countries cooperating, there's enough stability in that portion of Bolivia to set a trickle of oil going, and for Chile to receive its share. Let Peru and Penaranda grind their teeth. It's quite a victory, shame that it needs to be secret.

And yet, still not enough happens. Ibanez gooses his popularity by arranging extended furloughs. He lowers interest rates to stimulate the economy; he sets up credit agencies to pump money into business. He decrees wage increases.

But underneath the surface, Chile is all but bankrupt. The economy is still in ruins, still propped up by government fiat and wage and price controls. There are still shortages everywhere. As money printed to pump into the economy inflation takes hold, slowly but steadily and escalating. The crises and strains of the economy are not resolved. The manpower shortages of the military are still pressing, conscription rules are still widening.

Instead, a disquiet seeps slowly into Chilean society, a sense of a false peace, where everything is fine, and nothing is resolved.

It's almost a relief when Ibanez falls into a normal everyday scandal – an underground newspaper exposes his March Accord and embarrasses him with Villarroel. He's forced to repudiate it of course. But he's confident he can salvage matters.

It turns out that he can't. Villarroel, angered, launches a series of direct assaults on Argentine forces. Ibanez is forced to support him, as Villarroel intended. The conflict with the Argentines creates a diplomatic crisis; embassies are closed, relations broken. The odious Penaranda and the Peruvians see their opportunities to push into Villarroel's territories while the fool distracts himself.

The war continues to slowly heat up. The furloughs are ended, conscriptions enforced, the talk of demobilization fades away. On the home front inflation is a larger and larger problem each month, even with price controls. And outside the price controls, the black market is increasingly volatile. Unemployment mounts. There are daily complaints and demonstrations about shortages everywhere. There are bitter conspiracies, promoted by disenfranchised Nazis; claims that the Jews are hoarding. The consensus is someone is hoarding. Everywhere there's too much and never enough of everything.

The government controls the Newspapers and Radio Stations of course, the official ones at least. The secret police are Chile's only growth industry, on the lookout for spies, saboteurs, hoarders and trash talkers. The official line is that everything is good and getting better. Chileans embrace this optimism wholeheartedly. There's really no choice.

But underneath, there are underground newspapers everywhere, printing subversion. Temporary pirate radio stations mock Ibanez. Quiet conversations express reservations. Given the shortages, the only way to get anything, is through the black market. Chileans become adept at negotiating a suddenly flourishing criminal underworld.

Prostitution flourishes, as does bootlegging, gambling, homemade stills and breweries pop up everywhere. Theft and robbery are endemic; after all, the black markets need to find their goods somehow. The Chileans, caught in suspension, become a nation of pleasure seekers. Parties ignore curfews. Orgies of drinking, drugs or sex, whatever your choice, proliferate. Gambling houses promise wealth and opportunity. Soldiers, particularly, on increasingly short furloughs, feed a desperation for pleasure. The stories they bring home bring uneasiness.

The war isn't going away. And while it's not as bad as it was, it's not getting better. The stories come back that perhaps the Americans like Peru better, have chosen a different favourite. Reports of enemy build ups seep in, and rumours of new weapons that they shouldn't have, and Yankees in places that perhaps they shouldn't be, doing things that they shouldn't do. At the negotiation tables, the Americans shake their heads and give assurances to Ibanez ministers. But still you have to wonder. What's really going on?

To the Chilean nation, it feels like they're on a merry go round, going faster and faster, and everyone laughs and dances, everyone is happy and happier with each turn. There's a manic intensity to life, a hunger, as if deep down there's a feeling that nothing will last. But everything keeps going around and around, and nothing ever goes everywhere. The nation feels like it's holding its breath, like it's waiting for something. What happens next? What happens when the merry go round stops?

There's a joke that goes around Chile, as things get better and better, and worse and worse at the same time. We know that Ibanez is lying to us. But do we really want to hear the truth?

***

Bleeding Bolivia - December 1941 through April 1943

While Peru enters the period known as the 'Tranquility', Ecuador's lifeblood slowly leaches away in the 'Desperation,' and Chile searches for a way out of its 'Deception,' the Andean War comes to focus almost completely on Bolivia.

Initially, the region came under the American imposed ceasefire from December 1941 through May 1942. A temporary stasis sets in, as fighting dies down, but not completely away.

Three cornered negotiations begin between the Penaranda, Villarroel and Valpes factions. Unfortunately, Penaranda's and Villarroel's positions are utterly incompatible, and the United States refuses to recognize the only possible compromise candidate, Valpes, due to his Argentine connections.

Chile has won its way to a pre-eminent position, in control of the mining district. The United States looks the other way as Peru begin building up its forces for a campaign to take the district back for Penaranda. Chile's Ibanez, correctly believing that the loss of the mining districts of Bolivia would be a major blow and would allow the United States to tilt decisively against Chile, commences his own build up in the region.

In response, in the spring of 1941, hostilities slowly renew along the Peruvian/Chilean trench frontier, as the Peruvians attempted to force Ibanez to commit troops to the front and defuse his build up in Bolivia.

In turn, Ibanez, without the knowledge of their clients, the Villarroel faction in Bolivia, tacitly enters into an informal agreement with Paraguay and Argentina for a build-up of Argentine forces in Southern and Eastern Bolivia.

This is followed by the March 30 Secret Accord between Chile and Argentina, promising the cession of the rest of the Chaco, won in the Chaco War and including the oil reserves, to Paraguay. This accord takes place without informing either the Villarroel or Valpes governments in Bolivia.

Beginning in late February, hostilities resume. Although the mining districts are left intact, Peruvian and Chilean forces joust back and forth across the Altiplano.

On May 2, 1942, the combined forces of the Penaranda Regime of Bolivia, and the Peruvian military strike across a broad frontier, driving towards the mining district. After a month and a half of hard fighting, Peruvian forces are in control of almost the entirety of the Mining district. However, this control is tenuous.

Villarroel in retreating, evacuates most of the miners, and remains in control of the roads and rails for access. In addition, Penaranda is sidelined by the Peruvian military, despite increasingly bitter protests. Penaranda takes his dispute to the Americans, arguing that the Peruvian policy of holding the mining district directly and deploying his forces to supporting positions is itself an unlawful occupation. American representatives are uninterested in the dispute. Despite this, the American government acknowledges control of the mining district and formally recognizes the jurisdiction of the Penaranda regime over the whole of Bolivia.

This recognition turns out to be premature. By July 2, the Chilean counterattack is under way and the Peruvian line begins to collapse almost everywhere.

There are a number of reasons for this: The Peruvians are over-extended. Co-ordination between Penaranda's Bolivian forces and his Peruvian allies have largely fallen to pieces, with Bolivian units flat out refusing to support Peruvian units. In the east, a mop up operation to clear out Valpes remnants becomes a disaster as the Peruvians misjudge the sheer number of Argentine troops committed. In the west, a build up to take control of transport lines to the coast is taken by surprise and overrun. Finally, a general problem relates to leadership as a surge of officers come in from Lima and position reassignments are made all across the front - the result was that in some cases, communication lines are so confused that troops literally did not know who their officers were.

Through the month of July, Peru suffers massive casualties and massive reverses, is pushed out of the mining district, and reduced to piecemeal positions all through the Altiplano. Only around Lake Titicaca does the Peruvian position remain stable.

The only things that keep Peru's campaign from complete collapse are massive conscription and deployment of Quechua and Aymara Indigenous from both Peru and Bolivia, and massive urgent American aid supported by limited American intervention. The Peruvians are simply throwing money and bodies, in vast quantities, into the gap, and the Americans are dragged along.

By Late August, the Chilean counter-offensive stabilizes. At that point, the March Accord, dividing Bolivia between Argentine and Chilean interests, becomes known to the Villarroel government. Villarroel forces the Chilean regime to repudiate the Accord.

Later that month, Villarroel's forces, acting independently without Chilean support, re-occupy the oil district, splitting the Argentine mission. Hostilities between Villarroel and the Argentines draw in Chilean forces. Argentina and Chile break off diplomatic relations and close embassies.

At this point, the Bolivian theatre is a multi-cornered conflict, driven locally, with positions changing daily. The three outside parties and the three factions ally and fight each other for transient advantage. At times, Villarroel and Valpes forces fight Argentines and Chileans. Penaranda's troops fire upon Peruvians. Friends and enemies shift from one day to the next, one place to another.

The chaos proves a boon to the Peruvians, who, despite poor organization manage to hold on. Through August and September, Peru undergoes a dramatic reorganization of its forces, incorporating Penaranda's Bolivian units and the Bolivian government administration directly into the Peruvian command structure.

Penaranda's government ceases to exist, except as a legal fiction. Even Penaranda's personal staff is now Peruvian and he is entirely cut off from decision making, his very correspondence is vetted and revised at will by Peruvian officials.

Similarly, the Valpes faction, never financially or militarily well equipped, literally exhausts its resources with its transient acts of independence. There is a flurry of brief negotiations between Valpes and Villarroel to form a 'Boliviano' coalition, but this is vetoed by the Argentines, and Valpes is reduced to a catspaw.

By October, the only Bolivian faction which maintains anything like an independent presence is Villarroel's Presidency and administration. Indeed, during this time, Villarroel gains support from defections from the emasculated Penaranda and Valpes factions. However, the all-important mining district and road access to the sea is under the direct control of Chile, not Villarroel. He is a supplicant in his own country.

Unfortunately, by October, a number of factors are contributing to a Peruvian resurgence. Foremost, is that the massive conscriptions in Bolivia and Peru among the Aymara and Quechua are finally taking effect, as trained and equipped Indigenous and Mestizo troops and officers come into the field, particularly from the north. The wholesale reorganization of the Peruvian command, the dissolution of Penaranda's independent forces and incorporation as part of the Peruvian armies addresses some but not all issues of confusion.

Driven by necessity and long communication lines, Peruvian forces adopted a diffuse command structure with extensive local autonomy. Although the majority of the troops speak some Spanish, large numbers speak only dialects of Aymara and Quechua. The Criollo officer corps is attenuated, with most Criollo officers preferring the relatively safer trench war of the frontier. Safer for officers at least. Shortfalls in both non-commissioned and line officers are made up through extensive field promotions of Mestizo and Indigenous officers.

During this time, American observers send reports back of exotic, adventurous - informal officers. Captain Atualpha, Two Gun Echeverria, Singalong Huascar, Iron Head Taruka. These men commanded large numbers of troops and coordinated field operations among themselves with minimal direction from Lima, and only the sketchiest of field promotions.

By November, 1942, the Argentines are on the verge of withdrawing, but Paraguayan demands and a sudden weakness in the Chilean position renews their commitment. For the rest of the year, into the spring of 1943, the balance swings back and forth, as each countries supplies and manpower waxes and wanes.

Meanwhile, the Chilean/Peruvian frontier heats up to the point of more or less continuous warfare. There are no major offensives on either side, but as a key part of its strategy, Peru kept up pressure, hoping to exhaust Chile or force it to divert enough manpower from Bolivia to allow a decisive Peruvian breakthrough there.

In turn, Chile supports Villarroel's administration in its own campaign of massive conscriptions of Mestizo, Quechua and Aymara within Bolivia.

The effect of this on Bolivia cannot be underestimated. Towns and cities pass back and forth almost weekly. An American observer with the Peruvian campaign observes one town captured and lost five times in a month, counts half the buildings destroyed and cannot find a single structure unmarked by gunfire. As much as 25 percent of the Bolivian population is reduced to refugee status both within and without the country, with large numbers of Indigenous fleeing the conscriptions up into Peru. Within the mining district, the population is literally reduced to slave labour.

Bolivian society is in a state of disintegration, and the fracture lines extend deep into the combatant nations.

***

Brazil and the Vargas Regime

Brazil has always been the odd man out in Latin American history. Portugese, where every other state is Spanish. Unified, where the rest of Latin America broke into feuding states. Brazil achieved independence relatively smoothly, transitioning from colony to monarchy and then from monarchy to republic.

For much of its 19th and early 20th century history, Brazil us dominated by Latifundistas, big landowners and rural oligarchies. Its economy is based on cash crops - milk and cattle locally, coffee and rubber for export. For the most part, Brazil cruises along in splendid solitude, having little enough to do with its Latin American neighbors, staying out of international controversies, exerting itself minimally, and mostly on behalf of its European neo-colonial trading powers.

This glosses over things somewhat. Brazilian history, as almost any history, is rich and complex when we examine it. There are the stories of individuals and peoples, of rise and falls, struggles and ambitions, moments of high drama, crisis and resolution, and steady development and evolution. But for the most part, we have little need to explore it here. So forgive us, a superficial pass is all that is necessary.

But in the early 20th century, particularly from the 1920s on, the power of the Latifundistas is increasingly challenged by growing urban centers, and an increasingly restive middle class. This is, on the whole, an inevitable development.

Brazil is a country of vast hinterlands. Physically it is nearly the size of the continental United States. Even discounting the thinly populated and inaccessible regions of the Amazonas, Brazil is still larger than most European states. And more importantly, Brazil is relatively densely populated. The population was 10 million in 1870, 18 million in 1900, 27 million in 1920, and 34 million by 1930. In short, it can claim European levels of population density.

Remote from markets, with no significant regional economic rivals or partnerships, it is a matter of time before the disparate regional village and town economies begin to knit together, for cities to emerge and become magnets of population, for urban infrastructures to evolve in response to both the domestic and export economies, and for urban classes to seek a greater share of political power to go with their growing economic power.

Brazil will sooner or later come into its own. This is an opinion shared by many Brazilians, as the country casts about for an entry on the world stage, for its own 'place in the sun.'

It was this accumulating sense of national pride, this quest for national status that in the early years of the twentieth century leads to Brazil commissioning its own dreadnaught. At this time, Britain and Germany are engaged in their dreadnaught race, building super battleships for status and military security.

Brazil has no real need for a dreadnaught battleship. It has no overseas possessions or interests, is not significantly vulnerable to naval warfare, and has no regional rivals. From a common sense perspective, it's a gigantic waste of money. But it buys one anyway, for what seems to be no better reason than some misguided notion of international prestige. Its acquisition kicks off Chile and Argentina to commission their own new warships, for equally misguided reasons. In the ensuing naval arms race, Brazil commissioned three battleships.

This naval arms race is really nothing more than a historical footnote. But it tells us three things about Brazil between 1900 and 1920.

One is that Brazil has a shitload of money. Battleships, dreadnaughts, do not come cheap, navies do not come cheap. The rubber trade and the coffee trade bring in a vast amount of revenue. And somehow, the Brazilians, in an age before coherent economic or industrial policy, in an era before systematic infrastructure planning, can't seem to find a better use for it than shiny toys.

The second is that Brazil has aspirations; there is a clear yearning there to be someone, to represent something, to make a mark. This isn't really coming from the Latifundistas and the rural oligarchies, who are happy enough to tend their gardens. Rather, it is emerging from a newly establishing and newly rising urban class, from a national class that finds itself becoming a national force. Battleships are a statement. There is no real attempt to rival Germany or Britain, or dominate the South Atlantic. It's mostly "We're here!"

The third is that having announced itself, this new class, this new urban elite, this new Brazil, really doesn't have much of a clue as to what it was, or what it wants to do.

And there you go.

History is made by people, and sometimes it is just as superficial as that, along with the impersonal forces of economics and religion, class interests, geography and resources... we have neuroses and insecurity and ambition.

And so we have Brazil in the early twentieth century. Not really a Latin American country by its own reckoning, not quite a European nation by geography, a nation coming to know itself, driven by formless ambitions, convinced of its destiny, but with no idea of what that destiny is.

The years between World War 1 and the Depression are a mixed bag for Brazil. Following the war, there is a general worldwide recession. Trade and exports decline, the British and European market that Latin America caters to goes through a period of contraction. For Brazil, that means the end of the coffee and rubber booms, and a corresponding decline in the wealth and power of the rural oligarchies. But unlike other states, Brazil is large enough and organized enough that a decline in export markets can at least be partially offset by a developing internal economy.

Ambitious, lunatic ventures like a fleet of battleships are off the table. Nevertheless, the urban classes find themselves gaining ground against the rural oligarchies. It is hardly a smooth ride; the rural oligarchies are quite unwilling to surrender power. They might be willing to buy off the urban class with expensive toys, like battleships. But the real governance of the country, the real setting of policies.... That is going to be a source of conflict and controversy.

New World War – Page 165

Nor is it going to be straightforward - as the urban class becomes more aggressive and more aware of its interests, the rural oligarchies are bolstered by a revival of trade and the emergence of the United States as an increasingly dominant trading partner. In short, through the 1920s, Brazil was the scene of accumulating class and political tensions, as more and more factions in Brazilian society began to articulate and press their interests and agendas. It might have been interesting to have watched it all play out, see where the Brazilians would have gone, and what they would have done.

But then, in 1930, in Brazil, as happened everywhere else, the bottom dropped out of the world, the Great Depression was on. The slow struggle between the urban class and the wealthy landowners comes to a head.

The result, obviously, is revolution. This is Latin America's default response to class conflict: A strong man who will simply stop the arguing and run things. All too often, the strong man is the product or the pawn of the conservative oligarchies.

In Brazil, the strong man is Getulio Vargas, who would under various guises and regimes rule Brazil for the next fifteen years.

Vargas is an interesting man. Very much a creature of his time, that being the turbulent era of the Great Depression, when all the contradictions of capitalism are being laid bare. Vargas, like so many of the strongmen who rose up during this period, is a 'populist.' That is, he appeals to the urban masses, catapulted into a state of shock by the collapse of the local and world economies and who are desperately looking for a savior. He talks the talk; he speaks to their aspirations which tend to be jobs, money, a less predatory economy and something resembling a social safety net.

On the other hand, he is a fervent anti-communist. While recognizing and speaking to labor and the poor, he is also feeding from the hands of the wealthy and of the captains of industry, and even to some extent compromising with the Latifundistas and coffee barons. In modern terms, he would claim to be a big picture guy. In cynical terms, he promises everything to everyone, and tells them all what they want to hear.

And he is a bit of a fascist. That's an ugly word these days. But back in the dark days of the Depression, what seems pretty clear to everyone was that liberal democracy and old style capitalism has failed, and there are only two real models left standing: Corporate communism and state ownership as expressed in Stalin's Soviet Union, and a sort of state controlled and directed private enterprise under dictators like Mussolini and Hitler.

In 1930, Vargas runs for President and loses. A few months later, a populist and military uprising places him in the charge as a 'Provisional President', drawing support from a variety of factions, until the constitution of 1934.

The July, 1934, constitution essentially uses Mussolini's Italy as a loose model, attempting to centralize Brazil, and to co-opt labor and leftists under state controlled organizations, while at the same time, attempting to direct or regulate industrial concerns in state interests, but as often as not working the other way. From this time on, Vargas starts toning down the radical rhetoric. The left wing move away from him and become disenchanted. Unable or unwilling to fulfill leftist aspirations, he finds new friends on the right. By 1935 left wing opposition is banned outright, and then followed by a wave of state terror.

In the meantime, Vargas finds a base of support in the "Integralist" movement, also known as the 'Greenshirts.' The Integralist are your standard 1930s, Mussolini inspired fascists - they chose a shirt color by way of a uniform, like Hitler's Brownshirts, or the Latin American 'silver shirts' or 'dirty shirts' - cheaper and less provocative than a full military kit. They march a lot; they shout a lot; they embrace anti-Semitism as the thing to do. Their ideology is the usual incoherent mixture of anti-communism, populism and conservatism, but at its heart, what they believe in is an almost mystical notion of the 'triumph of will' over reality - the belief that sheer will power or wishing can transform the world and set things right.

Integralism is not Vargas creation. It was founded in 1932 by Plinio Salgado, typically, another failed artist/writer of the type that these movements seem to attract. In 1932, he was pretty late to the party. Hitler and Mussolini had been around since the 1920s. But once started, the Greenshirts take off fast - they appeal strongly to the German and Italian communities in Brazil, and draw heavily from these populations.

By 1935, they are holding their own mass paramilitary marches, beating up communists and engaging in the usual thuggery and street brawls. The relationship between Vargas and Salgado's Greenshirts is not unlike that between Hitler and Ernst Rohm's Brownshirts, and perhaps fated to go the same way. Their support enables Vargas to steadily consolidate his hold on power but ultimately, they are disposable.

Fast forward a bit to 1937. Vargas term is expiring in a year, and under his own constitution, he's barred from serving again. In November, he goes on the radio, announcing the 'Cohen Plan' a communist plot to take over the government. Cohen was a nice Russian name, wasn't it? The left has in fact had an uprising in 1935, the result of which was that Vargas was given new powers to crush them with. By 1937, however, the communists are a dead letter. The Cohen Plan is a complete fabrication.

Instead, Vargas announces the 'Estudo Novo' (New State) a lovely fascist term. He declares a state of emergency, dissolves the legislature, and essentially assumes dictatorial powers. There is a new constitution, and the short version of it is that Vargas was the boss. He spends the next seven years running the country as supreme ruler.

In December, 1937, having obtained supreme power, Vargas bans all political parties as unnecessary, including the Integralists. The Integralists were apparently not paying attention to what happened to Ernst Rohm and his brown shirts in Germany when Hitler decided he no longer needed them. They decide not to take things lying down. In May of 1938, they stage a rather half-baked coup attempt which ends badly for them. And that was all she wrote. Vargas is left as absolute dictator, master of all he surveys.

Vargas rise to power and career arc is not appreciably different from those of the European tyrants of the inter-war years. We see the same hallmarks of cynicism, populism, violence and treachery, all in the pursuit of absolute power.

Where Vargas differs is that in what we might see as the typical Brazilian fashion, he is not much interested in the world beyond his nation. He is all about making the trains run on time, so to speak.

Thus, Vargas, like previous Brazilian governments before him, looks upon the developments in Latin America with something quite close to utter indifference. The ferocious Chaco War in 1935 between nations on his border is nothing to do with him. So far as Vargas was concerned, it is mere newspaper fodder no more or less meaningful than the sports page.

Velasco Ibarra's trips to Sao Paulo in 1934 and 1937 are met with stony silence. Ibarra barely achieved a courtesy meeting with Vargas' foreign minister's assistant.

The outbreak of hostilities in the Andes is seen as almost as remote and irrelevant as the outbreak of hostilities in Europe. Actually, even more remote and irrelevant, since Europe is a major trading partner, and there are large numbers of Germans and Italians in Brazil. In contrast, neither Chile nor Peru nor Ecuador or all of them put together amount to a nickel's worth of trade for Brazil.

The position of Vargas in Brazil is neutrality in both theaters, even as the conflict escalates.

But neutrality is hard to maintain. Over the next few years, the Vargas government faces a series of situations which drag it into both theaters, despite its wishes.

The first is the emerging jungle and river war in the Amazon/Oriente interior of Peru and Ecuador.

****

Brazil and the Rain Forest War

Although Vargas and Brazil has no interest whatsoever in the Andean war, this disinterest does not keep the war at bay. The original causes of the fight were conflicting claims between Ecuador and Peru over rain forest territories, part of the vast Amazonian basin and fed the mighty Amazon River network.

Fed by the Andes Mountains, every river or stream that constitutes the Ecuadoran Oriente and the Peruvian Selva leads inevitably towards the Amazonas and the Brazilian territories. There, deep in the rain forest jungles, the demarcations of one nation to another are sometimes meaningless.

Of course, neither Ecuador nor Peru hold any designs on Brazilian territory. Even the very idea is repellent in Quito or Lima. A simple look at a map or comparative populations exposes that as a colossally bad idea. Even General Blandon, initially, has no urge in that direction.

The violation of Brazilian borders is not deliberate, not initially, and is simply an outcome of the see-saw war that Blandon fights as dry and wet seasons alternated, and as his forces alternately push and are pushed deeper into the interior.

Sometime in early 1941, the first incursions take place into Brazilian territory essentially unrealized, Blandon's forces stray across unmarked boundaries into territories, discovering their trespass accidentally as they encounter Brazilian missionaries and outposts. Initially, these incursions are unintentional/ But over time national borders mean less and less to Blandon.

The Brazilian government is initially unaware of these provocations, and even as they become aware, they underestimate them. They fail to respond, deeming such response too costly and prefer to look the other way. The violations of Brazilian territory, even in the remote Amazon becomes bolder. Resulting from this, armed and trained native bands, acting under Blandon or acting independently, terrorize their neighbors, creating internal displacement and refugees.

Eventually, by October, 1941, the disruptions and provocations that Blandon poses can no longer be overlooked. Stern messages were sent to the Ecuadoran Embassy, and forwarded to the Ecuadoran government, receiving only denials. Enrique Blandon is an Ecuadoran commander in the Selva, but he was nowhere near Brazil. And if he was or had been, it was purely an accident, for which apologies are proffered.

Rumors make it out from time to time that Blandon has contracted malaria or a jungle fever and is feverish and delusional. Others speak of mania. Still other Rumors suggest that he has gone native. No one in Quito is entirely sure of what is going on.

During this time, Velasco Ibarra can do little more than desperately try to persuade Vargas that the situation is a local and temporary one, that Blandon is under control and if rogue forces sometimes cross the border, that was not their doing. Whatever irritants there are can be smoothed, there is no need Brazilians to declare war. In the meantime, efforts to rein Blandon in become increasingly desperate and increasingly ineffectual. The Bonifaz regime is terrified that Blandon might lead them into a war, but finds itself with no options, except to deny, dissemble and hope that the problem would go away. Diplomatic relations between Brazil and Ecuador remain rocky through the period of the war.

Finally, in October, 1941, Vargas directs an expeditionary force from Manaus in the Amazonas to eliminate Ecuador's 'rogue elements.' In November, it disappears without a trace.

That same November, Vargas receives assurance from the Ecuadoran government and his own officers in the Amazonas that Blandon has withdrawn back across the border. However, it appeared he's armed a substantial number of the native population, with the result that the interior is more dangerous than it has ever been.

A month later, Japan attacks Pearl Harbor.

***

New World War – Page 171

The Rain Forest War - Fate of the Manaus Expedition

On October 18, 1941, an expeditionary force leaves the city of Manaus in Amazonas province to intercept a rogue Ecuadoran General, Enrique Blandon. The force consists of three river gunboats, all that are available in the city of Manaus, various small craft, and a handful of river barges. A spotter plane is deployed, but lost early in the expedition for unknown reasons.

The entire military garrison of Manaus, under the command of Major Augusto De Paula, consisting of four hundred enlisted men and officers, armed with small arms, machine guns, and field artillery pieces. Accompanying them are a substantial portion of the City's police force, a hundred in all, and approximately six hundred armed citizens with a variety of small arms. The expedition is provisioned for sixty days.

The expedition starts inauspiciously when, on October 19, 1941, several of the civilians became intoxicated, fights break out and the offenders are required to return back to Manaus. On October 21, 1941, one of the barges develops mechanical problems, and several craft accompany it to Manaus. October 22, a number of boats are caught on mud banks and low water. It takes most of two days to free them. By October 25, a number of the civilians have had enough, and a significant portion of the fleet turn back the way it came, taking a small portion of supplies. These reach Manaus on October 30. All told approximately two hundred civilians and fifty police return.

The remainder of the expedition continues onward. On November 1, 1941, the expedition is attacked from the shore by armed natives with rifles. Several men are shot, and several more are killed by friendly fire in the ensuing panic. After an initial volley, the natives retreat, but moments later, another larger group opens fire from cover, peppering the fleet. This fire continues for several minutes until the panicking expeditionaries are able to mount a machine gun to strafe the shoreline. The attack discontinues, but it is not clear any of the natives were killed. Overall casualties are thirty killed or injured.

From this point on, a permanent guard rotation is established, and machine guns are kept in readiness at all times. There is no further action on November 1 or 2, although several times, civilians fire into the brush.

On November 3, 1941, as the expedition is making its way along a curve of the river, the rear of the expedition sustains heavy fire from several concealed groups along both sides of the river bank. The result is mass panic, with civilians firing wildly in response, and attempting to rush forward to get their boats out of harm's way. There are a number of collisions. The military is trapped up front and unable to deploy its machine guns. Gunfire continues, raking the civilians, until finally, one of the gunboats is able to flank the expedition, sailing upwards it strands on a mud bank, and proceeds to rake both shores until fire dies away.

With fire suppressed, the fleet organizes defensively, while the several boats work to pull the gunboat off the mud bank and assess potential damage. This is complicated by intermittent sporadic fire from the shore. Total casualties are almost two hundred killed or injured, including friendly fire and boat mishap. The expedition has not even seen the enemy. The fleet sets anchor, and camps overnight, debating what to do next.

Major De Palma and his officers and NCO's are in a bind. Their orders are clear that they are to continue on and engage Blandon and his auxiliaries. But the spotter plane is missing, there is no local information. The number of injured civilians requiring medical attention seriously exceeds their medical supplies, and several die during the night. They need to be dealt with. They consider terminating the expedition, in order to accompany the civilians back.

After further consideration it is decided to continue with the expedition. The injured civilians, and any other civilians who wish to retreat, will go back to Manaus on boats flying the white flag. For protection, one of the gunboats, and a complement of fifty soldiers will accompany them. The remainder of the force shall proceed.

In the morning, the fleet splits. Two gunboats, three hundred and fifty soldiers and one hundred civilians steam forward deeper into Amazonas. The rest wave goodbye as they chug home, the boats festooned with white flags. None of them make it back to Manaus.

Late afternoon, the expedition comes across the remains of a large camp site, with a number of pits. Along the shore, mud has been trenched out, as if a large heavy boat has been moored. This is tentatively identified as the fearsome Matilde. A black plume is spotted in the distance, and the expedition proceeds towards it.

This turns out to be a bonfire in the lee of a lagoon. At this point, the Matilde appears from an inlet, and engages the two remaining gunboats. One of the gunboats is obstructed by the other, and so they are unable to bring full fire to bear. The Matilde fires two bursts of machine gun fire from each of its machine guns. Concurrently concealed fire from the jungle opens up.

General Blandon then ceases fire. He announces that the Brazilians are now prisoners of war and demands surrender, failing which the Brazilians will be obliterated. The survivors of the first gunboat surrender immediately, and the second shortly after, followed suit by the remainder.

The prisoners are processed in the lagoon, stripped of clothing and weapons, and tied together. Even the dead are stripped. Blandon and a small group of natives and white men are meticulous in inventorying and inspecting the captured boats, equipment and weapons. One soldier throws his weapon into the water, and is executed on the spot by one of the natives. Efforts are made to repair damaged boats and equipment. What was not salvageable is dismantled for parts or burned. At this time, the prisoners note several hundred armed natives.

They wait there for two days, during which time the prisoners are not fed. Any resistance results in immediate execution. Prisoners, particularly civilians, are interrogated for usable skills. Six boat mechanics are separated out. At the end of the second day, the third gun boat appears, bearing no apparent damage, along with most of the boats that departed under white flag. A few bear signs of rifle fire. There are no survivors with them.

Blandon advises that all prisoners of war will be transported by various routes to the town of Jaen. There they will be processed by the Ecuadoran government, and arrangements will be made for repatriation. On the third day, the native auxiliaries begin to disperse; taking with them selected groups of prisoners. None of these prisoners are ever seen again.

Blandon, with part of his native army, takes the remaining prisoners, the captured boats, including the three gun boats, and his own fleet and heads east, upriver, crossing over the Brazilian border into Peru. Many of his armed native auxiliaries are indigenous to Brazil and remain active in the general area, posing hazards to Brazilian officials, civilians and even other tribes.

****

Pablo from Manaus

Pablo thinks he is going to die. He never even really wanted to go on this fool's expedition. He would have preferred to stay home with the pretty girls.

Wander up and down the Amazonas looking for some imaginary Ecuadoran madman? There are always rumors and stories on the river, and most of them come to nothing. The foreigners that pass through Manaus are always looking for such things, lost cities, fabled treasures and whatnot. The folk of Manaus know better.

But the word comes in from Sao Paulo. An expedition is ordered, and as much as De Paulo drags his feet, eventually they go. All across the sleepy town, there is talk of Blandon. In a place like Manaus, there isn't much to talk about, so any gossip is seized on. And somewhere along the line, people get the idea to establish a support force, to assist the army with Blandon's bloodthirsty hordes. And so, the whole mad, drunken caravan assembles. There's even a parade and celebration to send them off.

For Pablo, it should be a vacation, a chance to party, and perhaps make some easy cash. He is a skilled mechanic after all, and it would be good to have an adventure out on the water, something to brag to the girls about.

Then, step by step, it all goes horribly wrong, first as comedy, with drunkenness and fights, and then, by stages progressively darker. Native villages and missionary outposts are deserted. Then gunfire from the shores, and the desperate panics they cause. Then the bloodbath.

Pablo wanted to go back with the others, but the soldiers decide he is necessary. That turns out to be a good thing. The others who tried to go back, he is certain now, they are all dead.

And now, he is a prisoner, among more natives than he has ever seen together in his life. They are all over, half naked savages, men strutting around with guns, women with their breasts bare, doing the work of the camp as always. It isn't until you watch carefully, that you started noticing these are not proper savages. They move about with purpose, they salute each other like white men, on the paints on their arms and chests were what look like military markings. One of the men bullies some others as he watches, and he realized that the paints the man wears are a sergeant's chevrons.

The prisoners are divided into groups, and by and by, a white man comes to question them. Pablo sees a chance and begins begging for his life, but the only answer to that is a rifle butt across the face from one of the savages. He and the others in his group quickly learn to simply answer the series of terse questions put to them. Elsewhere, you hear screams and sometimes a rifle shot, but you don't look. You keep your head down.

"This one!" the white man says pointing at Pablo. He barks something else in a native tongue, and brown hands seize him. Pablo begins to scream until he is pummeled breathless. He is dragged across the camp, begging for his life each step of the way, and thrown down into a small group.

A tall white man glances at him, and Pablo knows instantly this must be Blandon. His skin is bronzed now, and there are signs of tropical fever around his eyes. He's lost weight, and his skin hangs loosely on him. Instead of pants, he wears beaches and a penis sheath. But strangely, his boots are polished. He wears a short sleeved shirt, unbuttoned, and as he moves, Pablo sees scars along his chest, the second or third time he glimpses them, he realizes that they are carved in the shape of medals.

Beyond him is a large gunboat, or what was once a gunboat, now painted and festooned with camouflage, native symbols, he can see signs of extensive reckless work on it. The Matilde.

In front of him kneels Major Augustin de Paulo. There is something of an interrogation going on.

"...by the authority of the government of Brazil..." de Paulo is saying.

"There is no Brazil here," Blandon says, sounding reasonable. "There is no Brazil at all."

New World War – Page 177

"What?"

"It's all right," Blandon reassures him. "It took me a while to figure it out. What is Brazil? Can you eat it? Can you fuck it? Can you wipe your ass with it? No, none of that. It's just a lie men tell each other. Brazil. Ecuador. Just lies."

"This is Brazil," de Paulo insists. "This is territory of Brazil. This land. You are in Brazil right now and–"

"This?" Blandon, waves his hand. "Look around. This land belongs to the Indigenous. They lived here since God put them here. You think this is Brazil because some bureaucrats far away and a long time ago made a line on a map? No. It's theirs."

"You think you are better than them? What do you call them? Savages? That you are brave and strong because you have the guns, that they are worthless. They are inferior, less human, so you take what is theirs? But put a rifle in their hand, suddenly, they are as human as you are."

De Paulo opens his mouth to protest. Blandon draws a pistol and shoots him in the face. To Pablo's horror, the black man does not die immediately, but falls flopping to the ground, gurgling. A native steps forward and cuts his throat.

"Well," Blandon says conversationally to no one at all, as he holsters his pistol. "That was going nowhere."

He glances around; his eye falls on Pablo in the group of prisoners. He makes a gesture and says something in native tongue, and Pablo is dragged from the group. Pablo is sobbing with terror.

"Hey," Blandon says. He slaps the boy. "Look at me and calm down. I have some questions."

"Don't shoot me," Pablo cries. "I don't know anything. I don't know..."

"I'm not going to shoot you," Blandon reassures him. "Waste of a bullet and bullets are worth more than gold around here."

Pablo can't help but glance at de Paulo's body. Already flies are gathering. Blandon follows the gaze.

"He was an officer, he was entitled to the respect," Blandon explains. This doesn't make Pablo feel any better.

"You have some Spanish," Blandon says.

Pablo snuffles. "A little."

Blandon nods. "Can you read and write?"

Pablo nods. Blandon smiles.

"Good. I can use that," he pauses. "I hear you're a mechanic. Good with engines."

Again, Pablo nods. He struggles to control himself, to think.

"Boat engines? Gasoline or Steam?"

"Both," Pablo replies. He screws up his courage to offer a little more. "Best in Manaus."

That is a lie; he counts a dozen mechanics more skilled than he is. But if it helps keep him alive…

Blandon grins in satisfaction. He straightens up, seized Pablo's hair, and forcibly turns his head.

"You see, my Matilde? Is she not beautiful? All my wives are jealous of her, but they must suffer, because she is my first love. I have a mechanic, but sometimes he's sick. I could use another. To keep Matilde going, you see. It can be hard."

Suddenly, Pablo realizes he isn't going to be killed. He is being offered a job. A place on the ship, and away from these damnable murderous savages.

"Yes," he says, and then repeats it quicker, "yes! I'm good with engines. I can make her run good."

Blandon smiles reassuringly.

"Excellent," he says, "just what I wanted to hear. It's not just Matilde; I have a lot of boats. More so now. Lots of engines. Lots of work."

Pablo nods.

"You have tools with you? A kit?"

"Yes, Sir," Pablo says. "In my boat."

"Good," Blandon says. "Know any other mechanics here? You might be saving their lives."

At the cost of his own? How many does he need? But Blandon didn't wait for an answer.

"What else can you do?" Blandon asks. "Can you run a still? Whiskey?"

Pablo is surprised by the question.

"No," he says, "but Klaus had one. The German..."

Blandon barks an order to one of the natives, Pablo catches Klaus's name. Blandon turns back to him, grinning.

"Wonderful!" he says. "You've been helpful. Here's a thought. You wouldn't know how to make gunpowder by any chance?"

<u>Return to Table of Contents</u>

***

BOOK OF QUECHUA

From Inca to Obscurity

In 1940, no one cares what the Quechua think.

In the world of Latin America, with its liberals and conservatives, its reactionaries and leftists, cities and haciendas, with its carefully graduated degrees of whiteness, a caste system that distinguished between gradations of pure Hispanic and mestizo, the one thing that everyone who is anyone agrees is that the Indigenous, the Quechua, do not count. They aren't a factor. They don't matter.

This is mainly racism. In Latin societies, generally it's hard to go lower than Indigenous. Even the descendants of African slaves, pure or mixed, stand higher than the Indigenous in many countries. With the exception of Paraguay and perhaps Mexico, they are the absolute bottom of the caste systems.

Partly though, it's geography. The Andes Mountains, running the length of South America, literally from top to bottom, are one of the most formidable mountain ranges in the world, sporting some of the tallest mountains outside of the Himalayas. The Andes ranges divide South America in two, west of the Andes is the fertile coastal strip facing the Pacific, on the east is the balance of the continent. Melting snow from the ice caps along the Andes feed the plethora of rivers that all eventually join into the mighty Amazonas, and creates the immense Amazonian rain forest, the lungs of the world. Further south, they feed the River Plate and the basin that waters Argentina. Divided into several ranges, the Andes are host to a series of interweaving valleys and highlands, collectively known as the Altiplano, and including some of the highest inhabited regions in the world.

This is the home of the Quechua and their cousins the Aymara, the largest most populous Indigenous nations in South America. The homelands of the Quechua stretch across the highlands, from Ecuador, through Peru, Bolivia and Argentina. Their Aymara cousins are found in Peru, Bolivia and even the northern reaches of Chile.

Despite their vast numbers and vaster reach, their mountain homelands make them largely inaccessible. Spanish settlement concentrates on the coasts and the lowland strips between the foothills and the coasts. While the Spaniards conquered the inland and its mountains and valleys, they didn't have much use for it. The air is too thin, the weather too inclement, it is tough to get around, the mountain passes and passages were difficult, even for the Indigenous. Isolation and geographical barriers divide the Quechua into eighteen separate dialects, many unintelligible to each other. The Indigenous have always mostly left alone, left to priests and landowners, occasionally subject to conscription, or taxation, or labour levies, but mostly ignored and deemed irrelevant. Latin America passes them by.

And honestly, that isn't such a bad thing. Close contact with the Spanish and their heirs proves to be a uniformly bad thing (Paraguay excepted) for the Indigenous in the new world. The word genocide comes up a lot. The Quechua and Aymara are satisfied to be ignored and left alone by the Latin mainstream, free to live their lives and raise their crops in the manner their ancestors have done for centuries.

The Quechua and Aymara live in subsistence economies, growing what they needed. Their trade intercourse with the outside world is minimal. They don't grow cash crops; they don't really mine valuable resources. They have no economic significance, they don't contribute much to the GDP, but then they don't cost much and they don't demand much. They aren't hooked into the cash crop / resource export based economies are evolving under neocolonialism. There is no money to be made from them, or off them, or through them. So who cares?

It is true that there are a lot of them. But Latin American nations didn't extend them the vote. Voting, when it happened, tends to restrict to the white inhabitants of civilized areas, and usually not many of them. Enlightened liberalism of the era is barely considering that maybe poor urban dwellers or half breed mestizo should vote. But nobody thinks of the Indigenous. Most of the coups, the counter coups, the juntas, the petty little wars? Those are invitation only, of, from, by and for the white ruling class. Apart from bouts of conscription, they aren't even a factor for wars, Europeans have all the guns, and keep those close. So there is absolutely no significance to them, and no reason that there should be. If, one day, some intrepid mountaineer climbs up there and discovers the entire population vanished, the Latin American states where they lived would barely notice a hiccup.

It hasn't always been this way. The Andean peoples are one of the world's founding civilisations. It is one of the few places that independently invented agriculture seven thousand years ago, first squash, then potatoes, sweet potatoes, quinoa and many others. Every potato in the world is the gift of the Andean peoples. Metallurgy was invented independently there; the Inca brought the beginning of the bronze age to the new world. Their first towns and cities go back five or six thousand years.

The Quechua peoples or at least their language is thought to date as far back as 4600 years ago. Along the Andes civilizations rose and fell and rose again leaving massive ruins, and the Quechua are part of that story.

Somewhere around 1200, a branch of the Quechua establishes the Kingdom of Cuzco, little more than a city state, led by a Sapa Inca or 'paramount leader.' Cuzco begins to expand rapidly, by 1400, it evolves into the Inca Empire, and over the next centuries, the Quechua conquer their way from modern day Colombia to Chile, creating the greatest of the New World empires. The Quechua, or their subjects, sail as far out as the Galapagos, and as far up the pacific coast as Mexico making contact with Mayan and Aztec cultures and introducing bronze metallurgy.

New World War – Page 183

Then around 1525, it all goes to hell. The Conquistadors show up. Normally, this shouldn't have been a problem. The Inca are an Empire at their height and climbing. But along with the Conquistadors, comes European diseases, particularly smallpox. The Empire's efficient road system and networks allow diseases to travel like wildfire devastating the population. Among the dead is the Emperor, Huayna Capac.

Huayna Capac leaves behind a devastated Empire and two sons, Huascar and Atahualpha. So... there is nothing to do but have a devastating civil war, because obviously, enduring a series of horrific pandemics hasn't been enough. It is bloody, eventually Atahualpha wins, defeating and destroying Huascar's legions. But before he can enjoy his victories, he gets captured by the Spanish and murdered. The Spaniards turn out to be very good at exploiting the Empires flaws.

The Inca do not go down easy. The Spanish do their best to smash the Inca state and destroy the culture.

But in 1536, Manco Yupanqui took advantage of internal conflicts among the Spanish to break away and re-establish an Inca state in the interior that lasts until 1572. His son, Tupac Amaru, is executed as the last Inca.

A couple of hundred years later, in 1780, along comes José Gabriel Condorcanqui, an upper class Quechua with some claims to noble or even royal blood. 1780 is the era of the American Revolution, and both France and Spain are backing it heavily in hopes of breaking British power. But backing the United States and fighting a war against Britain is expensive, and that means more taxes, more hardship and more oppression among the subject peoples of the Empire.

Jose decides to rebel, renaming himself Tupac Amaru II, and claiming to be a direct descendant of the original. The uprising rages up and down the Andes, growing more ferocious. Tupac is captured and killed in 1781, but the rebellion continues, led by Tupac's relatives and associates, until 1782. Even after it is put down sporadic fighting continues through 1783. A hundred thousand Quechua die in the greatest native rising in Spanish history.

Almost simultaneously, there is another massive revolt in Bolivia in 1781. This one lead by an Aymara named Julián Apasa Nina, who takes the name Tupac Katari. Claiming to be the Viceroy of Tupac Amaru II, together with his wife and sister, they raise an army of 40,000 and twice lay siege to La Paz.

It isn't the end. In fact, there is a record of peasant uprisings, protests, and small revolts and rebellions among highland Quechua and Aymara, particularly in the post-Spanish era of the Latin American republics.

There is the Atusparia revolt in 1885. A village chief named Atusparia raises a peasant army and takes control of a province and holds out for several months.

Another famous one from 1915-1916 is the Rumi-Maqui Revolt (in Quechua - 'Hands of Stone', the nickname of the rebellion leader), led by a Peruvian Sargent-Major named Teodomiro Gutiérrez, in the Lake Titicaca region that called for Inca Restoration.

Mostly these rebellions fail to catch fire, they run out of steam, everyone eventually goes home. The leaders are either captured and executed; or they run away and change their names as they hide out. None of these ever amount to a threat to central governments.

There were reasons that it doesn't amount to a major challenge to Lima. Basically, it comes down to transportation and communication - among the Quechua of the Sierra highlands, as we've said; there are 18 dialects, mostly unintelligible to each other. The Aymara have another set of dialects. On top of that, the ferocious Andean ranges means that it's hard to get around. People stick to their own valleys and their own communities. Things happening in the other valleys generally tend to be ignored.

Nevertheless, the Andean region manages to produce a steady stream of colourful and exotic characters; bandits, mercenaries, con men, adventurers and scoundrels abound. The region is full of stories, local histories tell of flamboyant larger than life characters. There is one con man for instance, who became wealthy and eventually infamous by travelling from valley to valley, marrying a different woman in each valley, collecting dowries and lands. His funeral is attended by numerous and wives and dozens of children, I suppose because when you're an ass on that scale, it becomes endearing. It is easy to become a bandit or a rogue; you just leave your valley and start anew. The Andes are full of these local legends. But they aren't producing an intellectual or leadership class.

Outside the Andes? It doesn't matter. Because in 1940, no one cares what the Quechua think.

Everyone agrees that they don't matter.

Quechua Under Stress

For the Quechua, generally, their exclusion from mainstream society is not necessarily a bad thing. It preserves their language, their traditions, their way of life. Truth be told, their preference is mainly to be left alone.

And mainly, they are left alone.

Subject, occasionally, to taxes, subject to labour drafts, military conscription. Subject, occasionally, to having lands taken up by landowners. The 19th, and the 20th centuries eat into their lives in a hundred small ways. There are endless small irritations. Typically nothing so large or profound as to trigger massive rebellions. But there is a long history of local uprisings and resistance.

Between 1900 and 1930, there are records of 300 local uprisings in Peru alone. But there is no social or ideological structure to animate or motivate these risings, no unifying leaders or causes. They are responses to local irritants, and once the irritant is dealt with, the pressure goes away.

There are attempts to provide that ideology. In the 1920s and 1930s, Marxists and Socialists found the "Indigenismo" movement. This is an idealisation of the Inca Empire as a sort of socialist utopia.

From this, thinkers argue that the Indigenous, with their communal lifestyles are actual true socialists or proto-socialists. They are living the life; all they needed was the rest of the ideological building blocks which Marx and other socialist thinkers are willing to provide.

The 'Indigenismo' movement is essentially a coastal leftist fad. It is rooted in Rousseau's myths of the 'Noble Savage' and a rather idealized/ideological view of the Inca which only arbitrarily accord with actual history. It is current in the parlour debates and universities, but it doesn't really have tangible application to the

Indigenous. The sad truth is that is that most of these academics would be appalled to find themselves in a Quechua village, or to have Aymara in their living room.

One of the more enthusiastic 'Indigenismo' thinkers is Juan Manuel Lasso Ascásubi, a cousin of Neptali Bonifaz, who in 1922, attempts to launch a socialist revolution of the Indigenous from the Guachalá hacienda in Cayambe, Ecuador. It goes nowhere of course.

As far as the Quechua are concerned, urban intellectual Marxists are just another group of white men out to tell them how to run their lives. They are strangers, even less trusted than the Latifundistas and others, who are at least familiar and well understood.

The coastal intellectuals' love affair with the idea of the Quechua is not reciprocated. Marxist theory, ramblings on about proletariats and capitalism, don't really have a lot of application to day to day life. It is foreign stuff, to be treated with suspicion.

Beginning in the 1930s with the Bonifaz regime, this begins to change. Typically, intellectuals, when they become troublesome in their home country, would be encouraged to leave or exiled to some other state. But the Bonifaz regime is building a cold war, so Ecuadoran exiles weren't welcome in Peru, and vice versa. Bonifaz's regime doesn't want them going to Chile or Colombia where they're trying to stir the pot. As nationalism takes hold up and down the coast governments become reluctant to export their leftists. Governments become reluctant to accept troublemakers from their neighbours; and those troublemakers find it problematic to betray their nation by living somewhere else.

Instead, slowly, but with increasing frequency, the approach is internal exile. Annoying journalists or academics in Quito or Lima are invited to spend their time away from the big city, out in the countryside, far from anywhere that matters. Leftists, Marxists, socialists, intellectuals, social critics end up in the Andes, rubbing shoulders with the Quechua. Some of these 'Indigenismo' find themselves closer to Indigenous than they ever wanted to be.

But mostly, the exiled radicals and the Indigenous ignore each other. A displaced university professor is not going to end up in a hut in an Indigenous village. He doesn't want to be there, they don't want him there. Most internal exiles become guests at haciendas through family connections, many end up residing with the middle classes or Mestizo in the small towns and villages. But at least there is proximity. In normal circumstances, this would have come to nothing. And through the 1930s, there is no significant impact.

But the war when it comes in 1930 brings changes, particularly for the Quechua of Peru. Wars are expensive; this leads to taxes, including regional and local taxes and levees. Even when these are levied against the Haciendas and the Mestizo, these costs are passed on, in whole or in part to the local Indigenous. War demands mean shortages; it means disruptions, reduced services and arbitrary changes.

The Quechua live in subsistence economies somewhat disconnected from the commercial economies of the coasts and lowlands. That insulates them somewhat from the depressions and recessions of the outside world. The 1930s are tough in the Highlands, as they were everywhere else. But the Quechua weather it better than most. The disruptions and impacts of the war, even at a distance, added stress and hardship.

But even if a people are out of the actual War Zone, that doesn't mean that they're out of the war. The Quechua and Mestizo traditionally live in self-contained subsistence economies out of the mainstream, but the degree of self-containment varies over the years. It's the interactions and friction between the outer borders of the commercial Peruvian economy and the subsistence economy that produces the steady stream of protests, uprisings, rebellions and banditry that comes and goes, flares up and burns out.

War is a highly transformative and incredibly destructive thing. The central government is spending vast sums of money hand over fist on its war. That has consequences.

Suddenly, money and resources, personnel and priorities that might have gone to the Sierra normally, they're not going there any more, they're diverted, constrained, reallocated. The demands of the coastal elites on the Sierra are increasing dramatically. The margins of the commercial economy are pressing a lot harder, impinging more forcefully on the subsistence economy. Delicate webs of relationships and interactions, arrangements, the local balances are being disturbed and disrupted, sometimes outright broken everywhere.

People are unhappy, in ways they can barely describe, things happening a long way away and happening to other people are screwing up their lives. The world is changing, and none of these changes seem good, and there's a whole bunch of new things happening.

And then there is conscription. As Alba decimates entire armies in the north, as the trench war in the south turns into a meat grinder, as the Bolivian theatre opens up, Peru has a desperate need for manpower to replace its losses.

Racism is endemic in the Peruvian upper classes, and there is no particular desire for Quechua troops. But they need bodies, and those bodies have to come from somewhere. The Quechua have the disadvantages that they are not elites or middle class, to seek political exclusions. They aren't employed in the cash economy, in essential services or business. They are just this pool of available bodies that can be pressed into service, without adverse consequences.

Conscription, historically, in peaceful times was often a good way to deal with local trouble makers or other problems. Ship them into the army. But here Peru is forced to conscript literally tens and hundreds of thousands due to the pressure of war. This is extremely unwelcome. Losing a few obnoxious young men that everyone was better off without is one thing. Losing a substantial chunk of the manpower of a village? Losing fathers, cousins, brothers, that is hardship. Those men were needed to work the fields, to feed families, to keep things going.

Eventually, of course, the theory is that they will come back when the war is over. That doesn't help for farms that have to be worked now rather than later. And worse, a lot don't come back; they die. Or they come back early wounded or disabled.

The Quechua deal with conscription in the traditional way. They run away. There is a lot of draft dodging. Young and middle-aged men have a strong impulse to go visiting or travelling to other valleys when the draft officers come visiting. Draftees are motivated to sneak away after they are conscripted and then to hide out in their home valleys or other valleys, or to keep on moving. There are subterfuges and deceptions and a lot of traffic between communities.

There are more eligible people actively working to avoid or foil conscription, than are actually being conscripted.

All of this is intensely disruptive to the village life of the Quechua. The outside world is imposing itself, and the effort of dealing with that imposition produces more disruption and more complexity.

The Quechua have no investment in the wars. They have no sense of nationalism. That is for the European folk on the south. And they have no real tools to appreciate or understand the disruptions of their lives.

This is where the displaced intellectuals come in, the ideas and thoughts, the concepts of journalists and academics, thinkers and writers start to percolate, directly and indirectly. It isn't as if a Marxist is being invited to give lectures in a village. But rather, that Marxists rubbing shoulders in towns and haciendas talk to the people they knew, they gossip and argue with landowners and Mestizo. Concepts and ideas are picked up, fragmentary and imprecise, but still ideas. These eventually percolate from Mestizo, from traders and service people, from neighbours to the Quechua themselves.

But people do incorporate ideas. They pick things up; they adapt things to their perspectives, their notions, their world view. Marxist dialectic won't sell. But odds and ends will be picked up, pruned and added on to, welded together into something. Passed on. The role of an intelligentsia is often exaggerated. Certainly they're not a power in and of themselves, and their ideas are almost never accepted wholesale or unmediated. But stuff does happen.

It was hardly a comprehensive education. But rather a slow transmission of ideas and notions, as the Quechua struggle for tools to understand how their lives were being disrupted. It isn't really a radicalisation of the Quechua, although radical ideas and perspectives do travel, but rather, the beginnings of an awakening.

Still, the history was that the Quechua rise up in response to irritants, and relax again if those irritants went away. Village life is strong and reasserts itself. The War is a major disruption, making itself felt in many ways. That is a strong irritant. But radicalism doesn't offer a clear pathway forward, and eventually the war will go away, life will return to normal. In the normal course, leftism and radicalism would make little headway.

Normally.

Brazilian Diplomacy Prior to Pearl Harbor

Brazil is the four hundred pound gorilla of Latin America. With forty million people and a territory larger than the continental United States, it dwarfs every other Latin nation. As to the Andean conflict, it dwarfs Ecuador, Peru, Chile and Bolivia put together. Its involvement should be an instant game changer.

But its real enemy is geography. Its population centers are on the Atlantic coast, above the Argentine La Plata. Its interior is largely inaccessible, thinly populated and poorly serviced by infrastructure.

Theoretically, a Brazil-Ecuador war, or a Brazil-Peru war should be entirely one sided: A giant swat. But to send an Army to Ecuador or Peru, Brazil will have to ship thousands of troops on hundreds of river boats down the malaria and tropical disease ridden Amazonas, and ship equivalent amounts of food and water. After which point they enter the Selva or the Oriente, and pass over hundreds more miles of rain forest. After which point, they reach the jagged wall known as the Andes mountains, a near impassible range of mountains punctuated by valleys and passages. If they somehow make it over the Andes, then finally, they can confront the impetuous Ecuadorans or Peruvians and teach them a lesson, hopefully.

All for the low, low price of a measurable portion of Brazil's GDP. It is the same almost everywhere. Bolivia was protected by the Altiplano, a ten thousand foot high fortress, and remote from population centers. The Guiana's offers highlands. Venezuela and Colombia are shielded by several hundred more miles of rain forest. The only viable foe geographically is Argentina, and it is by far the most capable of putting up a fight, theoretically.

Hypothetically, Brazil has a navy that it could sail up and down the South American coasts. But Brazil has little naval tradition and the fleet is not well maintained. That in itself is another dubious proposition, particularly considering that Chile and Argentina maintain comparable rival navies.

Despite its size and power, war with its neighbors simply isn't feasible. It isn't cost effective. It is far too expensive by any standard. Particularly in the worldwide financial disaster that is the Great Depression.

These considerations are certainly on Vargas' mind, as he spends December considering what to do about Ecuador's wayward general Blandon, or his own lost expedition, and the slurry of reports of armed natives with military weapons and tactics in the deep regions of the Amazon basin.

Historically, the Vargas regime maintains a policy of strict neutrality with respect to the Andean conflicts.

Vargas regards the Ecuador/Peru war and the Peru/Chile war as two separate conflicts. His one certainty is he wants to be left out of both. This isn't a difficult proposition. It has no border with Chile, and its borders with Peru and Ecuador are mainly inaccessible and remote.

The Bolivian Civil War is a more troubling matter, one which seems to go towards the balance of power in the southern cone. This is an area somewhat less peripheral to Brazil's interests.

During the Chaco War, Brazil maintains neutrality, while offering some nominal support to Bolivia.

This is driven mostly by rivalry with Argentina. Argentina is a heavy, though covert backer of Paraguay. An unequivocal Paraguayan victory would have tilted tilt balances of power slightly towards Argentina. So it seems the thing to do is to throw some quiet weight behind Bolivia.

It isn't much weight, however. Bolivia is too remote and inaccessible for any kind of serious covert aid, there are no strong interests at stake, and the official position is neutrality.

The Chaco war ends in a matter that satisfies Brazil. Paraguay wins most of the Chaco but wins nothing of particular value. Bolivia holds onto the oil producing sections and remains intact. Argentina's ambitions are mostly frustrated. And best of all, the peace treaty effectively disarms both Bolivia and Paraguay, leaving

Brazil with impotent buffer states to the south between it and Argentina. Big rewards for very little effort.

Perhaps because the border states are now entirely impotent, the Vargas government is taken completely by surprise when the Bolivian Civil war breaks out in July of 1941. The official position, assumed quickly, is flat neutrality. Behind the scenes, the Brazilians find themselves ideologically sympathetic to General Villarroel's position, but not enough to be swayed.

The escalation of the Bolivian civil war in August and September is a further unwelcome surprise. Brazil formally protests the entry of Chilean troops into Bolivian territory. Ibanez moves shift Vargas' favor towards the Penaranda regime. Again, there's a degree of balancing going on. The perception is that Villarroel is allied not just to Chile, but to Argentina, and this requires Brazil to support his rival.

More than anything, Vargas is disturbed by the escalation of the war, and the possibility of its consequences spilling over onto his borders, whether this is in the form of refugees, border incidents, smuggling or the temptation of a commitment.

Vargas builds up forces along the border and increases security, but confines most of his activity to diplomacy.

When Valpes breaks away from Villarroel in Bolivia, the Brazilian government almost welcomes him as a palatable option. Valpes at least, promises to secure the frontier with Brazil.

In September, Vargas joins with the United States, Britain and Argentina in a four power effort to contain the Bolivian War, in the Montevideo Conference. Brazil joins Argentina in excluding the Villarroel faction from the conference, and supporting Valpes. This proves to be a mistake, as it becomes clear to the Brazilian delegates that Valpes is in the process of allying with the Argentines for support.

It also became clear that Argentina's foreign minister is making a major effort to corral the smaller Southern Cone countries under Argentina's leadership. At this point, Vargas' diplomats begin taking adverse positions. They shift support back to Penaranda from Valpes, leaving no clear favorite and no real means of resolution to the Bolivian conflict. Uruguay is excluded from Argentina's alliance by diplomatic pressure on both countries.

As a concession, Brazil is prepared to tolerate Paraguay's alliance with Argentina, but only on condition that Paraguay is to continue to abide by the Chaco Treaty, continues to remain disarmed with only a skeleton military force, and foreswears all further or future claims on the Bolivian Chaco.

Having stalemated Argentina's designs, and having guaranteed, once again, that Brazil's borders are secured by a ring of powerless, impotent buffer states, Brazil's diplomats return home, pleased with themselves.

Any joy is short lived, however. The Argentines, stung by Brazilian success in ensuring that Paraguay remains neutered, focus more and more effort on the Valpes regime, throwing money, increasingly overt diplomatic support, and weapons and soldiers into it the project.

By October, Brazil is expressing concern about Argentine advisors in Valpes forces overstepping their role. In November, Argentine 'volunteer brigades' in substantial numbers are actively fighting on Valpes side to stop Villarroel's offensive.

Of even more concern is Argentina's escalating influence in Paraguay. The Paraguayan armaments industry is reviving to arm the Valpes faction, paid for by Argentine money. The moribund Paraguayan economy is perking up rapidly, and with it, a wave of public optimism and enthusiasm.

But this also masks Argentina's increasing influence in Paraguay. Using that country as a conduit to Valpes's Bolivia, Argentine diplomats, soldiers, shipments and advisors enter Paraguay, many passing through, some remaining. Joint infrastructure projects are commenced to build rail and road connections through the Chaco. Of course, with military and police forces limited by Treaty, there are no extra troops to guard Argentine interests, and so increasing numbers of Argentine troops are being stationed in Paraguay.

By May of 1942, Brazilian diplomats are complaining that these Argentine troops outnumber Paraguay's own forces. The Paraguayan government and key parts of Paraguayan administration and territory are falling under the control of Argentina.

Argentina's participation in the Bolivian civil war continues to escalate. By May of 1942, Brazil claims that Valpes is nothing more than a shell or proxy, and the Argentine army is in de facto control of his faction. This is a clear exaggeration at that point in time. But it is also clear that as Argentina's role increases, Valpes own autonomy is declining.

For Brazil, all of this means that the security situation in the south is rapidly deteriorating.

Instead of neutered buffer states, there is a power vacuum that Argentina was moving into.

Reluctantly, between November, 1941 and May, 1942, the Vargas government finds itself forced to build up forces on its border, a move matched by Argentina, and both countries seem to be moving towards war despite themselves.

During this period, Vargas moves decisively to secure Brazil's security with the May, 1942 treaties known as the Washington Accords. For Brazil, Pearl Harbor proves to be a huge boon. The United States is gearing up for war, it needs resources.

Along the Amazon - December, 1941

Humans have an extraordinary capacity to endure the unendurable. A week after the bowel loosening terror of that awful day, life for Pablo has achieved something approaching normality. Every time he shuts his eyes, the images leap to his mind, the smoke, the smell of gunpowder and blood, the reports of machine gun and rifle, people screaming, not just people; companions, friends. Death and violence everywhere and strange unearthly savages.

The first day, he is in a funk of crazed fear and horror. The next, slightly recovered, he entertains fantasies of sabotaging the engines, of plunging a dagger or a screwdriver into Blandon's breast. But he quickly realizes he is too much of a coward. Instead, there is only shaking, quaking fear, a desperate refusal to look beyond the moment, a stunning willingness to obey. Pablo knows about slavery, everyone does. But it never occurs to him to realize that he himself has been made over into one.

Routine settles in. He checks the engines carefully, diligently. The maintenance has gotten sloppy, so he applies himself, looking for any sign of mechanical dysfunction, of any problem developing. A breakdown won't do at all. He prefers to be down there when he can, away from the savages.

Afterwards, he will be brought up on deck. There in the Pilot's house, Blandon will sit listening, while Pablo reads from the stack of papers retrieved from the expedition. There are all sorts, manifests, orders and warrants from de Paulo's kit, newspapers, journals, even a novel, badly translated, by someone named Conrad. Blandon listens, half smiling, as he watches the waters and shores, occasionally making a comment.

Occasionally crowds of savages gather along a river bank, and Blandon goes out and shouts and waves, his savage sergeants shouting brief translations. The savages continue to terrify him, though over time he becomes used to some, particularly a fellow named Montresor.

The Matilde cruises along, part of a huge armada of river boats of every type, including the now captured gunboats. Native canoes dart among the boats like mosquitos carrying people and objects back and forth, transmitting instructions. A few boats and canoes speed far ahead, scouting the river, returning with their findings as others rush out. Pablo realizes that his terror has abated when he finds himself simply gazing upon the wonder of it all.

Then in the evening, is meal time, when Blandon's crew of white and black men and savages gather up on the decks to sit and eat together, gossiping and joking in two or three languages. It is so peculiarly normal that Pablo at first struggles with this. Montressor usually sit by him, translating now and then. One night, Montressor casually lays his hand on Pablo's thigh. Pablo freezes, glancing around, but though a few notice no one seemed to consider the matter worthy of attention. After thinking things over rapidly, Pablo decides to leave Montresor's hand where it is and offers him a wan smile.

After about a week, when Blandon seems in a genial mood, Pablo regains sufficient bearings that he dares to ask questions.

"Where are we going?" he blurts out.

Blandon looks up, momentarily confused.

"Up the rivers. Dry season is coming; there are some folk I need to see to. Things to do."

"The war?"

Pablo is vaguely aware of the war between Ecuador and Peru. In a sleepy town like Manaus, such things are far away, but still worthy of gossip. He understands that Blandon is part of that war, but not how or precisely what he was doing in it.

"The war," Blandon agrees.

"Why did you invade Brazil? Why did you kidnap us?"

Blandon's brow furrows.

"Kidnap you?" he is genuinely puzzled. "You are among friends, comrades. You are fed, kept safe. Look, here you are like a brother, eating freely at the table. Where are your chains? Your confinement. You are here of your own free will. You're here because you've chosen, and we're happy to have you. But you are free, you can leave any time. Anyone can. People come and go all the time."

Pablo is careful not to look out over the boat across the shadowed jungle. The savages seem to come and go freely. The prisoners? Most of the prisoners are gone now, spilling their blood into the waters from cut throats. The minute he leaves, he is a dead man, not even Montressor could protect him. He knows better than to say any of this.

"And Brazil... It's just lines on a map that someone drew, a long time ago, and far far away. It's meaningless. You shouldn't give it any credence."

Those comments echo his final conversation with Major de Paulo. As reasonable as Blandon seems, he is still terrifyingly mercurial.

"I used to believe in that," Blandon says thoughtfully. "I see more clearly now."

"But why did you come here?" Pablo insists. "Why didn't you just stay where you were and fight your war? Why attack us?"

"We attacked you?" Blandon muses. "Somehow, I don't think all those gunboats were come to bring me flowers and kisses."

There is a muted round of laughter as his remark is translated among the savages. They grin at Pablo, shoving each other.

"As to the war," Blandon replies, "yes, we fought it, and we fight it still. But let me tell you a secret, in war, it's best not to be sitting where the other fellow is shooting. It's good to move around a bit. And to shoot him of course."

Again, a round of laughter.

"It was the wet season," he says thoughtfully, "so that brings certain conditions, and we must abide and spread wide. Advantage turns this way and that, and you turn with it or die. Sometimes you run, sometimes you advance. Now comes the dry season, the advantage shifts to us, so we go back."

Blandon leans back in his seat, resting against the side of the boat. "It's a tricky thing to manage an army, or a navy. The two things run together out here. You have to feed them."

"The schoolboys, they read in books, 'live off the land.' Like it was that simple. You have thousands of mouths to feed. The land will feed that for a day, for a week, and then what?"

He waves his hand airily.

"How do you feed them then? Well, you must move them. Move them here, move them there. All the time, the enemy wants to shoot at you, you want to shoot at them, but you must feed yours. You spread them out, easier to feed, but maybe get shot at more. So you move them further."

The dinner group goes quiet now, even the savages listening attentively, translating quietly to each other.

"There was this fellow, Alba. A little upstart. We all hated him, me along with the rest. We called him the Accountant. But I've come to realize, he was right. War is not about glory. That's for fools. War is about feeding your own, and what you do to make sure of that, where you put them, when you have to move, where to move."

"It's about numbers. So many rifles, but more important, only so many bullets. Each bullet you fire, that's it, can't fire it again. You don't want to run out of bullets, so you hoard them, like a miser with coins. You try to make sure each bullet counts."

He waves at the fleet, "we have boats. That's good. Boats have motors. Some steam engines, those are good, easy around here to fuel them. Some gasoline engines - for those, you have to worry. You count every gallon of gas, because when you run out of gas or kerosene or whatever, then your engine doesn't go, and your boat is no good."

"Of course," he tells his audience, "Klaus may help us with that, if he can build a still. That would be good. Then all we'd need is a fellow who can make bullets."

The man seems lost in his own thoughts. Pablo is almost irritated. The question he wants answered is 'Why?' Why? Why? Why has it come to this? Why has he intruded? Why is he here? Why is Pablo here? Blandon seems less a man than the working of fate and Pablo wants to know why fate is so capricious.

Blandon stares off into the distance.

"Why Brazil? You ask this, like the question has meaning. That black soldier, de Palma, he thought the same way. They fooled him, and he died for it."

Pablo freezes again; remembering the casual way Blandon pulled his pistol and shot the man in the face. The pistol is still at his side. Pablo's heart skips a beat. He can die just as casually in the next moment.

But instead, Blandon just shakes his head and continues.

"The way of it, is that there was this big empty space on a map. So some people, they look at that map, and they start drawing lines. Here's Brazil, they say, and this is Ecuador, and this is Peru. All just lines on a map. No care for who is living here. Those are just Indigenous, who cares?"

"But it wasn't real, just lines. It took me a long time to figure that out," he says. "But then some people look at those lines, and they think 'I own this, this is mine!'"

"The damned Peruvians are the worst. They just go 'Nom nom nom,'" Blandon holds up his hand to his face and makes an eating motion. "'Nom, nom, nom!' They're not even hungry, but they just go 'Nom, Nom, Nom.' They're greedy, they want everything they see, they devour. That's why we fight them."

He pauses.

"The way to a moral life, Pablo? It's simple. Don't eat when you're not hungry. There's no sin greater than greed."

"But there are greedy men everywhere. Ecuador. Brazil. You start hearing the stories of the Indians of the old times, or the not so old times. The rubber trade. Heartbreaking. Greedy men love weakness, it lets them go 'nom, nom, nom,'" Again, the 'eating' hand gesture. "There's no right and wrong with greedy men. Right is what you can take, and wrong is whoever you can take it from."

"Peru, Brazil," he says, "they look at these Indians. They don't see men and women. What's wrong with these Indians? They go around naked. They don't read the bible. They hunt and they fish, and they get along fine by themselves. But greedy men, they look, and they just see savages.

"What does that mean? It means they just see things they can take. It's not anything more complicated than that."

"Why? Why are these Indians so much less than men? Because they're naked? Because they just have a bow, and the white man has a gun? You give an Indian a gun, and you train him to use it like a white man... and he's just as good as a white man. Just as fine."

"I'll admit, I did not believe it myself. I did not think such a thing could be. I had to learn it. I will confess, I am not the man I used to be. But it's true. And that, my boy, begs the question. If an Indian with a gun is just as good as a white man, then what right over the Indian does that white man have? What should lines on a map by white men far away mean? Why should that mean more than the people that live on that place on a map?"

Blandon lifts his bottle and takes a drink.

"But then, it's not just guns. It comes down to bullets, and the white men always have more bullets."

Blandon grins and lifts his bottle in salute.

"I suppose I must toast the glorious nation of Brazil and its contributions to our cause. All the bullets we could want, and guns, and boats, a fine mechanic, and sisters for my dear Matilde. This is a generous bounty... Not that you intended to give it to us, not in this particular way. But a gift it is, and I'll make full use of it, as I slap the Peruvians."

"After that..." he shrugs. "Time doesn't pass the same way here; it doesn't mean the same things. After that... something I suppose, we'll find out."

New World War – Page 203

Pablo glances around at the men and women, white and native, who hang on Blandon's every word. Even Montressor, with his hand on Pablo's thigh is riveted.

But he's mad, Pablo thinks. He's stark raving mad. I'm a captive of a madman. He'll destroy us all.

Blandon shrugs.

"You probably think I'm mad, Pablo," Blandon says. "I'll destroy us all. That if you try to leave, you'll be executed."

Pablo's heart skips a beat. He is suddenly hot and cold, sweat breaking out all over his body. For a moment, he's convinced that Blandon is supernatural. Not a man, but some spirit of the Indians, incarnating in a mad Admiral.

Blandon shakes his head.

Suddenly, Pablo realizes he's stopped breathing. He draws a breath like a gasp, his eyes wide on the strange man.

"But you just give it time," Blandon tells him. "Time will open your eyes. You will see the truth, as I came to see it. You will not want to leave, because your place is here. You will see as I do. You will see that we are right, that our cause is right."

****

Brazil Enters the War... or at least A War... at Some point...

On January 28, 1942, Brazil officially severs relations with Germany, Italy, Japan, Ecuador or Chile.

On the same date, Vargas authorizes an expeditionary force of ten thousand men to the Amazonian city of Manaus to deter Blandon and, more importantly, to suppress his native auxiliaries. On February 2, 1942, this is reduced to 5,000. Budgeting.

During this period of time, Brazil begins negotiating a series of military, political and business arrangements with the United States.

Although technically neutral during the early months of 1942, Brazil permits the US to set up air and naval bases in return for the offer by the United States to encourage the formation of an iron industry. Air bases are located in Bahia, Pernambuco and Rio Grande do Norte. The city of Natal hosted a US navy patrol squadron, and the United States carries out anti-submarine operations from Brazilian ports and bases.

These military concessions are not free, but rather, the quid pro quo is the commitment of the United States to assist in the development and financing of a Brazilian iron and steel industry. This is hardly unusual, Brazil remains highly isolationist. Most of its interests and goals in its relations with the United States tend to be economic.

One of the most important of these is the 'rubber battle' or second rubber boom.

***

Brazil - The Rubber Battle

The Japanese takeover of Southeast Asia means that 92 percent rubber supplies to the US are cut off. This is disastrous; rubber is an essential war material. The United States is desperate to replace those losses; the war effort depends on it.

Brazil was once a major centre of rubber production, but this collapsed when Southeast Asia took over the market decades before. Now, Brazilian rubber is back in demand, and for Brazil, this means incredible wealth.

The Brazilian interior experiences its first rubber boom between 1880 and 1910. The boom brought immense wealth to Brazil, to plantations and entrepreneurs, and to the region. Cities and towns are founded deep in the Amazon, among them Manaus, Belem, Itacoatiara, Rio Branco, Eirunepé, Marabá, Cruzeiro do Sul and Altamira often sporting fabulous public works.

But there is a dark side to the rubber boom. Rubber extraction is a brutal and labour intensive undertaking, workers are paid poorly. Initially, the area's Indigenous are recruited or enslaved, devastating the population. One plantation recruits 50,000 Indigenous, of which 8,000 survives. In some areas, 90 percent of the Indigenous population is wiped out. The scale of brutality is devastating.

As Indigenous populations collapse, migrant labour streams in from all over Latin America, and from places as far away as Asia, Europe and Brazil. It is this new population of labourers and the educated and skilled technicians who accompany them who build the cities and towns that pepper the Amazonian river basins.

To the Indigenous population, the story is tragic. The rubber industry, and the massive influx of foreigners, bring new waves of disease that ravages native populations. Indigenous are displaced from traditional lands. Immigrant hunters and fishermen, with superior tools and numbers wipe out traditional fish and game. Indigenous who were not virtual slave labour are excluded from local economies. Everywhere across the Amazonas self-sufficient

thriving villages and tribes experience plague, starvation, dislocation
and misery. For the Indigenous, the rubber boom is an unmitigated
ongoing disaster, one that they are helpless to resist.

The rubber boom ends around 1910, with the development of
massive rubber plantations in Southeast Asia. The bottom drops
out of the Amazonian rubber economy. Towns and cities which
were some of the richest on the continent fall on hard times, with
entire populations melting away.

Suddenly, with World War II, the boom times are back. With
ninety per cent of its supply suddenly offline, the United States is
desperate to make it up, and Brazil is the only place to do it.

The problem is that the workforce has gone away. The cities and
towns and plantations all withered with the end of the original
Rubber Boom in 1910. Now, a full generation later, most of them
still stand, but as a shadow of their former selves. There are
perhaps thirty thousand rubber workers available in the entire
Amazonian region. Even they don't even have enough work to go
around. But over 100,000 bodies are required to meet America's
needs.

The 'rubber battle' constitutes a major fascistic industrial effort.
More than 65,000 workers are recruited and sent into the deep
Amazonas to harvest rubber for American industry, to join the
35,000 workers already there. There is a great deal of nationalist
and patriotic hoopla associated with this, but the underlying
activities are rather grimmer. Vast numbers, tens of thousands of
unemployed are forcibly relocated across the country to work on
the rubber plantations. Extravagant promises are made, that these
workers will be returned to their home towns or regions at
government expense, that they will be eligible for housing and
benefits comparable to the military. These promises are quickly
forgotten. They were never real. The important thing for Vargas is
to get workers out there by any means necessary.

But there is a problem. General Blandon's campaigns, extending
into the Brazilian Amazonas, have left a scattering of several
hundred, perhaps a few thousand, native 'auxiliaries' spread
piecemeal through the region. These are armed with military rifles

and trained with military tactics. As the Rubber Battle gets under way through 1940, there are more and more complaints of organized violent resistance by native communities. These complaints become increasingly urgent. As more immigration flows in, the resistance becomes steadily more violent. Unpredictable patches of the Amazonas become increasingly dangerous.

The Vargas government can only respond by increasing the military presence in the Amazonas, and launching punitive missions into areas of insurgent activity. Despite this, there are relatively few firefights. The insurgent Indigenous prefer not to engage directly. Frustrated soldiers, unable to distinguish between peaceful Indigenous and insurgents, turn their guns on both. The result is often a hardening of resistance and increasingly savage reprisals, or a migration of beleaguered Indigenous towards the borders.

Ultimately, Vargas is sanguine. He has a fully equipped army. The resistance is simply a few bands of Indigenous with small arms. Eventually, they'll run out of bullets and the problem would be solved.

Except for one thing...

****

The Rain Forest War - January 1942 - May, 1942

General Enrique Blandon's return to the command centre of Jaen in January, 1942, near the Ecuadoran Oriente comes as a shock. Blandon is almost unrecognizable, but he comes at the head of a fleet of gunboats and support craft of all descriptions and an army that is by now mostly native. Approximately a third of his force is European, but these are almost all fanatically loyal.

During the period of his absence, Blandon's command is superseded and a new institutional structure put in place. There is actually a document on file in the Jaen Commander's office relieving Blandon of command.

Blandon simply ignores all that and takes command of the entire town. He then proceeds to requisition every gun, every bullet, every can of food, every gallon of gasoline and anything else that can be carried away. Leaving a garrison in place to hold the town, he then proceeds to Ecuador's remaining satellite outposts, fortifications and supply depot stripping each bare, with no significant resistance. Among his acquisitions are two float planes. As he has only two pilots that he trusts, all other aircraft are stripped for parts or destroyed.

During this period, Ecuador's command becomes aware of Blandon's presence. By this time, he has become a major headache for them. His campaigns into the Peruvian Selva are not authorized, but they are tolerated and even supported.

The incursions into the Brazilian rain forests are another story altogether, provoking furious reactions from both Brazil and the United States. Diplomatically, the Ecuadorans respond with denials, evasions, confusion, apologies, offers of reparations, more denials; counter accusations against Peru, excuses and repudiations. Nevertheless, the problem doesn't go away. The disappearance of the Manaus Expedition is on its way to provoking a major crisis when Pearl Harbour hits and takes the wind out of everyone's sails.

The Bonifaz triumvirate has no idea what to do with him, or about him. Blandon ignores orders, or interprets them as he sees fit. His reports become occasional, sometimes professional, sometimes rambling monologues. At one point he is cashiered and a court martial in absentia is scheduled, but then cancelled and rescinded. At another point, he is almost promoted to field Marshall, before it is stopped. Repudiating him is considered, but the prospect of a Blandon running free without any restrictions at all is terrifying.

For what it was worth, Blandon is still part of the Ecuador command structure. He still considers himself part of that structure somewhat. And he will still obey orders, if he feels like it, if he can't interpret them to his liking, and if they appear to be in the political and military interests of Ecuador as he sees it.

So the agenda is to try and persuade him back into the fold, a strategy that is increasingly more fantasy than fact.

Through the next few months, Blandon remains in occasional communication in return for a trickle of supplies. The Triumvirate is able to dissuade him from attacking or looting the Peruvian town of Iquitos, at the time under effective Ecuadoran control.

Instead, Blandon shifts focus to the Peruvian outpost of Lamas, overrunning it in a night attack on March 20, 1942, massacring the population. Now in control of Lamas, Blandon hunkers down to wait, refusing to try for Tarapota, which he judges inaccessible and impregnable. He continues to focus on arming, training and building networks among the Indigenous population. This, together with his float planes gives him unprecedented information on enemy movements and deployments.

Peruvian relief expeditions are launched from Tarapota and Pucallpa, but efforts to coordinate are poor. Blandon catches the Tarapota expedition as it waits for Pucallpa, and destroys it on April 4. The Pucallpa expedition is harassed steadily until it arrives to confront a holding garrison by April 9.

In the meantime, Blandon takes his river fleet through tributary channels off the main river swollen by the wet season rains. In this way, he bypasses the Pucallpa relief expedition, to launch another night raid on the town, on April 16, in pitched battle. The town is overrun the next day, 1942, finally surrendering under fire from the four gunboats.

Survivors are corralled as hostages and put to forced labour. The road is impassable, flooded and washed out in sections, nevertheless, Blandon works to further disrupt the road, blowing up sections, mining other sections.

The Pucallpa relief expedition, upon learning of the fall of the town, and being misinformed that Blandon is deploying against it, makes its way to Tarapota.

By May, 1942, Peruvian forces in the region have been swept away. The sole remaining outposts are Tarapota and Atalaya, but Blandon controls everything between and is busily organising native militias to make the region permanently ungovernable for Peru.

But the reality of the Jungle War is that it is a see saw war, with advantage continually flowing back and forth. A lot depends on what manpower is coming in and when. Ultimately, the Peruvians are correct; it will be a war of attrition, with the eventual outcome not in doubt.

This is the expected map of the future.

But in April and May, 1942, increasing numbers of Indigenous refugees, both peaceful and armed, are trickling across the border, as Vargas' campaigns against the Indigenous slowly escalates. At first, this simply appears to be Vargas' response to Blandon's incursion. But over time, the reports include waves of new immigrants into the Amazonas and a revival of the rubber trade. Blandon, now at least somewhat in contact with civilisation puts the pieces together, including the potential impacts on Indigenous populations through the region.

Blandon has found his crusade.

***

New World War – Page 211

The Rain Forest War - May 1942 - December, 1942

The Brazilian campaign marks the final break between General Enrique Blandon and the Ecuadoran state, though neither side comprehends it at the time.

The native guides that Blandon initially recruited have become native auxiliaries, and then armed auxiliaries. As Blandon's expedition is forced to live off the land, as his troops succumb to disease and combat, he recruits and trains native troops to replace them. Recruiting among the natives opens him up to relationships and alliances among the tribes immersing him in their politics and worlds.

Alliances bring native militias into being. These militias require training, arming and direction, and while they serve him, reciprocation requires that he serve their needs as well. It was a two way street. The Jungle war, the conditions of isolation, of rainy and dry seasons, of diffuse irregular forces require adaptations, new strategies, new tactics, new doctrines.

It's not clear when Blandon's loyalties begin to shift. It likely isn't clear to Blandon at the time; this is the sort of thing that is usually realized only in hindsight. These shifting loyalties, and the demands and innovations of the jungle war transform Blandon himself as he evolves from a rather conventional and rather petty officer into... something else.

Blandon crosses back into Brazil sometime in late May or June. Early June is the last acknowledgement by Blandon of communications from Quito. Dispatches from Blandon to the Ecuadoran command continue into July, but take weeks to arrive and are maddeningly vague. The last known dispatch is dated early July and received in mid-August. During this period, there is no clear information on Blandon's movement or activities.

During this period, however, Brazilian military and provincial authorities note a substantial increase in incidents of native armed violence. On June 4, in Amazonas province, there is a full-fledged firefight between natives and regular army forces, the first time this has ever happened. Through the month of June, there are increasing reports of patrols being ambushed, supply centers raided, massacres at work camps, and attacks on boats. Abductions and disappearances reach record levels. Reprisals against Indigenous populations are ineffective.

The Rubber Battle continues, however, as the Vargas regime continues to pump more and more indigent and migrant labourers into the region by thousands. As reports of massacres trickle out, some of the indigent become reluctant to go. The Vargas government resorts to bribes and threats, including signing bonuses. Prisoners are given work release. For their part, migrants agitate for protection, and work camps are provided with armed guards, usually private.

Private Citizens' militias begin to operate in the region.

On July 12, 1942, a partially submerged flat bottom boat is found outside the town of Eirunepé. There is no sign of an engine, it appears to be poled or paddled. The boat is heavily camouflaged. Most disturbingly, a wooden platform appears to be a machine gun mount, although the machine gun is missing. This is the first confirmation of apocryphal reports that there are machine guns in the hands of the natives.

Violence continues to escalate through the month of July. On August 10, 1942 a convoy of Brazilian four navy gunboats is attacked by a pair of heavily camouflaged gunboats. Three of the Brazilian craft are sunk; the fourth retreats and escapes under fire. One of the attacking craft is identified as the Matilde. Blandon has finally reappeared.

In the resulting storm of outrage, the Ecuadoran government formally repudiates Blandon and strips him of all title and rank, he is ordered to present for Court Martial or be tried in absentia. This is a meaningless gesture, since they have no way to communicate with him. The Vargas government demands Blandon and all associates be handed over as war criminals. An equally futile gesture. As difficult as this makes things, there are no relations or areas of contact between Ecuador and Brazil.

The bigger problem is the United States. Blandon's actions make things extremely difficult for the Ecuadoran triumvirate and its efforts to salvage any kind of relationship with the Americans.

On Brazil's part, the native resistance is an embarrassment, and an obstacle to its economic and political alliance with America. Vargas is forced to substantially escalate his military commitment in the region. Private militias are dissolved or folded into the army. Military airfields are commissioned in several of the towns. The 100,000 workers of the rubber battle are to be protected by 18,000 soldiers, although it would take until early October to reach full strength.

Meanwhile, the situation in the Atlantic Ocean is also escalating. From January to July 1942, German U-Boats sink 13 Brazilian merchant vessels. In August 1942, a single U-Boat sinks five Brazilian vessels in two days, causing more than 600 deaths. The escalating deaths and attacks provoke a public crisis; businesses and property owned by ethnic Germans are attacked. Vargas formally declares war on Germany, Japan and Ecuador in August 22, 1942. The declaration excludes Italy, Chile or any Bolivian faction.

Even here, there is an element of calculation. For Vargas it is always a calculation. Large numbers of Italian and German immigrants, and the important position these immigrants hold in business and politics predispose Vargas towards the Axis. Vargas is quite sympathetic to Mussolini, whose tactics and policies inspired him. He is a pretty authoritarian guy at heart, and under other circumstances, would go down in history as just another fascist.

On the other hand, the allied blockade means that the only trade is with the US and Britain, so through 1940 and 1941, Brazil, tilts towards its own self-interest, and aligns with the remaining trading partners. War with Germany involves minimal risk, and maximizes the rewards from the relationship with the United States, and this becomes the focus of Vargas' war effort.

There is no particular impulse to act on war with Japan, apart from some actions against Japanese nationals.

Nor is any thought given to becoming involved in the Andean war. The declaration of war mandates that all Ecuadoran military personal or declared or undeclared allies are now officially combatants and subject to attack. Essentially, it means that Blandon, his men, and any armed Indigenous were liable to be killed on sight. But there's no thought to crossing the Andes on some incredibly expensive, militarily pointless venture.

Overall, Vargas remains slow to become directly involved in conflict. The Jungle campaign is expensive and cannot be rushed. Vargas opts to build that slowly and incrementally and actively works to de-emphasize that in the public eye. Too much attention makes it difficult to attract migrants to the region, and interferes with the Rubber Battle. The Rubber Battle is supposed to be an economic windfall for Brazil, not an actual battleground. There is little appeal to squandering the windfall, wasting all that money on unnecessary soldiers and weapons. There isn't a lot of profit to stumbling around the jungle shooting things, it is a cost. The military buildup is on the cheap, building up to enough to solve the problem, no more.

The public focus is on the war with Germany, it plays better in the newspapers, and it makes the Americans happier. Brazil becomes active in anti-submarine warfare and blockade patrol in the Southern Atlantic. July 2, 1944, the first 5,000 members of the Brazilian expeditionary force are sent off to Europe. Between 1944 and 1945, the expeditionary force grows to approximately 25,000 men, fighting under American command, a relatively tiny contribution considering the size of the country.

Meanwhile, Brazil attempts to navigate cost effectively through its trials and Blandon does his best to prosecute a futile war. Between August and December, 1942, there are hundreds of incidents, mostly small scale, but genuine fire fights take place repeatedly. The Matilde is sighted dozens of times, and some of these sightings are even real. Apart from guarding cities and work camps, and the occasional massacre of Indigenous, the Brazilian army is averse to taking risks and prefers to stay out of harm's way.

Also in August, Blandon opens yet another front when his manifesto arguing passionately against colonialism and for indigenous rights appear in a socialist newspaper in Rio de Janeiro. Although of uncertain provenance at the time, it is genuine. Blandon will follow up with a series of manifestos, polemics, letters and rants, sent to various news organizations, newspapers and radio stations throughout Latin America. Some of these will take several months to reach their targets. Due to censorship, many will not be published. But inevitably, a few manage to circulate officially and unofficially.

Prelude to Salitre, September, 1942-April, 1943

The aftermath of Pearl Harbor brings to the Andean Wars, if not actual peace, then at least a reduction in fighting for much of 1942. A de facto cease fire takes place along the northern frontier between Ecuador and Peru. On the southern front in the trenches between Peru and Chile, there is a temporary cessation of hostilities, and even though fighting slowly returns, there will be no major operations for a year and a half.

The cease-fire is not universal - in the Oriente, Enrique Blandon, only nominally under control, continues his campaign against the Peruvian forces in the Selva. The indigenous peoples of the Selva are in a state of low level rebellion. But the interior is far from the main theatres and thinly populated, so not much attention is paid.

In Bolivia, the Civil War continues, through endless permutations. The American demand for a cease-fire is almost meaningless, in the face of three competing regimes, and three foreign powers - none of which is prepared to surrender their position. Within the chaos, new factions arise, Indigenous rebellions, workers uprising, a soviet communist 'people's state' is briefly declared, cities and towns declare their neutrality or switch their allegiances, coalitions of bandits rise up present formidable adversaries and melt away the next day. Violence waxes and wanes. The Bolivian situation seems unsolvable. There is no compromise that lasts; only victory will end the tragedy, when one faction, one power, crushes the others.

As 1942 wears on, Ecuador is persuaded to gradually withdraw from occupied Peruvian territories. Eventually, within its own borders, it entrenches in the face of a regular stream of border incidents. But there are no more offensives, and Ecuador and Peruvian diplomats engage in protracted arguments, trying to resolve the question of the Oriente. As 1942 turns into 1943, the negotiations grow more difficult, as Peru pushes for war reparations and cession of the provinces of El Ora, Lojas and Zamorra on the southern coast.

New World War – Page 217

Ibanez in Chile has no more interest in war. Events have moved past the hope of victory. All he can do is work towards a status quo which secures his regime and his country.

For Lima, however, triumph is in the air. Following the Washington and Lima Accords, the United States begins to re-arm and re-organize the Peruvian military. In particular, between June 1942 and January 1943, the United States ships tanks, mobile artillery, trucks, fighter and bomber aircraft, all under the banner of Brazil. A flood of American and Brazilian advisors and trainers arrives with the new equipment. American planners become involved in strategy.

The most active ongoing theatre, the Bolivian front is least affected by the flood of materials. This was partly due to the inherent racism of the Criollo class in Lima, partly due to the chaotic nature of the theatre. Under the advice of the Americans, Peru holds back the new war material, preferring to build up for a major campaign.

Beneath all this, another reason for Peru to withhold the new materials from the Bolivian theatre is America's insistence on recognizing the Penaranda regime as the rightful government of Bolivia. Penaranda in turn uses the Americans as a wedge to regain his and his government's own autonomy. Although essentially remaining a puppet, Penaranda's agitation makes the Ramirez Junta cautious about transferring war materials which might ultimately end up in control of another government. Only a trickle of new arms and munitions go to resupply the indigenous forces fighting there.

Meanwhile, an increasing source of frustration for the American government is the rapidly escalating corruption that began to permeate literally all levels of society as American money and resources flowed in.

To be fair, it is not all graft and corruption, the Junta's decisions and allocations are heavily driven by internal politics and by the complex relationships between the Junta and Penaranda, between the Junta and its generals and supporters, between Criollo, Mestizo and Quechua, even between towns and cities. These issues are often opaque to the Americans, who neither understand nor care; they're simply frustrated.

But all these obstacles merely slow progress.

Peru, formerly all but exhausted, steadily rearms, and rearms with nearly state of the art American weaponry. By late 1942, the Peruvian high command, with American assistance, is planning a major offensive to end the War once and for all, and to rewrite the map of South America forever.

After protracted negotiations, the Americans agree to support a restoration of the original boundaries, pre-War of the Pacific - boundaries which would restore and recognize the lost Peruvian provinces. Which would grant Bolivia its long sought coast and create a buffer between Peru and Chile.

It will be the revenge for the War of the Pacific, also known as the Salitre (Saltpetre War). The Offensive will be called Operacione Salitre.

And it will be launched in the opening months of 1943.

****

Operacione Salitre, May-July, 1943

As planned by American advisors, Operation Salitre will constitute major, simultaneous coordinated offensives to decisively end the war.

In the South, an onslaught of tanks and mobile artillery, supported by intensive air power would break through the Chilean defences, driving towards Valparaiso and Santiago. Accompanying them will be air forces flying from captured landing strips, and the remnants of the Peruvian navy, to neutralize the Chilean fleet and hamper defensive operations.

In the East, a supporting campaign would evict Villarroel from the mining districts, and cut him off from Chilean support. The isolated Villarroel would fold without backers, leaving Peru free to wipe away the Valpes regime and evict Argentina. This will leave only the Penaranda regime as sole ruler of most of Bolivia.

Ibanez, facing with disaster on two fronts, would be forced to capitulate and seek terms.

After a series of delays and last minute reallocations, on May 18, 1943, Peru opens up with the heaviest use of air-power seen in the entire Andean conflict. Modern American-made aircraft engage in bombing and strafing all along the lines, with bombing missions as far south as Santiago and Valparaiso.

Following in the wake of waves of bombs were tanks and rolling artillery bearing down on Chilean lines.

The attack is initially successful. The Chilean lines are over-extended since the Landing and are only maintained at great cost. Now they're far too exposed and much too vulnerable. The Chileans are overwhelmed at points and forced to retreat.

Chile's situation is dire, by this time, manpower shortages are so severe that the age of conscription is lowered to fifteen for males.

Secondary conscription drives have recruited large numbers of women, mostly into military support roles, but there are actual women's combat brigades.

But Ibanez has two advantages. One is intelligence, the increasingly corrupt, politically riven Ramirez Junta leaks like a sieve, and Ibanez and his war cabinet are very well informed of the enemy's war plans, literally to the time and date of offensives, and the specific numbers of tanks and bombers.

The other is time, which the Chileans used it to prepare and harden defensive lines with concrete emplacements and hardened artillery. Behind the front lines, were further lines and layers of fortifications, mine fields and tunnels, the trench system beginning to approach the old French Maginot line.

Chile's sparse armor is utterly outclassed both in numbers and quality by Peru's imported American tanks. As the reports come in, Ibanez's Generals invest in constructing tank traps, barriers and anti-tank weapons. Chile's aircraft are obsolete and short of fuel, instead investment goes into manufacturing or adapting anti-aircraft weapons and munitions. There isn't sufficient time to fully arm or prepare, but there is time, and what can be done is done.

After Peru's initial successes, they find that the Chileans give ground, but only so much, retreating to hardened secondary positions enormous underground installations and anti-tank and anti-aircraft weaponry.

As June wears on, the offensive stalls out. American tanks and aircraft are much less effective than anticipated and attrition is dramatically higher. Even more war material is pulled from the Bolivian theatre to sustain the offensive.

Meanwhile, the offensive is hampered by Chilean fleet, lead the near obsolete battleship Almirante Cochrane, the pocket battleship Toro and the cruiser Almirante O'Higgins, each supported by a destroyer, a nest of support ships equipped with anti-aircraft weaponry.

The ships sail out into deep waters to avoid detection and then head in to choke points, offering heavy shore bombardment along the Tarapaca coast where land the Peruvians land based supply lines are most accessible. A number of support ships are heavily retrofitted with anti-aircraft weapons. The Peruvian air force is sent after the Chilean ships, diverting them from the offensive. They run into unexpectedly heavy fire. In the heavy fighting, the Almirante Cochrane is damaged and eventually scuttled. The Toro and Almirante Cochrane take lighter damage and withdraw with the destroyers and support ships into deep water beyond the range of the most dangerous aircraft.

The fleet offensive is cover for a secondary operation, a near suicidal raid called the "Little Landing" aimed at disabling the Airfields in Arica from which the Peruvian air force operates. The raid is costly and partially successful, reducing both the number of aircraft and the operating range into Chilean territory.

Despite territory won the Peruvians are taking enormous casualties, and steadily losing faith in American wonder weapons. Peruvian pilots fly higher and higher to avoid anti-aircraft fire, or restrict their bombing to the 'safer' regions, often bombing empty fields. Tank units also become more cautious. The Peruvian offensive grinds to a halt.

For the Chileans as well, the cost in lives is enormous. Ibanez war cabinet debates offering terms. Although the offensive was stopped, Valparaiso and Santiago are being bombed regularly. No one can see a way forward to any kind of victory. Only Ibanez stubbornness and the fear of an angry population, which has suffered too much, keeps the cabinet in line.

In the east, the concurrent Peruvian offensive in Bolivia starts much more slowly, hampered by shortfalls of fresh troops, armour or aircraft. The priority is reserved for the Chilean front, and the Bolivian campaign is further hamstrung when additional resources are pulled away as the Chilean offensive runs into difficulty.

By mid-July, after the Chilean front stalls out. Peruvian air and armour begins to shift towards the Bolivian front and a renewed offensive there.

Initially, the assault is successful. The important city of Cochabamba, held almost continuously by the Villarroel faction since the beginning of the civil war falls. Through the month of July, there is hard, brutal fighting throughout the mining district, but the Villarroel faction is pushed back steadily, losing control of the mining district. Only at Sucre, after a two day campaign against the heavily fortified town and entrenched forces are the Peruvians forced to retreat.

In desperation, Villarroel agrees to the March Accord, Chile makes further concessions, and Argentina throws its expeditionary forces into the mix, attacking the Peru/Penaranda regime. This produces the ironic situation where Villarroel allies with the Argentines, and is prepared to sell out even more of his country than Valpes.

The Argentines, for their part, maintain their support for Valpes as a counterweight to keep Villarroel in his place. Valpes and his faction are oblivious to these manoeuvres, aware only that he and Villarroel, and their backers, Argentina and Chile, have allied to stop the Peruvians.

By the end of July, the situation again reaches stalemate, this time with the mining district solidly in Penaranda's hands, and somewhere between half and two thirds of the country under Peruvian control.

Villarroel is literally hanging by a thread, and Valpes is not much better off. But Villarroel's forces have retained their order, Villarroel controls territory and most importantly, his lines to Chile and Argentina are open. Despite the battering, neither Villarroel nor Valpes are decisively knocked out of the war.

While the mining districts are taken, it's not clear that they can be held. The Chileans, nearing the point of demographic collapse, struggle to reinforce Villarroel for a new series of offensives.

In turn, starting late July and early August, Peru moves a substantial force of its crack soldiers from Chilean front to occupy and fortify the mining districts against counterattack. This move is as much political as military - General Gamarra, Commander of the Chilean front, is held responsible for the failure of the assault and a significant chunk of his core command - pureblood Criollo troops who are the backbone of the Trench war, are taken away from his command.

The reinforcements are controversial. The Penaranda objects to the Peruvian occupation of the district, demanding that the assignment should go to Bolivian units. Bolivian fighters are frustrated that their long sought prize is being handed over to Peruvian occupiers. There's a sense that the new Criollo troops have done no fighting for the prize, and that the assignment keeps the white men out of harm's way, while pushing the indigenous troops back to the front line. There are tensions between the primarily Criollo Peruvian soldiers, and the mainly Indigenous Bolivian theatre forces. A stream of negative reports begin to flow back to Lima about the quality and conduct of the indigenous conscripts.

The local population, including miners, are treated as hostile. The primarily Criollo force has no cultural or social bond with the Mestizo and Indigenous miners. Things go from bad to worse. On August 8, repression triggers a general strike. This is followed shortly thereafter on August 10 and 12 by massacres, as the occupation force turns its machine guns on striking miners and their families. Martial law is instituted, a campaign of savage repression imposed. Over twelve hundred arrests are made, many of whom are never heard from again.

It is in this context that Villarroel makes several raids, attempt to recapture or at least regain hold of parts of the districts. All of them fail. Sensing the antipathy between the new Criollo occupation troops, and the indigenous units, Villarroel's people attempt to reach out through their own Quechua contingents.

Despite gains, the offensive is treated as a disaster in Lima, with finger pointing everywhere. The reality is that even with American aid, the Peruvians are close to collapse, with their economy in ruins, their society riven by internal conflicts and dissension and their military under deep strain. The junta counted on a decisive victory, a triumph. They don't get it.

The Ramirez government uses the occasion to demand even more military and financial aid from the Americans, and privately blame American stinginess for the failure. A few more tanks, a few more planes, a little more ammunition and airplane fuel would have made the difference, they mutter to each other. But the Americans wanted to bleed them so that they'd be weaker and more amenable later on. It is at least a change from blaming each other as Generals are demoted or reassigned, Majors and Colonels promoted, and civilian members of cabinet removed.

General Gamarra, who is in charge of the Chilean front, is singled out for bitter criticism for timidity. If only he'd pushed harder, the Chileans would have collapsed. Look at how much better the Bolivian mission did, and that after he stripped their cupboards bare But Gamarra is too solidly established as commander in the Trench war, and cannot be removed, is demoted within the Junta's framework, and a large part of his most loyal core is transferred to Bolivian occupation duties.

In Bolivia, Penaranda blames a lack of Peruvian commitment, and opens secret negotiations with Villarroel, unaware of Villarroel's own outreach efforts, and proposes a grand Boliviano Confederation. Of course, neither has a pot to piss in without their respective backers, but discussions begin. At the same time, less successfully, Penaranda reaches out to both Valpes, against Villarroel, and separately to the Argentines to see what they have to offer.

General Estevez in turn blames Penaranda's meddling. General Estevez, nominally in charge of the Bolivian theatre, is removed without a replacement being appointed. He was successful enough for others to scramble for credit or control of his victories, but not successful enough or deeply rooted enough to hold onto his command.

The Bolivian operations are now officially directed from Lima, but in practical terms the elements of the Peruvian and Bolivian military in the theatre are virtually independent. At one point a shooting conflict breaks out between the Criollo occupiers of the mining districts and Quechua elements of the Bolivian army.

The Americans, find themselves appalled by the infighting. They attribute the failures to achieve goals, progress notwithstanding, to the pervasive corruption of the Ramirez regime. This is compounded by intelligence failures and leaks, again attributed to the corruption of the Ramirez machine. The renewed demands for money and materials are seen as further proof of the venality, greed and incompetence of the Junta. Peruvian troops are dismissed as cowardly and poor quality, incapable of executing a campaign.

American advisors almost lose faith in the Junta, and write back to Washington of the need for radical measures - either a commitment of American troops into the field to finally sort the war out, or some massive reform or restructuring of the Peruvian government.

Their opinions of Penaranda are no better; he is an untrustworthy, odious little toad scheming only for his own aggrandizement. The Peruvians are right; he belongs on a tight leash.

By August the verdict is in. All the blood and toil, the suffering and sweat, the lives and wealth squandered... and there's no conclusion. No one is happy. Everyone is desperate.

***

October 1943 – The Storm Builds in Peru

As September, 1943, draws to a close in Latin America, the writing is on the wall, and almost every observer is predicting that there will be peace by Christmas.

By this time, all of the warring parties are reaching their limits.

In the case of Argentina, the Junta is seriously reconsidering a Bolivian adventure which promises much, but has become as an ongoing drain threatening to bankrupt the country. Ironically, only British and American wartime purchases of wheat and cattle keep the country afloat.

Bolivia is a shambles; Ecuador, Peru and Chile are each exhausted and nearing points of collapse. For Ecuador, there is only the slow drag of negotiations in Washington, as diplomats plead for their country not to be dismembered. In Chile, Ibanez is desperately looking for a way out that would preserve his rule.

Only Peru is still willingly in the fight with a pipeline of American money and supplies, and a mighty flood of Indigenous conscripts. Through September and October, the balance steadily shifts towards Peru. But the Peruvian mission is evolving.

Statistics tell the story in Bolivia. Thirty-two per cent of all conscripts fighting for Peru are Bolivian nationals, and sixty eight per cent Peruvian forces. Eighty-five per cent of Peruvian/Bolivian forces are classified as Mestizo, Aymara or Quechua, with the vast majority of those being Aymara or Quechua. Less than four per cent of the Peruvian officer corps in Bolivia are Criollo, though of course the proportion is higher in Peru itself. More than half of the active officers in the Bolivian Theater are Quechua, Aymara and Mestizo holding field commissions or promotions, many of which go unrecorded in Lima.

Peru began the war with a professional officer corps composed exclusively of Criollo, or Spanish descendants. This corps was intended to control and direct conscript armies drawn principally from the Criollo and Mestizo populations. But the disastrous Ecuador campaigns, the vicious fighting with Chile and even internal coups have devastated the Criollo officer caste.

At the same time, the dramatic expansion of Peru's military and the casualty rates end up outrunning the professional resources. The new generations of Criollo officers are not soldiers, but former lawyers, accountants, landowners, rapidly promoted, and poorly trained themselves. They have almost no relationship with their mostly native troops. Particularly in the Bolivian theater they are highly dependent upon their native NCO's.

Within Peru, the Criollo caste, as represented by the ruling military junta, is hard pressed to retain control. In Bolivia, they find it difficult to scrape together enough officers to effectively direct the field operations. The war devolves onto the shoulders of Indigenous and Mestizo leaders, promoted officially or unofficially in the field, and sent into action, as the regular officers look on.

The Bolivian campaign evolves as a series of compromises and work-arounds. Cadres of officers and commanders emerge whose loyalty to each other is as great as or greater than to the high command. At times, control over this group is exercised through control or manipulation of supplies or through American advisors, which is effective, but which promotes bitter resentment.

The de facto leadership of Peruvian campaign forces in Bolivia devolves to a man named, Otoronco, known as Captain Jaguar, although the Captaincy was a field promotion at best. In reality, Otoronco is equivalent to a General, having assumed wide authority over a group of Mestizo and Indigenous officers.

Their relationship with the high command in Lima, which controls the flow of supplies, and sometimes with the official local command structure of Criollo officers is at times contentious, and a source of consternation, but as long as the war is going well, Otoronco and his peers are tolerated.

Nevertheless, between July and October, 1943, under the leadership of Captain Jaguar (Otoronco) and his colorful associates, Peru begins a series of tactical and strategic advances. Argentina suffers disastrous reverses; Chile's position falls apart steadily, until only the mining district is held by Ibanez forces.

In October, 1943, enough is enough. The Peruvians are unstoppable. All parties agree to a ceasefire, with Ibanez trying to negotiate the safe withdrawal of his forces, trapped in the mining district. Villarroel is left to negotiate on his own, and discovers that direct negotiations with Captain Jaguar and his associates are quite different from the hard line taken by Lima.

But October 22, 1943, is also the date of a military coup in Lima.

****

October 22, 1943 – Coup in Peru, Gamarra Overthrows the Junta

General Gamarra, field commander on the Chilean/Peruvian trench war front, moves decisively on Lima, ousting the ruling junta led by General Ramirez.

Coups always come as a surprise, but this one has been building for a long time.

The Americans in particular, are disenchanted with what they perceive as runaway corruption in Ramirez Junta. Heavy American support of and preference for Peru opens up a pipeline of money and supplies, one which the Peruvian infrastructure and officer corps is poorly equipped to handle. The result is the emergence of graft, sometimes massive graft, up and down the chain of command. The Americans steadily lose faith in what they perceive as wholesale mismanagement of phases of the Bolivian campaign.

Within Peru's military, Gamarra, engaged in actual fighting a real war on the front, and carrying on like a professional soldier, attracts American attention and support. As far as the United States is concerned, he is the only real soldier in the Peruvian command.

Gamarra through 1943, steadily becomes the lightning rod, attracting dissidents in the military, including the remnants of the navy, the emerging American-trained and equipped air-force and in Criollo society in general. Some of this dissension is motivated by professionalism, some by resentment, and some by a greater desire for spoils.

The end result that Gamarra's ascension is celebrated by just about everyone. Spontaneous celebrations burst out throughout Peru.

Ibanez in Chile was reported to have said "At last, a man I can talk with."

Gamarra is welcomed by the officers and men fighting in Peru. The acclaim is universal. Together with the ceasefire, it seems that the long bloody road has come to an end.

New World War – Page 231

Gamarra Takes Command

General Luis Gamarra moves into office as the President of Peru with great expectations.

Fundamentally, he is an old school Criollo, with all the values and shortcomings of his caste. In his career, he is noted for formality and discipline. Through the 1930s, he rose up in the ranks, but studiously avoided any association with politics. He serves with famous neutrality under both Sanchez Cerra and Benevides. As Ramirez military coup moves forward, he remains absolutely apolitical, earning a legendary reputation for personal integrity and discipline.

Inevitably, in late 1941, he is selected to command on the trench frontier, and successfully begins reorganizing, efficiently beating back several Chilean attacks, and earning the name 'Stone Wall' Gamarra.

Having finally taken the step into politics, his new regime acts decisively, sweeping the old order aside, and replacing it with... himself. Ramirez Junta consisted of an inner circle of high ranking officers, landholders and commercial leaders. This facilitated corruption, but was also an inclusive regime which tolerated and incorporated a wide range of opinions and relatively effective policies.

Stone Wall Gamarra's regime consists of ... himself. He sees himself completely in the Caudillo strongman mold. Power will not be shared; no other judgement or wisdom will come before him; his judgment is final. He will give orders and directions, they will be carried out, and all will be well. Questions and dissension are not tolerated. Gamarra has run the Chilean front as a disciplined, orderly machine. He sees no reason that Peru should not be run the same way.

In hindsight, much has been made of Gamarra's racism. He is famously reported to have said that he had not so much as spoken to an Indigenous person until he was thirty-five. But to be fair, his attitudes are not unremarkable for someone of his social class.

Unfortunately, Gamarra makes two mistakes on taking office.

The first is to completely dismiss concerns about the situation of the Quechua in the highlands. The Indigenous population is, at this time, undergoing unprecedented social stress, with refugee movements, massive conscription, war taxes and a shift from a barter to cash economy, erosion of traditional lands taken up by landholders, etc. Gamarra, consistent with much of Peruvian history, considers Indigenous matters to be local ones. He consistently refers problems back to the Church or landowners. He acknowledges unprecedented numbers of local and brushfire rebellions, but believes that these will settle on their own, or will be quashed in due time by the Army. These are how things are always done. Gamarra does not care what the Indigenous think.

Gamarra's second mistake will prove fatal. With the ceasefire, and the emerging peace, Gamarra sets about re-organizing his Bolivian command. He is already moving to post-war thinking; planning for the reduction and decommissioning of much of the Army and returning to a peacetime military and society.

To Gamarra, the Bolivian theater is an undisciplined mess. The forces lack the discipline and order that made his Chilean front a well-oiled fighting machine. Instead, the forces in Bolivia are barely one step above rabble. It's no wonder that the campaigns there are so chaotic. Clearly, the current advance in Bolivia is the product of luck, rather than prowess. It needs reform, massive reform.

What is needed is to reintroduce discipline and order. This comes in the form of a series of directives. Spanish is reinstituted formally as the spoken and written language of the Army. The Bolivian elements incorporated into the army are to be cashiered out to fend for themselves, all units suspended and commissions revoked. All field commissions and promotions are put on suspension, pending case by case review. In the meantime, a new command structure is to be put in place, drawn from Criollo officers reassigned from the now dormant trench war.

To ensure that the transition back to a professional army runs smoothly, Gamarra drafts up a list of 22 'trouble makers,' This shortly expands to 46, all of them Mestizo or Indigenous, and who have effectively lead much of the Bolivian campaign. These are to be arrested for insubordination, without notice or fanfare, by handpicked men sent out by Gamarra, and returned to Lima for trial. This operation is to be conducted quickly, quietly and will sweep away the old command structure in Bolivia, leaving the troops open to receiving his new officers.

Of course, nothing goes smoothly.

***

Peru/Bolivia, the Housecleaning….

Stonewall Gamarra's decisive moves are at first received with consternation but no real consensus by the officers in Bolivia. Some firebrands quietly advocate rejection or rebellion, others feel that negotiation was possible, others are committed to following orders, some feel that they have a future in Bolivia and some are simply relieved to be leaving the war.

Initially, there is no unified position, much less a rebellion.

There is considerable uncertainty and not a little resentment, but this is failing to coalesce in any meaningful way. Instead, the field officers of the Bolivian theater increasingly find themselves looking inwards to their own leadership, to the Sergeants, Captains and Colonels who were de facto generals. But among these, there is no certainty.

Rebellion does not seem like an option, considering that the flow of money, ammunition and weapons is under the control of Lima.

Nor does anyone have a clear notion of what the face of peace will look like. For many, there is simply a vague idea that it is over, that they can go home. Many soldiers and officers begin discussing their post-war lives, their returns to farms and families.

But even there, it will not be a matter of released Indigenous just going back to their villages. War has broadened experience and perspectives, has introduced machinery and weapons, new ways of thinking, literacy has spread, as have new political and economic ideas, ranging from the moderate to the radical. A group of Quechua talking about returning home also talk about all the things that they could do if they brought the truck with them.

In this context, the first few arrests of Gamarra's list take place without incident.

The fourth arrest, however, goes badly wrong. In La Paz, Gamarra's men closed in on a Mestizo Sargent named Oscar Santa Rosa. Santa Rosa, by nature a suspicious man, disputes the arrest. Gunfire broke out and Santa Rosa flees across town to the Bolivian police station, which is the headquarters of the newly re-established Bolivian army.

The Bolivian government under Penaranda never technically vanished, but it is emasculated. Gamarra by fiat restores Penaranda his army, but there is no chain of command whatsoever. The Bolivian Commander gives Santa Rosa sanctuary and refuses to acknowledge the jurisdiction of the Peruvian officers. Gamarra's agents then use their command authority to enlist local Peruvian forces on an attack.

The conflict attracts the attention of Two Gun Echeverria, in town attending a wedding. He assumes command of local forces, Gamarra's agents are captured and Gamarra's list is found.

In a state of high tension, Echeverria issues an urgent letter delivered by runners to all the names on the list. By the next day eighteen of these names are converging on La Paz. In the day following, twenty three Indigenous and Mestizo officers gather to review the list and documents, to hear Santa Rosa, to interrogate Gamarra's agents and to decide their course of action.

Debate rages through the night. By morning, decisions are made.

It is them or Gamarra, there are no other options. The Peruvian Army in Bolivia is in revolt. Jaguar Otoronco is elected Colonel and leader.

Captain Jaguar Otoronco

Baptiste Condaqui, aka Otoronco, aka Captain Jaguar, is a northern Quechua of uncertain provenance. In the normal course of things, he might have almost no impact on history whatsoever, perhaps a high ranking villager, perhaps an entrepreneur, perhaps a local bandit.

War changes everything for him. Conscripted initially for the Ecuador campaign, he receives more training than usual as General Markholtz builds up for his Second northern offensive. A capable Corporal, he's elevated to Sargent in the field, and receives an informal tutelage through the successes and failures of the campaign. Later, he is one of many Quechua sent south by Markholtz as he hoards his quality officers. He sees hard fighting with the outbreak of the Chilean war, and is elevated by field promotion to Lieutenant. Thereafter he's assigned to Bolivia, where his skill dealing with both Criollo officers and Indigenous conscripts makes him invaluable. Initially illiterate, he learns to read and speak passable Spanish.

In Bolivia, he ends up in the unique position of a Spanish commanding officer who speaks no Quechua and Quechua troops who speaks no Spanish. Although never formally designated as an NCO or Lieutenant, he receives a field commission to Captain, and becomes invaluable to the Generals of the Bolivian campaign. Repeatedly assigned to field missions, he meets and becomes the informal leader, of the informal officers who do the actual fighting. He rises rapidly, if informally, in the endlessly fluid campaigns of the Altiplano.

In many ways, his story is typical of the generation of men, Indigenous and Mestizo, who find themselves emerging in the Bolivian theater, a place where personal charisma and tactical ability counts as much or more than formal rank.

Under Ramirez, such elevations are tacitly accepted. With reorganization and the effective dissolution and absorption of the Bolivian army, the Ramirez Junta focuses on results and performance. This frustrates American advisors and more doctrinaire Peruvian officers, but it is a necessary compromise.

The Peruvian campaign is always plagued by logistical and communication breakdowns - there are a dozen different Indigenous dialects in use, in addition to Pidgins, Mestizo tongues and Spanish, and conscripts from across the country, illiteracy is endemic and training varies widely. It is simply not going to function on strict traditional lines. The only viable option is a decentralized, theater driven approach devolving authority to local commanders. It has inefficiencies, but as we've said, it is the only approach.

In this situation, men like Otoronco rise, and rise swiftly. Captain Jaguar Otoronco distinguishes himself as a tactician, and then as a strategist. He meets, forms bonds with, and learns from other officers, both formal and field commissioned.

Otoronco stands out for personal charisma and ability, but he does not stand out far. Rather, he is near the top of a cadre, a network of soldiers that extends from an inner circle of competent and freewheeling generals, all the way down to conscripted men.

This is the army that Gamarra is trying to bring to heel, and these men are all on the list that he wants arrested.

There was no consensus as to what to do about Gamarra's changes. But the discovery of the list and the fact that shots were fired at Santa Rosa galvanizes the group. The decision has been made for them.

It is about survival.

***

Bolivia Explodes in Rebellion

Once the decision is made, Otoronco and his allies move with breathtaking speed.

Even those who were able to attend the meeting are enlisted. Dissension and loyalists within the emerging new command structure are purged, sometimes violently. However there is little dissension. There is little Peruvian nationalism, and little loyalty to the formal command structure or government. Rather, loyalty and cohesion is local and personal.

The rebels begin by rapidly re-enlisting the Bolivian contingents decommissioned by Gamarra. The lines of command and authority are still fresh enough that they can be resumed. But the Bolivians are less interested in getting involved in what might be perceived as a dispute between Peruvians. Bolivian nationalism is not a force in any way, but Gamarra's regime is a long way away, and, as we've noted, loyalty and cohesion is local and personal.

In order to gain their cooperation and provide a unifying force for the rebellion, appeals are made along ethnic lines. The conflict is presented as one between Quechua and Criollo, and so the Bolivian Quechua have a duty to support their brothers.

Bolivian society has long been riven along these class and ethnic lines, with many of the Indigenous soldiers being initially unwilling conscripts. They were detached from and, if anything, even more antagonistic to the Spanish descended upper classes of their own country.

In short order, the rebellion becomes not an army rebellion, but an Indigenous rebellion. The mixed officer class of the Peruvian army in Bolivia makes it easier to enlist Aymara and particularly Mestizo in a broad based social rebellion.

So comprehensive is the ethnic call that General Villarroel finds his army dissolving out from under him, as his Indigenous and Mestizo soldiers and officers deserts in droves. Villarroel's Bolivian government, already a shadow of itself, becomes a wraith.

Otoronco and his allies consolidate with astonishing speed, but even as this is underway, Otoronco is already moving.

Taking everyone by surprise, any kind of hostility against Ibanez and the Chileans is abandoned. The mining district, hanging by a thread, is left alone, the Criollo occupation force surrounded and isolated.

Instead, Otoronco, Two Gun Echeverria, Singalong Huascar, Rumaqui Bastido race back along the supply lines, overwhelming and confiscating supply depots.

Initially, Gamarra completely underestimates the insurrection, issuing orders to nonexistent officers and dithering.

By December, 1943, armies of the rebellion are in control of three fourths of Bolivia and cross into Peru.

Somewhere in the Quechua Highlands, Andes Mountains

Otoronco paces back and forth. QuizQuiz Guererro and Two Gun Echeverria are off in a corner playing cards. Singalong Huascar is strumming a guitar. Ironhead Taruka and Manco Yanqui stood by the doorway, smoking cigars.

"This won't work," he says finally.

"I don't see why it shouldn't," Manco Yanqui replies, puffing away.

"You're not the one going out there," Otoronco says, "It's my neck in a noose."

"All our necks are in a noose," QuizQuiz Guererro mutters without looking up from his cards.

"That's why you're going out there," Yanqui says.

"There's thousands out there," Otoronco snaps. "Where are they all from?"

"All over," Yanqui replies.

"Almost time," Ironhead Taruka says, "Sun's coming over the mountain."

"Radio ready?" Yanqui asks.

"So I'm told," Echeverria says. "We'll find out."

"Bad idea," Otoronco mutters. "All we need is the fucking Criollo listening in."

"I forget, were you this much of an old woman yesterday?" Yanqui asked. "Every goddamned Criollo can listen in, and all they'll hear is some dumb Indigenous barking on the radio. But the ones who understand, they'll listen and nod, and then they'll cut the throat of the closest Criollo.

That's what we want, remember?"

"That crowd," Otoronco complains. "Most of them won't even understand."

QuizQuiz laughs out loud, one by one, the rest of them join in.

****

The Proclamation

Otoronco steps out onto the high platform overlooking the valley. It is packed. There are more people here than he's ever seen in his life. Not in the army. Not in the city. He raises his hands, slowly, silence descends on the crowd. They are waiting to hear him speak, a thought that thrills and terrifies him.

"Once," he yells as loudly as he can, in his own Quechua dialect, "we were a free people."

He waits, as shouters relay his words across the valley, their voices ringing out, rendering the words and phrases in different dialects, some familiar, some unintelligible, and even in the rolling vowels of Aymara. He waits a few beats for the shouting to die away. There is little response from the crowd.

"Before the Criollo," he yells, "we were free. We lived in peace. Our homes were warm, our bellies were full, there was enough of everything."

Again, the shouting repeating his words in different dialects. He waits it out.

"Before the Criollo," he calls, "we were one people, one nation, united. We were Tawasintuya, under the Inca, and we were mighty!"

This time, as the shouts work their way through the valley, there are rumbles of agreement. He feels a rush of relief.

"Then the Criollo come," he roars, "their boots go on our necks. They take our lands. They build their haciendas. They force us to work. Now we are poor. We are not one, we are divided. The Criollo do this."

He pauses, and before the cries die down, he shouts out again.

"The Criollo, they take our sons! They take our men! They take them away from our homes! We must run and hide! Or go away and fight! We die for Criollo! Our sons do not come home! They die far away! The Criollo comes, with taxes! They take our homes! They take our lands! They take everything! They leave nothing!"

His heart is pounding, despite himself, despite the practice, the careful phrasing they had all worked out, he is falling into it. The shouters were struggling to keep up, relaying his phrases, as they pile on top of one another. The crowds are responding, shouts of approval, shouts of anger.

He holds up his hands, gesturing for silence.

"We were mighty," he yells, "we were Inca, and the Criollo came and took it away. But we fought them then, under Tupac Amaru."

"The Criollo thought they won. But then the blood of Tupac Amaru rose up, and we fought the Criollo again. We are the Inca, and we do not forget! We do not forget who we are1"

"The Criollo now, they are worse than ever. The Criollo are greedy, they know no limits."

The crowd is screaming now, he has to shout louder than ever to make each phrase heard.

"But we never forget. The Criollo thought they purged the blood of Tupac Amaru, and the blood of the son of Tupac Amaru. But the people, they preserved the blood. From one child to the next, the line of Tupac Amaru preserved. Father to son, against the time of need. The time of rising."

There are chants beginning in the crowd. Again, they've planned for this, spreading chanters. But now it is a live thing, the chants being taken up by the throng, the words passing from person to person, pulsing. He can feel them; he can feel his chest swelling, his blood growing warm. These people, he thinks, my people. Enslaved for centuries, humiliated, degraded, shunted aside, robbed and used and abused, endlessly, generation after generation. My people, he thinks!

"This is the time of need! This is the time of rising! I am the son returned, I am Tupac Amaru!"

Suddenly, it is as if everyone gasps at once, he can feel the pause, the indrawn breath, the shock of wonder and revelation.

"I am Tupac Amaru!" he roars, and suddenly, the crowd roars back, thousands of voices all ringing as one, "Tupac Amaru! Tupac Amaru!"

"I am Tupac Amaru," he roars. "Come again! Come in time of need! Come for time of rising!"

That mysterious, cosmic moment where all voices speak as one is breaking apart. Some continue to chant, going in and out of harmony. Some simply scream. Others shout, benediction, cheers. The noise is overpowering.

"I am Tupac Amaru!" he roars. "We are one people. The Quechua, the Aymara, the Mestizo.

We are all one. Our enemy are the Criollo, the Capitalists, the Haciendas. We must come together! We must unite to defeat the Criollo who oppress us all!"

"I am Tupac Amaru," he roars. "Brother of Christ, sent now by God, as he sent my brother Jesus in his time. This is time! This is the time of deliverance, as God promised."

"I am Tupac Amaru!" he roars. "I am here to make the people one! To make the people whole!"

"I am Tupac Amaru!" he roars, believing every word. "I am here to free us from the Criollo. To lift their boot from our necks. To take our lands back. I am here to throw the Criollo into the sea they came from."

"I am Tupac Amaru. I am here to sweep away their false countries! I am the deliverance! I am freedom! I am the voice that shouts! The hand that makes! The fist that shatters! I am here to proclaim the one people united! I am here to proclaim the Inca Empire reborn!"

****

New World War – Page 245

Aftermath

Some fifteen thousand people, many of them refugees, soldiers, deserters from all over the Andes, bear witness to the proclamation of the self-proclaimed Tupac Amaru III and the reborn Inca Empire. Thousands more hear over the radio.

But beyond that, the news and proclamation spreads like wildfire up and down the Andes, from Ecuador to Bolivia and beyond. There were previous uprisings, but these were always limited, to a valley, to a province, to a locale, and eventually suppressed. The Andes themselves formed barriers to communication, the Quechua language divided into 18 dialects, many of them unintelligible.

But the Andean war has changed all that, bringing together conscripts from all over Peru and Bolivia, and sending draft dodgers fleeing from their own regions. The Quechua peoples, historically isolated from each other, are experiencing degrees and magnitudes of interaction and communication never before experienced.

And at the same time, they are experiencing degrees of disruption and dislocation beyond anything in the last century. The outside world was impinging in the form of conscription, land grabs, new taxes, technologies, population movements. The Quechua and Aymara are a stressed population, assailed by a world that previously spent generations ignoring and marginalising them.

Conditions are perfect for Tupac Amaru III's message to be heard and embraced. The speech is repeated again on radio. Runners carry it breathlessly across the Andes. The word spreads to the Oriente and Selva, to the Coast, from the docks of Guayaquil, to the mines of Bolivia. The word spread. The proclamation of the Inca Empire reborn galvanizes whole populations marginalised and oppressed for centuries.

For the former Otoronco, Manco Yanqui and their associates - the 46 names on Gamarra's list, the speech satisfactorily achieves their immediate objectives.

Dissatisfaction is enough to trigger an uprising, as it had in the Chilean naval mutiny of 1931. But without some unifying ideology or principle, dissatisfaction isn't enough. Dissension arises, indecision and argument sets in, people go off in different directions, a movement splits apart, and eventually gets crushed. The rebels are clever enough to see the risk, knew enough local folklore and history to see the way things went in the past. They realize that to survive, they need to appeal to something greater.

The speech unites and motivates the disparate Quechua and Aymara elements scattered through the Bolivian and Peruvian armies, both those in rebellion, and those nominally loyal. It provides a unifying banner around which all the fractured and isolated communities and factions could unite under and form a common identity.

The result is the rapid consolidation of a rather amorphous uprising or series of uprisings into a unified movement. More than that, it appeals to wavering military units, persuading them to throw in with the rebellion.

Elsewhere, of course, where Gamarra's control is more complete, Quechua units are rapidly disarmed or disbanded, and Quechua soldiers are summarily discharged. But these obviously punitive measures only antagonize many Indigenous and Mestizo who, for one reason or another, were loyal to the regime, or on the fence.

Gamarra's regime, at least initially, continues to control large areas of the Andes, and a large portion of the Quechua population. The official response of Gamarra's regime is that the rebellion was serious but not unmanageable. Gamarra himself believes this, he's well aware of the long history of local rebellions that have exhausted themselves and gone nowhere. This is a little larger than most, but not fundamentally different.

Gamarra has reason to be optimistic, he's become the clear favourite of the United States. He is receiving increasingly massive American aid and support. In the north, Ecuador has largely disintegrated and is in process of being absorbed into Colombia, and there is every reason to think that territorial issues there will resolve favourably. In the south, the Chileans are desperately looking for a way out, and Bolivia is a non-state. For Gamarra the war is all but won. Who cares what the Quechua think?

Peru has weathered native and military uprisings before, and they always run out of steam, fallen apart and are crushed. Gamarra sees no reason that this should be any different. Besides, this Indigenous uprising is clearly communist inspired, and the Americans hate communists.

He is wrong of course. Gamarra's racism blinds him. He doesn't appreciate just how many Indigenous, both Quechua and Aymara have been conscripted, or how effective they have become. He doesn't appreciate the degree of Quechua discontent through the Altiplano and the Andes, and to be fair, the Criollo caste have seldom cared about such things. He doesn't appreciate the degree to which the war has forced communications and connections among the Quechua and Aymara. He doesn't understand the degree of networking that has taken place among formerly disconnected peoples. He doesn't realize how the war has transformed everything.

Finally, although it is there staring him in the face, he does not appreciate the consequences of the depletion of the Criollo military caste in the wars. In Gamarra's mind, the Quechua are illiterate rabble. In Gamarra's world one good Criollo officer is worth twenty Indigenous soldiers. He believes that his army of the south has proven itself as the dominant military force of the Andes, but does not appreciate how brittle a trench war army is.

 On the eve of doom, Gamarra is tranquil. He is the product of a world where no one cares what the Quechua think.

That world is coming to an end.

****

BOOK OF ENDINGS

A Word in German - December 15, 1943

General Higinio Morinigo, President of Paraguay, looks out across the streets of Buenos Aires. He is in a good mood. Railways are being built, public works projects are proceeding, there is the hum of progress.

The partnership with Argentina has been good for Paraguay. The two countries have united for a common cause, stability and security throughout the region. Particularly security and stability in Bolivia, with a friendly government in La Paz. Both Bolivia and Paraguay have borne the scars of the Chaco War. But clearly, Bolivia has come off the worst.

Paraguay, like Argentina, supports the Valpes faction. Morinigo himself met Valpes and considers him a decent man, far better than his rivals. Actually participating in the war itself is out of the question. There is no money for it, his little nation is broke. The population will not stand for it, and in any case, the Paraguayan army is a mere eight thousand men. That is barely sufficient for home needs, no foreign adventures possible.

But Argentina has plenty of men to send to Valpes side, to fight for Bolivia. While Paraguay has no wish to fight, it has no objection to Argentines travelling through Paraguay, into the Chaco for Bolivia, or maintaining stations and camps in Paraguay to support the Bolivian mission.

The Argentines pay for the privilege, which is all to the good. And even better, the Argentines are willing customers for war materials manufactured in Paraguay. Argentines war effort provides a much needed infusion of cash into literally every aspect of the Paraguayan economy.

He looks forward to discussing new plans for the joint project. Railroad spurs to the Chaco Oil fields, and lines to the La Plata. A joint hydro-electric dam project his engineers are working on.

The door opens. President Ramirez enters, flanked by two armed guards who take up stations at the door. Morinigo only vaguely knows Ramirez, who only recently came to power in a coup. The previous President was Castillo. But luckily, at last with regard to cooperation, the two men are in accord, and the relations between the two countries are uninterrupted.

"My friend!" Ramirez pumps his hand enthusiastically. "Forgive me for being late. Affairs of state."

"I understand," Morinigo replies.

They exchange pleasantries finally sitting together at the table to discuss their matters.

"I know that we have an Agenda," Ramirez bubbles. "Railway lines, hydro-electric dams, military procurement. Important matters. And I'm sure you are eager to be briefed on our affairs in Bolivia. But I must share with you a brilliant proposal. We call it the Grand Confederation, a working arrangement between Argentina and Paraguay. And if all goes well, we hope that Bolivia and Uruguay join our Confederation. From there, who knows?"

Ramirez hands over a sheaf of papers, and smiling Morinigo takes them.

But as he reads through them, Morinigo's smile fades away in steady increments. The Grand Confederation is a customs union between Argentina and Paraguay, itself entirely unobjectionable.

But there is more. An integration of the two countries militaries, with Argentina in command. A currency union. A financial union. Integrations of government functions, a steady subordination of Paraguayan independence, and unification under Argentine control. The proposal relentlessly erases every line between the two countries, except only that Paraguayans would retain a national character, albeit as second class citizens, even within their own country.

"This will be the end of Paraguay," Morinigo speaks, his voice quivering with outrage.

"Nonsense," Ramirez says. "Paraguay will continue to exist... On maps at least. And there will continue to be a President of Paraguay, a few other posts. It's not so bad."

"Not so bad?" Morinigo snaps. "It's infamous! I'm sorry, but I must refuse!"

"General Morinigo," President Ramirez says, "this is not a proposal, it is the plan. Your consent is not required."

"Nevertheless," Morinigo replies. "It will not happen. I will not allow it."

"It's already done," Ramirez says. "It's been done for a while. We have twenty thousand men stationed in Paraguay? What's the entire Paraguayan army? Six thousand? What weapons does your army have? We could arrest the lot of them within a week. We already have the run of the place, every town, every city. There can be no resistance."

"The world will not allow it!" Morinigo protests.

"The world? Brazil? They won't be happy, but they'll live with it. We'll concede Uruguay if we have to. But they won't go to war. I think everyone's seen what a mess a war is."

Ramirez made a dismissive motion with his palm.

"And the Americans? They don't care at all."

"I won't sign my country away," Morinigo says stubbornly.

"I'm sorry to hear you say that," Ramirez opens a folder and took out a document. "But I see you already have."

"Forgery!"

"Of course," Ramirez replies calmly. "But duly witnessed as genuine, and therefore a legal and binding document."

He shuffles some papers.

New World War – Page 251

"And let's see... Your resignation, also signed. Your appointment of your successor. And a charming handwritten letter, in which you admit to serious ill health, long concealed, but which has proceeded to the point you can no longer do your duties. You retire to medical convalescence... That one was quite tricky."

"My resignation?" Morinigo breathes, "This is infamous. Let me see that!"

Ramirez passes it over. Angrily, Morinigo tears it up.

"I have copies," Ramirez says calmly.

"You'll never get away with this," Morinigo swears.

Ramirez lifts up a hand. A servant walks to the door and opens it. A pinch faced man walks in, in military dress uniform.

"Major Alfredo Stroessner," Ramirez says. "Actually, General now. Congratulations on your promotion, and your elevation to the Presidency."

"Thank you, Mister President. I look forward to our two great countries working together."

Morinigo is speechless. Finally, he sputters one word.

"Traitor."

Stroessner and Ramirez looks at him with barely concealed amusement.

"My family is German," Stroessner says. "There is a German word for this sort of occasion: Anschluss."

"General Stroessner," Ramirez explains, "has witnessed all your signatures, and can swear to their authenticity before a court of law, should it be necessary. And he pledges his cooperation and commitment to our new Commonwealth."

Ramirez stands.

"I am sorry to say, General Morinigo, but your work is done. Paraguay thanks you, Argentina thanks you. And now these gentlemen will take you someplace where you can be comfortable."

"People will ask questions," Morinigo says. "Some will not believe. Some will oppose you."

"Of course," Ramirez replies. "But it will take time. At first, no one will be quite sure what's going on. They'll wait for a while, before asking questions. The first questions will be quite soft. And in the meantime, General Stroessner will be in place, quietly making certain people disappear, discreetly retiring or reassigning officers, eliminating positions and people. Like a frog in a pan of water set on a stove to boil... by the time anyone reaches the point of acting, it will be too late."

Morinigo finds he has nothing left to say. The soldiers waiting to take him away are vicious looking toughs.

"Now," Ramirez says, "if you will excuse us...."

Morinigo is marched from his room. Stroessner slides easily into his place.

"Conquest," Ramirez muses, "at the stroke of a pen, and not a drop of blood spilled. Well, probably not much blood comparatively. If only the rest of the Bolivian adventure were so easy."

Peru and Gamarra

General Gamarra is often criticized as absolutely the wrong man for the wrong time, inflexible, doctrinaire, racist incompetent. The man who is stiff when he needs to be flexible, the man who is authoritarian when he needs to compromise.

This may be unfair. Better than anyone else in the high command, Gamarra recognizes that the Bolivian theatre is largely out of control. On taking power, he takes decisive, but not reckless action to try and bring it to heel. It's possible that he might succeed.

Of course, it's arguable that the situation is already past the point of no return. It is profoundly unlikely that he is going to be able to successfully arrest and repatriate all 46 named men from Bolivia. At some point, things are likely to fall apart and matters break. But the circumstances under which the arrests fall apart and the break are a matter of luck.

It could have gone any number of ways.

Gamarra might have snuffed potential rebellion before it ever emerges. Instead, his actions trigger it. It ends up going as badly as it possibly can.

Gamarra can be faulted for not reacting swiftly initially to the rebellion. But even Gamarra's harshest critics acknowledge the breathtaking decisiveness and speed with which the rebels organize and move.

His regime's rapid collapse in the face of the rebel's Peruvian campaign is blamed on Gamarra. But a number of factors are at work.

One is that, genuinely, Gamarra is an inflexible and doctrinaire commander. Well suited to trench warfare on the front, having fully adjusted himself to such warfare, he simply isn't suited to an open field theatre.

Another is simply bad luck - Gamarra has begun the process of reassigning and reorganizing the army, reassigning large parts of the officer corps from the trench front. The result is that the rebellion's invasion hits in the middle of the reorganization. Logistical and command breakdowns are everywhere.

The final truth is that the rebels really are that good - Tupac Amaru III, or Captain Jaguar, Singalong Huascar, Nicola Bandido, Two Gun Echeverria, Perdita Diabla, Cowboy Cachi, Mama Occla, QuizQuiz Guererro, Manco Yanqui - beyond the colourful theatricality, the Bolivian campaign produces not one, but a handful of brilliant campaigners, tacticians and strategists, men and women from all over the Andes who know each other and work well together, men and women who are flexible, adaptable and used to seizing opportunities, and beneath them are a competent battle hardened army of exceptional motivation.

There is nothing left in Peru to match them.

There is nothing left in Latin America to match them.

The Rain Forest War, The Rubber Battle - January 1943 to January 1944

The steady escalation of violence that marks the second half of 1942 in Brazil slowly subsides through the first months of 1943.

This is in contrast to the Peruvian Selva, where the government largely gives up on controlling the rain forests. By this time, the Indigenous insurgency is dominant there. The Peruvian government restricts itself to a few fortified outposts, and deals with the natives on a strict cash and carry basis, employing bribes to keep peace on the few operations it carries out, and otherwise leaving the natives strictly alone.

For Brazil, one reason for the decline in violence is simple attrition and resource limitations. There are plenty of Indigenous, but Blandon has only a limited supply of rifles for them, and only so many bullets to go around. Blandon's Indigenous uprising has no foreign patron and no cash reserves. There are small trickles of weapons; from smuggling, from the Quechua lands, from Brazilian sympathizers in leftist and Marxist circles, and from raids and captures. But mainly, it becomes increasingly important to hoard scarce ammunition.

Another reason for the decline in violence is a remarkably Brazilian solution. Parties simply agree to get along. Plantation owners and work camps discover that the simplest way to avoid trouble is to pay bribes and treat the locals respectfully. The army found that avoiding massacres is the best way to avoid revenge attacks. The army and Indigenous learn to respect each other's territories and timetables. Bribes, contributions, local arrangements, informal truces and treaties, evolve to keep things peaceful. Transgressions on each side are policed. In some cases groups are so committed to these arrangements that directions for operations or attacks from the Capital are outright refused, or more often, avoided. Some of the expeditions to suppress the Indigenous exist only on paper.

Informally, the operations budget for the Amazonian military command includes hidden line items for bribes at every level.

Yet another reason is the maturing Brazilian military commitment. By January/February 1943, the troop commitment was 18,000, with (unreliable) local militias potentially contributing another 6,000. This is something like one soldier for every three or four rubber workers. Or to put it another way, somewhere between four and ten times Blandon's estimated number of effectives. The sheer size of the military commitment acts as a suppressant.

Geographical scale is an additional inhibitor. The Amazonian region is the size of Western Europe, but with only a few thousands of combatants. It is a challenge to even find each other.

Finally, air power comes into play - 1943 saw the establishment of a series of military airstrips and supply stations that allow Brazil to regularly patrol the Amazonas from the air, and where necessary, to attack. Most of the aircraft are small scouts, including many float planes. But there are real military aircraft on call, bombers and fighters equipped for strafing. Blandon has no full defense to this, he has relatively few anti-aircraft pieces and little ammunition for them and these pieces are not effective against state of the art aircraft. Attacks on airstrips fail. Faced with his enemies' insurmountable advantage, his only options are camouflage, stealth, night travel and concealment.

Blandon keeps up a steady stream of manifestos and critiques, some of which find circulation. The plight of the Indigenous becomes a subject for passionate discussion on the Brazilian left.

This does not mean that violence abates completely. There are large numbers of small scale conflicts throughout the region, and chains of violent reprisal. There are large scale attacks on camps, raids on armouries and massacres. The Matilde and her sister patrol boats are involved in numerous altercations, although often these seem more piracy than combat.

There are major operations. On January 30, 1943, there is a massive raid on the town of Cruzeiro do Sul Acre, followed by an assault on the town of Eirunepé on February 4, 1943. Both towns are close to the border, and both informally declare neutrality. The purpose of these actions seems to be to keep the border open for passage for the Indigenous insurgency.

In April 2, there is a major attack on the town of Itacoatiara. Half the town is burned. This appears to have been triggered by a local massacre of Indigenous and abusive practices by some of the work camps and plantations. On this occasion large numbers of migrants join forces with the Indigenous to assault the power structure.

There are a handful of pitched battles between the Army and the Insurgency during this time. The most notable are the Battles of Putumayo of February 22, 1943, where Brazilian gunboats are ambushed and clash full on with the Matilde and her Sisters, which ends with a rout for government forces.

This is followed by the Japura Armoury Battle, of March 4, 1943, the Battle of Japura, March 28, and the Battle of Madeira, May 9, in which the Sisters and several other craft are sunk and the town of Manaus was protected, but from which the Matilde escapes unscathed. It is at Madeira that the air force comes into heavy play for the first time. Madeira, with one exception is the last large scale engagement by the insurgents. Thereafter, their river boats and forces are dispersed.

July 2, 1943, Brazilian aircraft spot the Matilde on the Purus River. Local detachments mobilize, and a number of aircraft patrol the area. On July 4, 1943, the Matilde is finally flushed from hiding and then destroyed by aerial bombardment. Enrique Blandon's death is announced.

This turns out to be incorrect as Blandon issues a flurry of letters and manifestos. If anything, he ups the ante, formally proclaiming the 'Free Confederation of the Amazona' and invites both Indigenous and Migrants to join. He even calls for an army uprising. But the reality is that he is coming to the end of his rope.

On August 17, 1943, there is an abortive attempt to take over the town of Manaus, and Blandon issues an address from the captured radio station. But this is the last major operation of the insurgency. The army recaptures the town almost immediately, and the body of a white insurgent is put on display to establish that Blandon is finally, once and for all, dead.

The insurgency goes quiet thereafter for the month of September with no incidents of any kind reported.

October, new manifestos from Blandon begin to appear. Renewed army efforts trigger firefights with the natives in October, tapering off in November. There are no activities after that.

By January, 1944, the Vargas regime pronounces the insurgency over, and takes the position that Enrique Blandon is finally dead, having passed away from accumulated injuries and malaria.

Over 50,000 die in the Amazonas region, of war and insurgency, exhaustion, overwork, brutal conditions and rain forest diseases.

This does not include the deaths suffered by the Indigenous population, which in some areas verge on genocide. In addition to deaths, there are massive disruptions, refugee movements, dislocations and disease outbreaks among the Indigenous population.

The reality is that there was never a chance. Blandon's Brazilian uprising is doomed from the minute it was conceived, a fact that he acknowledges in some of his own writings. The entire campaign is a mad, romantic futile gesture that wrought harm on the very people he tried to save.

The lucrative Rubber Battle continues past the insurgency into the remaining span of World War II and for a few months thereafter, until traditional sources of rubber come back on line.

The Brazilian rubber boom is over as quickly as it began, the tens of thousands of workers forcibly relocated, are abandoned. As few as 6,000, less than a tenth of those who go out ever manage to return home, and those do so at their own expense.

For Vargas, however, the 'Rubber Battle' is an unmitigated success, both economically for Brazil as a whole, and temporarily for the region. And it has the further effect of putting a final and definitive conclusion to the spillover of the jungle war between Ecuador and Peru into Brazilian territory.

Staying out of the Andean Wars is good for Brazil.

New World War – Page 259

World War II turns out to be good for Brazil, all in all, Brazil procures approximately 335 million dollars in lend lease, loans, grants, materials and economic development, substantially exceeding all the monies promised or provided to all of the Andean nations together, and more than five times the funds provided to Peru.

***

The Fall of Peru

By January/February, 1944, the government in Lima loses complete control of the Highlands and is facing army revolts across the country. To defuse these revolts, tens of thousands of Indigenous conscripts are summarily disarmed and discharged. In some cases massacres of unarmed men took place. If anything, this makes things worse. Singalong Huascar, Rumaqui Bastido and Manco Yanqui inflict a series of defeats on Gamarra's forces, pushing the Lima government on the defensive.

An alarmed American government increases the flow of money and war materials to Peruvian ports. American planes are deployed to bomb the rebels. Moves commence to send an American relief expedition to Peru. In the meantime, the Americans force Gamarra to accept a coalition government with the Junta he replaced and negotiate a ceasefire with Chile's Ibanez on generous terms.

None of this helps. On March 4, 1944, Manco Yanqui wins the Battle of Three Dogs, and Singalong Huascar reaches the Pacific, splitting Lima from the last functioning loyalist battle group, the 'Army of the Trenches.'

Three days later on March 7, 1944, the Naval base at Callao surrenders. The Captains of the cruiser Almirante Grau and the destroyer Garcia mutiny, refusing to accept the surrender. Instead, they put to sea, exchanging fire with Revolutionary forces on the shore. Peru's final destroyer, Palacio, undergoing repairs, is scuttled. The Almirante Grau and Garcia head for Chile, requesting Asylum.

On March 10, 1944, Tupac Amaru III marches into Lima. Over the next few days, he is joined by the other senior generals. On March 11, 1944, the heads of Ramirez, Gamarra and the rest of the former government are mounted on pikes at the entrance to the city.

***

The New Regime

After years of war, the sudden collapse of the Gamarra regime, and the onset of the Peruvian revolution is breathtaking.

As with all revolutions, the Inca resurgence is the result of long simmering tensions, bad luck, and dramatic mistakes. On the surface, the Gamarra Regime appears unassailable. Its enemies are on the verge of collapse, it is winning an almost complete victory in the Bolivian Theatre, its armies are the largest in the region and its patron, the United States, is the most powerful nation on Earth.

But beneath that facade, Peru is a tissue of rotten fabric, waiting to be torn away.

Historically, Peru is among the most regressive of Latin societies. A small Criollo class of Spanish descendants ruled a mestizo class of half breeds, while a large mass of Indigenous are either ignored or dominated in the interior. Class divisions are strict to the point of repression. These often result in outbursts and outbreaks of violence, banditry, local rebellions.

But none of these ever amount to anything, because of the divided geography and natural barriers in the country. Decentralized by god and nature, social conflicts or rebellions have little opportunity to spread and tend to die out locally. The central government rules just enough to keep everything in check, but Peru is still one of the most decentralized states in Latin America.

This allows the Criollo class to maintain its domination of Peru. But this results in a handicap. A diffuse and decentralized state, Peru always performs poorly in its wars, particularly the War of the Confederation and the War of the Pacific. The decentralization that keeps rebellions and social tensions from catching fire also make it difficult to fight a war.

Without the Andean war, that might have continued indefinitely, with social change and progress coming slowly to Peru. But that is an intangible and uncertain future. The Andean Wars did occur, and with it came irrevocable changes to every part and stratum of Peruvian society.

To begin with, as we've noted, the war devastates the Criollo officer class. The runaway casualties of the Ecuadoran and Chilean campaigns leave the traditional officer class, particularly the field officers and non-commissions, almost completely hollowed out.

Enlistment becomes recruitment, which becomes forced recruitment and then conscription. Field officers die in droves, or struggle for promotions or assignments to safe billets or in the High Command. Gaping holes appeared throughout the command structure, which are filled by Mestizo.

But the Mestizo appreciate neither being thrown into the field of fire, nor the class barriers that keep them from promotion or assignments to safe billets. Class tensions in the army are high and escalating. Even during the Ecuadoran phases of the war, discipline and insubordination rates are extraordinary. General Markholtz, for instance, writes casually of the weekly whippings list.

Massive conscription of Mestizo, then of Quechua, and then of their Bolivian counterparts, changes the character of the army, adding an endless new array of challenges and problems. Problems that the traditional officer class, as attenuated as it is, are simply incompetent to deal with.

Social cracks appeared everywhere. The Criollo class has always ruled by having a greater grasp or sense of class consciousness than any other constituency. But the Criollo class itself is decentralized and centrifugal. The demands of the war, and centralization, alienate many Criollo, particularly those outside of Lima. Although many benefit, particularly in Lima, from centralization and the war economy, many others suffer. Criollo society is left in a state of perpetual conflict and tension.

During the period of 'La Tranquillity' this dissension and conflict is smoothed over with what is essentially runaway corruption and graft. When Gamarra takes over, he brought a sense of unity through personal integrity and brutal ruthlessness. But the Criollo consensus is on the verge of shattering, there is no longer any coherent faith in the nation.

In turn, the desperate efforts of the Criollo to maintain control of their fracturing economy and society has the dual effect of raising Mestizo aspirations, while forcibly excluding them from opportunity. The elitist Criollo of Lima have no room for Mestizo except in the most subordinate positions; all their efforts are devoted to trying to enlist the decentralized regional Criollo of the provinces to fill out the ranks and help fight the war.

But these provincial Criollo in many areas are in economic and social trouble, and cope with this by 'kicking downwards', pushing back on the Mestizo. Preoccupied with their internal conflicts, the Mestizo are exclude and assigned the losers place.

As a result, the Mestizo class, the traditional supporters and underclass of the Criollo - the workers, the drones, the entrepreneurial classes, are completely alienated. Only a lack of class consciousness and regional diffusion prevents them from becoming a dangerous force.

The most traumatic effects are on the Indigenous themselves, particularly the Quechua. The Quechua up to the war are left largely alone, were isolated by mountain ranges and valleys, divided into 19 dialects unintelligible to each other, by illiteracy, local priests and landowners. All they want is to continue their traditional lives without interference from the government. Geographical barriers, communications issues, lack of organization and technology mean that rebellions remain local and ineffective.

But now change comes to the Quechua whether they like it or not. Massive draconian conscription depopulate whole villages, or sent thousands fleeing. Refugees from Bolivia move up and through. Runaway soldiers, exiles, refugees moved from valley to valley. The isolation of the Quechua groups is breaking down and they are increasingly conscious of their nation, of people like themselves, and of a world beyond. Unintelligible dialects are bridged with pidgin.

The outside world puts immense economic pressure on the Quechua as well. Forced labour became endemic. Taxes are imposed, sometimes by confiscations of crops, or by confiscations of land. Everywhere, the Quechua are assailed by a world that will not leave them alone, by a thousand small crises that never quite go away.

Old solutions, the nostrums of priests or the arrangements or negotiations with landowners become ineffective as the problems grow. Socialist and populist ideas filter in from outside, sometimes disseminated by leftists exiled to the interior, sometimes by soldiers stationed there, at other times by bandits, draft evaders or runaway soldiers.

The Quechua struggle with this influx of new ideas. Some describe this as the advent of socialism or socialist principles, but in truth, the Quechua are absorbing and struggling with a barrage of new concepts and ideas on every level, often distorted or fragmentary.

And as they do this, they attempt to incorporate and understand these ideas in terms of their own society, and do develop or remember their own philosophies. Prophecies and call backs to the old days of the Inca are common, and any political discussion or conversation of the Elders cannot help but at least allude to the prior Inca states and rebellions.

The truth was that before Tupac Amaru III ever begin his triumphal procession through the highlands; almost the entire of the Quechua can be characterized as being in a state of low level, diffuse, disorganized revolt.

When Gamarra takes power, he inherits literally thousands of letters from priests, landowners, police, local commanders complaining about the situation in their corner of the highlands. In most cases, these letters reassure Gamarra that the situation was in control, but hinted darkly at the future.

The truth is that the war has broken Peruvian society irrevocably, and there is no going back. Even without the Revolution massive changes would have been coming.

✳✳✳

American Policy in the face of the Inca Revolution

As is usual in the Andean War, American foreign policy with regard to the Inca Revolution is a day late and a dollar short. The consistent goal of American policy in the region from the start is stability, protection and preservation of American interests, and the exclusion of foreign interests, particularly those of the Axis. These turn out to be elusive. Time and again, the United States forms a position, and time and again, events outrun America.

The crucial problem with American foreign policy in the region is that they consistently see it as a matter of externalities - British influence, Nazi influence, American needs. They neither see nor understand the intrinsic nature of the warring parties or the indigenous roots of the conflict. In America's eyes, all that is needed was to get rid of the Nazi elements and then restore stability.

At the time of the Revolution, the Roosevelt government is able to implement a relatively successful policy, of, if not enduring armistice, then at least intermittent ceasefires and reduced levels of hostility. More importantly, American obtains clear guarantees from all parties protecting the property and investments of Americans, and American vital interests in resources, particularly copper and tin.

The overall policy goal is resolution of Regional conflicts through Peruvian hegemony in the Andes (as America's designated proxy), which will include the resolution of wars and territorial disputes, peacefully, or violently, in Peruvian favour. Peru, despite misgivings, seems the only logical choice. Ecuador simply has neither the population nor position nor resources to be a significant client. If every other matter is equal and there are no foreign influences at all, the US will favour Peru against Ecuador. It is a simple matter of relative scale and significance of investments.

Bolivia, of course, is by this time a non-state and battleground. Only Chile seems to be an alternate choice, but it is tainted by German influence since the Graf Spee incident.

The biggest concern is the spectre of Axis involvement in Ecuador, Chile, Bolivia and Argentina, and while each country in its own way attempts to distance itself from Nazi Germany, the taint remains.

To this end, the United States pursues a policy of overt neutrality and diplomacy, while deploying massive military and civilian aid to Peru. This, on its surface, is quietly effective, as Peru apparently grow stronger even as its rivals stagnate.

The Inca revolution, of course, comes as a complete shock and invalidates all of these plans. Seeing the Inca Revolution in Peru as the end of the war, Ecuadorans celebrate in the streets of Quito and Guayaquil. Velasco makes a premature announcement of peace and promises the imminent drawdown of the military and return to peacetime. He is embarrassed when Bonifaz publicly repudiates him. But the mood of Ecuador is reflected in Velasco.

Chileans publicly celebrates as well. Despite this, in Chile, Ibanez sees both disaster and opportunity, both for Chile and Bolivia. Villarroel, hanging on by a thread in Bolivia is less optimistic. The Argentines, badly battered in Bolivia, pause to rethink their strategy.

It seems that the Andes were now up for grabs again. Whoever can credibly replace the Peruvian regime as strongman and representative of American interests will literally inherit the region, or at least be beneficiary of new divisions.

Within days of the revolution, every state in Latin America, save Venezuela, is sending diplomatic missions to Washington to plead their respective cases and interests.

These include Argentina and the Valpes Bolivian faction, seeking either support for an Argentine hegemony, or dominance in Paraguay and Bolivia, or at least the assurance of an independent Bolivia outside of Chilean or Peruvian orbits.

Villarroel pleads his own case as an independent ruler of Bolivia, despite his patron.

New World War – Page 267

Colombia seeks recognition of its interests in Ecuador.

Ecuador, plaintively seeks a window of independence, and the recognition of the territories it fought for.

Chile seeks at a minimum a reinstatement of the outcome of the War of the Pacific, including possession of Tacna and Arica. But in his more enthusiastic moments, Ibanez sees in the communist Indigenous revolution the prospect territorial gains against both Bolivia and Peru and perhaps even Argentina, dominance in Bolivia, and ascendance as the regional power over Peru and Argentina.

This is a major shift, as only weeks before, private cabinet minutes in Chile involved what sort of negotiated peace is available, and whether Chile will be forced to cede territory to Peru, and how it might preserve some sliver of interests in Bolivia.

The Roosevelt government is treated to the ironic sight of a flurry of Nazi regimes rushing to Washington to plead their cases.

The most significant mission to Washington is from the newly minted Inca Empire.

The United States has already invested heavily in Peru; that is hard to simply walk away from. A force of 2,000 men were stationed as trainers and advisors in Lima under the Gamarra regime. As many as 10,000 American personnel were spread through Peru, in positions ranging from Engineers and Planners, to equipment operators, specialists, trainers, pilots, and so forth. The Roosevelt administration finds that these were all now potential hostages, vulnerable behind enemy lines.

The band of Cowboys and Caballeros who are now the new Inca Empire really have no idea of what the United States is, and only the vaguest idea of where it lies. Somewhere to the north, they understand. As a whole, they come from isolated, poorly educated regions. Nevertheless, they clearly understand that the American connection is an essential pipeline of supplies and arms. Manco Yanqui, who has gotten to know American pilots and quartermasters, has even named himself after the Americans.

But if the Revolutionary leadership is ignorant and ill informed, the levels below have enough educated men, and enough diversity of opinion and insight, that the newly minted government begins to have some notion of the importance of the United States. As a result, Tupac Amaru III, together with his war council, sends Manco Yanqui, Singalong Huascar, Sargent Santa Rosa and a contingent of trusted men known for their ability to read and write.

Their objective is to persuade a massively sceptical American government that all is business as usual, which calls for overlooking a forest of severed heads on pikes of former government officials, a great deal of irredentist native populism and leftist talk, and the alleged prospect of imminent pogroms of the now deposed Criollo caste. It is an uphill battle.

Manco Yanqui initially buys goodwill by agreeing without conditions to the repatriation of all American personnel, and guaranteeing their safety. There are further guarantees of safety for all American investments. Leftist language in Peru is toned down significantly in Washington. Perhaps the most positive impression that the Roosevelt administration takes is that the new ruling cabal are not communists, or even socialists, but bumpkins.

One lesson that the Inca delegation takes to heart is the sheer size and wealth of the United States. Halfway through, Manco Yanqui returns to Peru to impress upon Tupac Amaru III and their associates of the need for circumspection in dealing with America.

For their part, the Americans have other matters on their plate. The Asian Theatre, the second priority after Europe, is running hot. The Japanese Empire pushes into Burma and threatens the Bengali region. At sea the Allies are fighting the Japanese across the Pacific, regaining Island groups.

The main priority, consuming almost all the attention of the Roosevelt Administration, is in Europe. There, the Western Allies are fighting their way up the Italian peninsula, the Russians are driving the Germans back across the eastern front and preparations are under way for D-Day, the allied invasions of Normandy on June 6, 1944.

New World War – Page 269

Against these matters, the latest peccadillo of the Latin American Soap Opera warrants very little attention. At some point, that matter will have to be sorted out. But for now, matters were sufficiently muddy that the United States dithers. No clear decisions are forthcoming.

The Americans are prepared to let things drift a little longer.

***

A New Player on the Board

For Chile, in the aftermath of the Inca Revolution, everything is suddenly up for grabs.

The big question is what the new Inca Empire will do? Are they tired of war? Will they accept peace? On what terms? Will they demand Tacna? Arica? More? The revolution originates in Bolivia, and the Inca regime sits on a substantial portion of Bolivian soil. It is unlikely that they will simply let it go. But a fledgling regime is often weak. Are there opportunities for Chile?

Will the Inca accept the Chileans preserving a Bolivian puppet state made of the remnants the Revolution has not yet conquered? Is a direct partition of Bolivia between the two nations possible? Exactly how dangerous is the revolutionary regime? Ideologically, it is terrifying - an assembly of Indigenous and communists, all bent on murdering true white men and women in their beds. That isn't a good thing at all. It will be best for everyone; including all those bastard Peruvian Criollo yet unmurdered if that revolution is quashed quickly and brutally.

Is that possible? On the face, it seems so. It is only a portion of the Peruvian Army they are facing now, not the whole. The Chilean/Peruvian front is a shambles, and Ibanez foresees major breakthroughs. The Quechua are clearly reverting to impulses, descending to savagery. It could be done.

And what are the advantages to Chile quashing the revolution - clearly Peru would be ended as a threat once and for all. There would certainly be territorial acquisitions from Peru and Bolivia. Chile would inherit pre-eminence in Bolivia. If they are clear winners, then the dithering Americans will clearly find it in their interests to adopt Chile as their client.

These are the debates going on in Ibanez cabinet, and within Ibanez own mind. Decisions are forming quickly.

***

New World War – Page 271

The Inca Resurgent

Tupac Amaru III is the new Inca Emperor, the saviour reborn and revealed, and very little short of a god for the Quechua nations; but another reality is that he was more the head of a coalition of very capable leaders and warriors who emerge in the Bolivian theatre.

In a sense, he conducts as the head of a Politburo or the Chairman of a Board of Directors, or the Leader of a Cabinet. Willing to make decisions unilaterally, complexity intimidates him, and he prefers to have matters debated or discussed from different angles until a consensus, or at least a clearer picture emerges. In turn, the politburo members have their own trusted associates, friends and advisors; they are willing to listen as much as talk, particularly if they need ideas. Socialists, intellectuals and journalists find, if they are careful, that they can whisper in the ears of power. Relying upon Quechua traditionalism, a certain conservatism and decentralization is at work, which balances out the infusion of socialist ideas from exiled leftists.

In a sense, they were rebels without a cause. There is no clear ideology underpinning the revolution. Initially, it was a simple matter of survival and personal conflict. The appeal to Quechua nationalism was a matter of political calculation.

Beyond that, they aren't really sure what they stood for. They are against the Criollo bastards who sit safe and fat while other people bleed and die. They are for democracy, because it sounds good. They imbibe a variety of leftist, socialist and populist notions that seem to float around.

But they aren't strongly wedded to anything. Mostly, they are pragmatic and flexible in their approach. They want to reform society, to change it, to turn it inside out, but mostly, they are feeling their way.

It would be nice to burn all the Haciendas for instance, drive all the Criollo into the sea. And there are some efforts here and there in that direction. But in some places, the lords of the Haciendas are well liked by the local Quechua or Mestizo, so you leave those alone. The whole approach to pogroms tends to be decentralized, and all too often, too many people have too many friends or supporters, or the situation is more complicated over here. So while driving the Criollo back to Spain sounds good, the local ones are often tolerable and the feeling is that they should be left alone, that happens quite a lot. There are bloodbaths here and there, and some fires here and there.

But a national policy to purge the Criollo fails to gel, and the further things go the more complicated it gets. The old order is shattered, and Peru and Bolivia are undergoing irrevocable transformations, but the pathway is far from clear.

But if there is one thing that Tupac Amaru III and his confederates have in common, one decision that is clear for him to make, and one issue that all his confederates and advisors have in common: It was that they hate those Criollo bastards who were in charge, including the ones back home in Lima, but especially those bastards from Santiago and Valparaiso that they are still fighting. Prosecuting the war is a welcome diversion from thorny internal questions.

For the new Inca, the revolution is truly against the Spanish Order. And it seems that the perfect embodiment of that Spanish Order is Chile. The Revolution demands the whole of Bolivia, and the expulsion of Argentine and Colombian meddlers. The revolution demands the defeat of the Criollo of Chile and Ecuador.

****

Colombia, on the Sidelines of the War

Colombia, sitting astride both Pacific and the Caribbean spends most of the war sitting on the sidelines of the Andean conflict. Ironic, given that the roots of the Andean conflict can be traced all the way back to the Colombia-Peru War of 1933.

Although in practical terms, the war results in minor adjustments of borders in the Amazonas region; it amounts to a national humiliation for Peru. For Colombia, however, the outcome of the war means relatively little. Over, almost before it truly starts, there isn't the time or the inclination to drive militarization. The war ends satisfactorily; Colombia is left without unresolved issues.

With no territorial disputes or ongoing grievances the Colombian army withers, reaching a low of 16,000 men in 1937, working with mostly obsolete equipment. To this, we add another 5,000 police officers and a token navy of 2,000 men. Although Colombia theoretically has universal conscription, there is neither the budget nor the infrastructure for this.

This is astonishingly tiny, even for a Latin American nation of some nine to ten million people. The reason for this stretches far back into Colombia's history, into its revolutionary period and the formation and fall of Gran Colombia.

The struggle for independence is led by Simon Bolivar in Colombia, and Francisco Santander in Venezuela. Bolivar, of course, got to be the famous one. But these two men are crucial to the formation of the succeeding state. They also have utterly contrary political philosophies.

Bolivar is an autocratic centralist, he believes in a strong state, a limited franchise composed largely of the landowners and elite, and a close alliance with the church. Bolivar's followers and political movement evolve into the Conservatives.

Santander seeks a decentralized, relatively weak state, with limitations on the Catholic Church and a broad based franchise.

His followers become the Liberals. Thus begins the Liberal/Conservative split, and the broad division between Latin America's elites that we see throughout Latin America.

In practical terms, mostly it breaks down to a division between land based, traditional, elites - the haciendas, the Latifundista, the landowners, etc. for the Conservatives; and urban, trade based elites which usually include the marginal middle class, for the Liberals.

This conflict between Centralism and Centrifugalism, between Conservatives and Liberals, is nowhere more intense than at the heart of the revolution, in northern South America.

Peru clings to Spain for a while; Argentina and Chile are peripheral territories that have their own local revolutions.

But Gran Colombia, that's the big rock and roll, where the thunder meets the mountain. It's the richest of the Spanish colonies, accessible from the Caribbean, part of the heartlands of the Spanish new world. This is where Spain really fights to hold on, and where the revolutionaries fight hardest to break free.

The end result is the defeat of the Spanish. But following victory there is no real consensus among the revolutionaries, or between Bolivar and Santander, as to what kind of country they are going to have. Initially, Bolivar holds sway, forming Gran Colombia out of Venezuela, Colombia, Panama and Ecuador. Bolivar never learns the art of compromise, more comfortable as a general than as a politician, his autocracy causes his enemies to coalesce against him. Santander's followers pull Venezuela out of Gran Colombia, and Ecuador drifts off on its own. Only little Panama is left to Colombia. At least until Teddy Roosevelt comes along.

Bolivar drifts into obscurity, writing grandiose constitutions for imaginary Latin American super-states and lifetime presidencies. No one takes him seriously. He's much better appreciated once he's dead.

The political split between Liberals and Conservatives is preserved in each of the fractured nations, like flies in broken amber. Nowhere is this split more intense, nowhere is the bitterness more concentrated, than in the heartland of the revolution, the birthplace of the movements: Colombia.

Through the 19th century, the two factions struggle back and forth, dominating politics for roughly equal periods, with occasional interludes of military rule. This culminates between 1899 and 1902 with the Thousand Day War, a civil conflict based on party lines, with each rival party raising armies, enlisting child soldiers, and committing atrocitie. It kills a hundred thousand people. It is during this period that the United States breaks Panama off in order to build its canal.

Because Colombian society is so badly divided, the consensus is to maintain a small military force. The balance is complex, a powerful military is a game changer, giving clear advantage to one side or the other, neither side really wants to risk its enemy accessing that kind of power. Or the kind of bloodletting that a divided military could get up to in a civil war.

A military is expensive, most of the fluid capital or tax revenue to fund a military would come from the liberals, who are reluctant, to fund an institution whose membership would tend to be drawn from the conservative landholder class. As with every other aspect of Colombian society, the military is a fulcrum in a tug of war between the two parties.

The relative balances between Liberals and Conservatives evolves over time. As the economy developed, as different areas of the economy wax and wane, one side or the other grows or weakens. Banana and tobacco plantations in the 19th century encourage the ambitions of the large landholders and conservatives.

Coffee, grown by small landholders, represents a shift towards the Liberals. It climbs from 8 percent of the Colombian economy in the 1870s to nearly 75 percent in the 1920s. Coffee proves to be an incredibly lucrative cash crop, and through the 1920s, foreign capital floods into Colombia. In the 1930s, coffee turns out to be a depression proof' commodity, demand and prices remain steady. While much of Latin America, particularly Ecuador, is devastated by the Depression, Colombia floats along, entirely comfortable.

This evolution towards a 'single product' neocolonial economy is fairly typical of Latin America during this period, but it also marks a low level social conflict, the erosion of Conservative power and Liberal ascendance. Social consensus is always a fragile thing. This is the situation of Colombia, perched on the edge of Ecuador. Flush with cash, trapped in a single product commodity economy, with an ever widening gulf between bitter conservatives and rising liberals.

Alba's Last Battle

The shack is a rude affair, overlooking the hill; its roof is threadbare, signs that it has been abandoned for a year. Off and on, it has been a stop for Ecuadoran officers or messengers. For a few months it was a watching post.

Now it lies beneath the watchful eyes of two armies. To the north, the Ecuador Army supplemented by Colombian forces, to the south the new Inca Empire, a sea of Quechua faces. Colonel Alba and Captain Flores stand outside the cabin, watching two mounted men pick their way up the path. Or rather, Flores kept a watchful eye on the men. Alba takes the opportunity to study the Inca army with his binoculars.

"What do you think?" Flores asks.

"Not much in the way of artillery," Alba says.

"That's good then," Flores says. "A weakness we can exploit."

Alba shrugs.

"Depends. Artillery is slow to haul around, and it's fussy, time consuming to set up and use effectively. These boys, they're used to moving very fast. Like lightning. But light as feathers."

"So that's bad?"

Alba shrugs again. "It's the way they've learned to fight, and it worked well enough against Gamarra and his bunch."

Flores glances at his friend. "I can almost hear you thinking," he says, "clack, clack, clack, like a typewriter."

"I assume that they move, take their ground, and bring in the artillery later, once they've pinned their targets," Alba reflects. "Or maybe they don't even bother, bypass it altogether. What do you think?"

"I try not to," Flores replies. "Look, they're here."

The two men negotiate the final curves of the path, waving their arms in greeting.

The first is tall and thin, with a ready grin and a bushy moustache. Alba knows from descriptions that this is Manco Yanqui, a Quechua half breed, former bandit, former Sargent by appointment, field promotion to Lieutenant, then to Captain, de facto Colonel, and self-appointed General. Number-two man in the Empire

The second man is heavier, corpulent, smooth-faced with slicked black hair woven into a long braid. He rides a burro, clearly an affectation from a Catholic upbringing. He doesn't look Quechua. Bolivian, maybe Aymara perhaps, but the signs of the Indigenous are light on his features. QuizQuiz Guerrero. Many of the new Inca, even the Mestizo and Aymara, even the handful of white men who joined the banner, are fond of taking the names of Inca generals and emperors. It became confusing after a time, these men changed names like hats. QuizQuiz Guerrero was originally Ramon Hernandez, then Paco Galindo the second time he was conscripted, then Jesus Jordan when he'd been a white man.

And now... QuizQuiz does not stand nearly so high as Manco Yanqui. Barely in the first tier, on the upper edges of the second. Alba knows them both for sneaky, ruthless bastards. Manco Yanqui dismounts, practically leaping from his horse, and came over, a huge grin lighting his face. QuizQuiz follows with the slow meticulousness of a larger man.

"Ah," he laughs, shaking Flores hand heartily, "so this is the famous Colonel Alba, Napoleon of the North! I have heard so much about you! So good to finally meet you!"

****

Alba's Last Battle, Part 2

The four men sit at a table in the shack. Flores pours wine into standard tin ration cups. The wind whistles through gaps in the cabin walls.

"Is this poisoned?" Manco Yanqui asks casually.

Flores freezes.

QuizQuiz simply watches, observing everything, giving nothing away.

Alba simply raises his cup and swallows. He makes a face at the taste.

"Might as well be."

Yanqui laughs heartily and tosses the drink down with one swallow.

"Ah my friend, you should have been in Bolivia with us. This is like Ambrosia compared to some of the cat's piss that we swallowed then, and glad to have it. You are too refined for us simple peons. I am ashamed to be in your company."

"Ambrosia?" muses Alba, he lifts an eyebrow.

"Ha," says Yanqui to QuizQuiz, "I told you he'd be a clever one."

He turns back to Alba, "Yes, I've picked up a bit of learning here and there. I studied to be a Priest in my younger days. More money as a bandit though... and more women."

He winks.

"What of you?" he asks.

"The Criollo," he spat, "they called you an accountant. This while you were beating them like rented mules. How does one get from accountant to a Napoleon?"

Alba shrugs.

"It's not so different," he replies. "War is men, yes. But it's numbers too, and where you put them."

"So a battlefield is like a ledger?"

"As it turns out..."

Yanqui hoots with laughter. QuizQuiz maintains his cold gaze on Alba, weighing him.

Yanqui turns to his mate.

"What did I tell you, QuizQuiz? I was going to love this man like a brother!"

QuizQuiz nods, not so much glancing at Flores as his cup is refilled. His stare is like death.

"You know why I like you," Yanqui asks.

He doesn't wait for an answer.

"Because you look like an accountant, or a shopkeeper, you look all mild. But deep down, you and I are the same."

"We kill those fucking Capitalists and Warmongers who have had their boots on the necks of the common people. Stinking Aristos living off the blood of the proletariat. You and I, we fill graveyards with them."

"I go to Tupac, and I say, 'this man, this Alba' he has done such a service to us, killing all those generals and officers. Where would we be without him? I must meet this man!' And here I am, and here you are."

Yanqui takes the bottle from Flores, and drinks directly from the neck.

"Capitalists and proletariat?" Alba asks. "Are you a socialist then?"

Yanqui chuckles.

"Ah, you caught me. I hang around with learned men who use big words like that. They asked me in Washington, you know. President Roosevelt himself, he got up from his desk and walked over and took my hand and he said 'Yanqui, are you a Communist? I cannot abide Communists!'"

New World War – Page 281

"Well, this is the President of the United States, what can you say? I say, 'No Mister Roosevelt, I am no Communist, I am a simple boy who studied to be a Priest, it is just my English is poor, I get words from all over.' So he says, 'Ah, then all is well. But don't be a Communist.' I say 'Okay!' We are good friends now."

He leans back.

"Is just words is all. You make sure to say the right words. I have to be careful of that. They make all those Criollo scared that we are going to come and take their ill-gotten wealth and give it to the poor."

"I imagine it would," Alba replies dryly.

"Well," Yanqui says, "they shouldn't worry. I have gone to Washington and I know how things work. Not too much blood. The Americanos don't like that. The Criollo, most of them, they are safe. Oh there might be a little suffering here and there, but that's good for the soul. And they won't be lords of creation no more. But humility is also good for the soul too. So you see, we'll be doing them favours. The Americanos know this, so they like us."

"Good for you," Alba says.

Yanqui pauses.

"The Americanos don't like you. Something about your friend Mister Adolph? They don't like him at all. I mean, they don't like Communists. But especially, they don't like him. Funny isn't it. I have trouble telling them apart - I think the Americanos don't like Mister Adolph, he reminds them too much of something."

"So it goes. But there it is - The Americanos like us. They don't like you."

"What does it matter?" Alba says. "The war is over."

"Ibanez in the south," Yanqui says, "you should ask him if it's over."

"Ibanez makes his own decisions," Alba replies. "Ecuador wishes only to be left alone. We are in this war because of those Generals in Peru, the ones you spit upon, who had everything and wanted more. They wanted a part of our country, we said no. As simple as that. We defended ourselves."

Yanqui smiles.

"You defended yourselves all the way to the gates of Lima."

He whoops with laughter.

"We did what we had to do. And we will do it again," Alba speaks plainly.

"Our enemies were the same as yours," Alba continues, "those Generals in Lima. No friends to either of us. They're gone now, and we are happy to see the end of them. We have no quarrel with you. Leave us alone, we will get along fine."

"I am warned by the mighty Colonel Alba," Yanqui nods. He turns to QuizQuiz. "What do you think, my friend, we should get our tails between our legs and go home?"

The big man simply stares.

"There is no disrespect," Alba says. "We don't need to fight. Peru is a vast country to rule and we are happy to recognize your rule there."

"What about those poor Criollo in Peru," Yanqui asks, putting on a tearful face. "Ibanez makes much of their suffering under us. Do you have no class consciousness? No loyalty to your race?"

"I cannot say that any of those notions were present for Peru when they decided to take our lands."

"True enough," Yanqui sighs, "everyone talks about their souls, but it always comes down to filling their pockets."

"You keep your souls and your pockets," Alba says. "We'll keep ours."

"You think we only want a piece of your country?" Yanqui asks, grinning.

He pauses significantly. The smile fades away bit by bit into a ruthless coldness. "We want it all! What do you think of that?"

"A child wants everything it sees on the table, but its stomach is big enough for a plate. Peru is big enough for you. Why do you need more?"

"Human nature," Yanqui says, "perhaps we are greedy. Or perhaps your time has finally passed - all these little caudillos, all these little haciendas, little countries amounting to nothing."

"Centuries ago, we were one people, Quechua, Aymara, all of us one nation that stretched the length of the Andes themselves. Then you Criollo, you Spanish, you come and put your boots on our necks. You set yourselves up to rule over us, and then because you're all too greedy, you can't even abide each other, you set yourselves up in all these worthless little countries, each ruling over its own Quechua."

There's something like passion that comes into Manco Yanqui. He leans forward, and as he speaks he half rises from his chair. The easy demeanor fades as the light of fanaticism comes into his eyes.

"Well, it's time the Quechua were one people again, one nation. You think we'll stop and leave a portion of our people under bondage with you? It's time to sweep away all these little nations; you've shown you don't deserve it. It's time for the Quechua to join together, to come down from the mountains and be an Empire again!"

Abruptly, Yanqui catches himself. He settles back in his chair, takes a deep breath, and winks at Alba, whose posture and expression has not changed.

"History, Alba," he says. "I think it's on our side this time. Maybe our time has come back, and we are taking what is ours. Maybe we are the future."

"Mister Hitler, I think, talked that way. But talking is not the same as doing. We beat those who came before you. We can beat you. Ecuador will stand," Alba gazes calmly and levelly at the two Incans.

Yanqui's face betrays shock, then anger.

He glances at QuizQuiz who remains impassive, staring coldly at Alba.

Flores looks terrified.

Then Yanqui throws his head back and laughs uproariously.

"Tupac and I, we love you. We have the greatest respect. We honour you! You know how we will honour you? We have talked it over all of us, and decided!"

"Nothing but the best for the Colonel!" Yanqui leans over conspiratorially. "We are going to put your head on the tallest pike in Lima. That way, you can look down on all those Criollo dogs. We will raise you up so high the stench of their rot will not bother you. We might even make a hole in your skull, out your mouth, so it rains you can spit upon Gamarra and Ramirez and Markholtz and all the rest of those bastards. What do you think of that?"

Alba smiles slightly. "It's a high honor indeed.... But you'll have to take it first."

Yanqui puts on a sly grin, "Oh don't be like that. I have an axe in my satchel, we step outside: Whack! Whack! It is done. Everyone is happy, everything is easy."

He throws up his hands in mock horror.

"Don't tell me, you are going to make me work for it? I thought we were friends?"

"I'm told that it is all the sweeter if you have to sweat a little."

Yanqui seems to think it over, puts on a face and finally shrugs in agreement.

"This is true. The priest told me once, so it must be so. Personally, a little hard work? I'd rather someone else go do it."

"How about this then? We don't put your head on a pike, not even a tall one. The game is over, Alba, it's all done. You go home, we take the field, then we take the country. No shame in running away. I ran away lots. Never did me any harm."

Alba seems to consider it.

"No."

"Then this - there's rape, but there's also seduction. There's no reason this must be done the hard way. Join the Great Inca; we'll make a place for you and yours in it. Ecuador can be a special province; we will put it in writing. It won't be so bad, to be a part of something great. Better than being all of something small and forgotten."

Alba hesitates. Both QuizQuiz and Yanqui notice.

"I can't make such an agreement. I am sworn to Ecuador."

Yanqui replies, "and your capitalists have sold out to the Colombians already."

Flores looks nervous. Yanqui catches that, turning to Flores he winks.

"Yes," he says, "we know more than you think. You should learn to be more like your friend here. He's a cold customer, your Alba."

Yanqui sighs.

"All right, I think we are done. Today, we will take Ecuador. Tomorrow: Chile. Don't doubt that. I've fought Ibanez and beaten him, we'll keep beating him, and everyone else until we're done. You want to know our secret? We have no secret. It's the Criollo's secret not ours."

Yanqui pauses.

"The Criollo... They learn from everything... except their mistakes. That's why we are going to win."

***

A Metaphor

"So," asks Yanqui, as they were riding back down the path, "what did you think of this Alba fellow."

"I liked him a lot," says QuizQuiz.

"So did I," replies Yanqui.

"He's very smart," QuizQuiz says, "his position is good, and his men are solid. He understands war."

Yanqui nods.

"He won't be easy."

"You think so?" Yanqui pushes his lip out. "Well, we're here already, might as well test him out. If he proves a tough nut... well, there's other ways to crack an egg."

"Nut?"

"What?"

"You said he was a tough nut first, then you talked about cracking an egg... it should have been cracking a nut. To be consistent."

"No, no, Alba is the nut. Ecuador is the egg. You see?"

"Ah, it's a metaphor?"

"That's right."

"It still doesn't work."

Yanqui rolls his eyes.

✳✳✳✳

A Question of Pants

"I'm glad I wore my old pants today," Flores says.

"How so?" asks Alba.

"I think I shit myself," Flores replies. "That was terrifying."

"Hmmm," Alba muses thoughtfully, "they were testing us."

"What do we do now?" Flores asks.

"We win."

"Is it that easy?"

"Is there another option?"

***

Columbia, Sliding Down the Slippery Slope

Unfortunately for Ecuador, cacao is not a depression proof commodity. The Bonifaz triumvirate came to power with its cupboards bare. To sustain the country and to build the Ecuadoran military to the point where it can resist Peru, the Bonifaz government makes the rounds, seeking capital, loans, investment anywhere and everywhere, even from Nazi Germany.

During the 1930s, Ecuadoran diplomats and missions are a regular feature in Bogota. Bonifaz himself makes several state visits, as does Velasco Ibarra. Oddly, the Ecuadorans end up appealing to the different factions in Colombian society. Ibarra is the darling of the Liberals; Bonifaz makes common cause with the conservatives and the haciendas. Ultimately, it is Bonifaz' association with the Conservatives that led to Colombia keeping a degree of distance, through the 1930s.

June of 1940, war breaks out between Ecuador and Peru. Initially, to the Colombians, the war is a matter for the newspapers and for personal cheerleading. Bonifaz supporters among the Conservatives and Velasco supporters among the Liberals find a rare common cause. They join to pass a parliamentary vote of support to Ecuador in defending its borders. This support doesn't extend to financial contributions, supplies or soldiers. But Colombia did turn a blind eye to a trickle of private contributions and volunteers.

War is an expensive proposition. Within the first year, Ecuador has exhausted its financial resources. In the second year of the war, Ecuador has gone deeply, deeply into debt. Velasco is forced to return to Bogota, cup in hand, to beg for assistance of any sort. It isn't a bad strategy, buoyed by coffee revenues, Colombia is literally the only state left in the region with anything resembling both financial resources and sympathy for Ecuador.

The difference between 1939 and 1942 is really with Ecuador not Colombia. Ecuador is, to put it bluntly, having a fire sale. With finances in desperate straits, Velasco is forced to go to Bogota and seek lines of credit to keep Quito afloat. These lines of credit are initially on extraordinarily high interest rates. As Ecuadoran administration burns through it, new lines of credit are secured with liens and pledges against future tax revenues.

As that is used up, financing is secured through a long term assignment of customs revenues in Guayaquil. Colombian customs officials and then Colombian soldiers are assigned to Guayaquil to monitor and then to secure revenues. Guayaquil becomes a city of shared jurisdiction. The initial phase of Colombian involvement is mostly arm's length and lead by and through the Liberal factions which are revenue oriented.

Over time, the interests of the Conservative factions becomes ascendant. This takes place through two separate channels. One is the shift in economic support and financing from high interest loans and revenue assignments to grants of mineral and land rights, which leads to affiliation between the Ecuadoran and Colombian hacienda classes. In particular, the Conservatives of the Ecuadoran legislature are aligning politically with the Conservative factions of the Colombians. In response, Velasco becomes increasingly ambivalent about the relationship, creating splits within the Ecuadoran government that only Bonifaz himself can paper over.

The other is through the increasing involvement of the Colombian military in Ecuador. By slow increments, Colombia's relatively small military becomes involved in Ecuador, first as a relatively small contingent supporting the customs auditors in Guayaquil. However, as Ecuador's military is committed to the front, Colombian forces are deployed in support or garrison roles. By 1942, this is somewhere between 3,000 and 5,000 men.

Colombian troops are active, primarily in noncombat roles, in Ecuador. The war to the south and the involvement with Ecuador, as well as the overall framework of World War II, becomes the foundation for a dramatic expansion of the Colombian military. By 1944, the Colombian army expands to almost 45,000 troops. The

Navy to 5,000 sailors. The police force to 10,000 officers. The nucleus of a professional air force has been formed.

Colombian involvement with Ecuador is a diplomatic thorn for Colombia in its relations with the United States. When World War II breaks out, the United States became almost the sole trading partner for Colombia. The revitalization of the American economy and the massive demand that an American war economy brought boosts the Colombians.

Americans, however, are prone to looking askance at the Colombian's involvement with an Axis power in its own back yard, an issue that the Colombians repeatedly have to finesse, even as they engage more and more deeply with Ecuador.

Colombia breaks off diplomatic relations with the Axis powers following the Pearl Harbour attack in December, 1941.

On November 26, 1943, following a series of incidents involving the sinking of Colombian shipping by a German U-Boat, Colombia declares war on Germany and Japan in November of 1943. However, unlike Brazil, Colombia contributes no troops to the overseas war effort, and allows no American bases on its territory.

In March of 1944, Colombia has its sole engagement with the forces of the European Axis, when Colombian naval units in the Caribbean attack and sink a Nazi submarine from Germany.

By May of 1944, the increasingly strained affiliation between the Colombian and Ecuadoran governments is breaking down. The Liberals are about to throw in the towel. Quito cannot pay its loans coming due to Bogota, the assignments of tax revenues and futures are simply not materializing or not worth the cost of investment. The disastrous deployment of Colombian troops in the battle of Lojas is taken as a major sign of bad faith, and the source of a huge rift. The final straw is the uniform American hostility to engagement.

As the Liberals prepare to abandon Ecuador, the Conservatives respond by hanging in more ferociously. But this brings them into direct conflict with two of the three ruling members of the Ecuador triumvirate. Once again, only Bonifaz direct intervention maintains a tenuous truce. But by July of 1944, Bonifaz ill health and illness leads to a stroke.

At that point, the Liberal government attempts to withdraw entirely from Ecuador and a recall order goes out. This triggers an abortive military coup from officers in the city of Pasto. Pasto is the Colombian city nearest Quito, and becomes the centre of their Ecuadoran operations. Pasto's population benefits from this involvement, and assignment to Pasto is a plum position for upcoming officers. The military command in Bogota wavers.

Colombia's President Pumarejo is forced to back down on withdrawal plans, a dramatic humiliation for the Liberals. Instead, Liberals and Conservatives agree to a 'Review' of Ecuador/Colombia relations. The Liberal Agenda, of course, is withdrawal.

In contrast the Colombian Conservatives grow more engaged and their influence over Ecuador becomes dominant. In particular, their alliance with Conservatives in Lima allows them to control the Legislature. In the wake of Bonifaz departure, both Velasco Ibarra and Luis Alba are pushed out. Ecuador becomes a de facto colony, not of Colombia, but of the Conservative party of Colombia.

***

Battle of Lojas, May 22, 1944

The battle of Lojas is the first major conflict of the new Inca
Empire on its northern frontier. It's also notable for being the last
major battle of the Ecuador Republic and the final engagement of
Colonel Alba.

Going into the battle, the Inca have numerical superiority, with
roughly 45,000 men at arms. This is divided almost evenly between
infantry and cavalry, with almost no artillery. The Inca are led by
the generals Manco Yanqui and QuizQuiz Guerrero. The
Ecuadoran forces, led by Colonel Alba, consist of approximately
18,000 men, including 3,000 cavalry, and 4,000 artillery.

In addition, there is a contributing force of 6,000 Colombians,
whose presence is contingent on not participating in the
engagement. The rules of engagement mean that the Colombians
are not to see direct contact with the enemy, except in the case of
following up on a total rout, or covering an urgent retreat. By this
time, 20,000 members of Colombian forces are in Ecuador, in
garrison and non-combatant roles, freeing up Ecuadoran troops for
front line duties. This occasionally produces tensions within the
military sphere, and many Ecuadoran troops and civilians resent
the Colombians.

The Inca Empire's objective is to roll back Ecuadoran positions,
take the province of Lojas and from there split Guayaquil from
Quito. The ultimate strategy is to move through the Ecuadoran
highlands enlisting the local Quechua. In the south, the plan is to
isolate Guayaquil from the rest of the coast and ultimately overrun
the country. To do this, they have to move up the valley and
foothills which were the gateway to Lojas. The Incan generals opt
for maximum mobility, selecting a light, manoeuvrable force, with
the intention to outflank and overwhelm the defenders.

The Ecuadorans have the advantage of local knowledge of the
countryside and well established positions. According to legend,

there is a parlay between the Ecuadoran and Peruvian commanders before the commencement of hostilities.

The battle opens with the Peruvians engaging along a wide front, with scattered fire fights. Almost immediately, the Ecuadorans make effective use of artillery to confine the offensive. Manco Yanqui brings up a major offensive on the foothills to the right of the valley, in order to secure a pathway. However, Alba anticipates this and focusses most of his artillery on that front. Manco at that point commits a substantial portion of his forces, but is able to spot the trap and withdraw without excessive casualties.

Alba then counterattacks, walking artillery barrages up the main body of the Peruvians and committing Cavalry as follow up. Infantry then streams down the foothills, leaving the Peruvian force split and part of it caught in the jaws of a pincer. Manco Yanqui is then forced onto the defensive, maintaining integrity of his forces and withdrawing. At this time QuizQuiz Guerrero's force, is moving to the west, attempting to perform a flanking manoeuver. This eventually takes him directly into the Colombian contingent.

The surprise is mutual, the Colombians were not expecting to see combat, and Guerrero is not expecting an entire undeployed reserve force appear out of nowhere.

Of the two, Guerrero adapts more quickly, pressing the Colombian force which begins to collapse, having only operational orders to cover a retreat. Alba is forced to deploy infantry to repel Guerrero's force and protect the withering Colombians, weakening his own centre.

Manco Yanqui then counters with an attack on weakened centre, but did not count on Guerrero being stalemated so quickly. In order to take advantage of the rapidly shifting battlefield, he splits his infantry from his cavalry, sending the cavalry against the centre, and leaving the infantry to defend against Alba's eastern attack.

Meanwhile, QuizQuiz and Alba exchange a series of feints up and down the flank. Finding no weaknesses, and badly overextended, QuizQuiz is forced to withdraw and consolidate his forces. Manco Yanqui, is now trapped between Alba's forces, and is also forced to withdraw from the centre, but would be moving into Alba's artillery bombardment corridor. The position is untenable. There is no choice but to expose his forces and risk a bloodbath.

After an exchange of messages between the Inca commanders, QuizQuiz withdraws from the field entirely, taking up position as a reserve force to support Manco's two wings as they consolidate. Alba permits Manco to withdraw under light fire, moving his forces forward, to command the battlefield. By the end of the day, Ecuadoran forces have achieved a clear tactical control of the battlefield.

Manco Yanqui, legend has it, sends a white flag and a bottle of wine to Colonel Alba, and the Incans move to a secure defensive position. The battle is concluded.

The Battle of Lojas is notable for unusually light casualties on both sides, in part because of forbearance shown. At points, Alba halts artillery barrages to allow the Peruvians an opportunity to recover their wounded. In turn, Peruvian field medics give Ecuadorans equal care on the battlefield.

The battle has been called 'The Finest Battle of the Andean War', and is renowned as a study in rapid organized movement and virtuoso command of the battlefield. The British General, Montgomery of El Amein describes it as 'more a brilliant chess match than a military contest.'

Tupac Amaru III, upon hearing the description of the engagement, wept that he was not there to have seen it himself. Neither Manco Yanqui nor QuizQuiz Guerrero suffer any loss of status within the Empire from the battle.

Aftermath

Alba pours the wine over the mass grave of the soldiers. This is the part no one ever talks about in war, he thinks to himself.

For every battle, a graveyard.

Flores crosses himself, as a good Catholic should.

"At least we won," Flores says. "It's finally over."

Alba grunts. So many dead, he thinks.

"For now," Alba slowly replies.

Flores eyes narrow.

"You think that they'll be back?"

Alba nods.

"You heard them," he says. "They have a cause. They won't let go."

"Well, we'll just beat them again, like we do every time."

The bottle is empty, its final drops spill from its mouth. He tosses the bottle into the mass grave, into the arms of the dead. Once Ecuadorans, once Colombians, once Inca... now just dead.

Flores watches the trajectory of the bottle, sees it land and bounce among the corpses, coming to rest in the crook of an arm.

"Waste of good wine," he opines.

Alba shrugs.

"It's been poisoned."

"How do you know?"

Alba turns to go, "I met them."

***

New World War – Page 296

A Toast

"Do you think he'll drink the wine?" Manco Yanqui asks.

QuizQuiz Guerrero shrugs.

"It would be a shame if he did."

"He's good at what he does," says Yanqui finally.

QuizQuiz thinks it over.

"But limited," he says finally.

"Yes..."

They ride along a little further thinking.

"These northern Quechua, they're not so eager to rise up," Manco offers.

QuizQuiz nods.

"Not like Lima," he says thoughtfully, "the Criollo there never stopped fighting. Up here, things settled down, they were allowed to go home. The old ways came back, they settled in. They are victims of False Consciousness."

Manco Yanqui chews it over. "I think you are right, they fall back into the old ways, into their villages and haciendas. They went back to sleep on us. I noticed the troops, almost no Indio. They weren't fighting for the Criollo."

"But they don't fight them either. They've gone to sleep. We must wake them up," QuizQuiz suggests. "Once they wake, then Alba and his masters will crumble like a fistful of dried mud. Their whole nation is rotted from within, he and his are brave men guarding a rotting mansion.

"Take the Sierra then," Manco says. "Slip the highlands out from their grasp, valley by valley?"

"It can be done," QuizQuiz replies. "Perhaps a little slower. Alba's fine with an army, but I don't think he's suited for other kinds of fights. He is stricken with False Consciousness himself, it limits him."

"He doesn't speak Quechua," Manco laughed. "I'll bet you that. He'll have a hard time keeping the highlands in line, and the harder he tries the more he'll lose."

QuizQuiz nodded.

"I should leave you to it?"

"I have some ideas," QuizQuiz says.

"I'll trust you to it," Manco Yanqui says. "I'll speak for you to Tupac. Anyone you want?"

"Chiriki," QuizQuiz replies. "He's from the north, he knows the country some. He's good with the dialects."

"Echeverria?"

"That maniac? Why not send Diabla up too? They're a pair of hammers. This isn't right for them, hold them back until the time comes."

Yanqui nods.

"We want them in the south, we need to finish that shit Ibanez. That's a mistake the Criollo made, they picked too many fights - Ecuador, Chile, Bolivia; always picking new fights. One at a time, that's the way. Finish Santiago, clear things up down south, then we turn north."

"It will be ready when the time comes. We'll have the highlands," QuizQuiz says. "The next time we bring an army north, we'll walk into Guayaquil... and everything else."

"What's your assessment of the Colombians?" Yanqui asks suddenly.

QuizQuiz pauses a long time, the two of them ride together quietly.

"Pretty," he says finally. "Young. Clean uniforms. Nice guns...."

He spits.

New World War – Page 298

"No discipline. Cowards. They weren't ready, you could tell, they didn't know what to do. Middle of a battle, and they didn't think it would come at them...."

"Assholes," he concludes.

"They were surprised," Yanqui agrees. "Like they were there to watch the show, but not play a part. They fared poorly."

He thinks for a moment.

"They're deep in Quito and Guayaquil. That could be a problem."

"To hell with them," QuizQuiz says. "They have no stomach; they stand around and let others fight for them. When we take Ecuador, they'll scurry away like the Criollo shits they are. They'll go home and give each other medals for their bravery running away."

Yanqui grunted.

"Have a care," he counsels, "the Colombians may not be worth spit, but behind them are the Americans."

"Assholes," QuizQuiz says. But he nods.

****

New World War – Page 299

The Fall of the South, May 22 through November 14, 1944

"The trouble with Ibanez was that he seemed doomed to learn from everything except his own mistakes." Velasco Ibarra, October, 1949.

The disruptions of the Inca Revolution seem to provide Ibanez with a golden opportunity. In Bolivia, Ibanez forces suddenly have time to entrench in Villarroel's enclave, retake the mining district, and consolidate their transit routes to the coast.

There's even a successful campaign against Argentine forces in the south, inflicting a string of defeats, and freeing up troops to face off against the Inca in Bolivia.

It is on the frontier that the greatest opportunity lies. The Peruvian army occupying the trenches is the last bastion of loyalists to the Gamarra and Ramirez regimes. The Inca revolution has demoralized the soldiers there, left them undermanned and under strength, short of ammunition and with a command structure in shambles.

Ibanez orders a buildup in anticipation of a major offensive. But he is struck with indecision. What if the attack fails? The record of the trench war has been brutal and inconclusive, and one promising offensive after another has turned into a meat grinder, to no real effect.

There is also America to consider: Which way will they go? The Revolution potentially alienates the Americans from Peru and gives Chile an opportunity to curry their favour. But renewing aggression might not be well taken by them. They are too big a factor to dismiss lightly. As a result, Ibanez hesitates and continues to hesitate.

The apparent defeat of the Inca Empire in May 22, 1944, at the Battle of Lojas decides it for him. Ibanez takes this as a sign of weakness of the Inca, and with the recklessness of a gambler, he decides to throw all in. On May 24, 1944, Ibanez launches an offensive.

The result initially is a breakthrough. The long established trench lines of the Peruvians fall apart and the remnants of the old regime break. Chilean army groups surge towards Lima.

Unfortunately, the Inca are preparing their own offensive in Bolivia, which begins in the dying days of May. By early June, Villarroel's enclave is overrun and Villarroel himself captured.

****

Perdita Diabla and the Argentine Campaign

Is not a handsome woman. She has a broken nose and a scar down the side of her face. There are a lot of stories about how she got those, most of them terrifying, but they're all lies.

The truth is that when she was a child, she fell down carrying a bucket.

But that's not an exciting story.

Her teeth are stained brown from chewing tobacco, she spits a lot, and she has a flat way of looking at you. It makes a person wonder if they're going to live through the next five minutes. But she can ride a horse like she was born on it, or drive a truck as if she's done it all her life, and a knack for figuring out where the enemy is and how to hurt them.

She had a husband once, but he's dead. She had children, but the civil war took them all. She has sisters though, and nieces and nephews.

One day, she shows up at a camp, a simple Aymara woman, speaking broken Spanish, asking for a rifle.

In a month, she is running the place.

There is an officer, of course. A Criollo, who is supposedly in charge. But when he speaks, even the ones who understand Spanish look to Diabla and wait for her nod.

She is one of the Indios fighting for Villarroel. Then at some point she's fighting for Villarroel and his Chileans. Or maybe it's just for Chileans. Perhaps, the way they strut about, it was always for the Chileans.

She sees brothers and sisters, Quechua and Aymara, on both sides, fighting for Penaranda or Villarroel as chance has thrown them. Or perhaps fighting for Chile or Peru. From where she stands looking up at the officers and their dizzying heights, they all blend together. She can see no difference between the Criollo factions and nations. They're all just white men, offering nothing but their willingness to shed Indigenous blood.

It's hard to kill for men like that, and harder to die. Out in the field, away from the eyes of white officers, she is... flexible. She obeys the white officers well enough, she's aware of the risks and consequences of insubordination. But if an officer is too demanding? Well accidents happen.

Her family are all in graves, after all; folk who wanted nothing better than to be left alone. But the Criollo had to have their civil war. Now she has a Criollo name, and she's going to teach them what it means.

Under Villarroel's command, she fights Valpes and his pretend regime in the lowlands. She likes that well enough. There are few Aymara here; mostly the ones that are sympathetic. There's Guarani and Mestizo. But mostly, no one is interested in fighting, except for Valpes, and he's no good at it.

Until the Argentines come like a plague. The devil-damned Argentines, with their fine uniforms and finer boots, their expensive kits and weapons. Criollo so white and European, their arrogant noses held so high, it's as if their mothers have just arrived from Spain.

They fight a wealthy man's war, with their fine boots and their fine weapon and money for bribes. Each victory invites more of them as if to partake. Each setback draws more to replace their losses. Always more and it comes clear to her that Valpes is just another puppet of masters far away.

When she catches an Argentine, she makes an example. Her officer is disturbed, but he's learned his place by now, so he keeps his mouth shut.

 When Gamarra makes his list, her name is not on it, of course. But she hears of it quickly enough. She senses the sea change that comes with it. The Criollo have betrayed their Indio soldiers. She is not surprised, they are Criollo. Treachery is in their blood. How long before her own masters do the same?

When Otoronco begins his revolt, she is one of the first to join. She meets Singalong Huascar and Two Gun Echeverria in the town of Potosi to pledge her allegiance, and brings an army with her.

When the revolt becomes a revolution, she is a true believer in the new Inca. She is there when Otoronco proclaims himself Tupac Amaru II; it is a glorious moment to witness.

Initially, through May, in the confusion of the Revolution, the Chileans strike, advancing towards Lima, and mounting a new offensive in Bolivia, with their dog, Villarroel. Perdita Diabla is content to pull back and let the despised Criollo murder each other.

Valpes Government on its own amounts to little. Even Ramon Valpes loses heart, from what her spies tell her. It hollows out, like a gourd, barely more than a skin or a regime. As Valpes regime hollows, the Argentines puff out, more of them, more resplendent, richer, fatter, whiter.

She is almost amused as the Chileans sweep down upon the Argentines. White men killing each other, what could be finer? But she's seen it before, with every setback, the Argentines double down; send more men, more arms.

She knows this. She's seen it among men. The gambler's sickness. The urge to try to make up each loss by throwing more in.

The campaign turns to the Chileans. Without their native Boliviano auxiliaries, without the Quechua and Aymara to guide them along paths, to dig their trenches, to carry their supplies, to shoot their guns for them, the Chileans are strangely helpless.

They come in numbers yes. They come well-armed with plenty of bullets and fine boots. But it's not their country and they don't know it.

There is a saying; Singalong Huascar is loved by his men, as Perdita Diabla is feared by her enemies. She has no mercy.

The final Chilean expedition in Bolivia falls apart. The Chileans start to flee, officers on their horses, enlisted men on their boots, throwing down their weapons, abandoning their kit. Diabla and her fellow revolutionaries pursue, taking up what was abandoned, and using it against the foreigners.

If one in ten makes it back out of Bolivia, it's not her doing and not her mercy.

****

June 9, 1944 - The Last Stand of Gualberto Villarroel

"It's over," Villarroel thinks. He pours himself another glass of wine. He is alone in his Presidential office. Everyone is gone, he's sent them away. Everything is falling apart. Elsewhere, in Chile, in Ecuador, even Brazil, the fighting goes on. But not here. Bolivia is finished. Bolivia is lost. There is no point in keeping men around to die. There is a pistol and a cavalry sabre on the desk next to him.

The Chaco, Sorzano, the odious Penaranda, the fucking Chileans, the Peruvians, that shit Valpes, the bastard Argentines... all of us fighting each other. For what? In the end, it turns out to be the Indigenous. Who would have thought?

He almost wishes them well. Surely they can't fuck it up more than the rest of us did.

He drains the glass.

Then he picks up the pistol, a German Luger. Nice gun, reliable. He'd always liked it. He won it from David Toro in a game of cards. That had been a night to remember. German Busch had been there, Quintalla, all better men than he. He remembers the camaraderie of that night, the easy conversation, the smell of tobacco and the flavor of wine and a tear forms in the corner of his eye. He sticks the pistol in his mouth, feeling the barrel lightly touch the roof. He waits. He puts the pistol down and sighs.

He's not half the man German Busch was, he thinks. He's a coward.

In the end, German shot himself. He'd never bent, but in the end, he'd broken. Still, he'd been a hell of a man.

Abruptly, his eyes fill with tears. He's made such a hash of it all. What would they think of him? He'd tried to be strong, he'd tried to do the right thing, tried to stand up for his country. But how had that turned out, he'd sold his country by inches, a little here to the Chileans, and a little more, then a little to the Argentines, one compromise after another, selling his own soul a bit at a time.

If only it had been German, and not him. German would have done right. Or David. Or Quintalla. They'd have all stood up. Not one of them would have sold out like he had, an inch at a time. They were heroes, and he... He was a fool and a failure.

Abruptly, reaches for his handkerchief and blows his nose. He wipes his eyes, and stares at the pistol.

Suicide is against the will of the Catholic Church. If he kills himself, he'll go to hell.

Or worse, the Chaco.

Ah Bolivia, he thinks. Poor, poor Bolivia. There was no place on earth so beautiful, so bountiful, so magical. Bolivia, blessed by God.

Cursed by man.

It is to weep for.

He stares at the bottle; pours himself another glass. There was a goodly supply of wine. Maybe he should just barricade himself and drink till he passes out?

For some reason, he thinks of poor Paz Estenssoro, the socialist. That last wine-sweetened conversation they'd had in the Brothel. The warm friendship; the play of wit and ideas Then less than an hour later, he'd sat there like a coward, the Luger in his hand, watching as Penaranda's thugs dragged him out on the street and shot him like dog. He'd sat there and done nothing. But Paz died standing, protesting, arguing; he hadn't backed down.

Would it have been different for Bolivia if it had been Paz that the Nazis rescued instead of him that day? It didn't seem like it could have turned out worse.

He always tried to be a good man, to do the right thing. But he'd been a coward that day. Maybe he's been a coward all along.

New World War – Page 307

Maybe, he thinks, finally, it is time to be a man. He has known so many good men, all better than him, all dead. Maybe it's time.

He stands and takes up the cavalry sabre in one hand, holsters the pistol, and marches from the Presidential office, down the hall, the stairs, until he is standing in front of the building. He pulls out the pistol and waits. Sword in one hand pistol in the other, this is the way to die, he thinks.

He stands there for ten minutes. No one comes. A truck appears at the end of the street, stops, and drives the other way.

Ten more minutes. He wishes he'd brought a bottle of wine down.

Half an hour. He goes inside and comes out with a chair. He sets it down beside the doorway, sits down and waits.

An hour or so passes, and finally they come.

A group of dusty horsemen ride up, their ponies tired. They wear colourful sashes and bandoleers, as the Quechua officers do. He knows who they are. They don't come too close, perhaps thirty yards. Instead they sit on their horses, watching and quietly discussing among themselves.

Villarroel's mouth is suddenly dry. He wants to call out to them, curse them, challenge them. But the words won't come. So he waits.

Finally, they seem to come to a decision. One of them rides up to within ten yards.

"That's far enough," Villarroel calls, pointing his pistol.

The rider halted. He leans forward in the saddle a bit. Then he reaches back and scratches his ass.

"I think it is," he says. "I can see you're a bold man. We're looking for the Presidential Palace? We're told it's around here somewhere?"

"This is it," Villarroel replies, a little hoarsely.

"Ah, thank you," he called back over his shoulder. "We found it!"

The man turns back to Villarroel, leaning forward.

Many thanks," he says grinning, "I am Rum Maqui Bastido. It means Stone Hand Bastard. You've heard of me, perhaps?"

"I have," Villarroel replies.

He wants to say more, to fling curses, challenges, to go down fighting. He should shoot Bastido, but the man makes no moves. He licks his lips.

"Excellent! And you are?"

"General Gualberto Villarroel, the last and final President of the free Peoples of Bolivia."

Bastido grins and slowly dismounted. He turns back to the other horsemen. "It's him; I told you I was right. Nicola, you owe me!"

The assembled horse riders cheer and clap.

Bastido returns his attention to Villarroel, seeming not to care at all about the pistol pointed at him.

"General Villarroel," he says cheerfully, Villarroel can see stained and missing teeth in that grin, "good of you to come out to meet us. That's Iron Head Taruka, Nicola Bandita..." he rattles off the names of the others, as they wave or call out cheerfully, their horses shifting. "Manco Yanqui, he wanted to come, but commitments... you know. Tupac, well, he's too busy."

For the first time, he seems to notice the weapons.

"Nice pistol," he squints. "Good sword. You know how to use it?"

"I've used it before."

"Chaco?"

Villarroel grunts.

Bastido steps closer, peering.

"Well," he says, "looks like you're all ready for a fight. A brave speech? Valiant last stand? Go down cursing? All that kind of thing?"

Villarroel curses himself. He has nothing to say, no fine words.

"Something like that," he squeezes out. He feels stupid. He's had all these clever, bold things to say in mind. Heroic lines that might survive him. That at least would let his enemies know that a real man dies, an honorable man dies. And now? He squawks like a crow, his mind a blank.

Bastido nods, leaning forward on his horse.

"Very good," he says. "I approve. Die like a man, that's how I'd like to go. Or drunk in a brothel, that's not bad either. Personally, I could go either way. But you've picked a good one."

Bastido pauses, while Villarroel tries to think of some famous last words, something to be remembered for.

"Not like that asshole, Penaranda," Bastido says. "It's a good way, you've chosen. I like it. Nicola, she's a dead shot. I've seen her shoot the balls off a mosquito at a hundred yards. I didn't even know mosquitos had balls, but there you go. She'd probably just pull out her rifle. But I'll tell her to stand down. There's no virtue in that. Women, they don't appreciate these things."

"Penaranda's dead?" Villarroel asks.

Bastido looks surprised. He holds up his hands.

"Oh no!" he says. "We caught him! Not sure what we'll do with him. Funny story: When we caught him, he was trying to get away; he was in this hidden compartment, in a truck full of pigs. You want to know how we caught him?"

"The pigs objected," Villarroel says.

Bastido laughs out loud, and he keeps laughing, until he is bent over, tears roll down his eyes. Villarroel waits; he isn't sure how to feel. This isn't going the way he hoped.

Bastido turns around, and yells back to his companions.

"Penaranda! He said 'the pigs objected!'"

There is a round of laughter from the horse riders.

Bastido turns back.

"I like you," he says, then he shrugs. "It's going to be a shame to kill you. Life! So full of tragedies."

He peers carefully.

"Have you been drinking?"

Villarroel blinks. At first, he thinks of denying.

"How does that matter?" he snaps.

Bastido puts up his hand.

"No judgment. Wine is god's gift to man. It's his way of saying 'sorry about women.' I do not condemn. Wine pleases the stomach; it gladdens the heart and steadies the hand."

"It's just..."

"What?" Villarroel demands.

"I haven't had any all day."

"So?"

"I'd really like a drink. Maybe before we start? It would do me good. You'll die, but you've had yours. I might die, but I haven't had any. That's not fair."

"You can drink after."

"Not if I'm killed. Fine if I kill you, then I sit back and have a bottle, and I toast the brave man I put an end to. That's a good way to do things. But then, what if you get lucky? I get killed. Then I die, and I go to my grave thinking, 'I should have had that bottle first.' It would be a tragedy."

"I don't think it matters," Villarroel grunts.

"It's not good to kill a man on an empty stomach," Bastido says.

"You want to eat first?"

"Wine fills a stomach," Bastido tells him.

"If it's all the same," Villarroel says, his hand is beginning to shake. He can feel his legs trembling. "I'd rather just get on with it."

Bastido rolls his eyes.

New World War – Page 311

"You Criollo," he replies. "Always in a hurry. Business, business, business. Can we never have a moment to enjoy? No! It has to be right away! You think the Lord will mind if we wait a little? I think he's patient."

"I'm not patient."

Bastido folds his arms stubbornly.

"Well, I want a drink. I'm not going to kill a man while I'm sober. People will talk," he stares down at Villarroel. "You going to shoot me? I'm not even reaching. You go around shooting unarmed men?"

"You're armed."

"But I'm not reaching, so it's the same thing."

"You could reach."

"I need a drink first. Steadies my hand."

"What about them?" Villarroel waves at the horse riders watching them.

Bastido glances over his shoulder.

"They all want a drink too," he said. He calls back. "Hey, what first? We drink, or we kill this Criollo?"

The shouts come back one way or the other, but the consensus seems to be to drink first.

"I'm sorry," Bastido says almost apologetically. "It's been a long day. We all really just want to have some wine. We kill you later, I promise. Hell, why don't you drink with us? We all pour some cups, relax a little; then we can come out and finish you off. You can have your sword and your pistol; we can make a real fight of it, so you know you died like a man."

"I don't think so," Villarroel replies.

"Oh come on, Man," Bastido complains. "This is not fair. This is very unfair. You've had a drink. You probably had a whole bottle, sitting back and relaxing. Drinking from a fine wine glass, even, like a gentleman, not even from the bottle. Here we are, we're tired, we're hungry. And you say 'no!' How are you even a Christian?"

"What?"

"A Christian? Were you even baptised?"

"Of course I was. What are you talking about?"

"Christ," Bastido repeats. "You have not heard of him? The good lord, he turned loaves into fishes, and he passed out the wine. The good Samaritan, he found a man by the road, tired and dusty. He gave him a drink."

"Aren't you a good Samaritan? He would give us a drink. Why are you being like this? It's all over, Gualberto, it's all done with. The war is over, your cause is lost. It is just this. Do you really want to be your last act to be refusing some weary travellers a sip?"

Villarroel is suddenly tired.

"Fine," he said, he holsters his pistol.

Bastido smiles.

"Excellent," he waves back at the riders as they approach.

Villarroel's cavalry sabre droops; it is hard holding it up. They are probably going to shoot him. Like a joke. His great last stand is going to end as a joke. Like his whole life.

"Now," Rum Maqui Bastido says, "you come up and have a drink with us. Yes? It's no good to drink alone."

***

The Chaco and the Altiplano

For a time, the Argentines are almost swept away, retreating from Santa Cruz, towards a series of fortified towns and villages near the border. But as the Chileans fade away, they come surging back - more men, more horses, more trucks, more tanks and field artillery pieces, more supplies. Heading into the teeth of the Revolution.

Two-Gun Echevarria pushes from Sucre, marching to La Santa Cruz, which is all but abandoned. From there he and his forces drive for the Bolivian Chaco-

At the Gran Chaco, the Argentines invest heavily in holding the Bolivian oil fields. It's hard fighting. It's almost the Chaco war all over again, but Echevarria has the benefit of many veterans who have already seen the Chaco, and so he knows what mistakes to avoid.

The Paraguayan veterans, on the other side, are reluctant to volunteer for Argentina's war and are largely absent; freeing the Argentines from any wisdom they might offer. The fighting is brutal, but the Argentines are slowly pushed out of the Bolivian Chaco. And then pushed back far enough into the Paraguayan Chaco to put them in the worst possible position.

Singalong Huascar and Perdita Diabla take the southwest. She is given the mission of sweeping away Valpes cardboard regime in the lowlands. Or perhaps she simply decides on it. There aren't many on the Revolutionary Council who are willing to argue with her; when she sets her mind to a mission.

Between the two of them, Huascar and Diabla, once enemies, now occasional bed mates, push back, almost to the Argentine border, splitting the invaders.

On the right, Diabla clears the lowlands, but then faces a string of fortified towns at the edge of the Altiplano - Villazon, Tupiza, Atocha, Cotagati, Uyuni, San Pablo, Villa Martin, all the way north to Sabaya. They're anchored by garrisons and staging camps across the border in Argentina, in La Quiaca and Tartagal, stretching all the way back to the City of Salta.

These fortresses are near impregnable, secure in the highlands, reinforcing each other, a launching point for the Argentines to sweep down into the Bolivian lowlands all over again, even to cross to the Chaco and take Huascar from behind.

For a week, Diabla rides the length of the fortresses, testing their defences, conferring with scouts, interrogating prisoners and speaking with the local Quechua, all unhappy with these new occupiers.

Jujuy, Argentina, late June, early August

Lieutenant Mattias Shmidt is tired of Bolivia. He much prefers San Salvador, the capital of Jujuy province, where at least you can walk down the street without worrying about being shot in the back.

He smiles at a pretty girl passing by, and she smiles back.

That didn't happen in Bolivia. The people were dour. The women didn't smile at you. No one smiled at you, unless their hand was out for a bribe, or they had a knife ready to slide between your ribs.

Officially, they were invited as guests and allies of the officially recognized, legitimate government of Bolivia. That seems so straightforward on paper, until you talk to captured officers, insisting on the legitimacy of their own version of Bolivia's government, or Chileans or Peruvians, or Quechua, or Aymara, or even, god help us all, Valpes people, at which point you admit that you have no idea what the hell was going on.

He didn't really understand why they were, or why Buenos Aires seemed intent on digging itself deeper and deeper. Even in his own short time, he'd seen the commitment escalate.

It was only through luck, and his own reputation as an experienced Bolivia hand, that he'd managed to wangle his way to a staff position back in Jujuy. He'd have preferred a position in Salta, or even Buenos Aires. But you take what you can get.

Besides, the place isn't so bad. The Depression hit San Salvador de Jujuy hard, and the Bolivian adventure literally pulled the town back from the precipice. As soldiers and supplies had gone north, money flowed into the city, revitalising the economy. San Salvador and Salta are some of the biggest boosters of the Bolivian adventure. The local newspapers compete in their extravagant puffery.

Mattias, however, is not impressed. He's been to Bolivia, the place was a shithole. Its cities and towns were crap before the Civil war and now half of them were in ruins. The best thing to do would be to go back to Buenos Aires, and leave the Bolivians to murder each other.

The sun is setting, the evening is coming on. It will be dark before too long. He hurries along to the telegraph office. It's closed, but he is a staff officer, and he's on a mission. He bangs on the door until an operator comes. The man is balding and skinny, with coke bottle glasses, and a permanent hunch from sitting at the telegraph. He's not impressed in the least by Schmidt's uniform.

"Go away," he says, "I'm having dinner."

"That can wait," he holds himself stiffly and thrusts a paper forward. "These have to go out tonight, requisition requests, from the General himself."

It doesn't have the desired effect.

"Doesn't matter," the operator tells him. "The telegraph is down. Again."

"Will it be operational tonight?" Schmidt demands.

The operator laughs.

"Who's going to go wandering about in the middle of the night looking for a break in the line," he demands. "If that's what's wrong. Could be anything. It might be fixed tomorrow. Or it might be in a few days."

The operator shrugs. "That's the way it is."

"But these requisitions have to be sent!" Schmidt says. "Immediately."

"It won't be by telegraph," the operator replies. "Don't you soldiers have radios?"

"It has to be secure," Schmidt snaps.

The operator is indifferent.

"Send it by train then," he tells Schmidt. "It'll get there in a day or so. If it's so important, deliver it yourself. Now, go away, I can do nothing for you, and my dinner is getting cold."

The door shut.

Schmidt stands there. One thing is true; it is past time for dinner. Schmidt heads back to staff offices.

Perhaps it's not such a bad thing, he muses. Delivery by train? A train delivery will need a trusted man as courier. He wouldn't mind a trip to Buenos Aires. And perhaps it can lead to a reassignment back at headquarters.

As these thoughts run through his head, at first he doesn't really notice the pop pop of gunfire. In Bolivia, he'd be running for cover at the sounds. But it doesn't feel natural here, so at first he thinks it's just soldiers loosing a few rounds.

But then it continues, the volume escalating. He hears the screams, and the beginning of sirens.

Schmidt's heart begins to pound; he starts to run clutching the requisitions in his hand. Not here, he thinks. Not here. It can't be here. They're well away from the border, and the garrison here is half of the size of the entire Bolivian expeditionary force. They're the reserves, the back-ups, the suppliers.

A huge explosion lights up the sky, a pillar of flame rising up. He can hear the sound of artillery fire. What are we shooting at? Then an instant later, he wonders if it's our artillery or theirs.

 As an officer he has a sidearm. Did he remember to load it? He checks, relieved. Bolivia habit, he thinks, always have one in the chamber.

He can't understand what's happening.

People are in the streets now, running in every direction. He pushes against the crowd, his pistol raised high in the air. The night is full of screams. He smells the wisps of smoke. Somewhere, something is burning, perhaps a building, perhaps a lot of buildings.

Should he make for the garrisons or the barracks rather than staff headquarters? Headquarters should know what's going on, but the garrison might be safer.

Is it the Chileans? He'd exchanged plenty of fire with them in Bolivia, but the two nations left each other completely alone in their respective territories. Had they decided to start something? That was madness. They already had their hands full with two wars.

If not the Chileans... Brazilians? Impossible.

A plane flies low overhead, so low that people duck. For a moment, it reminds him of the handful of pieces of obsolete junk that littered Valpes airfields, pushed to the side.

Bolivians? Madness! The place is a shambles, a backward mess of feuds and factions. Besides, there's no news from the forts. Surely, they'd have reported an attack. And anyway, any attack on the forts is doomed to fail, they could hold out against anything the natives could throw at them. And even if they were pressed, reinforcements were just across the border. It made no sense.

A coup then? Someone is taking over in Buenos Aires? Some kind of struggle between generals? But who? And which side does he need to be on?

A truck passed by filled with Argentine soldiers. He waves and yells, but takes no notice. They careen around the corner.

And that's when he notices the gunfire coming down the street. Staff headquarters is barely a block away, but even from this distance he can see the building is burning. The pop pop of firearms is continuous. Change of plans, he needs to get to one of the garrisons. They're scattered all over the city. You can't just displace the residents of course, so if you are bringing troops and supplies, you put them where there was room to spare. He tries to think of the closest ones.

He hears shouts. Bolivian accents? Indigenous? How did they get past the Forts? And why didn't we get warning? How do they think they'll succeed here, they're twice the numbers of any fort in Boliva, three times.

New World War – Page 319

And then the epiphany comes. They bypassed the Forts; they ignored them and came here. Juju isn't set up as a fort, its supply station, units scattered all over the city and surroundings, no defensive placements at all. They're going to try and take the City, and if they can, then they can roll up the forts, the entire Bolivian expedition will come crashing down.

By the holy mother, if they take the city, they could take Salta. Hell, between the railways and the rivers, they could march all the way to Buenos Aires.

The sounds of battle are everywhere. Screams and cries; guns and artillery. Smoke is thick in the air, and beneath that, the smell of cordite and gunpowder is overwhelming.

They're just Indigenous, Schmidt tells himself. He knew their kind in Bolivia, lazy, shirkers, good for stabbing in the back, but not for a fight. Raiders who strike and run away. He is starting to plan, to adjust to new realities. He dismisses the nearby garrisons, they're in town, swamped with civilians. They'll be next to useless. He needs to make his way to the barracks near the armoury on the outskirts, rally a defence, and run the Indigenous off. Once the resistance organizes, they'll retreat. How many officers are left? Maybe it's just him. He'll be a hero.

He'll need a car. Or a horse. Or something.

Almost out of nowhere, a group of Indigenous on horseback appears before him. He gapes. The leader is the ugliest woman he's ever seen, brown weathered face, broken nose, scar and smoking a cigar.

For a moment, they stare at each other.

Then she levels her rifle.

***

New World War – Page 320

Chile - The Final Battles, June to October, 1944

By mid-June, the only active Chilean presence in Bolivia is the well defended mining district, but that is cut off. Chilean forces there have no ability to break out or counterattack, and can only die on the vine.

In the meantime though, even as the noose closes in Bolivia, Ibanez's offensive in Chile overruns Arequipa. From there, Chilean forces push their way through Nazca where they encounter but overcome heavy fire. By mid-June, the Chileans reach Chincha, on the edges of the Lima province and barely a couple of hundred miles from Lima itself.

The Chilean strategic objective is to take Lima, either crushing the revolution right there, or if fighting continues, establishing a puppet Peruvian government in Lima, and demonstrating control of the country to the Americans.

In order to take the city, the offensive carries massive numbers of artillery pieces and munitions. Ibanez has learned from Alba's mistake. Alba was able to fight to the gates of the city, but lacked the heavy firepower to enter it. The Chileans are carrying that heavy firepower, even if it means a loss of speed of advance. The compromise between artillery and speed is deemed acceptable, and even as far as Chincha, it proves out.

For Chile and Ibanez, all the suffering finally pays off. Victory is in sight.

Unfortunately, the same issue that plagued previous Chilean offensives comes to the fore. The offensive outruns its supply lines. This produces several temporary halts, as the offensive waits for its baggage trains to catch up. By Chincha however, those supply lines fail completely.

The inevitable Inca counterattacks take place on a wide front ranging from Chincha down to Antofagasta.

For Chile, it is an unprecedented military disaster. The bulk of Chile's expeditionary force is separated and scattered along the coast, like a string of broken pearls.

The remnants of the Chilean navy attempt to provide support from shore bombardment, and there are amphibious rescue operations, to little effect. The scattered army groups fight to re-join, but even where units manage to reunite, they find themselves short of ammunition, food, medical supplies and even water.

The Inca strike south across Argentine territory into Antofagasta, routing under-equipped and unprepared Chilean forces in a series of small battles. By August 18, 1944, after a pitched battle, the city of Antofagasta falls, and the province is in their hands.

From there the Chilean forces stumble through a series of military disasters, disintegrating as they go. On September 1, the Inca push into Coquimbo. September 10, the last remnants in Bolivia surrender. September 14 sees the obliteration of the largest surviving army group in the north, and any hope of reformation and rescue.

The last hope of the Chileans is Argentine intervention, and Ibanez send a series of urgent missions to Buenos Aires pleading for help and offering increasingly grandiose concessions. The Argentines for their part are less and less enthusiastic.

****

Cry for Argentina

The attack on San Salvador de Jujuy cripples their military presence in the north. Through the month of August, the Inca Generals, Diabla and Huascar, occupy the Argentinian Altiplano; establishing a series of fortified positions and essentially wipe out the Argentine mission in Bolivia.

The occupied Argentine highlands are used as a back door, attacking adjacent Chilean provinces, all the while the Argentine junta struggles to prepare a response.

The Argentine northern forces are badly split, with a major army group bogged down in the outer edges of the Paraguayan Chaco, while reserve forces attempt to consolidate at the City of Salta, to prepare a counterattack.

In Buenos Aires the Argentine junta is in complete disarray, with recriminations and screaming matches back and forth over who is to blame for the Bolivian disaster, or to blame for going into Bolivia in the first place. President Pedro Pablo Ramirez is replaced by his colleague and rival, Edelmiro Farrell.

The new President Farrell threatens to declare war directly on the Inca, but despite Chilean urging, hesitate to take that step. Other members of the junta cite the lack of preparation and the need to gear up for war. The record of countries leaping into war unprepared, France and England against Germany for example, is not a good one. Russia was unprepared for war with Germany, and it suffered greatly. Only the United States has done well, and there it has oceans between it and the enemy, to allow it time to be ready. Argentina does not have an ocean between it and the Inca Empire. Rather, there are direct river and rail pathways from the Altiplano to the gates of Buenos Aires. Farrell's protege, Juan Peron, counsels diplomacy. The consensus is to buy more time.

Farrell demands immediate withdrawal of Revolutionary forces from Argentine territory. This is the minimum he can safely do, while trying to organize a rapid armament. The response from Lima is ambiguous, alternately denying incursion, promising to withdraw, and accusing Buenos Aires of invasion. Diplomatic missions fly back and forth between Buenos Aires and Lima, continually revising their positions and arguments with every development.

 Buenos Aires complains to America about the invasion of their sovereign territory. But considering their occupation of Paraguay and their record in Bolivia, they receive little sympathy.

Diplomatic missions to Brazil are fruitless. The Vargas regime has witnessed Argentina's meddling in Paraguay, Bolivia and Uruguay along their borders, they are unimpressed, to say the least. There is little sympathy and no help. The best that can be achieved is an agreement for a drawdown of forces along the border, which frees up troops to be rushed to Salta. Anything more will require major concessions, Vargas is a hard bargainer.

The Argentine Junta attempts to stir up war fever over the occupation of their sacred national territories. But the urban Argentine population in Buenos Aires, weary of the endless disasters and losses of the Bolivian adventure, sapped and demoralized by the Depression cannot bring itself to care about the goings on in a remote, thinly populated province. Although newspapers frantically beat the war drums and appeals to patriotism are everywhere, attempts to institute a call up of troops result in a series of anti-draft riots only barely contained by martial law.

Juan Peron, who has cultivated support among unions and labourers, is arrested by Farrell, but soon released on promise of support.

The hasty and ill prepared counterattack on the occupied Altiplano, fails utterly on September 28. Principle reasons for the failure include micro-management from Buenos Aires, poor coordination among local commanders, lack of flexibility, a failure to understand the highlands geography and carefully chosen entrenched positions, all leading to massive casualties. This is followed a day later by the collapse of the Argentine army in the Chaco when Echeverria finally attacks.

Within days, the Inca counterattack, taking advantage of logistical breakdowns and bottlenecks. Supply chains are so poorly organized, that some Argentine detachments are literally without ammunition. Inca forces break through Argentine lines at various points, these breakthroughs are used to flank. Argentine force discipline collapses, as some units are surrounded, and others retreat.

By October 4, the city of Salta in the north has fallen to the Inca Revolution. Panic grips the Argentine nation. The newspapers and radio stations, the remnants of the civilian political establishment in Buenos Aires turn their fury on the General Farrell. His resignation comes the next day. In his place, Juan Peron becomes the new President of Argentina.

On October 7, Tupac Amaru III and Manco Yanqui request a Peace Summit with the President of Argentina.

Peron accepts.

****

October 6, 1944, Outside of Jujay

Perdita Diabla was not kind to the city of San Salvador. Entire districts have burned down, public buildings shelled to rubble. A substantial chunk of the population is fled, another chunk living in makeshift tents and shelters of the watchful eye of the Inca soldiery.

But the airfield is intact, and many of the leaders of the revolution have gathered. Among them, storied names, Nicola Bandita, RumMaqui Bastido, Two Gun Echeverria himself, QuizQuiz Guerrero down from the mountains of Ecuador, Singalong Huascar, Cowboy Chiraka, Iron Head Taruk, Perdita Diabla and of course Manco Yanqui and Tupac Amaru III. There were others, but they were mainly in the field. The ones gathered here are delegated the authority to make war or peace.

The night is cool; they sit on their packs, huddling under blankets, in a rough circle, in what has become the traditional way. There is a fire blazing in the centre, and a boy proudly tends it. This is the way they all learned to talk to each other when they were fighting for the Peruvians, or for Penaranda or Villarroel. This is the way they gathered, when the Criollo weren't looking, so they didn't need to fight each other. This is the way they'd formed the revolution.

Behind them were the clever boys, as Yanqui liked to call them. They were all sorts, Quechua quartermasters, Criollo historians, geographers, map makers, mechanics, accountants, perhaps two dozen advisors, some old and trusted, some recent but clever and brought specially for this occasions.

There is an informality to the old soldiers. They greet each other, exchange jokes, catch up. A fermented beverage, Chicha is passed around. For a while, the conversation is informal.

Then Tupac stands up, walks over to the fire, and tosses the remainder of his drink onto it. The flames roar and hiss loudly.

Everyone goes quiet.

He goes back to his back and sits down.

"All right," he says. "These new Criollo, these folk of La Plata. What about them?"

"Dogs," says Diabla. "They're dogs. They're rich and they're full of themselves. The fancy themselves Masters, and they came to our lands because they thought they could take it. But you kick them hard; they curl up and run away."

"Huh," Tupac replies.

"Weak," Echeverria offers. "Not well lead. No stomach for a real fight."

"There are," QuizQuiz Guerrero says, "quite a lot of them though."

He raises a hand. A Mestizo steps forward.

"How many of them are there?" he asks.

"Fourteen million," the Mestizo says. "I can tell you..."

"That sounds like a lot," QuizQuiz says. "How many of us?"

"Ten or twelve million. But…"

"Hum," QuizQuiz says. "That is a lot."

"I can see why they decided to pick a fight with us," Huascar offers. "They thought they could take the country. Like they did with Paraguay, they come in as friends. Then one day, they are running things. That's how it was with Valpes, they made him their dog."

"Friends like that are enemies," Tupac said. "The worst kind, they cut your throat while you sleep, and smile at you as you bleed to death."

"They have big stomachs, and big eyes. They see something, they want it. That's how it is with the Criollo, and these Argentines, these folk in Buenos Aires, they're Criollo through and through. Like the Chileans," Nicola offers. "Capitalists."

"Greedy," someone offers. "Greed fills their hearts."

"I find," Tupac says, "the Chileans are brave enough. They fight hard. What about these Argentines. How are they?"

This leads to a round of discussions of various battles, reminisces of campaigns, only some of which talk about the Argentine expedition.

One at a time, Echeveria, Huascar and Diabla are invited to recite their campaigns, the details pored over, questions are asked, particularities of weather and geography examined, the motivations and decisions or Argentine commanders debated and the merits of Argentine soldiers discussed.

"Jujuy," Tupac says, "and Salta. They fell so easily? They fought better in Bolivia. Even in Chaco they fought better. How is it that they fight so well there and so poorly in their homes?"

"Poorly prepared, poorly led."

"It's a matter of initiative, when they are about their own plans, they're capable. But there's no flexibility, they don't adapt. If something goes wrong, they don't know what to do. If you attack, they do not know what to do. They fold."

"Yes," Tupac says. "That's the thing with white men. Always, they have plans. They make good plans, it makes them dangerous. But they're nothing without their plans, take that away, and they fall into confusion."

"We let them come after us," Echeverria says, "it will be bad. Better to attack first. Someone has to choose the battle, better it's us."

"There's a lot in what you say," Tupac admits. "But they chose to battle at Salta."

"They didn't choose," Perdita replies. "They reacted, we scared them; they struck without thinking or planning."

Tupac nods.

"It's not good to have a foe that outnumbers you. Let him pick his time, it's not good. Even if we win, we'll bleed. Maybe it's better to attack first and finish him? What say you?"

Around the circle, one by one, hands go up, except for Guerrero and Yanqui.

"A battle," Manco Yanqui speaks up, "is one thing. To win a battle, that is a good thing. But unless you put them down good, your enemy will always come back. How do we conquer these Argentines?"

"Big country," Rum Maqui Bastido offers. "A lot of land between here and there."

"There?"

"Buenos Aires."

"It's all river country," Perdita says.

"Like the Chaco?"

"No, nothing like the Chaco. Rivers all over, flat lands, leading all the way to Buenos Aires. We have the maps."

"And railroads," Huascar says. "Railroads everywhere. We could ride to Buenos Aires."

"I like railroads," Taruka offers. "I like that I know exactly where they go. The trouble is, you ride the rails? Your enemy knows exactly where you will be. That's tough."

"You don't have to ride them, where there's a railroad, there's a road. There's a path you can travel."

"But then we're walking! My poor feet!"

"Once you have a foothold though," Chiraka says. "I grew up near a railroad. I worked them as a boy. The rails are good. If you can hold the end, you can ship supplies through, men, as much as you want. If you can get a hundred men to hold an end for a day, at the end of that day, you can put a thousand men anywhere you want. Ten thousand. You can ship everything back and forth."

"It's just getting your foothold that's hard?" someone asks.

"What about the rivers?"

Maps are brought out and passed around. The discussion goes on, examining riverways and railroad tracks. Questions are asked about navigation, barges, pathways along rivers and rails. Through it all, the shape of a campaign, a strategy begins to form, much as it has done for the campaigns against Peru, against Chile, Villarroel and Penaranda. Suggestions are made and discarded, ideas taken up, tested, refined.

Tupac listens and nods as arguments break out, whether the war is feasible, how many men it will take, how they are to be supplied, how long it will take them to move.

Finally, he turns to Manco Yanqui.

"Brother," he says, "you are troubled?"

Yanqui pauses, choosing his next words carefully.

"In the north," he says finally, "I met Alba. We fought, and I took his measure. Capable in a narrow way, a fool in ways that matter. He ruined his nation."

Tupac nods expectantly.

"Alba knows how to win battles," he says. "But he doesn't know how to fight a war. The man is narrow. His vision is narrow. His gaze does not rise above his footsteps."

"Huh?" Tupac grunts.

"How many times did he beat the Criollo in Lima? A dozen times? More? He smashed every army they raised up against them."

"Sounds like a fine man to me," Nicola says. "If I'd been up there, he might have won the battle; but I'd have won his pants."

Everyone laughs.

"But look at how he fought," Manco says. "He could have stayed home, bled them out. He could have won all his battles without leaving his lands. He goes all the way to Lima, but if he can do that and win as he goes, he could just as easy have stayed home and won, just the same."

Manco raises a hand.

"But he fights battles, not a war. When he goes out to Lima, he makes them afraid, he makes them angry. They never stop trying after that. He could have stayed home, and eventually, they would have tired and given up. But what he did to them, they would never give up."

"All his victories," Yanqui said, "did nothing but harden his enemy's hearts and resolve. They would never give up. He made it so he could not win."

"He wanted too much," Tupac says. "It is the failure of the Criollo, they always want too much. They go too far. Always. Look at Gamarra."

"Capitalists," Bandita says, spitting at the fire. She's spent a lot of time with leftists. "Alba's the son of a shopkeeper. It's about greed."

"I see what you are saying," Echeverria says. "But we've already crossed the border. Its La Plata land we sit on now, La Plata cities we've already burned. Yes, they had it coming. But that's not the point. You talk about Alba and Lima. Well, it's just like Lima now. We've gone so far, there's no turning back."

"Alba went home," Diabla says. "He didn't go all the way to Lima, he went to its gates and left. We need to go to Buenos Aires, but all the way. Not be like Alba, to go to the gates and turn around. We need to burn it. It's the only way. It's like Alba and Peru; it's them or us. Better to do it now, at our choosing, than later when they come at us."

"Should we be Alba?" Yanqui asks. "Do we have the Criollo disease? Are we greedy? Are we capitalists? Do we reach for too much?"

"Do we have a choice?" Tupac asks. "We know what the Criollo are like. They will not let us abide."

"I think," QuizQuiz says, "that the lesson of Alba is not his hunger; all Criollo are like that. But his stomach; Alba tried for more than he could eat. That was his mistake."

Tupac nodded.

"We all came in airplanes to get here," he continues, "some of us, it was their first time. Me, I've been in planes many times now. Some of us have been further. Manco, he's been all the way to America."

"When I'm in a plane, I look out the window, and I see how big the world is. I see towns and cities, and they are like specks. Mountains are but rock. And yet, as big as the world I see, I've learned the world is bigger."

"We talk of war with Argentina. But their lands are as big as all our lands put together, their numbers greater than all ours. That's a big meal. Can we sit down and eat it? Should we?"

Diabla replies. "It's not the same. The Andes are mountains, hard country. It's a big land, but it's a flat land full of rivers and roads, easy country, all the way to Buenos Aires. We could walk there in our sleep."

"Right now, they're soft and weak. And if we act, they'll fall apart. If we leave them be..."

Before Singalong Huascar responds, Tupac holds up his hand.

"We have made plans to fight tonight. But plans are one thing, the question is before us. If we fight, can we win? I have no wish to go to the gates of Buenos Aires and then walk away like Alba. I have no wish to lose a war that we didn't need to fight."

All the hands went up even Yanqui and Huascar.

"They're soft and foolish yes," Huascar says. "But they can toughen up. Fighting toughens you. If they hold on, they'll toughen. Then what?"

Yanqui whistled.

"You remember what you said about war?" Manco Yanqui asks Tupac.

Tupac closes his eyes for a moment. "War can make you strong, but it can make you tired."

"We've been fighting wars for long time," Yanqui said.

"We're strong."

"Sooner or later, we'll get tired."

"And they might get strong, as we get tired? That would be bad," Tupac says.

"If it was just La Plata," says Huascar, "I wouldn't be bothered. It's as we talked about, it's a good river country, all railroads and waterways, easy country to march through, and a city with no defense."

"But?"

"Brazil. Will Brazil stand by as we gobble up Argentina? Will the Anglo? What about the Americans? Yanqui's been there. I look over in Asia, over in Africa, in Europe. The Germans, they say we'll just take bite, a little fight. The Japanese say the same. But look at them. They win all their wars, but each just gets them the next war. Do we fight the whole world?"

"Let the world come," Diabla says, "we'll make them bleed. Too long we have Criollo boots on our throats. Never again."

There is a chorus of assent.

Tupac holds up his hand, the voices quiet.

"You know," he says. "I've been to Lima. And to Potosi. And Sucre. And La Paz. Callao. You know what? It's all beaten to shit. Everywhere I go, ruins. The cities of our ancestors are in better shape. Maybe it's time to stop fighting, and start building again."

"The Brazilians never bothered us. Maybe they won't. But if we take a shit in their back yard, maybe we'll have to fight them. Maybe not."

He looks over to Manco.

"Manco, you know the Americanos. You've talked with the President. You've seen their cities. Are they on our side?"

"For now."

"Do you trust them?"

"They were on Ramirez's and Gamarra's side before us. On Ibanez's side before that. There's no trusting tem."

New World War – Page 333

"Can we fight them?"

"I'd rather not."

"I think we should study these Americanos a bit more," Tupac reflects. "They sound difficult."

He pauses for a moment, and then shifts.

"Hum," Tupac rumbles. "It's a big world. Maybe the Argentines will be easy to beat, and maybe they won't be. But either way, we'll have to go back to our people and tell them we want them to march to a place they never heard of and fight people they don't know. And maybe we tell them that there might be another fight after that; and another fight behind that one..."

"...Maybe we just go home," he concludes.

"And if they come after us?"

"Didn't someone say they were cowards?" Tupac asks. "Dogs, that's the word I heard. Kick them and they curl up."

"Dogs bite, if they think they see an advantage."

"They do," Tupac agrees.

"We need to hold this ground," Diabla insists. "High ground. If we hold the Altiplano, they can't touch us."

"Sensible," Tupac says. He looks around.

The hands all went up.

"Salta and JuJuy?"

"Give them back. This close, they're hostages, we can come and burn them if we need to," Echeverria offers.

"They're just Criollo towns," Huascar says.

Tupac looks to Diabla. She shrugs and spits in the dirt.

Tupac nods.

"So we give them back a couple of crumbs, but we say, "this piece of pie, we're keeping.' Will they agree?"

"Will they have a choice?"

"Their pride will hurt," Yanqui says. "But they're dogs. Let's throw them a bone."

"Like?" Tupac asks.

"Chile," Yanqui says. "Give them the low southern part. We have no use for it. There's nothing down there worth having. It's just rocks."

"We don't have it to give to them," laughs Chiraka. "Not yet, anyway."

"Even better," replies Yanqui. "Let the dogs think they've won the bone. Let them toss their heads with pride, as they do half our work for us."

"Would that work?" Echeverria asks.

"I heard this about in Europe," Yanqui says. "Russia and Germany, they like to fight. One day, it looks like they're going to fight. You know what they do instead? They each take a big bite out of Poland. No more Poland, but Mister Adolph and Mister Stalin, they're fat and happy."

Tupac Amaru II nods in agreement.

"We will do that then. We will keep what we've took; we'll give them back what we don't want. And in exchange, we'll let them fight Chile with us, and they can keep the parts we don't want."

He looked around. All hands went up.

"Summon their head men," Tupac Amaru II orders. "We will talk peace."

"And if they won't agree?"

"Then we'll go down their rivers and rails and burn Buenos Aires to the ground."

"Fair enough," Yanqui says.

***

New World War – Page 335

The Fall of Chile

September 27, Ibanez is overthrown by a military coup, fleeing to Argentina. The new military junta in Chile undertakes desperate measures to reorganize a defense.

Nevertheless, the last pockets of Chilean forces in the north surrender or are obliterated by October 1. On October 4, 1944, there is fighting in Valparaiso.

By October 16, raids reach as far south as Maule and beyond. A sense of widespread panic and hopelessness overcomes the Chileans. Massive numbers of refugees flock to the cities of Santiago and Valparaiso or flee further south. The Chilean army, its command structure in disarray with Ibanez overthrow, lurches from one disaster to another. The Navy futilely scuttles up and down the shorelines, occasionally bombarding, but more often silently witnessing.

On October 31, the city of Valparaiso surrenders without siege to an Inca army under Iron Head Taruka, under condition of safe treatment. Inca forces take the coastal town of Concepcion, and continue to drive south.

***

November, 1944 - Stab in the Back

On November 1, 1944, the Argentines, unable to mount an effective offensive against the entrenched Inca occupying its Altiplano, turn south in a surprise attack against a weaker target. Argentina occupies the Chilean capital, Santiago, flooding it with troops and installing Ibanez once again as the head of a provisional regime. The rape of Chile begins.

Members of the Chilean Junta escape south to the town of San Bernardo, reconstituting the remnants of their government. The Chilean Army is in a state of collapse. The Navy remains active but is unable to affect proceedings.

Instead, the collapsing government makes plans to take the Navy and re-establish themselves as a provisional government in exile deep in the Pacific, on Rapa Nui and the Juan Fernandez Islands. None of these Islands offer usable harbours or facilities, but they do represent a fig leaf of unconquered Chilean territory.

The last reachable safe harbour, literally the only reachable neutral nation in the world, is Uruguay and its port of Montevideo. But to reach it they must sail around the Cape Horn and up past the Atlantic coast of Argentina. But there is no other choice. The Government in Exile sets sail, begging for British or American assistance, or at least recognition.

On November 6, representatives of Argentina and the Inca sign the Santiago Accord (actually signed in La Paz).

The accord essentially endorses and recognizes Argentine rule in Paraguay and Inca rule in Bolivia. The boundaries of the Chaco established by the 1935 Chaco war are confirmed.

Chile is characterized as a belligerent power and as penalty is to cede the occupied northern areas, including Valparaiso and Concepcion to the Inca as sovereign territory. Inca occupied portions of Argentina are ceded to the Revolution as well.

In return, Argentina is granted the southern Provinces, and the whole of Tierra del Fuego on behalf of Chile.

A rump Chilean state under the leadership of Carlos Ibanez, and including an enclave of the city of Santiago and rail connection to Argentina, is recognized, but under Argentine occupation as a 'trust,' similar to the nominally independent status of Paraguay. Ibanez attends in La Paz to witness the Santiago Accord, but refuses to sign on behalf of Chile. Peron simply signs on his behalf.

Ibanez's puppet government formally joins Argentina and Paraguay; in the Argentine lead Grand Confederation. The Inca, in return for the Grand Confederation formally abandoning Valpes and relinquishing any further claims on Bolivia, grants its recognition.

Chile has, for all intents and purposes, ceased to exist, divided between two powers.

Through the first weeks of November, with Incan collusion, Argentina begins to occupy the southern provinces of Chile. The Incan Empire, for its part, continues south past Santiago, leaving that city in Argentine hands, consolidating its gains, until the two countries reach agreed borders.

On November 11, 1944, the Inca forces are approaching the town of San Bernardo. Some army units are surrendering to the Inca rather than fight. The last remnants of the independent Chilean government join with the Navy, abandoning the mainland with a fleet of warships and support vessels, petitioning the US, Britain and the Soviet Union for recognition as a government in exile.

****

The Last Fleet

On November 11, 1944, the last remnants of the Chilean state - the Navy, a few shreds of the army, the ruling junta, cabinet members, generals, bureaucrats, prominent citizens, the wealthy and the desperate, their wives and children and hangers on, and a handful of refugees leave San Bernardo heading for sanctuary in Uruguay. There is a sense of panic in the town, already crowded with refugees. Wild rumors, inspired by the heads mounted on pikes around Lima, circulate about the atrocities of the Quechua, tales of rape and mutilation. People are desperate to escape, the ships are overcrowded.

The fleet consists of the battleship, Almirante Latorre, the obsolete battleship Almirante Cochrane; the former German pocket battleship Graf Spee, now renamed the Toro, and the destroyers Almirante Condell, Aldea, Hyatt and Serrano. In addition, the former Peruvian warships, the cruiser Almirante Grau, and the destroyer Garcia, are now part of the fleet, though they retain Peruvian crews and captains. Accompanying them are two passenger ships, the Moreno and Santiago, a fuel ship, and two supply ships.

The remainder of the Chilean navy, all of the smaller ships, the support ships and anything not deemed seaworthy are already sunk or scuttled. These fleeing refugees are all that remains of a century of glorious naval tradition.

As the fleet is underway, Ibanez is on the radio, returned President of a reconstituted Chile, pawn of the Argentines, ordering the fleet to surrender to his authority. The captains and admirals ignore him. Spotter planes, perhaps from the Inca, perhaps from Argentina shadow the fleet as it heads out to sea, but mercifully the expected bombs do not drop.

November 12, 1944, outside the range of aircraft, the destroyer Serrano, the most intact, well supplied and well-armed of the destroyers, with a heavy contingent of Marines, is assigned to Rapa Nui, to safeguard the last remnant of free Chile. The rest of the fleet continues on for the Cape Horn, rounding Tierra del Fuego, evading the southern Argentine naval group, heading deep into the Atlantic to avoid interception.

The slowest ship, the Almirante Cochrane, falls behind and is diverted to the Falklands, with a diplomatic mission to Port Stanley, to again plead for recognition from the British and American authorities. This takes place on November 20 through 22.

The effort only exposes the Almirante Cochrane's position to the Argentine navy. On November 24, 1944, the old battleship is intercepted by an Argentine naval group which includes the American made battleship Rivadavia, the cruiser La Argentina and two destroyers. After a tense standoff, the Cochrane surrenders without conflict.

On December 2, 1944, thirteen hundred miles north, a float plane from the second Argentine naval group, operating out of Puerto Belgrano, sights the Chilean fleet. The Argentine naval unit gives chase, catching it on December 4, 1944. The Argentine fleet consists of the battleship Morena, a second Rivadavia class battleship, two Italian made cruisers, the Almirante Brown and Veinticinco de Mayo, two British made destroyers, the Buenos Aires and San Juan. The Rivadavia class battleships are arguably the most powerful warships in South America.

The Argentine fleet paces the Chilean fleet, demanding surrender. The Chileans refuse. The fleet commander, on board Veinticinco de Mayo radios Buenos Aires for permission to fire.

While awaiting response, the Peruvian ships Almirante Grau and Garcia declare neutrality, and request permission to depart. This is relayed to Buenos Aires, and eventually the word comes back that permission is granted, but Uruguay is off limits. The Peruvian ships head for Brazil.

Following this, the ultimatum is delivered: Surrender or the Argentines will open fire.

The Toro fires first, striking the Moreno with a series of vicious broadsides. The Almirante Latorre joins the barrage, hitting the besieged battleship from the other side. Under heavy fire, fires break out over the Moreno and its return barrages are inaccurate.

The Almirante Brown moves to the rescue, attacking the Toro. Leaving the battleships to duel, the Toro sinks the Almirante Brown decisively. The Veinticinco de Mayo also comes in, but keeps its distance from the Toro; the two ships exchange fire ineffectively.

In the duel of battleships, the Moreno begins to pound the Almirante LaTorre. The Toro alternating between barrages at the Veinticinco de Mayo and the Moreno. The Argentine destroyer Buenos Aires engages the Toro, taking damage and giving it.

The older Chilean destroyer Almirante Condell, joins the battle against the Moreno, but takes heavy damage and begins to list. It will be the second ship lost in the engagement. The Chilean destroyer, Hyatt, also attacks the Moreno.

The civilian ships of the fleet try to escape north, pursued by the Argentine destroyer, San Juan. In turn it is pursued by the Chilean destroyer, Aldea. The two ships exchange fire inconclusively.

As night falls, the two forces separate. A frenzy of radio negotiations take place between the Chilean exile Government, Peron personally in Buenos Aires and British intermediaries. The southern fleet, led by the Rivadavia is dispatched north at full speed, leaving the Almirante Cochrane behind with a prize crew, but will take at least a day to arrive. Meanwhile British warships in the area are converging.

During the night, the Moreno is found to be taking on water and beginning to list. Most of the ships are damaged, particularly the Almirante Latorre. But the Latorre and Toro are still capable of fighting. They move to re-join the civilian ships, while the Argentine destroyer San Juan returns to the Argentine fleet. The two groups are just outside firing ranges, moving slowly pacing each other.

At five in the morning, Peron makes his decision. The Chileans may proceed to Montevideo, under escort from the San Juan and Buenos Aires to ensure their good conduct. Once at Montevideo no further operations will be permitted, and any Chilean personnel or ships will be interdicted. The Moreno and the Veinticinco de Mayo will return to Puerto Belgrano. Sea patrol duties will be reassigned to the Rivadavia group.

The Chileans proceed north, directly to the River Plate basin and Montevideo. Before they arrive, the encounter the Argentine cruiser, Puerredon and the destroyers Mendoza, Tucuman, San Luis and Santa Cruz, but there are no hostilities, and the ships proceed into port in Montevideo.

The Moreno, likewise barely makes it back to Port Belgrano with a skeleton complement, much of the crew having been evacuated. The battleship never sails again. Chile's Almirante Cochrane is confiscated by Argentina, but after assessment, the ancient battleship is judged effectively obsolete and scrapped. Publicly, Argentina declares victory.

As to the Chilean warships, the Almirante Latorre is assessed as extremely badly damaged, and the Chilean exile government has no wherewithal for repairs, it is scrapped as well. The Toro is damaged, but the Brazilian government becomes interested in acquiring it. The Exile government sells it to Uruguay as the Garibaldi, under which it is repaired and rendered seaworthy. It sets to sea past Argentine and British warships, and ends up at a Brazilian Port, where it is sold and reflagged, renamed Amazonas. The German crew is awarded Brazilian citizenship, but eventually by 1960 most have returned to the homeland.

The remaining warships remain under interdict in Montevideo, the Exile government holds onto them for a while, but cannot afford the cost of a navy, and the Argentines have made it clear that any exile ship living Uruguayan waters will be interdicted or sank. Ibanez attempts to negotiate for their return to his puppet government, but this goes nowhere. The balance of the navy is pledged or sold outright to Uruguay for operating funds. The Serrano in the Pacific is sold to the new Philippine state following American recognition of the Exile government.

***

Ecuador and Colombia, The Aftermath of Lojas...

The battle of Lojas leaves the Inca with certain respect for the Ecuadoran soldiers and command structure and considerable contempt for the Colombians. In both cases, this is to influence future decision making.

In particular, the Inca determine to have more control over territory before full scale combat. Among other observations, the Inca note that despite sympathy and interest the expected wave of uprisings among Quechua and Mestizo failed to fully materialize. Ecuadoran society, and its social and economic classes, are managed more consistently and effectively than Peru.

The Ecuadoran Quechua are simply not in the same state of crisis. Substantial enlistment work will be needed. Following the battle, the Inca Empire in the north switches to smaller unit engagements rather than set piece battles, actively working to enlist the local populations in advance, and focussing on intelligence and continuing movement.

Over the next few months, the Revolutionary Inca advance steadily, if erratically, into the highlands and foothills, giving way frequently but always returning. Ecuador's logistics and support network begins to break down, and Alba is forced to continually reconsolidate his positions - a game he called 'Andean checkers.'

But the campaign is typically confined to the Sierra and of low intensity. In Guayaquil and Quito there is a sense after Lojas, that they will be left alone. The steady erosion among the Quechua is easy to overlook. But it's a false peace.

The reality is that the Inca have not forgotten about Ecuador. They've just chosen to set it aside while they deal with major campaigns in the south against Chile and Argentina. The Inca Politburo learned from Peru's mistakes of too many wars on too many scattered fronts. Ecuador's time will come; it is a nation of the Quechua, and in the new ideology of the revolution, to leave a portion of the Quechua people under European thumb is utterly intolerable.

In Ecuador, the celebrations over the victory at Lojas is marred by Colombian fury. The Colombians feel that Alba directly placed their forces at point position on the front lines, in direct contravention of instructions and agreements. The Colombians demand Alba's removal as commander. The legislature agrees. Bonifaz and Velasco flatly refuse

The scandal is eventually papered over, but it creates a rift between Bonifaz' junta and the Colombians. In turn, the Colombians find themselves increasingly allied with the Conservative opposition in the Ecuador legislature.

As the Colombian's invest in Ecuador, the shattered economy begins to rebuild. Conditions are still terrible, but no longer so utterly desperate. Ecuadorans, teetering for so long on the edges of financial disaster and catastrophe find themselves tolerating the subordination of their society, so long as it brings a little relief.

June 18, 1944, President Bonifaz suffers a debilitating stroke. Velasco Ibarra, the Prime Minister, immediately assumes Presidential duties, despite protests from the legislature. Eventually, Ibarra's position is confirmed for a maximum of one year, but is contingent on Bonifaz recovery and return to office. This is an outcome no one believes in, but at least the compromise offers stability.

However, on July 30, Bonifaz passes away, without ever regaining consciousness.

At this point, Ibarra, disregarding the previous compromise, goes to the legislature, seeking formal appointment as President until such time as elections can be held at some unspecified date. The Legislature refuses.

In protest, Ibarra tenders his resignation, and to his shock and horror, it is accepted. This marks the end of the

Bonifaz/Ibarra/Alba triumvirate which has ruled Ecuador since 1931.

The new Interim President, Alfredo Moreno, supported by the legislature, takes immediate steps to ensure that the final member of the triumvirate, Alba does not launch a coup. General Enrique Gallo is appointed supreme commander of the armed forces, and beneath him, Alba's command is divided between Alba and three other commanders. Logistics, Navy and Air force were also separated from the army. The Ecuadoran military is reduced to a series of segregated local commands, with a governing committee lead by Gallo deciding on strategy. Alba is not on the committee.

Two Colombian generals are accorded observer status on the committee, representing supporting contingents in Guayaquil and the rest of the country. Alba is left as the supreme commander for the conduct of the war, subject only to Gallo theoretically. But in practical terms the title is now without authority. The measures are intended to foreclose any political ambitions Alba might have.

Alba's defensive war in the Altiplano continues to go poorly, even as he is hamstrung for resources. Frustrated, Alba begins to complain and write directly to the President and members of the Legislature, which earns him several reprimands.

General Gallo, an old school military man, from the traditional ruling class, fails to appreciate the significance of the situation in the interior.

***

Quito, Ecuador, September 8, 1944

It is warm out, and dry for once. The park is full. Flores and Alba sit on a park bench watching children playing. It is nice to see children playing. Most adults have little to cheer for.

Flores brings lunch, a bottle of wine, a couple of sandwiches. Flores is nervous, without seeming to, he keeps looking around. The two men eat and drink quietly.

After half an hour, when Flores is reasonably sure that they aren't being watched, he quietly pulls a folded piece of paper from his valise under the guise of fiddling with the wine bottle.

"Take a look at this," Flores says quietly.

Alba makes no secret of the document. He boldly holds the paper in his hands, noting the Presidential seal and the date of September 9, and reads it.

"I've been removed from Command," he says finally. "By order of President Moreno, effective immediately."

Alba shrugs.

"It's been coming for a while," he says thoughtfully. "Cordova's running the Altiplano. Moreno's in Guayaquil. The Colombians are everywhere. I'm not even getting memos any more. Every time I send a memo, I get a reprimand back."

Alba grunts.

"Cordova! We're losing the Sierra, the whole of the highlands, it's being nibbled away. But Cordova, what's his bold new strategy? Make some examples! Don't spare the rod! Let the Haciendas lead!"

"Far cry from Supreme Command," Flores says. "You can't tell me it doesn't hurt."

"Since the old man had his stroke, it's all gone to hell," Alba says. He looks again at the paper. "So I'm now on detached command, stand by and wait for new assignment. What does that even mean? Do I take a vacation? Just sit at home and wait?"

"Not for long," Flores says. He passes another sheet of paper.

Alba reads it, his face carefully blank.

"This is a warrant for my arrest and extradition: War crimes. It mentions a criminal complaint sworn before a judge in Bogota."

Alba stares at the paper. His free hand clenches his knee, he hunches forward.

"Calm, my friend," Flores says, looking around casually.

"What is this?" Alba said. "Where did you get this?"

"We still have friends," Flores says softly. "Even in the President's office. Clerks and typists, there's a young secretary who is quite fond of me. She slipped me the file copies. Later on, I will see her tonight. Tomorrow morning, she will slip them back in the files, no one the wiser."

"What is intended to happen tomorrow," Flores says, "is that sometime during the day, you will be relieved of command, and sent home to wait your new orders. Then when you are sitting at home, perhaps towards evening, there will be a knock on your door. Then you will be on a plane to Bogota... And then that's the last anyone will hear of dear Colonel Louis Larrea Alba, Napoleon of the Andes."

"I imagine that sometime after your disappearance, the paperwork will vanish from the files, and it will all be a great mystery."

"Lojas," swears Alba. "It's Lojas. They've been after me since Lojas."

"One of those Colombians at Lojas," Flores says, "must have had an important father. Maybe a few of them had important fathers, more than a few. It must have sounded so grand for sons of privilege, good for a political career. Be a soldier! Exotic adventure in a foreign battlefield! Win a few medals, be a hero, all the while kept carefully out of harm's way. So brilliant. Too bad war is such a messy thing."

New World War – Page 347

"Manco Yanqui," Alba laughs softly. "The clever bastard, he wins in the end."

"Personally," Flores says, "I'd take my chances with him, he seems a cheerful fellow. But those Colombians... they know how to carry a grudge."

Flores shudders.

"Cheer up though," Flores offers. "Maybe it's not personal after all. I read this thing about lions one time, when a young lion takes over a pride, the first thing they do is kill the old lions. Embarrassing for the Colombians to have someone like you hanging around. You make them look bad, just by existing. And who knows what you might get up to, who you might talk to..."

"Still," he concludes, "I'd still prefer to take my chances with Manco Yanqui."

"This wouldn't happen under the old man," Alba says.

Flores grunted. "That isn't quite true. The Colombians were slowly taking over despite Bonifaz. Still, at least he'd never been as cravenly servile as the milksop, Moreno."

"I should speak to Velasco," Alba says. "Maybe he can do something. He's still got some pull."

"Luis," Flores says, "Velasco's gone."

"What?"

"Gone."

"Dead?" Alba wonders, his voice tentative. "Missing? I hadn't heard anything."

"Last month, after the Legislature refused to appoint him to replace the old Man, remember? He resigned? They appointed that weasel Moreno as President, elevated Gallo? He went on that mission to Bogota? Except that he flew to Caracas instead, and never came back."

"I hadn't heard this!"

"No one is advertising it," Flores replies. "His household is still running; his servants are still on staff. He sends letters back to his household, they post it from there."

"Does Moreno know?"

Flores shrugs.

"I imagine he does. But no one is talking about it. Think of what it would be like if the news got out? The former head of government making a run for it? That's not going to fill people with confidence."

"He never told me," Alba whispers. He is surprised by how much it hurts. They'd worked together for years, and while they'd not always gotten along, it still bothers him.

"The former number two and three men," Flores muses. "The first time you were caught talking to each other, even suspected of talking to each other, that's a bullet in each of your brains."

"That's not Ecuador."

"Yes," Flores agrees. "But that's Colombia. Have you paid attention to who is really running things lately?"

"So what now?" Alba says. "The legislators? The newspapers? Who do we go to?"

Quietly Flores retrieves the papers and tucks them back in his satchel.

"These need to go back," he says. "I hear Caracas is nice this time of year. Venezuela, I like the sound of it."

"We can't run," Alba says. "I can't run. Not after fighting so hard for this country."

He shakes his head.

"Look around you," Flores says. "It's done. Ecuador's finished. It's over. Moreno? That shit Gallo? The legislature? Just finger puppets now. The Colombian vultures have taken everything."

Alba lets out a long sigh.

"It all comes to this," he says finally. "Ten years of work. All that planning. All that fighting. All those lives lost. And... nothing."

Flores shrugs.

"Why did we even bother? I don't even know. We should have all just stayed home. Let Peru take the Oriente. No one even cared about it but the Indigenous who lived there. Just lines on a map. No one would have died; everyone would have got on with their lives. Now, everything is ruins, it all ended in destruction for everyone, even Peru. In the end, it all went to the vultures. Why were we all so determined? What was the point?"

"Was pride our sin? We thought we were saving our country, but we've lost it completely. All this suffering, and it comes to this, we've lost everything. Why? Why should we have bothered? We should have just let it go."

For a while, neither of them speaks.

"Maybe God knows how things turn out," Flores murmurs. "But men don't. We do what we must."

Alba sighs, a long and heartfelt sound.

Flores pats his hand.

"In the game of cards," Flores says, "sometimes you get lucky, sometimes you don't. But when it comes, you need to know when it's time to leave the table."

"You're not the only one with a warrant from Bogota on your head. I got very lucky, a card turned up my way, just one card. I shared that luck with you. Now I say it's time to leave the table. I'm leaving."

"If you go in tomorrow, that's your choice. But if you do, know that twenty-four hours after you walk into headquarters, you'll be a dead man. Your choice."

Flores glances at him. "All I'm saying is that I hear the weather in Caracas is really nice this time of year."

****

Colombia, Marching off the Cliff

Oddly enough, the effective political takeover of Ecuador by the Colombian Conservative faction defuses tensions with the United States. America perceives this as a reform or cleansing of Ecuador from the Nazi taint.

The United States is even beginning to discuss the historical claims of Gran Colombia as a basis for a union between the two states - a union which will provide a credible bulwark against the communists in Peru.

Almost half a century ago, the Americans took Panama away. But now the winds have changed, and it looks like they'll give Ecuador to Bogota. And who could defy the mighty Americans?

It is in this context that Colombia reacts to the Inca encroachment on Ecuador by committing even more aggressively. With clear deliberation, Colombia's conservatives, as represented by its military, backed by the most traditional elements of its polity, and with the apparent support of the United States commit to facing down the Inca Empire.

Why not? If you think the Americans will fight your battles for you?

It does not go well. The Inca move up through the highlands, engaging in a multitude of small coordinated actions which take apart Ecuadoran supply lines and forward bases.

Up until September, 1944, Alba maintains a coherent defensive strategy, slowly giving ground. But after his removal, things begin to fall apart rapidly.

The military, backed by Colombia, stages a coup. Moreno is removed, the legislature is dissolved.

Ecuador's new President, Manuel Borrero, has no appreciation for the complexities of the Interior. Alba's replacement, General Gallo, is an old school Criollo, utterly racist and entirely incapable of dealing with the situation.

He assigns the Quechua highlands to General Cordova, a reactionary. Cordova's punitive approach rapidly alienates the Quechua, the Mestizo and even some of the Haciendas. The local population turns hard against Quito and the Inca make steady inroads.

By December, 1944, much of the interior is under the control of the Inca. Quito is cut off from Guayaquil. The Amazonas, or Oriente, region is entirely lost. The rump Ecuadoran government is reduced to fragments: Guayaquil and Quito, the coastline and the northern provinces.

In any event, this rump government has largely ceased to exist, with Colombians occupying or controlling all significant civilian positions.

Borrero is replaced by Arroya, who is replaced by General Gallo, who remains head of a nominal government, but is entirely under the control of Colombian advisors. Colombian advisors' are inserted at key points in the military structure. Those who object tend to disappear. The legislature is dissolved and replaced with a Colombian-appointed legislative advisory council.

Ecuador expires, not with a roar, but barely a whimper.

In Veracruz, Luis Larrea Alba weeps for his lost nation.

By January and February, 1945, Quito and Guayaquil, both cities now firmly under the control of large Colombian delegations and military contingents, are under siege by QuizQuiz Guerrero.

Tupac Amaru III formally offers safe passage to the Colombians back to their own country. Accepting such an offer, however, would amount to a political disaster for the Colombian Conservatives.

Instead, the Colombian military embarks on its first and only major military campaign in the war, when it launches a series of columns from Pasto to rescue and break the siege of Quito. At the same time, it implements a massive program of resupplying Guayaquil by sea with troops, artillery, medical supplies, ammunition and food.

The result is a disaster of epic proportions. QuizQuiz Guerrero, wielding a northern army force half again larger than the entire Colombian military, catches the Colombians en route to Quito on Ecuadoran soil and obliterates them in a one sided bloodbath on February 14, 1945.

Thereafter, Guerrero marches north, crossing the Colombian border on February 16, and taking the city of Pasto on February 20. The battle of Pasto is a rout. The Colombian army, unprepared and with no real fortifications, break and flee in a disorganized fashion. Quito falls on February 21, 1945, adding to the sense of panic. Nine days later, Guayaquil surrenders.

QuizQuiz Guerrero continues to sweep north through the Colombian highlands, assigning detachments to the interior and coast as he goes. The Colombians put up no organized resistance.

Appalled, the Americans in Panama commence air attacks on Inca forces in Colombia, with raids extending as far south as northern Peru. These have little effect. Washington declines to commit ground forces, focussing instead on the European and Pacific theatres.

The coastal city of Bueneventura falls.

Finally, the Roosevelt administration will take no more. It announced that if Inca forces enter the city of Cali, the United States will declare war. QuizQuiz Guerrero continued to advance. On March 4, 1945, Manco Yanqui and Tupac Amaru III fly by airplane to a landing strip just miles from the city of Cali, to stop the advance. More members of the Inca politburo attend over the next few days.

There are rumours of meetings with American representatives.

On March 11, 1945, under the watchful eye of American and Colombian observers, an Inca soldier plants an Inca flag some 500 yards south of the city of Cali.

Later in the day, there is a radio announcement that the Inca cease their advance and agree to an armistice, with the line running from Buenaventura, to the outskirts of Cali, to the southern shore of the Rio Guavaria. The northern campaign has halted.

New World War – Page 353

There is a tense moment when everyone waits for the next move by the Americans. But they are occupied with their own active fighting in Europe and Japan.

Roosevelt dies on April 12, 1945 and Truman is sworn in, having been Vice-President for only 82 days. Germany surrenders in two months, on May 7, 1945. Japan's surrender comes September 2, 1945.

In the meantime, American troops are not directly engaged in fighting anywhere in South America. The Colombians have played both sides of the fence, and the U.S. doesn't mind seeing them punished for it. They've been an unsatisfactory ally. Perhaps, they'll learn a lesson. In the meantime,

Washington is considering that perhaps this new Inca Empire is someone they can do business with. Copper and tin are far more important than coffee and chocolate.

The battle line become an armistice line. Hostilities cease. The Colombians will not relinquish their claim on the captured territory, but have no ability or inclination to pursue it, and the Americans will not fight this battle for them. There are no further hostilities.

The Andean wars are over.

✳✳✳

AFTERMATH

The New Inca Empire

The New Inca Empire is built upon the former states of Peru, Ecuador and Bolivia, and incorporating parts of Argentina, Chile and Colombia. Roughly 3,000,000 square kilometers, or 1,200,000 square miles, it remains relatively small to medium sized state of less than twenty million people.

The end of the Andean wars brings major challenges. The economies of the coasts are shattered, and the European descended ruling classes are in disarray. Key sectors of their societies suffer demographic depletion. The Criollo classes permanently lose their monopoly on power. On the other hand, the now dominant Quechua are largely unprepared for rule.

The United States initially perceives the Inca as a communist empire and hemispheric threat. Ignorant bumpkins, but in the emerging cold war, ignorance is not an excuse for communism. The initial approach is to attempt to isolate the Empire in hopes of bringing a counter-revolution. The Inca are shut off from international sources of capital, and restricted from trade. The Inca respond to this by gearing up a command economy, a natural outgrowth of the war economies which evolved in the predecessor states. The period of American imposed isolation is as critical to the formation and evolution of the Empire as the war itself.

The fears of a Criollo or Latin genocide fails to materialize. The Empire is simply too physically diverse, with too many local constituencies. However, the great Latifundista landholdings are consistently expropriated, and their owners pensioned off. The great estates are either divided up in land reforms, or administered by new managers. A substantial number of more modest landholdings escape confiscation, some remain, some are sold. There is a migration of the disenfranchised Latifundista class to the coasts and cities.

Great fortunes and conservative bastions are targeted for dismantling. On the other hand, the educated middle class is largely untouched, serving the new regime as it served previous interests. The new regime still needs doctors, lawyers, shop-owners, teachers, etc. The new Quechua lords have little experience with ports, commerce or an export economy; so many persons engaged in this economy continue their work, attempting to negotiate arrangements with the new regime.

The European Latins find themselves experiencing a loss of social and caste status, but for many, there are relatively few economic impacts and very little political persecution. The ruling elites largely discredited and destroyed themselves. The subordinate elites are hollowed out by the wars. The ones who were left generally are in possession of skills which are in demand and can negotiate a degree of security for themselves.

Even then, there are simply not enough of them. The Mestizo find themselves moving into occupations and roles previously shut to them. Urban and resource extraction working classes and Mestizo find their lives improved. In particular, near slave labour conditions in the mines are addressed with new rules regarding miner's rights, working conditions and pay. Mines which become uneconomic are shuttered, but later reactivate as commodity prices adjust. Overall, social mobility increases, and the position of the lower classes improves.

Displaced from power, their traditional world views turned inside out, one result is a remarkable flowering of Criollo culture, and an explosion of novelists, writers, playwrights, and artists of every kind, some celebrating their new masters, many mourning and romanticising a lost era.

For the Quechua of the highlands, the true revolution is trucks. Military surplus vehicles find their way back home into many villages and communities. In addition to transport, trucks and truck engines are put to literally dozens of community uses. These are followed by steam and combustion engines, increasingly manufactured and tailored to the needs of the interior. The remnants of Henry Ford's plant become the nucleus of a heavy manufacturing and industrial sector in former Ecuador.

The proliferation of engines and machines into the highlands changes the traditional Quechua and Aymara ways of life. Communities take advantage of the new machineries to accomplish tasks ranging from construction to irrigation. New farmlands open up, marginal lands revitalize or are repurposed, roads and travel routes are developed. Communities begin to produce surpluses and products which find their way into the mainstream economies.

Historically, the Indigenous of the highlands were outside the economy. The gradual entry of the Quechua into the mainstream economy produces an economic boom. For the highland Quechua, the adoption of increasing numbers of machines produces an emerging class of mechanics to run and repair the machines and to adapt them for various purposes. These mechanics proliferate and diversify, becoming machinists, inventors and engineers. New generations of machines and engines are designed for the purposes and needs of the highlands.

Geographically, the Inca is a state occupying a vast amount of difficult territory. To hold the country together, the Inca are forced to invest massively in infrastructure up and down the coasts, in the highlands, the interior lowlands and between all these regions. In addition to road and communications, there are massive local projects - hydro-electric dams, regional electrification, water channelling for irrigation and local water systems. All this is massively expensive and consumes state resources, but has to be financed internally.

As the Highlands merges together, as communication and transportation unite isolated communities, and as it joins the 'mainstream' economies, Quechuan and Aymaran nationalism and identity develop. A form of 'pidgin' Quechua evolves to facilitate communication between different dialects, and this becomes the basis of a 'Standard Quechua.' A syllabary alphabet is developed and literacy begins to spread widely.

Even during the nadir of American/Inca relations, there is still an active trading relationship. American requirements for tin and copper in particular means that the two regimes have to maintain trade. The United States invested heavily in many of the former states, and this creates conflicts and resentments. Many American enterprises are expropriated or purchased at substantial discounts; compensation disputes drag on for decades in some cases. Lack of access to American technology slows the development of the Inca state - telephone systems for instance remained mired in the 1930s, industries such as oil extraction also lag behind.

The New Inca Empire remains a quasi-communist autocracy under Tupac Amaru III, Manco Yanqui and their successors. Despite fears of communism, in practice the Empire operates a mixed economy which involves local businesses supported or directed by the state. The reality is that unlike, for example, China, where the revolution is ideological in nature, the founders of the Inca revolution are pragmatists without any particular ideology. To form their Empire, they've appealed to indigenous revanchism, and readily embrace leftist ideology. But fundamentally, they are not interested in ideological purity - they care about what works best, and at every level, are inclined to experiment, innovate and adopt what works. Tupac Amaru III and Manco Yanqui are both the focus of cults of personality around each. But neither attains the level of personal power of a Mao or Stalin. Instead, the Inca rulers constitute a diverse politburo of the old soldiers, expanding their ranks over time as conditions warrant.

Oddly, in the early days, the Inca's best relations are with its neighbours. Brazil because geography means both contact and conflicts are difficult, and on the other side Argentina because, ironically, contact and trade is easy. Argentina becomes a major trading partner, and Argentina's isolation means that they have both a strong need for partnership, and no special advantages.

Relations with Brazil, however, go sour as the 1940s come to an end. Brazil's pogroms and actions against the Amazon's native population leaves increasing numbers of refugees flowing across the border into the Inca portions of the rain forest. This results in tensions, and eventually the Inca respond by arming and supplying Brazil's Indigenous population. The resulting conflicts are eventually resolved in the early 1960s.

Support and arming Brazil's native population leads to similar initiatives in Colombia, Venezuela, Guyana and Central America. These are resolved in different ways.

In Guatemala, a Mayan insurgency overthrows the government and leads to a Mayan revival state, heavily supported and subsidized by the Inca and the Soviet Union, and in its own cold war with Honduras.

In Colombia, in the midst of La Violencia, an indigenous 'state within a state' emerges, FARC, controlling much of the interior, fuelled by a deranged fusion of extreme Marxist ideology and Indigenous tribalism. Initially seen, and perhaps actually developed, as an Inca stalking horse, FARC quickly becomes its own mad little kingdom.

In Venezuela and Guyana the result is a slow and awkward process of reconciliation and integration of Indigenous into mainstream society and economy and social reforms.

The Inca are also active internationally in the non-aligned and anti-colonial movement through the early period. Despite efforts, the Inca are not particularly successful in forming alliances with communist China or the Soviet Union. Soviet interest and commitment waxes and wanes pragmatically as the cold war proceeds. To the Soviets and Chinese, the Inca are simply not true communists, but a false path. The Chinese are hostile. The Soviets deal with the Inca when they see some strategic advantage, but truthfully, there isn't much, that's about it.

As Europe and Japan recover from World War II, the Inca's international and trade relationships expand. This eventually leads to a thawing of relations with the United States and detente in the 1960s and 1970s, and to a wave of 'Inca-mania' in the youth counterculture of the time. Around this period, beginning in the late 1960s, the Inca begin to integrate increasingly into the world economy.

In the 1970s, the old politburo, one by one, begins to retire or die off. With the passing of Manco Yanqui in 1984, the wartime generation largely hands the reigns over to its successors. The Empire begins to experiment with liberalism, supporting local and provincial elections, and establishing a legislative advisory body. During this period, focus shifts from state development to individual liberty and prosperity. The Empire continues to liberalize.

In a few years, the Soviet Union will dissolve. China will have its Tianamen Square. The world changes but the Inca endure.

****

Colombia, descent into La Violencia

For Colombia, the brief flirtation with war is a national disaster of catastrophic proportions. Within Colombia, the frequent refrain is that it would have been better for the lost territories to fall into the sea, or the population eradicated by atom bombs or plague, than what happened. An undersized, poorly organized, poorly trained, politically driven Colombian army, operating with little more than delusion and grandiosity, went head on against the battle hardened Inca and was obliterated, falling into one disgrace after another. This is the culmination of years of increasing involvement and entanglement in Ecuadoran affairs, all of which literally imploded overnight.

Along with military disaster is the loss of investment. Tens and hundreds of millions of dollars' worth of loans, of tax and customs assignments, of mineral rights, logging rights, outright land grants, an immense portfolio of Colombian investment vanish overnight without a nickel to show for it. All across Colombia, banks and investment partnerships go bankrupt. The nation plunges into financial disaster.

The Ecuadoran venture explodes in every possible way, financially, militarily, politically, and the explosion runs straight down the fracture lines of the Conservative and Liberal divide. For Colombians, there is only one question:

Who is to blame for this Catastrophe?

The real enemy is not the Inca, but the party on the other side of the table. Colombian society splits.

 La Violencia begins.

The Colombian civil war starts almost immediately. On May 1, 1945, President Pumarejo was assassinated in the 'Pasto Coup' by a group of disgruntled military officers. The officer's junta lasts a week before ongoing riots in Bogota and American pressure force their resignation. Civil disruption and strife, including massive purges in several major cities leaves Colombia in a state of chaos.

In August, 1945, the United States, under the new President Truman, demands that the Inca Empire cease to meddle in Colombian affairs and vacate the whole of Colombian territory it has overrun. The Inca decline, citing the Roosevelt declaration and resulting armistice as well as the ongoing collapse of state order in Colombia. It has nothing to do with them, they proclaim.

Matters vacillate back and forth, as the United States closes in on Japan. Driven by Manco Yanqui, the Inca pursue a relationship with the United States, offering favourable terms for tin and copper from the former Bolivian and Chilean territories. Facing an entrenched foe in the Andes, and unreliable allies in the region, the Americans accede and the Colombian front settles down as an armed frontier. The borders remain to this day as a 'ceasefire line,' and Colombia and the Empire remain in a technical state of war.

The civil war, 'La Violencia' continues on an internecine basis until 1962, characterized by continuous actions of death squads and paramilitaries operating covertly, riots, state purges, and rebellions.

Between 1946 and 1949, in response to massive numbers of refugees pouring into Panama, the United States occupies Colombia. Thereafter, Colombian refugees are expelled from Panama, and the Panamanian border is sealed. A patchy, barely functional Colombian state is established with American support.

The reconstituted Colombian state stands on its own until 1951, when new waves of rioting and assassination, bring about a stateless period. The United States leads an international mission, composed mostly of Americans with some Venezuelan and Mexican constituents and Brazilian support to stabilize the country, which ends in 1952.Estimates of the fatalities of La Violencia range from 300,000 to 500,000. As many as a million Colombian refugees flee into the Inca territories, and another half million flee to Venezuela, before the situation finally stabilizes.

An indigenous Marxist movement, FARC, eventually gains control over a large part of the interior, creating a violent pseudo-state somewhat resembling the Khmer Rouge of Cambodia.

Colombia maintains a state of cold war with the Inca Empire, and refuses to recognize the territories lost to the Inca. The border demarcation is the cease fire line, and remains an armed no man's land. Colombia intermittently refuses to recognize Panamanian independence and lays claim to the Panama Canal, depending on which government is in power.

In the 1950s and 1960s, the United States backs discussions for Venezuelan and Colombian (but not Panamanian, the big dog doesn't give up its bone) unification. Occasionally Guyana is part of these discussions, but they fail to go anywhere.

The Real La Violencia

In real history, even without the disruptions of an Andean War, political violence between Conservatives and Liberals was on the rise in Colombia through the 1940s.

This escalated slowly to the "Pasto Coup" in July of 1944, when Conservative Army officers staged an uprising and actually took the President, Alfonso Pumarejo, hostage. It only failed when the officers in Bogota refused to go along with it. By 1946, Pumarejo was out and the Conservatives had taken power. Assassinations began of Liberal politicians.

The result was the civil war, 'La Violencia' which officially lasted from 1946 through to 1958, and killed as many as 300,000 people, injured as many as 800,000 and produced as many as a million internal refugees.

The stories of La Violencia will curl your hair, particularly of the hideous forms of torture and murder developed. The Colombian Necktie was only of the tip of the iceberg. During La Violencia, no outside nation even tried to intervene. It remained an ongoing bloodbath, an orgy of fear, murder and torture.

***

Argentina's Grand Confederation

Argentina is often called the 'Italy of the Andean War.' It is not generally considered a compliment.

Say that to an Argentine, and the response is that Argentina did far better in the Andean wars than Italy managed to do in either of its World Wars.

The remark is generally understood as an observation that Argentina's role in the war amounted to minimal participation and naked opportunism.

Say that to an Argentine, and they'll simply respond that it worked.

Argentina's effort in the war consisted of a disastrously failed intervention in the Bolivian civil war, an opportunistic land grab on a collapsing state, and a treacherous takeover of an ally. The truth is that Argentina failed its way into success.

Argentina's performance in the Bolivian Civil war is substandard. The Argentine soldiers are poorly motivated, and their equipment obsolete. Still, the focus of Chile and Peru on each other, and the relative remoteness of the Argentine venture, allows the Argentine forces to eke out a few victories, to hold strategic positions, and to act tactically and strategically in Bolivia, either on their own, or through the Valpes faction. There is not much success, but enough to encourage the Argentines to keep in the game, to hold the promise of some ultimate success and reward.

Argentina's greatest successes came in allying with one side or the other in battles, playing spoilers, or exploiting opportunities that were left open. If the military side of the venture is disaster prone, the diplomatic side is active and aggressive. Argentina's diplomats and generals are in constant contact with Lima and Santiago, perpetually bargaining and negotiating, at times holding out for the most generous bid, the most enticing offer. Militarily, this produces one catastrophe after another.

The costs are thousands of Argentine lives, almost entirely in the Bolivian campaigns, some small territorial adjustments in the north, and massive expenditures which catapult the Argentine state deep into debt and destabilizes the economy for generations. But in comparison to literally every other participant of the Andean wars except for Brazil, Argentina gets off lightly.

On the other side of the scales, although Bolivia is utterly lost, Argentina manages to acquire both Paraguay and the southern Remnants of Chile, at minimal cost. Apart from a few territorial concessions, the fictions of these nations remain, but for all practical purposes, they are incorporated into Argentina.

Paraguay's loss of independence is not well received by Brazil, which takes decisive steps to block any Argentine maneuvering with respect to Uruguay. Relations between Brazil and Argentina become chilly, and both countries enter a cold war. Brazilian foreign policy is substantially more hostile to Argentina than to the new Inca Empire.

America and Britain maintain trade and diplomatic relations with the Argentine Grand Confederation. They insist on Chilean and Paraguayan autonomy. The United States continues to maintain recognition of the rump Chilean exile government, to Argentina's annoyance.

Argentina, like Spain, is eventually allowed in from the cold in the 1950s. The escalating cold war with the Soviet Union forces the United States to revise its foreign policy. Argentina poses a challenge - a fascist expansionist dictatorship in a key strategic position in the southern cone. America is aligned with Brazil, Argentina's enemy. But it also can't tolerate Argentina aligning with the Soviets. The result is an awkward partial thaw in relations, supporting the regime while maintaining the hidden threat of military invasion.

The Paraguayan nationalist movement never really goes away. Argentina responds with consistent repression, including persecution of the Guarani Indigenous and regular disappearances of Paraguayan dissidents. A major Paraguayan revolt in 1975 is put down only with difficulty. The issue remains an international black eye.

Unlike the Inca Empire, which literally rebuilds an economy from the ground up, and unlike Brazil, which is the beneficiary of heavy American investment, Argentina is never required to embrace social or economic reforms. Occasional attempts at reform, such as Peronism tend to lose their way and eventually be co-opted by reactionary forces. The Argentine society and economy tends to be a regressive extrapolation of trends and conditions from the 1920s and 1930s.

Beginning in the 1960s, Argentina falls behind, and in the current era is the most backwards and regressive of the Latin states, roughly equivalent to Francisco Franco's Spain. In the modern era, Argentina continues to struggle.

Brazil

Brazil never saw any advantage to involvement with the Andean War, and so its participation is both reluctant and absolutely minimal, focusing solely on regaining and enforcing control of its Amazonian region. Although Brazil declares war on Ecuador, it never takes any overt action against Ecuador beyond liquidating Enrique Blandon's mad crusade.

The outcome of the Andean wars have little direct impact on Brazil. Indirectly, it leaves much of South America consolidated into three dominant states: Brazil, the New Inca Empire, and the Grand Confederation of Argentina. Of the three, Brazil is by far the most tolerable to American and Western interests. The Marshall plan which rebuilt Europe also includes funding to reform and expand the Brazilian economy, and the United States invests in a military partnership as well.

The Andes constitute a major strategic barrier, so little threat is posed by the Empire. The principle rival is Argentina. However, even though Blandon has been eliminated, he leaves behind an armed, radicalised Indigenous population in the Amazonas. It is thought this would dissipate, the weapons rusting away, the bullets having long run out. This proves mistaken. Native populations retain their weapons in good working order and preserve ammunition, or manage to find new sources. Armed outbreaks begin in 1946 and occur sporadically into the 1950s. This results in ongoing campaigns against native populations.

In 1947, the Inca Empire begins to supply weapons to the indigenous peoples. Indigenous conflicts occur on an extremely intermittent basis. There are a number of incidents between Brazil and the Empire. Eventually, Brazil is forced to negotiate a compromise with the armed indigenous tribes of the Amazonas, instituting the 'Reservacion' system which provides for local autonomy for indigenous people, and rules to manage the development of the region.

With the resolution of its indigenous issues, most of Brazil's population and economy remains in the South. Brazil is considered to be an advanced, developed state with strong ties to Europe.

The Exile Government of Chile

During the Argentine Anschluss, surviving members of the Chilean junta make their way from San Bernardo to a naval base, where they board the destroyer, Toro. The remaining ships of the Chilean navy (the ones not scuttled) find their way around Tierra del Fuego, seeking sanctuary in Uruguay.

During the journey, there is an inconclusive naval battle with Argentine forces. Upon reaching Montevideo, exile Government's navy is sold off ship by ship to Brazil, Uruguay and the Phillipines for operating capital.

Based on their continuing territorial claim to Rapa Nui and the Juan Fernandez Islands, the United States recognizes them as the legitimate government of Chile and sponsors their seat in the newly formed United Nations. Over time, the fleet is either scuttled or the ships sold off to other states.

The Exile Government consisting of approximately five thousand people, many with dual citizenship continues to exist today. Of these, only a few hundred live on Rapa Nui and the Juan Fernandez Islands. Rapa Nui declared independence in 1972. The exile government continues to agitate internationally for the restoration of the Chilean state and its territory.

CATO (Caribbean Atlantic Treaty Organization)

The United States forms CATO (Caribbean Atlantic Treaty Organization), with membership including the United States, Colombia, Venezuela, Brazil, Panama, as well as Britain, France and the Netherlands as represented by their Guiana and Caribbean holdings, and the Caribbean / Central American states of Guatemala, Honduras, Nicaragua, the Dominican Republic and Cuba, patterned after NATO, CENTO and SEATO.

CATO's stated purpose is to contain the twin threats of communism and fascism in the western hemisphere - as represented by the Inca Empire and Argentina. It is dominated by the US even more than NATO was, and over time undergoes a certain amount of dissolution.

France pulls out in 1956, reducing its commitment to nominal membership. In 1959, Britain also voluntarily reduces to nominal status. Revolutions between 1959 and 1961 take Guatemala, Cuba and the Dominican Republic out of the alliance. Brazil becomes formally non-aligned in 1967.

In the 1970s, CATO fades to a consultation structure, with all of the individual nations retaining their own military prerogatives, and eschewing American political and military leadership.

In the 1980s, CATO sees a revival, with the enlistment of Colombia, El Salvador, Honduras, Guyana, Haiti and several newly independent Caribbean microstates, and a more aggressive US posture in the region, deriving partially from stresses arising from the drug trade.

****

Historical Persona of The Andean Wars

Colonel Luis Larrea Alba

Together with Benigno Flores and Velasco Ibarra, are allowed to depart Quito, flying to Caracas in Venezuela, where they receive political asylum. Alba remains in Venezuela and is part of the Ecuador 'Government in Exile' until 1947. Thereafter he moves Argentina, where he serves as a military consultant to the Argentine Junta until 1953. Retiring, he takes a staff teaching position at the Argentine military college until 1957. Departing as a result of criticism of the Argentine Junta, Alba relocates to Rio de Janeiro, remaining there until 1964. At the age of seventy, he accepts an invitation to visit the Incan Empire as an honoured guest. While there, he tours his old battlefields, eventually re-enacting the March on Lima, before crowds of thousands of celebrants. He is awarded the designation of Hero of the Empire, an honour previously reserved for the leading officers and generals of the revolution. He retires to Quito and lives there peacefully, establishing a reputation as one of the foremost military historians of his day, until passing away peacefully in 1986. He is buried with full military honours. In Ecuador, there is a folk tale that even today, Alba only sleeps and will come forward when called. In the iconography and official histories of the Incan Empire he is the forerunner to the revolution. The Quechua Jazzpunk fusion band, Colonel Criollo is named in honour of him.

***

Velasco Ibarra –

Serves for a term as provisional President of the Ecuador Government in Exile, until being voted out in 1946. In 1947, he renounces Ecuadoran citizenship and becomes a citizen of Venezuela. Once again he becomes a prominent newspaperman and columnist, crusading against corruption and injustice. He is twice elected to the Venezuelan legislature, and is briefly nominated as a Presidential Candidate until American pressure forces his withdrawal. Thereafter he relocates to Mexico in 1957, continuing his career as a writer. Passionate and idealistic, but unable to restrain his temper, he is eventually asked to leave Mexico in 1963, and relocates to Uruguay and then Brazil. In 1967, he returns to Venezuela, where he stands for President in 1969. In the fractured election he takes office as a compromise candidate and rules for a stormy 18 months before being forced to resign. Thereafter, Ibarra moves to Paris, and remains there until his death. He never stops writing and commenting on Latin American affairs, his columns are among the most widely read in newspapers throughout Latin America.

Colonel Benigno Flores

 President of the Ecuadoran Government in Exile following Ibarra's ouster, until 1951. Flores eventually re-locates to the United States, becoming an American citizen in 1955, and is well known as an anti-communist crusader. He marries an American heiress, in 1958, divorces in 1964, remarries in 66, divorces again in 1967. Remarries in 1970, and becomes involved with the Cuban expatriate community in Florida. Runs for Governor of Florida in the 1970s. Is involved in a bribery scandal in 1981. Dies in 1982. He's best known for his autobiographical accounts of the Andean War.

Carlos Ibanez

The former Dictator of Chile briefly heads the Chilean rump government under Argentine supervision. He does not get along well as a puppet leader, and resigns within six months. Thereafter, he remains under house arrest in a villa outside Buenos Aires for five years. In 1950, he is released. In 1956, he becomes heavily involved with the Chilean independence movement. After three years of being a thorn in the side of Argentine authorities, he disappears one night, walking his dog. The Argentine government consistently denies any knowledge of his disappearance and whereabouts. Chileans independantistes consider him a martyr.

***

Elroy Ureta

Peruvian General. The person history holds to be almost singlehandedly responsible for the Andean Wars. During the fall, he flees to Colombia and remained there the rest of his life. Ureta becomes a cultural icon, the very model of the Latin American military martinet - blundering, incompetent, arrogant and dishonest. Caricatures of Ureta are a staple in Latin American newspapers for decades, used to represent a variety of issues. Ureta the person fades away into obscurity, writing angry letters to newspapers and denouncing his numerous critics. He dies of a heart attack penning a rebuttal to a high school textbook edition chronicling the Andean wars.

***

Ernesto Montagne Markholtz

Peruvian General. As the revolution sweeps Peru, Markholtz chooses to abandon his northern Army command and flees from Peru to Colombia, from Colombia to Cuba and from there to Madrid, Spain. Markholtz gets along famously with Francisco Franco, and is awarded a lifetime pension. He spends the rest of his life writing books denouncing Alba, Ibanez, and his fellow Peruvian Generals, and justifying or excusing his own conduct. He dies in 1969 a bitter angry man.

✳✳✳

Oscar Penaranda –

President of the United Republic of Bolivia. During the revolution, Penaranda is taken prisoner and remains in captivity for seven years. Upon release, he returns to Bolivia, and is eventually recruited into government work, becoming a senior administrator. Although he often encounters Villarroel in the course of their respective duties, the two men never speak to each other. Penaranda retires from regular government work in the 1970s, although he continues to consult occasionally.

✳✳✳

Gualberto Villarroel

Prime Minister of the National Bolivian People's State, the second government of the Bolivian Civil war. Following the fall of Bolivia to the revolution, Villarroel refuses to evacuate with the remainder of his government to Santiago, and meets the forces of the revolution alone, outside his Presidential Palace, armed only with a revolver and an antique cavalry sabre. He is met by a column led by Rum Maqui Bastido. The two men speak privately, get stinking drunk together, and Villarroel formally dissolves the state of Bolivia. Thereafter he spends two years in prison before being released. He lives in Lima under house arrest for two more years, before being allowed to return to Bolivia. In the 1960s, Villarroel's status in Bolivia increases, and he serves several terms as the Mayor of La Paz. In 1961, he meets with Ramon Valpes, and the two men reconciled. However, he never makes peace with Oscar Penaranda and the two men never speak. Despite his involvement with Bolivian and Imperial politics, he never discusses of the war. Upon his death in 1988 he is accorded a state funeral. His memoirs are published posthumously.

✳✳✳

Ramon Valpes

President of the Popular Republic of Bolivia, the third government during the Bolivian Civil war found his government dissolving out from under him by the Argentine state. He relocates to Paraguay, where he becomes a civic leader. In 1963, he dies in a horse-riding accident.

***

Tupac Amaru III,

Baptiste Condaqui, aka Otoronco, aka Jaguar Otoronco, aka Captain Jaguar. First 'Inca' or emperor of the reborn Inca Empire. In 1949, in response to border hostilities with United States allies, Colombia, Brazil and Argentina, he enters treaty of peace and friendship with the Soviet Union. Instrumental in supporting the Guatemalan revolution and subsequent Mayan state. He is active in rearming and supporting the Indigenous resistance movement of the Brazilian Amazonians. He is also involved in supporting, overtly and covertly, Indigenous and Mestizo movements throughout Latin America, and a supporter of Asian and African independence movements, most notably in French Indochina. In 1962, following the Cuban Missile Crisis, throws out Soviet advisors and reopens relations with the United States. He loses confidence in the Soviets as an effective challenge to American hegemony. In 1963, embarks on an Imperial tour of America, including Disneyland. Following this in 1964, hosts the first state visit from the American President. Dies 1967 of a ruptured appendix.

***

Manco Capak Yanqui–

The second great Inca, taking office in 1967, following the sudden death of Tupac Amaru III. Yanqui initiates structural reforms to the Inca economy and government, including the political system. He also introduces various forms of democracy to local governance. Tiring of rule, he institutes a governing system wherein the Inca will be appointed by and represent the High Council for a

term of 12 years. Existing members of the High Council will sit
until they die or retire, after which new members will be appointed
for twenty year terms. Despite weaknesses, the system endures to
the present day. Manco Yanqui pursues a policy of continuing to
reduce tensions with the United States, and detente with Argentina
and Brazil, while becoming active in the world non-aligned
movement. In particular, he helps broker the 'Reservacione'
agreement which ends the intermittent hostilities between Brazil
and its indigenous population, and establishes massive trust
territories in the Amazonas for local governance. He is the
signature figure of the 'Inca-mania' that overtakes the American left
in the late sixties and early seventies. He steps down from power in
1981. Dies in 1984.

***

Montressor Blandon & Pablo Oliviara

In 1945, two men appear in French Guiana. One is a Brazilian
citizen reported missing or dead, Pablo Oliviara, of Manaus. The
other claims to be Montressor Blandon, son of General Enrique
Blandon, but is eventually determined to be a Peruvian nationale
Indigenous person from the Selva, bearing the Christian name
Baptiste Mollea. They are in possession of a number of personal
papers of Enrique Blandon from the Jungle war. After being taken
into custody, they are released and the papers returned to them.
They eventually move to France, where they publish an edited
manuscript of Blandon's war diaries in 1952, 'On the Rivers.' This
book is hailed as an important contribution to the appreciation of a
little understood aspect of the Andean Wars. This is followed in
1957 by a compilation of Blandon's anti-colonial writings 'Light
Comes With Dawn.' This is a major success and becomes an
influential book in the anti-colonial and Indigenous rights
movement. Several more publications ensue, and a cottage industry
spawned in Latin America tracking down his lost manifestos.
Blandon and Oliviara become major figures in the counterculture
of the 1960s. In 1974, however, serious questions arise as to the
provenance of some of the manuscripts attributed to Enrique
Blandon. In 1976, Blandon and Oliviara admit to writing some of
the published works, attributing it to Enrique Blandon's name. In

1984 a Brazilian man comes forward claiming to be Enrique Blandon, and bringing suit for royalties. The case fails to proceed. Montressor passes away in 1992, and Pablo in 1994.

CHRONOLOGY
MAJOR THEATRES AND CAMPAIGNS OF THE ANDEAN WARS

THE GREAT NORTHERN CAMPAIGN - PERU/ECUADOR –

APRIL – JULY, 1940

April, 1940 - The Secret Sorzano-Ibarra treaty between Bolivia and Ecuador for mutual support in war is exposed.

May, 1940 - Peruvian Northern Commander, General Elroy G. Ureta, in June, 1941, demands that President Prado declare war on Ecuador and authorize invasion. Prado equivocates.

June 2, 1940 - Ecuador Front - The Great Northern Campaign, General Ureta takes the initiative and invades Ecuador.

June 3, 1940 - Ecuador Front - The Great Northern Campaign, Alba orders a general mobilization to defend against the invasion.

June 8, 1940 - Ecuador Front - The Great Northern Campaign - Peru overruns the port city of Puerto Bolivar and moves on the town of Machata, where the Ecuadorans are preparing a last stand.

June 14-20, 1940 - The Great Northern Campaign - Peru attacks Machata, where the Ecuadorans have made their stand. After a week of fierce fighting, Ecuadoran forces withdraw but Peruvian forces have taken massive casualties.

June 14-21, 1941 - The Great Northern Campaign - Alba, the Ecuadoran general, uses battle of Machata as a distraction, using the time to redeploy forces from Lojas, cutting off overextended supply lines, and flanking Peruvian forces in both Machata and

Puerto Bolivar. One day after conquering the town, the Peruvians are forced to retreat and abandon both towns.

June 24, 1940 - Ecuadoran Front - The Great Northern Campaign, Ecuador achieves local air superiority. Peru's retreat becomes a rout, as the badly overextended and under-supplied forces begin abandoning vehicles and equipment.

June 28, 1940 - Ecuadoran Front - The Great Northern Campaign, Alba chooses to give Ureta battle near the Zamilla river on the border. After a morning of hard fighting, the Peruvians surrender. The Great Northern Campaign is over.

***

THE RAIN FOREST WAR - PERU/ECUADOR – JUNE 1940-JUNE 1941.

June 5, 1940 - Rain Forest War - The Great Northern Campaign, Peru's Army Jungle division and Chinchipe Army Group cross the Napo and Maranon rivers, attacking Ecuadoran outposts, but encounter immediate resistance from well-established battalions dug in.

June 15, 1940 - Rain Forest War - The Great Northern Campaign, the Chinchipe army group dissolves into uncoordinated units, most of who are in retreat.

June 18, 1940 - Rain Forest War - The Great Northern Campaign, Ecuadorans cross the river, taking Peruvian towns Jaen and Bagua, as the remnants of Peru's Chinchipe Arm, continue to retreat.

July 14, 1940 - Rain Forest War - the last Peruvian forces of the 'Great Northern Campaign' and the Chinchipe army group are trapped at the town of Yurimaguas, on the Rio Huallaga, where the Ecuadorans win decisively.

July 26, 1940 - Rain Forest War - Blandon leads Ecuadoran forces into the Peruvian rain forest territories, ostensibly in pursuit of fleeing enemy, but in reality in response to Alba's victories in the March on Lima.

August, 1940 - Rain Forest War - Blandon's forces move through the river systems into Peruvian territory, finding little organized resistance and overwhelming defenders.

September 2, 1940 - Rain Forest War - "Sack of Pucallpa" Blandon, leading a force of Ecuadorans and natives, attacks the Peruvian military outpost at Pucallpa, burning and looting the entire town.

October, 1940 - Rain Forest War - Blandon overruns 3/4 of the Peruvian Selva (Amazon) leaving only Madre de Dios province in Peruvian hands.

October 31, 1940 - Rain Forest War - Peru is rebuilding the military base at Pucallpa in the rain forest, as part of a campaign to eradicate Blandon's guerilla forces.

December 18, 1940 - Rain Forest War - Blandon is recruiting heavily among Peruvian indigenous populations for auxiliaries and support along the Ucayali River.

December 23, 1940 - Rain Forest War - Blandon attempts to mount a raid against entrenched Peruvian forces at Pucallpa. This turns into a major fight. Blandon discontinues further actions against Pucallpa.

March/April, 1941 - Rain Forest War - in coordination with the Second Northern Campaign, Peru begins a counterinsurgency campaign against Blandon in the Selva.

April/May, 1941 - Rain Forest War - in response to Peru's counter-insurgency campaign, Blandon is distributing his forces more and more widely and emphasising mobility. The forces begin crossing into Brazilian territory, at first accidentally, then deliberately.

June 1941 - Rain Forest War - Rainy season gives way to dry season. The rain forest theatre is now a diffuse battleground across three states. Blandon is now headquartered in Brazilian territory.

***

THE SOUTHERN FRONT – CHILE / PERU

JULY, 1940 – FEBRUARY, 1941

July 2, 1940 - Chile - Chile rebuffed in attempts to broker peace negotiations, declares war in an ill-advised move, but takes no further action. Instead, Chile proposes an immediate ceasefire.

August 8, 1940 - Chilean Front - "Battle of Tacna" After a long period of dithering Ibanez orders an attack against defended Peruvian positions. It goes very badly.

August 15, 1940 - Chilean Front - "Battle of Arica" taking advantage of Chilean disarray, the Peruvian forces push south into their former province of Arica.

August 24, 1940 - Chilean Front - Peru pushes into Tarapaca launching attacks on Antofagosta, deep into Chile

August 28, 1940 - Chilean Front - Chilean forces receive reinforcements and counterattacks.

September 30, 1940 - Chilean Front - The Chileans fall back from Tacna, retreating to their province of Arica.

October 9, 1940 - Chilean Front - A new Chilean offensive overruns Tacna, reaches Moqueguera, and attempts to establish a front along the road to Lake Titicaca.

October 18, 1940 - Chilean Front: Peruvians push Chileans out of Tacna. Chilean forces collapse.

October 30, 1940 - Chilean Front - Southern front stabilizes and trench warfare begins to set in, approximately 40,000 on each side. December 31, 1940 - Chilean Front - Mobility in the south comes to an end.

January 9, 1941, - Chilean Front - with the 'New Year's Offensive.' An addition of 15,000 fresh troops to the front inspires the Chilean generals to launch a human wave offensive against the Peruvians. Casualties were appalling.

January 21, 1941 - Chilean Front - end of the "New Year's Offensive" the Chileans have lost 13,000 men.

February 20, 1941 - Chilean Front - Chile and Peru agree to a cease-fire on the front, not precluding operations elsewhere.

****

New World War – Page 382

ALBA'S MARCH ON LIMA -ECUADOR / PERU – JULY – NOVEMBER, 1940

July 10, 1940 - March on Lima - Colonel Alba of Ecuador leads an expeditionary force in the famous 'March on Lima' a bold attempt to knock Peru out of the war.

July 24, 1940 - March on Lima - "Battle of Chiclayo" Alba's expeditionary force overwhelms and routes a Peruvian force.

July 30, 1940 - March on Lima – An Ecuadoran relief convoy of approximately 10,000 men leaves Tombes to resupply Alba's forces.

August 1, 1940 - March on Lima - "Battle of Trujillo." Alba arrives at attacks the Central Army Command at Trujillo. The Central command is taken by surprise.

August 23, 1940 - March on Lima - "Battle of Huarez" the relief convoy is only days away, Alba leaves Huarez, traveling back along his road to give battle. Peruvian forces are caught between Alba's main force and his relief convoy.

September 5, 1940 - March on Lima - "Battle of Calao" Alba reaches to the town of Calao, site of the Peruvian naval base outside of Lima without further incident. After an exchange of fire, Alba chooses his field of battle. The Peruvians fall into a trap. Alba defeats and destroys a force three times his size.

September 9, 1940 - March on Lima: Colonel Alba of Ecuador and General Benevides of Peru agree on peace terms. At this point, Peru is fighting a two front war, and losing badly on both fronts.

September 12, 1940 - Peru - President Prado and General Benevides are overthrown by General Ramirez. The Peruvians repudiate peace terms.

September 14 - 19, 1940 - March on Lima - "Battle of Lima" Four days of artillery shelling and sortie fail. Alba orders a retreats.

September 20, 1940 - March on Lima - the Ecuadorans begin their retreat through Peruvian territory. In the south, the Chileans retake Arica, and attack the Peruvian province of Tacna once again.

September 21, 1940 - March on Lima - A second Ecuadorian supply convoy, led by General Enrique Gallo, leaves Tombes.

October 4, 1940 - March on Lima - "Rape of Huarez" the Ecuadorans loot and burn the Peruvian town as they pass through.

October 14, 1940 - March on Lima - General Gallo's Ecuadoran relief forces meet up with Alba. Reinforced, Alba digs down in the town of Cajamarca and waits for the pursuing Peruvian forces to catch up.

October 20, 1940 - March on Lima - "First Battle of Cajamarca" Huanaco Army group attacks prematurely. The Peruvians are decimated and forced into a rout. Alba pursues.

October 24, 1940 - March on Lima: "Second Battle of Cajamarca" The retreating Peruvian Huanaco army links up with a Lima army coming up the coast. After two days of battle, Alba retreats, burning Cajamarca behind him. The Huanaco/Lima army follows slowly but does not give battle again.

November 6, 1940 - March on Lima - Alba returns to Ecuador, the campaign is over.

***

THE SECOND GREAT NORTHERN CAMPAIGN - PERU/ECUADOR – MARCH – APRIL 1941

March 4, 1941 - Ecuadoran Front - The Second Northern Campaign, by General Markholtz. Peru invades.

March 26, 1941 - Ecuadoran Front - The Second Northern Campaign, Alba counterattacks from mountain strongholds in Lojas towards the coast.

April 4, 1941 - Ecuadoran Front - The Second Northern Campaign, Markholtz counterattacks, with an inconclusive battle.

April 11, 1941 - Ecuadoran Front - Second Northern Campaign, Alba counterattacks and inflicting heavy damage. Markholtz forced to retreat.

April 13, 1941 - Ecuadoran Front - Second Northern Campaign, Alba's forces close in Markholtz manages to break out of trap, and retreats.

April 16, 1941 - Ecuador Front - Second Northern Campaign, Markholtz disengages and focuses on consolidating his position.

April 20, 1941 - Peru - General Rodriguez issued a directive relieving Markholtz of command and demanding his return to Lima. Markholtz ignored both orders.

***

THE LANDING, THE GREAT LAND/SEA OFFENSIVE - CHILE/PERU APRIL – JUNE 1941

April 11, 1941 - Chilean Front - April Offensive, Ibanez sees an opportunity, repudiated the cease-fire and launched a massive attack across the front, promising victory in ninety days.

April 22, 1941 - Chilean Front - April Offensive, Chilean forces have overrun four of six objectives.

April 27, 1941 - Chile - The Chilean government begins planning 'The Landing.'

April 29, 1941 - Chilean Front - April Offensive, Chile splits the Peruvian defenders into three groups.

May 4, 1941 - Chilean Front - April Offensive, the over-extended Chilean offensive stalls. Peruvians have reformed their ranks. Penetration into Tacna is uneven, leaving Chilean forces exposed. The offensive fails.

May 26, 1941 - Chilean Front/War At Sea - The Landing, Chile attacks from the sea in a massive amphibious operation supported by the bulk of the Chilean navy.

May 28, 1941 - Chilean Front - The Landing, Peruvian troops and local militia are engaging the new invasion, but are heavily outnumbered, and bombarded by offshore batteries.

May 29, 1941 - Chilean Front/War at Sea - The Landing, Peru commits most of their remaining naval resources, including their submarines, and most of their aircraft to trying to dislodge the beachhead.

May 31, 1941 - Chilean Front - The Landing, Chileans have landed 24,000 troops behind Peruvian lines, attacking south. Heavy fighting.

June 16, 1941 - Chilean Front - End of the Landing, major operations conclude. The battle lines stabilize, the Peruvians dig in to a new zigzag line that now extended over 180 miles.

August, 1941 - The bold gamble that is the Landing has not paid off. Peru has not been knocked out of the war. The Trench War grinds on.

***

THE RAIN FOREST WAR - ECUADOR/PERU, JANUARY-SEPTEMBER, 1941

January, 1941-May, 1941 - As the rainy season wears on the campaign in the Oriente/Selva/Amazonas swings slowly back towards General Blandon and his Ecuadoran Expedition

June, 1941 -The coming dry season features a renewed effort by Peru to rid itself of Enrique Blandon and his cursed Matilde.

July, 1941 - The road to Pucallpa is once again open.. Pucallpa is to be a fortress and launching point. The northern military bases at Lamas and Tarapota also expand.

July/October, 1941 – Blandon establishes overland dry-season routes.

July/October, 1941 – Peruvian forces, heavily supplied from Pucallpa and Tarapota push deep into the rain forest. Blandon has no choice but to withdraw further and further down the major river systems, slowly pursued by the Peruvians.

***

BOLIVIAN CIVIL WAR – JULY 1941 – DECEMBER 1941

July 18, 1941 – the American Ambassador provides Bolivian President Penaranda with a forged letter purporting to disclose a Nazi backed coup attempt. Penaranda resolves to purge his rivals once and for all.

July 21, 1941 – During a raid on a brothel in La Paz, Bolivia, socialist Paz Esstorensa is executed by Penaranda's officers. The murder is witnessed by Major-General Guilberto Villarroel.

July 23, 1941 – A general strike is called to protest the murder of Esstorensa and demand the resignation of Penaranda.

July 24, 1941 – Villarroel declares a rival National Unity Government from a radio station. Fighting breaks out between Villarroel and Penaranda factions.

July 25, 1941 - Villarroel's forces in La Paz, Bolivia, are forced to retreat. The rival National Unity Government establishes itself in Sucre, Bolivia's second largest city.

July 31, 1941 – Bolivia divides between the Penaranda and Villarroel governments

July 31 / September 8, 1941 – Heavy fighting throughout Bolivia.

***

BOLIVIAN CIVIL WAR - CHILEAN/PERUVIAN INTERVENTIONS – AUGUST-NOVEMBER 1941

August 13, 1941 – The National Unity Government is split when Villarroel announces he will seek Chilean military assistance.

September 1, 1941 - Ramon Valpes, a member of the National Unity Government, breaks away over Chilean involvement, establishing a third rival government, the Free Bolivia Movement in Santa Cruz.

September 2, 1941 – Calamity Summit, at Calama Base in the Bolivian Altiplano. President Ibanez of Chile meets with President Villarroel.

September 2-22, 1941 – Supplied with Chilean arms, and backed by increasing numbers of Chilean troops, Villarroel's National Unity Government goes on the attack.

September 8, 1941 - in response to news of the build-up of forces at Base Calama, Penaranda's government signs a mutual defense pact with Lima, Peru.

September 22, 1941 – In response to the Chilean intervention, Peruvian military forces enter northern Bolivia.

September 27, 1941 - the Battle of Titicaca officially commences, resulting in a major defeat of Peruvian and North Bolivian armies and opening the Peruvian Altiplano to Chilean forces.

October 10, 1941 - Chilean forces penetrate as much as one hundred miles into Peruvian territory on a broad front.

October, 1941 - Overwhelmed by the combined advance of Chile and the Villarroel government, Penaranda's government withdraws to La Paz, where Villarroel lays siege.

October 29, 1941 – La Paz surrenders to Villarroel. By this time, the Penaranda government has moved its seat officially to Cobija in the north.

November 10, 1941 – After weeks of heavy fighting the critical mining districts are under the control of the Bolivian Villarroel administration, which pronounces the nationalization of mining assets, and resumption of operations under workers collectives.

November, 1941 - Villarroel is reaching the limits that he can effectively push north with his forces, Penaranda's remnants are too entrenched.

November 15, 1941 - A sortie by Villarroel's forces against the rival Valpes government in the city of Santa Cruz is decisively defeated.

****

New World War – Page 388

BOLIVIAN CIVIL WAR - ARGENTINE INTERVENTION – NOVEMBER-DECEMBER, 1941

November 16-23 - Valpes forces in the south encounter a series of sorties and feints by units of Villarroel's campaign. Valpes soldiers uniformly perform poorly. Only against Santa Cruz itself are Villarroel's men decisively thrown back by Valpes forces.

November 23, 1941 – Argentina intervenes in the war. With Villarroel almost on top of Santa Cruz, an Argentine expeditionary force almost ten thousand strong crosses the Bolivian border

November 24, 1941 - Villarroel formally asks for Chilean assistance, including contributions of trucks, artillery and air support.

November 25, 1941 - the Chileans drive into Peru id contained.

November 25-29, 2011, Villarroel reaches the gates of Santa Cruz, Valpe's capital, once again encountering stiff resistance. Unable to breach the city, he begins the 'Four Day Siege.

November 28, 1941 – The Argentine expedition arrives at Santa Cruz. Shots exchanged between Villarroel's forces and the Argentines.

November 29, 1941 - the battle begins in earnest. Fighting is savage; casualties reached 3,000 on both sides,

November 30, 1941 - Villarroel's horse stumbles into a gopher hole, throwing him and resulting in a broken leg. His forces retreat.

December, 1941 - With Villarroel out of commission, his faction is paralyzed. Coalition members defect, and the political balance shifts towards Valpes, now for the first time a serious contender

November 30 / December 7, 1941 - the Argentine expeditionary force, after consulting with Valpes and eventually receiving further orders from Buenos Aires, embarks on a campaign to recover territories lost to Villarroel.

December 7, 1941 – The Valpes/Argentine coalition avoids the heavily defended mining district and the cities of La Paz and Sucre, eventually reaching the southern boundaries of Penaranda's rump forces in Bolivia.

December, 1941 - Despite Chile's and Villarroel's reverses, the Villarroel regime remains in control of the key cities,

***

RAIN FOREST WAR - FIRST BRAZILIAN INCURSION - SEPTEMBER, 1941/ FEBRUARY, 1942

September, 1941 - the Brazilian government begins to receive reports that Ecuadoran and Peruvian forces are crossing into Brazilian territory.

October, 1941 – Blandon's provocations can no longer be overlooked by Brazil.

October 18, 1941 – Brazil's Vargas government sends an expeditionary force down the Amazonas from the town of Manaus, to secure Brazilian borders and evict trespassers.

November 4, 1941 – Brazil's Manaus expedition disappears without a trace.

November, 1941 - Vargas receives assurance from the Ecuadoran government and his own officers in the Amazonas that Blandon has withdrawn back across the border.

January 28, 1942 - Vargas authorizes an expeditionary force of ten thousand men to the Amazonian city of Manaus.

February 2, 1942 – Vargas expeditionary force is reduced to 5,000. Budgeting.

***

THIRD NORTHERN CAMPAIGN – PERU ECUADOR, SEPTEMBER-DECEMBER, 1941

September 6, 1941 – Peruvian General Markholtz launches the Third Northern Offensive.

New World War – Page 390

September 7, 1941 – The Peruvian Junta in Lima votes to court martial Markholtz for insubordination, for his unauthorized offensive. The resolution is not acted on.

September 6 / October 4 - Peruvian forces overwhelm the coastal provinces of Ecuador and then push inland.

October 20, 1941 – Battle of Portoviejo. Alba counterattacks. Markholtz outruns his supply lines, and prodigious expenditures of men and ammunition have taken their toll.

October 24-31, 1941 - Faced with organized counter-offensives, Markholtz offensive degenerates into a series of independent units which were, one after the other, overcome.

November 1 – 30, 1941 – The November Campaign. Ecuador forces regain control of Ecuadoran territories and expand to re-occupy Peruvian territory, Peruvian oil districts.

December 1, 1941. There are no significant Peruvian military assets or structure in the left in the north.

***

<h1 style="text-align:center">THE "CEASEFIRE ERA"</h1>

<h1 style="text-align:center">DECEMBER, 1941 - OCTOBER, 1942</h1>

<h2 style="text-align:center">Pearl Harbour Event – December, 1941</h2>

***

THE "DESPERATION" OF ECUADOR
DECEMBER, 1941 - OCTOBER, 1942

December 7, 1942 – Pearl Harbor Event – America demands a ceasefire. Ecuador announces it will comply with the ceasefire but will hold its military forces, including those on Peruvian territory in place, pending negotiated resolution of all matters in dispute.

December 7, 1941 through October 31, 1942 - Ecuador receives roughly six million dollars in American non-military goods and non-repayable loans.

February 11-14, 1942 - Ecuador experiences its first great currency collapse of the Bonifaz era.

April, 1942 – freeze on military purchases as a result of the ceasefire ripples through the economy and causes industrial production to decline by 70 percent.

July 1942 - Flood of imported cheap American or Colombian goods feed a thriving black market. The economy is roughly where it was during the worst of the Depression.

April 22, 1942 – Bonifaz attempts to halt the runaway currency collapses and hyperinflation with the imposition of wage and price controls.

April 27, 1942 - Wage and price controls become even more punitive when Bonifaz decrees that businesses will be forced to sell products at the government rates.

April 28, 1942 - Several days of fierce rioting break out in Guayaquil and Quito.

May 2, 1942 – Bonifaz and Ibarra declare martial law and re-launch a new Ecuadoran currency.

May, 1942 – the Bonifaz regime attempt to deal with the rural crisis by engineering a system of labor conscription - temporary forced labor granted to the haciendas or landowners.

May 1942 – Repression begins. Several newspapers are openly critical of the Bonifaz regime, and are subsequently shut down.

June 9, 1942 – Financial crisis erupts again.

July 27, 1942 – Financial crisis erupts.

July 28, 1942 - A vote of non-confidence in Velasco Ibarra's cabinet is narrowly avoided. Then on

August, 1942 - Different sources place anywhere from five to fifteen per cent of Ecuadoran troops are classified as deserters or irregularly reporting, and the 'refused' become a political issue.

September 11, 1942 – Financial crisis erupts, the Bonifaz regime is almost bankrupt, and takes an entire week to re-establish stability.

September 13, 1942 - The 'revolt of congress' occurs with a bare majority calling for the resignation of President Bonifaz.

September 16, 1942 – Bonifaz shuts down Congress.

September 21, 1942 - Ecuador announces that it will begin staged withdrawals slowly from occupied Peruvian territories, but will continue to hold disputed territories.

September, 1942 - Although a ceasefire is in place, Ecuador's Blandon continues internecine warfare through the Amazon/Oriente/Selva region beyond the reach of the central commands.

October 10, 1942 - Congress is reconvened, but it is notable that over a third of the sitting Congressmen are removed from their seats, banned for 'treasonous sympathies.'

***

THE "TRANQUILLITY" OF PERU, DECEMBER, 1941-AUGUST, 1942

December, 1941 – Peru accepts the American imposed ceasefire conditionally, but refuses to withdraw its forces from Bolivia and Chilean territory.

January, 1942 – Peru is admitted to the American lend/lease program, and direct financial aid commences.

March and April, 1942 - Peru's economy and resources are being integrated into the emerging American war machine.

May 23, 1942 - A Brazil-United States political/military agreement 'The Washington Accords' sets the stage for a tacit arrangement which among other things, provides for direct American military aid to Brazil.

May 30, 1942 - The 'Lima Accord' in which Peru and Brazil formalize a trade and political alliance. The United States begins arming Peru.

August or September, 1942 – The Peruvian Junta begins planning to end the war decisively.

***

CHILE, THE 'DECEPTION' –

DECEMBER, 1941 - OCTOBER, 1942

December, 1941 – Ibanez accepts the American demand for a ceasefire and asks that all parties return to their original borders and presses for recognition of the Villarroel regime as the legitimate government of Bolivia.

December 14, 1941 - Chile breaks relations off with Germany, Italy and Japan. Ibanez formally outlaws the Chilean Nazi party while giving former Nazis an amnesty.

February, 1941 – Chile enters into a trading pact with the United States for supply of Chilean copper, and Bolivian tin through Chilean ports.

March, 1941 – On the Peruvian/Chilean trench frontier, hostilities slowly resume as the Peruvians attempts to force Ibanez to commit troops to the front and defuse his build up in Bolivia.

March 30, 1941 - Secret Accord between Chile and Argentina, promising the cession of the rest of the Chaco, won in the Chaco War and including the oil reserves, to Paraguay.

May-September, 1942 – The trench war frontier between Bolivia and Chile remains relatively static, with low level warfare and exchanges of artillery

August 27, 1942 – The exposure of the March Accord creates embarrassment in Santiago for the Ibanez government.

August 28, 1942 – Ibanez is forced to repudiate the March Accord, while attempting to maintain relations with Argentina.

September 15, 1942 – In Bolivia, Villarroel engages in a direct assault upon Argentine forces. Argentina and Chile break off diplomatic relations and close embassies.

October, 1942 - the Chilean/Peruvian frontier heats up to the point of more or less continuous warfare.

****

BOLIVIAN CIVIL WAR, "BLEEDING BOLIVIA" – DECEMBER 1941-SEPTEMBER 1943

December 1941 - May 1942 - Following Pearl Harbour, the United States demands a ceasefire in the region. In Bolivia, temporary stasis sets in, as fighting dies down, but not completely away.

February 20, 1942 – Low level hostilities resume between Peru and Chile in Bolivia.

March 30, 1942 - Secret Accord between Chile and Argentina, promising the cession of the rest of the Chaco, won in the Chaco War and including the oil reserves, to Paraguay

May 2, 1942 - The combined forces of the Penaranda Regime of Bolivia, and the Peruvian military strike across a broad frontier, driving towards the mining district.

May - April 15, 1942 - After a month and a half of hard fighting, Peruvian forces are in control of almost the entirety of the Mining district.

May, 1942 - Brazil claims that Valpes is nothing more than a shell or proxy, and the Argentine army is in de facto control of his faction.

July 2, 1942 - the Chilean counterattack is under way and the Peruvian line begins to collapse almost everywhere.

August, 1942 - the Chilean counter-offensive stabilizes. Villarroel discovers and forces the Chilean regime to repudiate the March Accord.

August, 1942 -Villarroel's forces, acting independently without Chilean support, re-occupy the oil district.

August and September, 1942 - Peru undergoes a dramatic reorganization of its forces, incorporating Penaranda's Bolivian units. Penaranda's government ceases to exist, except as a legal fiction.

October, 1941 - The only Bolivian faction which maintains anything like an independent presence is Villarroel's Presidency and administration.

October, 1942 - Peruvian resurgence in Bolivia. Massive conscriptions in Bolivia and Peru among the Aymara and Quechua are finally taking effect.

October, 1942 - April, 1943, the balance swings back and forth, as each countries supplies and manpower waxes and wanes.

November, 1942 - The Argentines are on the verge of withdrawing, but Paraguayan demands and a sudden weakness in the Chilean position renews their commitment.

***

THE RAIN FOREST WAR, BLANDON RETURNS HOME, JANUARY, 1942-MAY, 1942

January, 1942 - General Enrique Blandon return to the command centre of Jaen, consolidating his command over the interior. March

20, 1942 - Blandon without authorization, attacks the Peruvian outpost of Lamas, overrunning it and massacring the population.

April 4, 1942 - Peruvian relief expeditions are launched from Tarapota and Pucallpa. Blandon catches the Tarapota expedition as it waits for Pucallpa, and destroys it.

April 9, 1942 - The Peruvian Pucallpa expedition, harassed steadily, arrives to confront a holding garrison.

April 16, 1942 – Blandon bypasses the Pucallpa relief expedition, to launch another night raid on the town.

April 17, 1942 - The Pucallpa is overrun, finally surrendering under fire from the four gunboats.

May, 1942 - Peruvian forces in the region have been swept away.

April - May, 1942 - Increasing numbers of Indigenous refugees, both peaceful and armed, are trickling across the border from Brazil.

***

THE RAIN FOREST WAR - 2ND BRAZILIAN INCURSION –

MAY 1942 - DECEMBER, 1942

May or June, 1942 – Blandon crosses over into Brazil.

June 3, 1942 - Last acknowledgement by Blandon of communications from Quito, now entirely renegade.

June 4, 1942 - Amazonas province, a full-fledged firefight breaks out between natives and regular army forces, the first time this has ever happened.

June, 1942 - Reports of patrols being ambushed, supply centres raided, massacres at work camps, and attacks on boats. Reprisals against Indigenous populations are ineffective.

July 12, 1942 -partially submerged flat bottom boat is found outside the town of Eirunepé.

July 18, 1942 – Final dispatches from Blandon to the Ecuadoran command continue, received August 22.

August 10, 1942 - A convoy of Brazilian four navy gunboats is attacked by a pair of heavily camouflaged gunboats. One of the attacking craft is identified as the Matilde. Blandon has finally reappeared.

August 12, 1942 - The Ecuadoran government formally repudiates Blandon, he is ordered to present for Court Martial or be tried in absentia.

October, 1942 - The work force of the 'rubber battle' has reached 100,000 workers, protected by 18,000 troops.

January-July 1942 - Atlantic Ocean, January to August 1942, German U-Boats sink 18 Brazilian merchant vessels. Vargas formally declares war on Germany, Japan and Ecuador in August 22, 1942.

August and December, 1942 - Hundreds of violent incidents in the Rain Forest mostly small scale, but genuine fire fights take place repeatedly.

August, 1942 - Blandon opens yet another front when his manifesto arguing passionately against colonialism and for indigenous rights appears in a socialist newspaper in Rio de Janeiro.

****

PERU/BOLIVIA/CHILE - OPERACIONE 'SALITRE,' MAY - JULY, 1943

May 18, 1943 - After extensive American armament and training, including new rounds of conscription, the Ramirez Junta launches a pair of major offensives along the Chilean frontier and in the Bolivian theatre.

May 18-June 30, 1943 – Peru attacks. Initially successful, Chilean lines are overwhelmed, and Chileans retreat to hardened secondary positions. For the Chileans, the cost in lives is enormous.

May 24-July 4, 1943 - A concurrent Peruvian offensive in Bolivia is initially hampered by a shortfall of resources.

New World War – Page 398

July 4, 1943 - July 18, 1943 - With the Chilean front stalling and settling, air and armour shifts towards the Bolivian theatre, and the Peruvians advance.

July 8, 1943 - Battle of Cochabamba. City falls to Peruvian forces.

July 16-18, 1943 - Battle of Sucre, a two day campaign against entrenched forces of Villarroel and the Chileans.

July 20, 1943 - A hasty Argentine-Chilean coalition saves the Villarroel faction from collapse. But the Peruvians are now in overall control of 60 percent of the country.

July 31, 1943 - Peruvian Divisions are rotated from the Chilean front to occupy and fortify the mining districts. A stream of negative reports begins to flow back to Lima about the quality and conduct of the indigenous conscripts.

August 8, 1943 - A general strike is declared among the mining communities in response to punitive repression.

August 10, 1943 - A crowd of striking miners and their families are machine gunned, 400 killed.

August 12, 1943 - A second massacre of miners, 180 casualties.

August 18, 1943 - A wave of over twelve hundred arrests breaks the strike. Many of those arrested are never heard from again.

***

REVOLUTION IN PERU, OCTOBER 1943-JANUARY 1944

But November 22, 1943 - Is also the date of a military coup in Lima. General Gamarra, field commander on the Chilean/Peruvian trench war front, moves decisively on Lima.

November 28, 1943 - To ensure that the transition back to a professional army runs smoothly, Gamarra drafts up a list of 22 'trouble makers.' This list shortly expands to 46, all of them Mestizo or Indigenous.

December 2, 1943 – One of Gamarra's arrests goes badly wrong. In La Paz, Gamarra's men are captured and Gamarra's list is found.

December 3, 1943 - In a state of high tension, Echeverria issues an urgent letter delivered by runners to all the names on the list.

December 4, 1943 - Eighteen of these names are converging on La Paz.

December 6, 1943 – Twenty-three Indigenous and Mestizo officers gather to review the list and documents,

December 7, 1943 – The assembled Indigenous and Mestizo agree on revolt. Jaguar Otoronco is elected Colonel and Leader.

December 25, 1943 – At an assembly in the Andean Highlands, broadcast by radio, Jaguar Otoronco proclaims himself the new Inca, Tupac Amaru III.

January, 1944 - Armies of the rebellion are in control of three fourths of Bolivia and cross into Peru.

January/February, 1944 - the government in Lima loses complete control of the Highlands.

February, 1944 - An alarmed American government increases the flow of money and war materials to Peruvian ports. American planes are deployed to bomb the rebels.

February 14, 1944 - Americans force Gamarra to accept a coalition government with the Junta he replaced and negotiate a ceasefire with Chile's Ibanez on generous terms.

March 4, 1944 - Manco Yanqui wins the Battle of Three Dogs, and Singalong Huascar reaches the Pacific, splitting Peru in half.'

March 7, 1944 - the naval base at Callao surrenders. The Captains of the cruiser Almirante Grau and the destroyer Garcia mutiny and put to sea.

March 10, 1944 - Tupac Amaru III marches into Lima. Over the next few days, he is joined by the other senior generals.

March 11, 1944 - The heads of Ramirez, Gamarra and the rest of the former government are mounted on pikes at the entrance to the city.

****

New World War – Page 400

END OF THE BOLIVIAN CIVIL WAR –
MARCH, 1944 - SEPTEMBER, 1944

March, 1944 - Chilean forces Bolivia reinforce Villarroel's enclave.

April, 1944 - Villarroel and his Chilean allies a successful campaign against Argentine forces in the south, inflicting a string of defeats.

May 30, 1944 - Inca counteroffensive in Bolivia.

June 9, 1944 - Villarroel himself captured.

June, 1944 - Villarroel's enclave is overrun.

July, 1944 - Two Gun Echeverria defeats Argentine forces on the Bolivian southeast, enters the Paraguayan Chaco.

July/August, 1944 - Singalong Huascar and Perdita Diabla campaign in the southwest.

September, 1944 - Final Chilean remnants in Bolivia surrender.

***

THE ARGENTINE CAMPAIGN –
AUGUST - OCTOBER, 1944

August, 1944 - Perdita Diabla crosses from the Bolivian border, striking at Argentine supply bases, reaching the town of San Salvador de Jujuy.

August-September, 1944 - the Inca Generals, Diabla and Huascar, occupy the Argentinian Altiplano.

August-September, 1944 - Occupied Argentine territories are used to strike at Chile, bypassing Chilean defences. Chilean forces begin to fall apart.

September, 1944 - Argentina's reserve forces attempt to consolidate at the City of Salta, to prepare a counterattack.

September 28-29, 1944 - Argentina's hasty and ill prepared counterattack on the occupied Altiplano, fails utterly

October 4, 1944 - the city of Salta in the north falls to the Inca Revolution. General Farrell resigns; Juan Peron becomes the new President of Argentina.

October 7, 1944 - Tupac Amaru III and Manco Yanqui request a Peace Summit with the President of Argentina. Peron accepts.

October 10, 1944 - Argentine-Incan Armistice. The Inca withdraw from Salta and Jujuy but remain in control of the Argentine Altiplano.

****

FINAL CHILEAN OFFENSIVE, APRIL 1944 - AUGUST, 1944

April/May, 1944 - the last remnants of the old Peruvian government are the army occupying the trenches. Ibanez in Chile orders a buildup in anticipation of a major offensive.

May 22, 1944 - Ecuador's victory at the Battle of Lojas decides Ibanez. Sensing weakness, he commits to the offensive.

May 24, 1944, Ibanez launches an offensive. The result initially is a breakthrough.

June, 1994 - Ibanez's offensive overruns Arequipa. From there, Chilean forces push their way through Nazca where they encounter but overcome heavy fire.

June 17, 1944 - the Chileans reach Chincha, on the edges of the Lima province and barely a couple of hundred miles from Lima itself. Victory is in sight.

July-August, 1944 - The offensive outruns its supply lines. This produces several temporary halts, as the offensive waits for its baggage trains to catch up.

August-September, 1944 - The inevitable Inca counterattacks take place on a wide front ranging from Chincha down to Antofagasta. It is an unprecedented military disaster.

***

FALL OF CHILE,
AUGUST-NOVEMBER, 1944

August, 1944 - The Inca strike south across Argentine territory into Antofagasta, routing under-equipped and unprepared Chilean forces in a series of small battles.

August 18, 1944 - After a pitched battle, the city of Antofagasta falls, and the province is in Inca hands.

September 1, 1944 - The Inca push into Coquimbo.

September 10, 1944 - The last remnants in Bolivia surrender.

September 14, 1944 - sees the obliteration of the largest surviving army group in the north, and any hope of reformation and rescue.

September, 1944 - Ibanez sends a series of urgent missions to Buenos Aires pleading for help and offering increasingly grandiose concessions.

September 27 - Ibanez is overthrown by a military coup, fleeing to Argentina. The new military junta in Chile undertakes desperate measures to reorganize a defence.

October 1, 1944 - The last pockets of Chilean forces in the north surrender or are obliterated.

October 4, 1944 - Fighting in Valparaiso.

October 16, 1944 - Raids reach as far south as Maule and beyond. A sense of widespread panic and hopelessness overcomes the Chileans.

October 31, 1944 - The city of Valparaiso surrenders without siege to an Inca army under condition of safe treatment.

November 1, 1944 - The Argentines cross the border. Argentina occupies the Chilean capital, Santiago, flooding it with troops and installing Ibanez once again as the head of a puppet regime. Members of the Chilean Junta escape south to the town of San Bernardo, reconstituting the remnants of their government.

New World War – Page 403

November 6, 1944 - representatives of Argentina and the Inca sign
the Santiago Accord (actually signed in La Paz), dividing the
Southern cone between the two of them.

November 11, 1944 - As Inca forces are approaching the town of
San Bernardo; the last remnants of the independent Chilean
government and Navy flee into exile.

****

ECUADOR'S LAST STAND –
MARCH 1943 – MARCH, 1945

March, 1944 - Colombia has its sole engagement with the forces of
the European Axis, sinking a German submarine. It begins an
armament campaign.

May, 1944 - The increasingly strained affiliation between the
Colombian and Ecuadoran governments is breaking down.

May 22, 1944 – Battle of Lojas. Forces of the Inca Empire invade
the Ecuadoran province of Lojas, confronting a force of
Ecuadorans with Colombian reserves. During the battle, the
Colombian reserves are badly mauled.

May, 1944 - The disastrous deployment of Colombian troops in the
battle of Lojas is taken as a major sign of bad faith, and the source
of a huge rift.

June-December, 1944 – The Inca empire focuses on consolidation
and on the southern theatre. In the north new strategy of
subverting the Sierra interior is adopted.

June 18, 1944 - President Bonifaz suffers a debilitating stroke.
Velasco Ibarra, the Prime Minister, immediately assumes interim
Presidential duties.

July 30, 1944 - Bonifaz passes away, without ever regaining
consciousness. Ibarra threatens to resign, demanding to be
appointed President. The Legislature refuses and accepts his
resignation.

August to September, 1994 – With the loss of Bonifaz and Ibarra, Alba is demoted.

September 9, 1944 – Alba is removed and flees to Venezuela.

****

THE FINAL NORTHERN CAMPAIGN, ECUADOR-COLOMBIA/INCA - SEPTEMBER, 1944 – MARCH, 1945

September to December, 1944 – In the Ecuadoran Sierra, things begin to fall apart rapidly. A new campaign strategy of repression and punitive measures against the Quechua backfires.

November 3, 1944 - The Ecuadoran military blames its reverses on civilian meddling. Backed by Colombia, they stage a coup.

December, 1944 - much of the interior is under the control of the Inca. The rump Ecuadoran government is reduced to Guayaquil and Quito, the coastline and the northern provinces.

January and February, 1945 - Quito and Guayaquil are under siege by QuizQuiz Guerrero. Tupac Amaru III formally offers safe passage to the Colombians back to their own country.

January 24, 1945 – Desperate to salvage the situation, Colombia launches a series of columns from Pasto to rescue and break the siege of Quito.

February 14, 1945 - QuizQuiz Guerrero, wielding a northern army force half again larger than the entire Colombian military, catches the Colombians en route to Quito on Ecuadoran soil and obliterates them in a one sided bloodbath.

February 16, 1945 – Inca forces under QuizQuiz Guerrero cross the Colombian border.

February 20, 1945 - The battle of Pasto is a rout, with the Colombian army, unprepared, breaking and fleeing in a disorganized fashion.

February 20, 1945 - American forces in Panama commence bombing attacks on Inca forces in Colombia, with raids extending as far south as northern Peru.

February 21, 1945 - Quito falls to the Inca adding to the sense of panic.

February 22, 1945 - The coastal city of Bueneventura, Colombia, falls to the Inca

February, 1945 - QuizQuiz Guerrero continues to sweep north through the Colombian highlands, Colombians put up no organized resistance.

March 1, 1945 - Guayaquil surrenders.

March 2, 1945 – The President Roosevelt of the United States, issues the Cali Declaration, announcing that if the Inca enter the city of Cali, then the United States will declare war.

March 4, 1945 - Manco Yanqui and Tupac Amaru III fly by airplane to a landing strip just miles from the city of Cali, to stop the advance.

March 11, 1945 - An Inca soldier plants an Inca flag some 500 yards south of the city of Cali. The Andean wars are over.

***

THE WAR AT SEA –

ALL MAJOR NAVAL CONFLICTS

DECEMBER, 1939 - DECEMBER, 1944

December 13, 1939 - Battle of the River Plate - first naval battle of World War II. The Nazi Heavy Cruiser, Admiral Graf Spee, fights a British navy squadron. Heavily damaged and the Exeter was disabled. The Graf Spee puts into port temporarily at Montevideo, and within a few days, makes for Chile, where it is renamed the Toro.

June 6, 1940 - War at Sea - The Great Northern Campaign, the Peruvian cruiser Coronel Bolognesi and the destroyer Villar, along with a troop transport and support vessels enter the Ecuadoran Gulf of Guayaquil.

June 7, 1940 - War at Sea - The Great Northern Campaign, Ecuadoran gunboat Calderon encounters the Peruvian destroyer, Villar, on its way to Puerto Bolivar, the two ships exchanging fire all the way, until the Calderon was able to retreat into local river channels.

June 9-12, 1940 - The War at Sea - The Great Northern Campaign, the Coronel Bolognesi enters Guayaquil harbor and demands surrender.

June 28, 1940 - War at Sea – The Great Northern Campaign, Coronel Bolognesi enters Guayaquil harbor and commences to shell the city, taking minor damage from aerial bombing.

July 7, 1930 - War at Sea - Chilean battleship, Almirante Latorre and two destroyers, the Aldea and the Hyatt, enter the Gulf of Guayaquil ostensibly to protect shipping.

August 16, 1940 - The War at Sea - the Almirante Latorre opened fire on the Coronel Bolognesi on the direct orders of President Ibanez. In Peru, the battle was called the 'Treachery of Guayaquil,"

August 21, 1940 - War at Sea - the surviving Peruvian are dispatched for an attack on the Chilean naval base at Coquimbo.

August 28, 1940 - War at Sea - "Battle of Coquimbo" under a cover of heavy fog, the attack is carried out, catching the Chileans by surprise.

November 8, 1940 - War at Sea - the Chilean battleship, Almirante Latorre catches the Peruvian cruiser Almirante Grau and destroyer Palacio in open waters.

February 21, 1941 - War at Sea - the Chilean ship, Almirante Latorre on coastal bombardment and blockade of Lima, is struck by several aerial bombs.

May 26, 1941 - Chilean Front/War At Sea - The Landing, Chile attacks from the sea in a massive amphibious operation supported by the bulk of the Chilean navy.

May 29, 1941 - Chilean Front/War at Sea - The Landing, Peru commits most of their remaining naval resources, including their submarines, and most of their aircraft to trying to dislodge the beachhead.

January-July 1942 Atlantic Ocean, January to August 1942 - German U-Boats sink 18 Brazilian merchant vessels, causing Vargas formally declares war on Germany, Japan and Ecuador in August 22, 1942. The declaration excludes Italy, Chile or any Bolivian faction.

May 28-June 4, 1943 - The Little Landing.' Under heavy pressure from the Peruvian 'Operacione Salitre,' Chile commits its navy, the old battleship, Almirante Cochrane, the Pocket Toro, and the cruiser, Almirante O'Higgins, and support ships equipped with anti-aircraft weapons on a counterattack.

November 26, 1943 - following a series of incidents involving the sinking of Colombian shipping by a German U-Boat, Colombia declares war on Germany and Japan, unlike Brazil, Colombia contributes no troops to the overseas war effort, and allows no American bases on its territory.

March, 1944 - Colombia has its sole engagement with the forces of the European Axis, when Colombian naval units in the Caribbean attack and sink a Nazi submarine from Germany.

March 7, 1944 - The Peruvian naval base at Callao surrenders to the Inca forces.

November 11, 1944 - As Inca and Argentine forces overrun Chile, the last remnants of the Chilean government and the Chilean navy flees the town of San Bernardo, beginning an arduous flight to sanctuary in Uruguay.

November 22, 1944 - After stopping at the Falklands, the ancient Chilean battleship, Almirante Cochrane is intercepted by Argentina's fleet and surrenders.

December 4-5, 1944 - Argentina's Moreno battle group intercepts the exile Chilean fleet. Fighting breaks out. After an inconclusive battle, the battered Chilean fleet is allowed to proceed. The Argentines declare victory.

A Note and More Books by the Author

If you've skipped to the end, looking for an apology, well... Sorry? Also, no refunds.

Thank you for taking the time out to read this pair of books. If you've made it all the way here, then I'm just going to assume you liked it. It's an unconventional approach to an alternate history story, but I like it. If you're looking for similar, but briefer, alternate history takes, let me recommend **Bear Cavalry, Dawn of Cthulhu** and **Fall of Atlantis**.

What else do I have to offer? Some kick ass Doctor Who Pirates history, a trilogy of horror collections, an audiobook, novels, you name it.

If you liked this, could I suggest you leave a review wherever you got it. Mention it on your blog, or your Facebook. Say nice things. If that's too much, just toss me a couple of stars. Writing is a solitary, lonely pursuit and actually getting some feedback or appreciation is a wonderful thing.

But there's more to it. It's about trying to get out there. There are a lot of people writing a lot of books, and it can get hard to get noticed. Reviews help.

And speaking of writing more....'

Check out my Website, denvaldron.com

***

ALTERNATE REALITIES
A Trilogy or Strange New Worlds

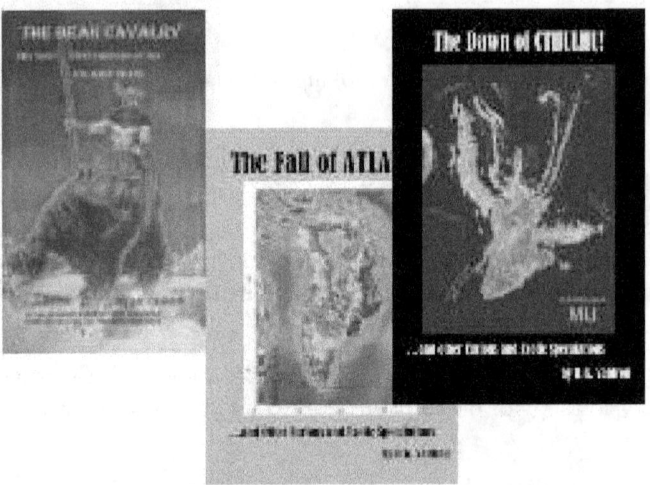

The Dawn of Cthulhu - The Secret History of H.P. Lovecraft's Cthulhu Cult; Lost Continents Found – real and legendary; The Monsters of Sesame Street, is a light hearted examination of Muppets as if they were actual animals.

The Fall of Atlantis – Retroverse, An Accidental Cinematic Universe of 50s Sci Fi movies, Greenland Without the Ice, Rome Crosses the Atlantic, and the Rise and Fall of Atlantis, an ecological catastrophe.

The Bear Cavalry, the True (Not!) History of the Icelandic Bears, an off the wall, short novel about the Viking domestication of bears, their evolution into a medieval cavalry Bonus novelette, The Sharebear Apocalypse.

HEARTS IN DARKNESS
A Trilogy of Horror Collections

Giant Monsters Sing Sad Songs – The connection between the author of the Necronomicon and a boy in Providence; a girl who meets the last Sasquatch, a poet who shares abandoned Tokyo with a Kaiju, and more…

What Devours Also Hungers – The unkillable killers in masks are recruited into the army, vampires and their hunters, clever serial killers, monsters, ghosts and more….

There Are No Doors in Dark Places – A childlike cancer that talks to its owner; A single mother drawn into dark magic; A man who turns into a different monster each night; and many more.

New World War – Page 412

A Dark Fantasy of Murder and Redemption

There's a City where all the races come together uneasily, now descending into civil war.

There's a Mermaid, murdered cruelly her people distraught and crying out for justice.

There's an Orc, the lowest and the worst, her mission: Solve the murder, before it all comes crashing down.

She finds something else... the world's first serial killer.

Available only as an Audiobook

New World War – Page 413

The Strangest, Most Surreal, Space Opera Ever Created

LEXX – Star Trek's Evil Twin

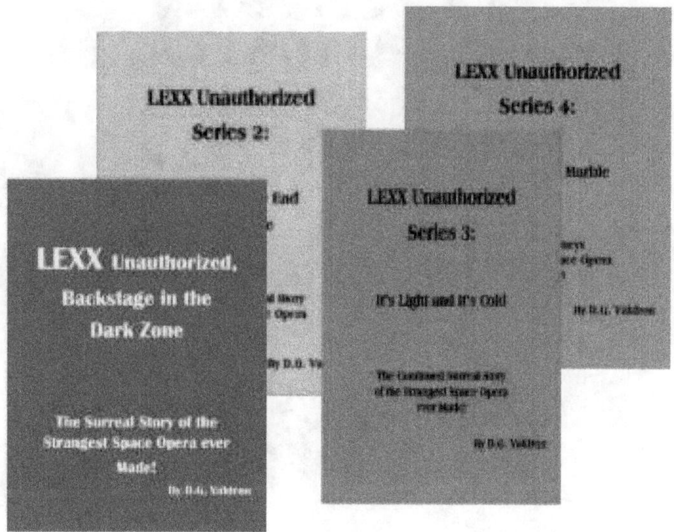

LEXX Unauthorized about the making of a show about a giant space bug that blows up planets, the cowardly security guard who is its captain, and the undead assassin, runaway love slave, and robot head who form its crew.

Originally billed as 'Star Trek's Evil Twin,' the cultiest of cult sci fi, LEXX's forte was black humor, startling visuals, big ideas, and a sensibility that had more to do with surrealists like Jodorowsky or Bunuel than mainstream science fiction. One of the most innovative science fiction series of all time.

New World War – Page 414

The Pirate Histories!

What's a Pirate's History, you ask?

Well, there's the official, sanitized, orderly histories that are approved by and all about the powers that be.

Then there are the Pirate's histories, the things that they don't want you to know about, or that they don't care about, things that are great and marvellous and intriguing... but unapproved.

It's a history of secret and forgotten corners of the Whoniverse. The first woman Doctor, the first black Doctor, animations, audios, stage plays and fan films.

New World War – Page 415

Drunk Slutty Elf
and Other Stories
Hilarious Science Fiction and Fantasy

plus the sequel
DRUNK SLUTTY ELF
AND ZOMBIES!!!

Two volumes of savage, satirical, subversive wicked, funny, frantic science fiction and fantasy. Demented ghost hunters, frustrated aliens, horny giants, drunken elves, sneaky ghosts, wayward barbarians and many more.

New World War – Page 416

AXIS OF ANDES
NEW WORLD WAR
A History of WWII in South America

Berlin, 1937, Adolph Hitler and his cabinet meet with a strange delegation from Ecuador. The delegates from the small South American nation beg for help, fearing an impending invasion from their rival, Peru. What happens at that meeting sets in motion a chain of events that lights the entire continent on fire. By the time it's done, millions are dead, nations are in ruins, and the map of Latin America will be changed beyond recognition.

www.ingramcontent.com/pod-product-compliance
Lightning Source LLC
Chambersburg PA
CBHW060424310726

48977CB00001B/45